Published in Great Britain 2015
by Mills & Boon, an imprint of Harlequin (UK) Limited,
Eton House, 18-24 Paradise Road, Richmond, Surrey, TW9 1SR

MILLIONAIRE PLAYBOYS © 2015 Harlequin Books S.A.

Paying the Playboy's Price, Exposing the Executive's Secrets and *Bending to the Bachelor's Will* were first published in Great Britain by Harlequin (UK) Limited.

Paying the Playboy's Price © 2006 Emilie Rose Cunningham
Exposing the Executive's Secrets © 2006 Emilie Rose Cunningham
Bending to the Bachelor's Will © 2006 Emilie Rose Cunningham

ISBN: 978-0-263-25225-5
eBook ISBN: 978-1-474-00404-6

05-0815

Harlequin (UK) Limited's policy is to use papers that are natural, renewable and recyclable products and made from wood grown in sustainable forests. The logging and manufacturing processes conform to the legal environmental regulations of the country of origin.

Printed and bound in Spain
by CPI, Barcelona

Emilie Rose lives in North Carolina with her college-sweetheart husband and four sons. Writing is Emilie's third (and hopefully her last) career. She's managed a medical office and run a home day-care, neither of which offers half as much satisfaction as plotting happy endings. Her hobbies include quilting, gardening and cooking (especially cheesecake). Her favourite TV shows include *ER*, *CSI* and Discovery Channel's medical programmes. Emilie's a country music fan because she can find an entire book in almost any song.

Emilie loves to hear from her readers and can be reached at PO Box 20145, Raleigh, NC 27619, USA, or at www.EmilieRose.com.

PAYING THE PLAYBOY'S PRICE

BY
EMILIE ROSE

To the Black Sheep.
Long may we baa and may the pasture
always be as green.

One

"Is our uptight account auditor ready to be corrupted? Your bachelor's coming up next."

Juliana Alden downed her complimentary champagne with the grace of a beer-guzzling dock worker in hopes of drowning the second thoughts swarming around her midsection like angry bees. She discarded her glass on a passing waiter's tray and grabbed another for courage before facing Andrea and Holly, her two best friends and cohorts in tonight's foolhardy scheme.

"I've never felt more naked in my life. I will never grant the two of you carte blanche with my wardrobe again. My nightie covers more skin than this slip dress."

She yanked the thin strap of her dress back onto her shoulder *again,* and then tugged downward on the short hem, which barely covered her hips. Sneaking out the club's back door gained appeal with each passing second, but if she bolted Andrea and Holly would never forgive her. Then again, they were the ones responsible for garbing her in a dress that could send her father into cardiac arrest if he ventured out of the cigar room long enough to see it, so their opinions were suspect.

Andrea waved away her objections. "You have the figure for it and red is a great color on you. Don't wimp out now, Juliana."

A sea of screaming, nearly hysterical women surrounded them, bidding on the men being auctioned off in the name of charity with the same ferocity as the shark feeding frenzy Juliana had witnessed at a nearby aquarium. She'd bet her monthly pedicure the walls of the prestigious Caliber Club ballroom had never reverberated in quite the same way before. The pandemonium only increased her doubts about the plan the three of them had concocted over quesadillas and, clearly, one too many margaritas.

Praying for courage and finding none, Juliana took a deep breath and then another sip of champagne. What in the world had possessed her to believe she could cast off thirty years of being a Goody Two-shoes to bid on the baddest bachelor on the auction block tonight? She should have started with a smaller rebellion, but no, she'd chosen to launch a massive insurrection on her first attempt.

As an account auditor in her family's privately owned banking chain, she was cautious by nature. She worked a predictable job and drove a sensible sedan. She found comfort in following the rules, having her life add up in precise, orderly rows and in steadily ascending the career ladder the way her mother had before her.

But the sudden pressure to marry for the good of the company had shaken that ladder and made Juliana feel more like a commodity being bartered in the merger negotiations between Alden Bank and Trust and Wilson Savings and Loan than a human being.

"I can't believe I let you talk me into this. Maybe I'm not

ready for the tarnish-your-halo type of man. Perhaps I should choose someone a little less…" At a loss for words, she shrugged. How could she describe the man whose picture in the bachelor auction program had given her hot flashes?

"Studly?" Holly asked with a wicked grin.

Understatement of the year. Juliana nodded.

Bachelor number nine took the stage and Juliana's heart cha-chaed erratically. The crowd of usually dignified ladies hooted, whistled and stomped their expensively shod feet. If any man could tempt a woman to take a few risks and break a few rules, that one could. Looking completely at home in the spotlight, he flashed an I-dare-you grin and encouraged the already rowdy crowd to make more noise by clapping his hands and swinging his hips to the loud music like the head-lining performer he'd once been.

The man knew how to move. She'd grant him that. A shiver skipped down her spine.

His tight black T-shirt stretched across broad shoulders, molding a well-developed chest and encircling bulging biceps. Jeans, faded in those intriguing places she ought to be embarrassed to look at rode low on lean hips, and he wore cowboy boots—something you didn't see often in the port city of Wilmington, North Carolina. Given that every other man who'd crossed the stage before him tonight had worn a tux, the bar owner's casual attire screamed *renegade*—coinciden-tally, the name of his bar and the word emblazoned across the back of his shirt.

Juliana's pulse boomed so loudly she could barely hear the MC's long-winded introduction. Had the woman never heard the old cliché "silence is golden"? If she'd hush and let people *look* at Rex Tanner, then her job would do itself. What woman wouldn't want to be carried off in those muscle-corded arms or be coerced by that naughty I'm-gonna-get-you smile?

"'Feel the power between your legs—one month of Harley and horseback-riding lessons,'" Andrea read aloud from the program. "Juliana, if this guy can't show you what you've been missing, then I'm going to check to see if you still have a pulse. He's exactly what you need to derail you from your mother's insane idea."

Juliana gulped the remainder of her drink. The bubbles burned her nose and brought tears to her eyes. "I'm still not convinced there's anything wrong with my mother's suggestion. Wally is a nice guy."

"You're not in love with him and he's boring," Holly stated.

"More effective than a sleeping pill," Andrea added. "And he's a pushover. You'd be wearing the pants in that relationship."

And that was a problem? The woman-in-charge role had worked for Juliana's parents. "I love you both for worrying about me and I understand your concerns, but logically, Wally is a good choice. He's steady, even-tempered and ambitious—like me—and he's the only man I've ever dated who understands the demands of my career and the hours it requires. We can talk for hours without an awkward silence."

Andrea snorted. "About work. What happens when that subject gets old or, God forbid, you're still with him when you retire? Are you going to discuss credits and debits in bed? I know you, Juliana. Once you commit to a job—or a marriage—you'll never give up on it. Forget logic for once in your life. This is your last chance to see that there can and *should* be more than convenience to a relationship."

Last chance. The phrase stuck in Juliana's head. Her last chance before agreeing to marry Wallace Wilson—son of the owner of the bank poised to merge with Alden's—in a sensible, but loveless match.

She shifted uneasily. Okay, maybe her friends had a point. Wally wasn't Mr. Excitement, but he was kind, pleasant-looking and steadfast. If she married him, they'd probably have predictable Saturday-night-duty sex for the next fifty years. On the other hand, routines were good and sex wasn't everything. It certainly shouldn't be the basis for something as important as marriage. Emotions were volatile and unpredictable. Similar ethics and mutual respect were far more important and dependable qualities. If she married Wally, they'd develop other shared interests and love would grow over time like a safe investment….

Wouldn't it?

Of course it would. If she had doubts, all she had to do was look at her parents. They'd married almost four decades ago to join two banking families, and they'd remained married when many of their friends had divorced.

The archway leading toward the exit drew her gaze again. Should she escape before diving off the bridge of sanity? No. A promise was a promise. But she truly hated going first. She turned back to her friends. "Swear to me you won't back out. You will buy bachelors tonight no matter what."

Holly and Andrea smiled angelically and raised their right hands as if taking the oath on a Bible. Juliana didn't trust those smiles. While her friends' lives might not be as methodically plotted out as hers, tonight's escapade was totally out of character for all three of them. Surely one of them would come to her senses before the evening ended?

The microphone screeched, jerking Juliana's attention back to the hunk commanding center stage—the one she'd been trying hard to ignore. How could any woman resist him? The man was a Grade-A gorgeous devil from his thick black ponytail to his worn low-heeled boots. He wouldn't need to read an instruction manual to know how to pleasure a woman—assuming that woman could be pleased.

But purchasing the cowboy's package would take more

than recklessness and champagne courage. It meant flagrantly disregarding her mother's wishes—something she'd carefully avoided until now for fear of the repercussions. But Juliana had to admit the proposed engagement combined with her thirtieth birthday had left her wondering if there was more to life. She'd promised Holly and Andrea she'd investigate the possibility before meekly agreeing to the future her mother had planned for her.

That didn't prevent Juliana from wondering if she'd taken on a bigger challenge than she could handle when she'd selected her bachelor—a man the complete opposite of anyone she'd dated in the past. She said a silent prayer that the rebel's price would exceed the limit she, Andrea and Holly had agreed upon, and then she could choose a less intimidating man.

Coward. If you do, then your plan will fail.

Her plan was beginning to sound more than a little like tequila madness. For once in her life, Juliana had decided to break the rules and, since she didn't have the first clue where to start, she'd chosen Rex Tanner, a hell-raising rebel who she hoped would lead her astray. For the next month, she'd put herself in his corrupting hands and then once she had this last fling out of the way and she was certain she wasn't missing out on anything worthwhile, she could marry Wally with no regrets.

"Go home before you get into trouble."

Juliana nearly tumbled off her flimsy sandals at her bossy older brother's growled warning. She refused to admit she'd like nothing more than to turn and run as fast as her heels would carry her. To annoy Eric, she raised her numbered fan, offering the first bid on Mr. Too-Hot-To-Handle.

Andrea and Holly grinned and gave her thumbs-up. Juliana didn't dare glance across the room to where her mother, the charity event's chief organizer, watched with an eagle eye.

She tilted her head back to glare at her brother. "How much trouble can a month of riding lessons cause? Go away, Eric."

"I'm not worried about the horseback-riding lessons because you already know how to ride. It's the other half of the prize that concerns me. You'll kill yourself on a motorcycle. Be reasonable, Juliana. You are not the most coordinated person on the planet."

The barb stung—mostly because it was true. In fact, these days she limited her exercise routine to swimming because then she wouldn't fall off anything and get hurt when her mind strayed to work issues.

Eric attempted to take her numbered paddle, but Juliana snatched it out of his reach and stabbed it into the air. "I'm thirty years old—too old for you to be telling me what to do."

"Somebody needs to. You and your friends—" he glared at Holly and Andrea "—must have been out of your minds to come up with this plan. Buying men, for crissakes. If you want to support the charity, buy Wallace and not this—"

"Hunk," Holly interrupted, earning a scowl from Eric.

Juliana pasted on the placating smile she reserved for difficult customers. "Actually, Eric, our mother came up with the bachelor-auction idea. Andrea, Holly and I are merely supporting her efforts."

"Dammit, Juliana, you can't handle a guy like him. He'll chew you up and spit you out. Use your brain. Buy Wally. He's…*safe*." He snatched at Juliana's fan again and once more she jerked it away.

Safe. Those four letters said it all. She'd played it safe her entire life and where had that gotten her? Ahead in her career, but pathetically far behind in her personal life. She'd never fallen head over heels in love or even lust, and she couldn't help wondering if she was capable of such intense emotions. Not that she wanted the heartache, but was it too much to ask for bells, whistles and earth-moving orgasms? For a woman like her—one who trusted cold, hard facts more than fickle emotions? Probably. But for once in her life, she didn't want to play it safe.

She glanced at the man on the stage. *Safe* didn't make her skin tingle or her breath quicken. She shoved the paddle into the air this time holding it high above her head and slightly behind her. Her brother was taller, but he was as conservative as she was. He wouldn't make a scene or wrestle her to the ground to keep her from bidding.

"I don't want to buy Wally. Saturday-night suppers? How unimaginative is that? Besides, I already have a standing dinner date with him on Fridays. What's wrong with having a little fun? You should try it sometime."

And then she winced. Eric had been very publicly jilted a few months ago and fun was probably the last thing on his mind. She suspected his heart hadn't been broken, but his pride had to have taken a serious blow. The worst part was that since he'd failed to marry into the Wilson banking family, her mother had decided Juliana should.

She waved her paddle—a little more desperately this time. "Eric, I have carefully thought this out, and I know what I'm doing, so leave me alone."

"*Sold* to number 223," the MC shouted from the stage. "Pay up and collect your prize, young lady."

Juliana's stomach plunged to her crimson-painted toenails. She looked from Eric to her mother's horrified expression. Andrea and Holly clapped and cheered. Juliana didn't need to double-check her number to know she'd won the rebel, and she had no idea how much she'd paid for him—a true shock for someone who tracked money for a living. Slowly lowering her arm, she swallowed and briefly closed her eyes as a bolt of unadulterated panic zigzagged through her. She wasn't ready to face the stage and the consequences of her virgin voyage into mutiny. She might never be ready.

Dizziness forced her to inhale. She faked a smile for Eric and anyone else who might be watching. "Thank you for your concern, big brother, but aren't you supposed to be behind the curtain getting ready for your turn on the block?"

Eric flinched and paled. A smidgen of guilt pricked Juliana for verbally jabbing his sore spot with a deliberate taunt. Her brother was not happy their mother had shanghaied him as a bachelor. But Eric wasn't Juliana's problem right now. She had her own catastrophe-in-the-making to handle. Dread ballooned inside her.

With her brother's muttered curses and Andrea and Holly's "Go get 'ems" ringing in her ears, Juliana made her way to the table in the corner of the room and handed over her check to collect her…*gulp*…prize.

Her mother, with fury in her eyes, met her there. "Juliana Alden, are you out of your mind? And where in the world did you find that disgraceful dress?"

Juliana's insides clenched tighter as all her doubts ambushed her at once. She *must* have been temporarily insane to agree to Andrea's suggestion that they celebrate their thirtieth birthdays by spending part of their trust funds on something wild, wicked and totally selfish.

No, not insane. Desperate. If she couldn't feel the heart-pounding passion other women whispered about with a man as blatantly sexy as the rebel, then she was a lost cause, and she'd be better off with a man like Wally who wouldn't expect more than she could deliver.

But while Juliana admired her mother's business acumen and hoped to emulate Margaret Alden's career success, the two of them had never been close, so confessing the tangle of emotions driving her decision wasn't a viable option.

"Mother, I have always done everything you've ever asked of me, but tonight, this—*he*—is for me."

She glanced beyond her mother's shoulder. Juliana's prize stalked toward her in long purposeful strides, and the hairs on her neck rose. Why did she feel like cornered prey? Determined not to be cowed by the cocky challenge in his eyes, she assumed the debutante pose her mother had drilled into her—tall and regal, chin high—and hoped her knees weren't visibly knocking beneath her scandalously short hem.

From a distance of ten yards—and closing far too quickly—the rebel's dark gaze drifted over her, making her intensely aware that she wore nothing but a thong beneath the thin dress.

Had she ever met a man who oozed this much sexuality? Definitely not. Her pulse fluttered irregularly and her skin tightened and warmed.

"What about Wallace?" her mother whispered angrily.

With great effort, Juliana tore her gaze away from her prize and refocused on her mother. "I will very likely spend the rest of my life with Wally. Neither of you should begrudge me a month of riding lessons."

Her mother's lips flattened. "One month and then I fully expect you to come to your senses. The Wilsons are a fine family and Wallace has impeccable manners." Her mother could be describing a pedigreed pooch, but then her mother would probably prefer a well-trained lap dog to a real man. "Be assured your father won't be as understanding."

No, he definitely would not. He'd be whatever her mother told him to be. As much as Juliana loved her father, she wasn't blind to his faults.

"Hey, babe." The deep gravelly voice sent goose bumps parading over Juliana's skin. She ignored her mother's shocked gasp and faced the man who'd come to a halt a yard away. The heat in his naughty smile and coffee-colored eyes robbed the strength from Juliana's knees. He offered his hand. "I'm Rex and I'm going to teach you to ride."

Ride what? Or whom? The questions popped involuntarily into her head and she couldn't breathe. Her teeth met with an audible click when she closed her mouth. She had definitely bitten off more of a challenge than she could chew. Rex Tanner was bigger, sexier and far more intimidating up close than he'd been onstage or in the tiny two-inch picture printed in the program. Even in her heels, Juliana's eyes barely reached the level of his mouth. What a mouth. And boy, did he look like he knew how to use it.

That is what you wanted, isn't it?

No. Yes. No. Ohmigod, Eric was right. I can't handle a man like Rex Tanner.

Yes, I can. And I will.

The corners of his lips quirked upward as if he were used to dumbstruck females.

Embarrassed, Juliana pasted on a polite smile. Her fingers trembled as she slid her hand into Rex's. "Hello, Rex. I'm Juliana."

Warm, callused skin abraded her palm as he grasped her hand, and when he slid his other arm around her shoulders, pulled her closer and turned her toward the photographer, every cell in Juliana's body screeched in alarm at the searing press of his flesh against her side and his long fingers curved over her bare shoulder.

"Smile, babe," he whispered in a voice as rough and piercing as a rusty nail. She felt the impact deep in her womb.

His leather-and-outdoors scent enveloped her, and his nearness made her woozy. She blamed the stars in her eyes on the camera's flash and knew she lied.

As soon as Octavia Jenkins, the newspaper reporter

covering the event, and her photographer sidekick departed, Juliana quickly disengaged and scrambled to make order out of her chaotic response. The temptation to discover how those long, slightly rough fingers would feel on the rest of her skin was a totally new experience and a step in the right direction *if* she found the courage to follow through with her plan.

If? You have planned this for weeks. You are absolutely committed to following through. No backing out now.

Overly conscious of her mother's disapproval and the stares of the other patrons aimed at them, Juliana met Rex's gaze.

"Why don't we get out of here?" Her words gushed out in a breathless invitation instead of the firm request she'd intended.

A bone-melting smile slanted his lips. "That's the best offer I've had all night."

After delivering a lengthy, censuring look, her mother pivoted and stormed off in a regal huff. Juliana turned in the opposite direction and headed for the exit before she could turn coward and ask for her money back. Without looking over her shoulder, she knew Rex Tanner followed. She could feel him behind her, hear the rhythmic thud of his boots on the marble floor, see the jealous glares of the women they passed directed toward her and the appreciative appraisals aimed at him. Many of those women were married and some were old enough to be his mother.

Rex reached past her to push open the club's front door, and a blast of sobering air smacked Juliana's face as she stepped outside.

Dear heavens. She'd bought herself a bad boy.

What was she going to do with him?

And how far was she willing to let this experiment go?

Bought by a spoiled rich chick with more money than sense.

Rex studied Juliana's arrogant bearing and questioned his

sanity in agreeing to his sister's crazy suggestion to use the bachelor auction to publicize his bar. If the bank note weren't coming due in sixty days, then nothing could have persuaded him to get back on a stage in front of screaming women.

Been there. Done that. Burned by it.

Self-disgust didn't stop him from appreciating the tasty morsel in front of him as she swished her red-wrapped hips away from the noise and chaos inside. Her lingerie-style dress looked like something she'd wear to bed instead of to a swanky country club, and the dark curtain of hair bouncing between her shoulder blades glowed with the same rich patina of his old guitar.

For the first time since moving to Wilmington, he found himself attracted to a woman, but everything about Juliana, from her cultured southern voice to her expensive clothing and the chunk of change she'd dropped on him tonight, screamed money. Rich gals like her didn't settle for rough-off-the-ranch guys like him long-term, and he'd had enough meaningless encounters to last a lifetime. When he'd left Nashville and the groupies behind, he'd sworn he'd never use or be used by a woman again. As long as Juliana realized that she'd bought his auction package and nothing else, they'd get along fine. But before he followed her wherever she was headed, he needed to be certain of one thing.

"Hey, Juli," he called as they reached the semicircular stairs leading down to the parking lot.

She jerked to a halt and spun to face him. Her bright blue eyes nearly made him forget what he was going to say.

Her chin inched upward. "My name is Juliana."

Stuck-up or not, she didn't look like the kind of woman who had to buy men. "Yeah, sure. You have a jealous husband who'll be gunning for me?"

A confused frown puckered her brows. "A husband?"

"The guy trying to stop you from bidding," he clarified.

"That was my brother. I'm not married."

"'S'all right then as long as you're over twenty-one."

Her long lashes fluttered and a pleat formed between her eyebrows. "You have jealous husbands chasing you?"

She'd ignored his comment about age. "Not anymore."

Her red lips parted and her chest—a damned fine chest—rose. "But you did?"

"Yeah." Most guys didn't take it well when they found out their wives had slept with another man. Rex hadn't taken the news that some of the groupies were married well, either—especially since the info had often been delivered via their husbands' fists after the intimate encounters.

He thought he heard Juliana wheeze as she turned to descend the steps. He'd have to be dead not to appreciate her long, sleek and sexy-as-all-get-out legs atop those red heels. She stopped abruptly at the base of the stairs with a distressed expression on her pretty face.

"Problem?"

She touched long slender fingers to her temple and then against her throat. "I rode with friends. I don't have a car, and I want to…" She looked past his shoulder and panic flared in her eyes.

He turned and spotted the pearl-clad dragon lady who'd organized the event and an uptight-looking man coming through the front door of the club. Understanding dawned. "You want to get out of here?"

"Yes, and fast."

"Did you write a bad check?"

Impossible as it seemed, her regal posture turned even starchier, as if he'd insulted her. "Of course not. Please, get me out of here."

These days he avoided ugly scenes. "My bike's this way."

Her eyes nearly popped out of her head. She gestured to her skimpy attire. "I'm hardly dressed for a motorcycle ride."

He ought to leave her, but dammit, he'd agreed to this stupid auction and he would follow through. Besides, he wouldn't wish the dragon lady on anybody. "I don't see any taxis. If you need to make a fast getaway, then I'm your only option. Where to? Home?"

She grimaced. "Anywhere but there."

"Let's go." He grabbed her elbow and towed her toward his Harley. She jogged to keep up. When they reached the side of his motorcycle—one of a handful of items he'd kept from his past—he tossed her his spare helmet and waited to see that she knew how to fasten it before donning his own. "Hop on and hold on."

Seconds later she'd mounted the bike behind him and gingerly clutched his waist, but she kept several inches between them. He twisted the throttle. The engine roared and the bike surged forward as he released the clutch. Her squeal pierced the deep growl of the Harley, and then her arms banded around him with close to rib-cracking force, erasing the gap between them.

Big mistake. Having her naked legs wrapped around his hips with the heat of her crotch pressed snugly against his butt just might melt a few brain cells. And if he couldn't ignore the softness of her breasts mashing against his shoulder blades and concentrate on the road, then he'd end up wrapping the bike around a telephone pole.

Warm, humid air rushed past them, fluttering her short skirt and baring more of her toned thighs. He forced his eyes away from the tantalizing sight and back on the road. Where could he take her? The shorter the ride, the better. The roar of the engine made asking impossible. Might as well take her to his place since he and Juliana needed to compare calendars and set up the riding lessons.

Pride filled his chest as Renegade's lights came into view. He'd bought the vacant riverfront building in the historical district eight months ago. It had taken a lot of sweat and most of his cash to turn the downstairs into a business and the upstairs into a home his sister Kelly and her girls could visit. He'd opened his doors four months ago, but business hadn't been as brisk as he'd hoped—hence his participation in the auction.

He pulled into his narrow private driveway, automatically counting the empty parking spaces out front as he passed. If he wanted to stay in Wilmington near his sister, then he had to turn a profit soon and pay off the bank note.

He parked, climbed from the bike and removed his helmet. Juliana remained seated. She fumbled to unfasten her chin strap and then pulled off her helmet. Rex rocked back on his heels with a silent whistle of admiration. Now there was a centerfold-quality picture—minus the staples—guaranteed to keep a man up all night. Mile-long legs straddling the Harley's black seat, red strappy heels, skimpy dress, beautiful face, tumbled hair. A hot package.

But good-looking women had caused him plenty of trouble before, so he tamped down his physical response and offered his hand. Gingerly, she curled her soft fingers around his and then struggled to draw her leg over the seat. A glimpse of her candy apple–red panties hit his belly like a fireball.

He caught her elbow as she wobbled on her heels on the cobblestone sidewalk. The evening breeze plastered the silky fabric of her dress against her puckered nipples. Was she wearing anything besides those panties under there? His pulse revved faster. *Forget it, Tanner.*

She scrubbed her arms and her tiny silver purse sparkled in the streetlights like rhinestones under stage lights. "Could we go inside?"

He motioned for her to precede him. When he reached past her to open the door, her scent, an intoxicating mixture of flowers and spice, filled his lungs. She stepped inside and looked around.

What did she think of his place? He'd played on Wilmington's TV and film industry. The bar's theme was movie rebels and renegades—men Rex had identified with back when he'd been a teen who couldn't wait to break free from family ranching tradition. He'd escaped the day he'd turned eighteen but, seventeen years later, the guilt of his bitter parting words still haunted him.

The bar itself took up most of the back wall. He'd filled the floor with tables—too many of which were empty on a Saturday night. The waitresses leaned against the back wall.

"You don't have any memorabilia from your music career in here."

The comment stopped him in his tracks. Juliana knew who he was even though he'd deliberately excluded his recent past in the auction bio. Had she bought him for the braggin' rights of bedding Rex Tanner, former Nashville bad boy? She wouldn't be the first with that goal. And as appealing as the idea of hitting the sheets with Juliana might be, he didn't want his old life intruding here. "No."

Her assessing gaze landed on him. "Wouldn't it be wise to trade on what people know of you?"

And be known as a has-been for the rest of his life? No thanks. "My music career is over. If people want a honky-tonk they can go elsewhere. Can I get you a drink?"

"No, thank you. May I stay here for an hour or so? As soon as the auction ends, I can call a friend for a ride."

"I'll take you home after we schedule your lessons." Her eyes widened. "I have a truck if you don't want to get back on the bike."

"Thank you, but I think I'll stay with one of my girlfriends tonight. She can come and get me. My car is at her place anyway. We rode to the auction together."

Why would a rich chick need to hide? She looked over the age of consent, but looks could be deceiving. "How old did you say you were?"

She hesitated. "I didn't say, but I'm thirty, if you must know. Didn't your mother ever teach you that it's rude to ask?"

His mother had taught him a lot of things. And like an ungrateful SOB, he'd thrown her lessons back in her face. "Aren't you a little old to be running away from home?"

"You don't understand. My parents…" She trailed off and took an anxious peek over his shoulder as if she expected them to burst through the door. "They won't understand about tonight."

"I don't have to know the whole story to know running's not going to solve anything." A lesson he'd learned the hard way.

"But—"

He held up a hand. "And I don't want to know the whole story. I'm here to give you riding lessons. That's it."

How did she manage to look down her nose at him when she was a good six to eight inches shorter than he was? "Fine."

He considered leaving her at the bar and going to his apartment to get his calendar, but she and her sexy dress had already caught the attention of the guys in the back corner. The men were regulars, friends of his deployed brother-in-law, and Rex didn't want anything to happen that would keep them from coming back. "Upstairs."

He waved to Danny, and pointed toward the private entrance leading to his apartment. From the wiseass smirk on his manager's face, Danny probably thought the boss was about to get laid. The thought sent a Roman candle of heat through Rex's veins. He doused it. He'd dodged every advance thrown his way since opening, and he wasn't about to get sucked into that drainpipe now.

Rex pulled his keys from his pocket, unlocked the door and motioned for Juliana to precede him up the stairs. If she wanted more than Harley and horseback-riding lessons from him, then she'd be disappointed.

Two

Who'd have guessed that after all these years of not getting hot and bothered that she could get turned on by something mechanical? Although Juliana suspected the motorcycle ride wasn't entirely to blame for her discombobulation.

"Have a seat." Rex prowled around the den of his apartment flicking on lamps to reveal a very masculine decor of cappuccino-colored leather and dark wood. The furniture looked expensive but not new. Relics from his days at the top of the country-music charts?

Juliana perched on the edge of the sofa tallying sensations and classifying the wide range of emotions she'd experienced tonight. *Safe* wasn't among them. She had an inkling this might be the beginnings of lust, but she couldn't be sure.

Fingers of wind had ripped at her clothing and tried to pull her off the bike when Rex had raced the motorcycle down a long, straight section of road. The scream bubbling in her throat had been caused by terror mixed with a smidgen of excitement. Each time he'd leaned into a curve, her heart had pounded so hard she'd thought it would explode. He'd probably have bruises tomorrow from where she'd clutched him so tightly. By the time they'd arrived at Renegade she'd practically burrowed under his skin.

And she'd liked it there.

Rex's abs had been steady and rock-hard beneath her knotted fingers, and the rough texture of jeans had abraded the sensitive skin of her inner thighs and the tender flesh between her legs. The heat of his broad back had seeped through his T-shirt and her thin dress to warm her breasts more effectively than any caress she'd ever experienced. When he'd climbed from the bike, her legs had been too weak to follow. In fact, they still hadn't quit shaking.

Which caused her extreme reaction? Fear or physical attraction? She didn't have much experience with either. In the past, she'd always been drawn by a man's intelligence more than his physique, but her reaction to Rex had nothing to do with his brain. She hated to admit she was shallow enough to look forward to exploring this new terrain.

He sat beside her on the sofa, opened a calendar on the coffee table and then angled to face her. The outside seam of his jeans scraped her knee and thigh. A shiver worked its way to the pit of her stomach and settled there like a hot rock.

"I usually work nights, so your lessons will have to be late mornings or on my days off. Which works for you?" The flirtatiousness he'd displayed at the auction disappeared behind a no-nonsense businesslike demeanor. Since she was counting on him to lead her astray, that wasn't a desirable development.

"I work weekdays."

"Doing what?"

With him sitting this close and holding her gaze that way,

Juliana had a hard time remembering what consumed most of her week. His scent and proximity had the oddest effect on her ability to think clearly. Funny, she lived for her job… What was it again? Oh, yes. "I'm an account auditor with Alden Bank and Trust."

His narrowed gaze traveled slowly from her face to her bare shoulders, over her dress and then her legs. Her body reacted as if he'd touched her by tightening, liquefying.

So this was animal attraction? She'd heard others talk about it, but she'd never experienced the sensation. She wanted to pick it apart and study the components the way she would account entries during an audit. Flushed skin. A tingle in her veins. Accelerated heart rate. Dampened palms.

"You don't look like any bean counter I've ever met." His skeptical expression robbed the words of any compliment and hit a sore spot. After earning an MBA from the local university, Juliana had accepted a position in the family bank's home office. She'd had to work doubly hard to prove her worth and quiet the rumors of nepotism, and she'd been proving herself ever since. But this wasn't work. She wanted Rex to see her as a desirable woman, not as a highly credentialed bank auditor.

"I've always been good with numbers." She downplayed. It was people skills she lacked. Growing up, her brother had been the socially adept one who'd held the titles of class president, homecoming king and every other desirable position. Juliana had been an ugly duckling who'd preferred books and horses to people. Andrea and Holly had been, and still were, her only close friends.

Rex thumped a beat on the table with his pen, drawing her attention back to his big, rough and scarred workman's hands. She'd listened to his music and it amazed her that such strong, masculine hands could pluck a guitar so beautifully.

"We'll meet after you get off work on Mondays and Thursdays, my days off. That'll give us a couple of hours of daylight."

She caught herself watching his lips move, blinked and refocused on his eyes—dark, knowing eyes that seemed to look right inside her.

"I've leased a smaller bike for you," he continued, "but you can't drive it until you've earned your motorcycle learner's permit and mastered a few basic skills."

The unexpected turn of the conversation pulled her from her corporeal exploration. "A learner's permit?"

"Required by North Carolina law. I'll give you the booklet tonight. Start studying. You'll have to take a written test at the Department of Motor Vehicles."

Her prize package required her to take a test? That hadn't been in the fine print, and she *always* read the fine print. "I work fifty to sixty hours a week. When am I supposed to find time to study and take a test?"

"Before the end of the month—unless you want the newspaper to report that you couldn't pass."

Her competitive instincts stirred. She hadn't taken a driving test in fifteen years, but she'd always been an excellent student. "Fine. Twice a week at six o'clock for four weeks."

"I'll let the reporter know." He closed the calendar and planted his hands on his knees. "Listen, Juliana, Renegade needs all the publicity it can get out of the newspaper series. You might not have noticed but the place isn't packed."

"I noticed. Business accounts are a large part of my job. Empty tables mean reduced revenue and reduced revenue means—"

He leaned toward her. Her mind went blank and her heart leaped in anticipation. She snatched a quick breath, wet her lips and lifted her mouth, but Rex didn't kiss her. Instead he dragged a fluffy pink boa and a small pink purse from beneath his sofa cushion and sat back again.

She blinked in surprise. *Had she bought a cross-dresser?* "Yours?" she squeaked.

The rugged lines of his face softened and his eyes warmed, turning her insides to mush. "My nieces'."

Shock receded. The rebel had nieces. And judging from his expression, he had a soft spot in his heart for them. The idea of using him to further her um...*physical* education had been a lot easier when she'd believed him to be one-hundred-percent bad boy, a heartless seducer of innocents, a man who'd get the job done and not think twice about it. Now the images of reckless rebel, concerned business owner and doting uncle tangled in a confusing mass in her head. But instead of turning her off, the combination intrigued her and made her want to know more. Not a good idea since this was a short-term project.

He stood and tossed the dress-up items into a wicker basket in the corner. "Let me make one thing clear. You bought horseback and Harley riding lessons and you're going to get them. But riding lessons are all I'm offering."

Half-dozen heartbeats later, his meaning sank in. Mortification burned over her skin like a desert wind. Was she so transparent? He couldn't know that she wondered how he'd kiss, how he'd taste and, more specifically, how she'd react to his embrace. Could he?

She wobbled to her feet. "I—I appreciate your candor."

"You ready to call for your ride yet?"

He couldn't wait to get rid of her. How embarrassing. Had she ever had a date so eager to show her the door? "Certainly."

The evening was not going as she'd anticipated and she had no idea how to get it back on track. What did she know about seduction? She'd counted on him doing all the work.

Why hadn't she developed a backup plan?

* * *

"So is he as great as he looks or is he all beauty, brawn and no brains?" Holly asked as Juliana climbed into her friend's Jeep outside Renegade.

"He's not just a pretty face." His dedication to his nieces and his business savvy in using the auction and the monthlong newspaper coverage as advertising proved Rex was more than an empty-headed pretty boy. "Did you get your firefighter?"

Holly abruptly reached for the radio and flipped through the stations. "No."

The rat. Had she and Andrea chickened out after sending Juliana into the bidding wars like a sacrificial lamb? "You promised you'd buy him."

"No, I promised I'd buy *a bachelor* and I did. The firefighter went for more money than we agreed upon—although *you* certainly broke that rule, didn't you? Besides, Eric was desperate."

Juliana recoiled. "Eric! *My brother, Eric?*"

Holly darted a glance in her direction and nodded.

"You cheated."

"No, I didn't. I wanted a man who would give me candlelit dinners and take me dancing. Eric's package promises Eleven Enchanted Evenings."

Juliana didn't like the blissful smile on Holly's face—not in connection to her brother. "But it's *Eric.*"

"So?"

"You wanted romance. Eric is no Prince Charming to your Cinderella. I'm having really icky thoughts of my brother kissing you good night, and I don't want to go there." She shuddered.

"I know you don't want to believe it, Juliana, but Eric is as much of a hunk as your rebel."

"Ick. Ick." She stuck her fingers in her ears. No matter what her friend said, Holly had cheated by taking the safe way out.

She unplugged her ears. "You and Andrea convinced me to go out on a limb and buy Rex. There is no risk involved in buying someone you know. Did Andrea also turn coward? Who did she buy?"

"Clayton."

Sympathy squeezed Juliana's heart and she sighed. "So she's really going through with it, then?"

"That's what she said." Holly didn't sound any happier about the situation than Juliana.

"I hope he doesn't break her heart again."

"I hope your rebel doesn't break yours. Those were some serious sparks between you when he walked you out."

Sparks? One-sided sparks, maybe. Rex Tanner didn't seem the least bit interested in fanning the flames Juliana could feel licking at her toes. At the moment, she had no idea how she'd change his mind, but given what she knew of his past, it shouldn't be too difficult.

"You are completely off base with that observation, my friend, and my heart will be just fine, thank you. Remember, my time with Rex Tanner is limited. He'd never fit in with my long-term career goals, and I seriously doubt an anal-retentive bank auditor whose idea of adventure is trying a new shade of nail polish would fit in with his."

Rex peeled his gaze from Juliana's behind for the fifth time and shook his head. Jodhpurs. He should have expected as much from a high-society chick who wrote five-figure checks without blinking.

"Next time wear jeans." Her formal riding attire was a far cry from Saturday night's scanty, sexy dress, but her jodhpurs looked as if they'd been spray painted over the luscious curve of her butt, and her sleeveless cotton blouse conformed to the shape of her breasts like a lover's hands. She'd pulled her shiny hair back with a clip and perched one of those prissy black velvet hard hats on her head—the kind horse-jumping folks wore. The siren-red nail polish was gone and so was most of her makeup. She looked better without the war paint. And why was he noticing? Her smooth skin had nothing to do with riding lessons.

"The boots are okay, and I can live with the hat."

"Please stop. Your flattery will turn my head," she replied with a hint of sarcasm, making him wonder if he'd read her lingering glances wrong Saturday night. "If I can find the time, I'll buy some jeans before Thursday."

He paused with the saddle midair. "You don't own a pair of jeans?"

"No. Casual Friday at the bank never gets that casual. You certainly have a lot of requirements for this package that weren't included in the description listed in the program."

"Most of it's common sense." He settled the saddle and saddle pad on Jelly Bean, the palomino mare he'd bought for his nieces. "Putting on a western saddle is similar to an English one. Here's how you secure it."

After demonstrating, he unfastened everything and stepped back. "Your turn."

Juliana tackled the task, but the mare tended to be lazy on hot summer afternoons. She bloated her stomach to prevent the tightening of the cinch around her belly. Juliana lacked the strength to make Jelly Bean exhale.

Positioning himself behind her, the way he did with the girls, he reached around to help her pull the leather strap. Having his arms around an attractive woman made his veins hum. He tried to ignore it. Unlike with his petite three- and five-year-old nieces, Juliana's taller frame lined up against his like a spoon in a drawer. Or a lover in bed. The mare shifted, bumping Juliana and her tightly wrapped behind against him.

Within seconds, her pants weren't the only tight ones. Rex steadied her and then stepped back, putting several yards and the hitching post between them. "Try the bridle next."

Juliana definitely knew her way around a horse. She rested the mare's muzzle against her breasts while she eased the bridle over her ears and brushed her forelock out of her eyes, and then she rewarded Jelly Bean for cooperating with a stroke down her golden neck and a scratch between her perked up ears.

He envied the horse being pressed between Juliana's breasts. Unacceptable. The auditor was off-limits. "Mount up."

She lifted her foot a couple of feet off the ground until the pull of fabric across her hips restricted her movements, and then she put her boot back down and looked at him over her shoulder. "Would you give me a leg up?"

Was there more than a legitimate request for help in her words? A tentative smile quivered on her lips—nothing seductive about it. In fact, he'd swear he saw nervousness in her eyes.

Get over yourself, Tanner. What does it say about your ego that you suspect every woman you meet of trying to get into your pants?

"Sure." As he did with the girls, he clasped Juliana's waist and lifted. Bad move. He didn't need to know that her waist was tiny or that her body heat would penetrate the thin fabric of her pants. He yanked his hands free so quickly Jelly Bean— the calmest horse he'd ever encountered—spooked and side-stepped. Rex lunged forward again, expecting Juliana to fall off, but she grabbed the saddle horn and managed to stay on.

"Is this another test?" More sarcasm. Okay, he'd definitely read her wrong.

She shifted in the saddle, and then stood in the stirrups and sank back down. She repeated the motion a couple of times. "This saddle feels odd, but comfortable."

Tugging at the suddenly tight collar of his T-shirt, he

looked away, cleared his throat and shifted his stance to ease the pinch of his jeans. The last time he'd seen a woman move like that, she'd been riding *him*. How long ago had that been? Too long. And hell, he couldn't remember her name or what she'd looked like.

There had been a lot of nameless encounters in his past—not something he was proud of now, but at the time he'd been floating on a wave of fame, taking the women who fell at his feet for granted and using them to make himself believe he was finally somebody. He'd been somebody all right. *Somebody stupid.*

His bandmates had used booze or drugs to come down from a post-performance high. Rex had used women—a practice that now disgusted him. He was damned lucky his carousing hadn't landed him in the morgue or given him an STD the way his father had predicted. Most of Rex's father's lectures had gone in one ear and out the other, but thank God the safe-sex one had stuck.

Rex had had a lucky escape, and he planned to put his sordid past behind him in a new city with a new career. He'd be the kind of brother he should have been to Kelly and an uncle Kelly's girls would be proud to claim. With their father deployed overseas, they needed someone they could depend on when their mom needed help.

Back to business. "The seat of a western saddle is deeper than an English one. It conforms to your shape." *And a damned fine shape it is.* "Take the reins in your hand with only one finger between them."

She did as he instructed, but looked unsure.

"Western horses move away from pressure and they prefer slack reins," he explained.

She stared down at him with a doubtful expression. "If my reins are slack how am I going to control the horse?"

"Use a soft touch. Your fingers and wrist work the bit, and rely on leg cues more than the bridle." Which drew his attention back to the length of her legs and the curve of her butt. If he didn't get his brain out of his briefs, she could get hurt. That kind of publicity wouldn't help the bar. "You know how to use leg cues?"

"Yes."

"Then signal her to walk."

Jelly Bean started forward. Rex kept pace beside them. A light evening breeze carried Juliana's perfume downwind, filling his lungs with her scent every time he inhaled.

He cursed his uncharacteristic distraction. Usually, he had tunnel vision. He saw what needed doing and didn't waver from his set course. His career and the destruction of it were perfect examples. He'd wanted to make it to the top and he had, and then, after his parents had died, he'd wanted out, but contracts had held him prisoner. Before leaving Nashville, he'd made sure he'd burned all his bridges. He shook his head to clear it. *Focus.*

"What's wrong?" she asked.

"Your motion. You're perching on top of the saddle instead of sinking into it, and every one of your muscles is strung as tight as a bow. Relax your upper body and your legs. Slump into the saddle."

"All my life I've been taught to sit up straight, and you're telling me to slouch?" Her haughty tone was exactly what he needed to remind himself of the differences between them.

"Not exactly, but you have to relax here." He quickly tapped the base of her spine with a fingertip. "Here." He nudged her thigh with his knuckle. "And here." His palm brushed her lower abdomen. He quickly withdrew it. Her body heat scalded his skin. He stepped away from the horse and crossed to the center of the riding ring. Ten yards wasn't enough distance to douse the fire smoldering in his gut.

"Cue her to jog when you're ready." Juliana nudged Jelly Bean into a slightly faster gait. Juliana tried to post, rising and lowering in the saddle from her knees as she would if riding English. "No posting. Sit."

She did and probably rattled a brain cell or two as she— and her perfectly shaped breasts—bounced along.

Rex ground his molars. He'd been attracted to a lot of women, but not this way. Had to be because he knew this relationship—like the ones in his past—would go nowhere. Falling back into old, bad habits was not part of his plan. "Scoot."

"Wh-at do you m-ean sc-oot?" The jarring broke her words into fragments. The mare snorted her displeasure.

"Rock your hips from the waist down." She looked at him as if he'd asked her to fly. In frustration he said, "Match your moves to the horse's. Like you're with your lover."

Her lips parted and her cheeks turned the color of a ripe peach. She jerked her face forward to stare straight between Jelly Bean's ears, but within seconds she had the correct motion. "Sorry. It's been a while, but I think I have it now."

Been a while? Riding a horse or with a lover? *None of your business, bud.* But the image of Juliana as his lover, straddling his thighs and arching to take his deep thrusts flashed in his mind. Heat oozed from his pores and his lungs stalled.

"Yeah. You got it," he croaked.

Keeping his distance from the bean counter was critical. She knew who he was, knew about his past. Worse, he feared she had the power to bring the self-centered SOB he used to be out of hiding. He couldn't allow that to happen.

When the man turned off the charm, he *really* turned it off. Juliana sighed. Rex hadn't given her a single sign of encouragement. And darn it, she didn't know how to flirt without looking like a bimbo with something in her eyes.

She reluctantly climbed from the mare's back. Was she so unattractive, so lacking in basic feminine charms that even a man who'd reportedly had women in every town his tour bus had rolled through wasn't interested? Ouch.

She had to find a way to get her plan back on track. In accounting, that meant understanding the parameters of the investigation, and the only way to achieve understanding was by asking questions, beginning with the nonthreatening ones and easing into the intrusive ones. She likened the practice to putting a jigsaw puzzle together, borders first.

"I don't suppose you'd consider selling Jelly Bean?" Not that she had much time to ride anymore, but this evening with a light breeze stirring her hair and the setting sun on her skin reminded her how much she missed having a horse in her life.

"She's not mine to sell. I bought the mare for Becky and Liza."

"And Becky and Liza are…?"

"My nieces."

"You bought them a horse? Did you also buy this property so they'd have somewhere to ride?"

He shook his head and his rope of shiny hair swished between his shoulder blades. The urge to tug the leather tie loose and see if the strands felt as thick and luxurious as they looked was totally out of character for her, but her neatly clipped-above-the-collar world hadn't allowed her to experience a man with longer hair without the width of a desk and the professional wall of her position at the bank between them. The men she'd dated in the past had all been the preppy, Ivy League type. Like Wally. Clean-cut. No rough edges.

Rex had rough edges aplenty.

"Farm's not mine. I rent the barn and a few acres from the owner. Her husband died last year. She leases the stable and the surrounding land to pay the mortgage."

"What made you choose to locate your business in Wilmington? We're not exactly horse country."

He flashed an irritated glance in her direction. Oops, had she sounded too much like a bank investigator? For a moment she thought he'd refuse to answer. "My brother-in-law is with Camp Lejeune's 4th Marine Expeditionary Brigade antiterrorism unit. I wanted to be nearby to help my sister with the girls when he's deployed. He's in Baghdad now."

Another chink in his bad-boy shell. What other discrepancies would she find if she looked past his rebel veneer? And did she really want to know? Her dislike of unanswered questions outweighed the need to keep her emotional distance. "You grew up on a ranch in tornado alley?"

"Yes," he barked in a mind-your-own-business voice and then took the reins from her and led the mare into the shade of the small four-stall barn.

Juliana's gaze immediately drifted to his firm behind in faded denim. When she realized what she was doing, she jerked her eyes back to the breadth of his shoulders. In the past, she'd been more concerned with a man's character instead of his looks, but she had to admit Rex had great packaging.

The smell of oats, hay and fresh shavings, and the hum of insects brought back memories. Until she'd turned seventeen, she'd spent almost as much time with her horse as her books, but when her old gelding had died of colic, she hadn't had the heart to replace him.

"Did you miss the ranch when you were touring?"

For several moments, Rex ignored her question while he exchanged the bridle for a halter and cross-tied the mare in the stall. He shoved his hand into the caddy carrying the brushes and stabbed a soft bristled-body brush in her direction. "Yes. Groom her."

Juliana couldn't imagine leaving Wilmington or Alden's

behind. For as far back as she could remember, she'd wanted to work in Alden's headquarters. The building's two-story foyer, with its marble pillars and the wrought-iron railings on the second-floor balcony, had been her own personal castle. She'd loved visiting after hours with her father, listening to the echo of their footsteps across the marble floor and the overwhelming silence of the place after the employees and customers had left for the day.

Because she'd wanted to stay near home and friends, she'd chosen to attend the local state university—much to her mother's dismay—rather than go to an Ivy League school out of state like so many of her classmates. The University of North Carolina at Wilmington had been her father's alma mater, and for once he'd spoken out against her mother's decrees and supported Juliana's decision to go to school locally and serve an internship at Alden's.

"Did you ever think of moving back?"

His gaze met hers over the horse's withers. The grooves beside his mouth deepened, drawing her attention to the dark evening beard shadowing his square jaw and upper lip. "You bought riding lessons not my life story."

Touchy, touchy. But she dealt with hostile people all the time. Digging into someone's accounts and revealing discrepancies didn't bring out the best in anyone. She'd learned to hold her ground and keep asking the questions until she had the information she needed. What exactly was she looking for here? She didn't know, but she'd keep digging until she found it.

"No, Rex, I didn't buy your biography, but if we're going to spend approximately sixteen hours together over the next four weeks, then we have to have something to discuss besides the weather. The story of my life would put us both to sleep, and since I imagine napping is frowned upon when riding or driving, I thought we'd try yours. You're welcome to volunteer other topics if you choose."

Scowling, he removed the mare's saddle and saddle pad, and deposited both on the top of the stall's wooden half door, and then braced his hands on either side of it. His shoulders, clad in another Renegade T-shirt, looked as stiff and broad as the beams supporting the barn roof.

"Yes, I missed the ranch. And I wish I'd gone back. But, I didn't. By the time I wised up, my sister had married and moved away and my parents were dead." He delivered the information in a matter-of-fact tone. His warning not to offer pity or sympathy came across loud and clear, but the ill-concealed pain in his voice brought a lump to Juliana's throat.

She ducked under the cross-tie, hesitated and then laid her hand on the rigid muscles of his back. "I'm sorry."

He flinched and stepped out of reach, then ducked to pick up the grooming caddy. Heat zinged through her from the brief contact, crackling and popping along her nerve endings in an unsettling manner. She lowered her arm and closed her prickling fingers into a fist. Before she could separate and label the avalanche of sensations, he straightened and turned. The emptiness in his eyes made her chest ache.

"Don't be. I got what I deserved. Groom the mare. I'll put the tack away and get her oats. We have to meet the reporter at Renegade in thirty minutes." He shoved the grooming box in her direction, snatched up the saddle and bridle as if they weighed nothing, and left.

Juliana stared after him. If Rex thought snarling like a wounded beast would put her off, then he'd miscalculated. The glimmer of softness he tried so hard to conceal had piqued her curiosity, and once Juliana had a puzzle to solve, she never gave up until she had every piece in place.

Three

"So tell me, Ms. Alden, why would the heiress to a banking empire need to buy a date?" Octavia Jenkins, the reporter, asked.

Heiress. Rex's chair wobbled precariously. He nearly fell over backward. Fighting for balance, he rocked forward. The front legs of the chair hit the floor with a thud. Up until now, he'd been completely relaxed. His half of the interview had gone well. He'd plugged the bar, served the reporter a selection of tasty appetizers and avoided discussing his aborted career.

"Your family *owns* the bank?" Rex asked. His first impression after the auction had been that Juliana had more money than sense, but he hadn't expected it to be *that* much money. Holy spit.

Juliana shifted in her seat and glanced around the restaurant as if checking to see who'd overheard his question. "I told you I worked for Alden Bank and Trust."

"You never told me your family *owned* it." And owned him,

or at least the note on his business. It would be her family's minions who would padlock Renegade's doors if Rex couldn't pay off the note. And he'd lose everything—his apartment and his business—since he'd invested all he had into Renegade. "You never told me your last name."

"You never asked."

He hadn't asked because he hadn't wanted to get involved beyond the lessons. So much for detachment.

The reporter looked up from her furious note-taking with a hungry glint in her eyes and a flush on her cocoa-colored skin. Rex had seen that look often enough in the past to know it meant trouble. "Were you trying to keep your family connections a secret?"

Juliana hesitated. "What would be the point? Every eligible male in the southeast knows who my family is."

And that, Rex deduced from Juliana's flat tone, was an issue. Had the banker's daughter experienced the degradation of being dated for what she represented rather than who she was as a person? He tamped down the empathy budding in his chest because he didn't want to have anything in common with Juliana. But she'd put a chink in the wall he'd worked so hard to build between them.

"Which leads us back to my original question, Ms. Alden. You should have men standing in line to wine and dine you. Why buy one?"

Juliana looked every inch the poised southern belle as she lifted her chin and smiled—a smile that Rex noted didn't reach her eyes—at the reporter. "My mother is the auction organizer. I wanted to support her efforts."

Bull. Rex didn't know how he knew it, but something in her voice and in her beauty-queen bearing told him that wasn't the real reason Juliana Alden, *banking heiress,* for crying out loud, had bought his package. His *auction* package—he clarified when a neglected part of his anatomy twitched to attention.

"And why did you choose Rex?"

Yeah, why him? He silently seconded Octavia's question. Lacing his fingers on the tabletop, he awaited Juliana's response.

"He's new in town and I've never ridden a motorcycle." More bull. He'd bet his Harley on it.

"You're playing welcoming committee?" He didn't bother to sugarcoat his disbelief.

"Is there something wrong with being neighborly?" She eyed him haughtily, but the tension in her features told its own tale. What was she hiding? Curiosity coiled in his gut.

Octavia persisted. "This had nothing to do with your recent thirtieth birthday, coming into your trust fund and your friends Andrea Montgomery and Holly Prescott also buying bachelors?"

Juliana paled and her eyes widened slightly. She inhaled a long breath and then slowly released it. Rex knew because the slow rise and fall of her breasts distracted him. He cursed the arousal strumming through his system, blinked and shifted his gaze back to her face.

"Only because each year Andrea, Holly and I do something to celebrate our birthdays. And yes, this year we each came into our trust funds, but since we all have well-paying careers, we don't really need the money. We decided to donate a portion of the money to a charitable cause, and the auction to support the disabled children's camp seemed as admirable a choice as any. Have you heard about the boat Dean Yachts has offered to design, build and donate to the cause?"

Octavia Jenkins waved the diversion aside. "I'll do a feature on that later. I want to talk about you." Leaning forward, she grinned mischievously and tilted her head conspiratorially toward Juliana. "You're a banker and he's a biker.

You can't get much more different than that. Taking a walk on the wild side never entered into your plans?"

Color rushed to Juliana's cheeks. She darted a panicked glance in Rex's direction, and then ducked her head and fussed with the silverware beside her plate. "No. That wasn't it at all."

Well, I'll be damned. If her guilty expression hadn't clued him in, then her rushed, breathless answer was a dead giveaway. The beautiful bean counter was lying through her perfect white teeth. And for some crazy reason, the prospect of Juliana getting wild *with him* turned him on like nobody's business.

Forget it, farm boy. Too risky.

"If you say so." Octavia closed her notebook and stood. "Well, that's all the questions I have tonight. I'll see you next week."

Rex rose. His mother had managed to drill some manners into his thick skull. He sat back down after the reporter had left and studied Juliana until she squirmed in her seat. She just didn't seem the type to rebel. And wasn't thirty a little old to get started on rebellion?

She bolted to her feet. "I should go, too."

Determined to get the truth out of her one way or another, Rex followed her outside, keeping pace beside her so he wouldn't be distracted by the sweet curve of her rear. The moon had yet to rise, but he could see well enough in the streetlights to know he was beginning to like the fit of her riding britches a little too much.

"Why did you buy my package?" he asked as they neared her car.

She turned on the cobblestone sidewalk. "I told you."

"You're off the record now. No reporter in sight. Let's have the truth, Juliana. Why me?"

Her face flushed with more than indignation. She shifted uneasily. "I beg your pardon? Are you calling me a liar?"

"Admit it. You fed that reporter a load of manure."

If she stood any straighter, her spine would snap. "Mr. Tanner—"

"Rex," he corrected and moved closer. Without the killer heels, the top of her head barely reached his chin.

She retreated, bumping into the lamppost behind her. Milky light streamed over her, painting ribbons of silver in her dark hair. A soft breeze ruffled the strands around her face. She tipped her head back and her lips parted on a shaky breath, and her pink tongue slipped out to wet them.

"*Rex,* then. Why would you suspect I had an ulterior motive for bidding on you?" Her damp lips and breathless tone hit him like the business end of a cattle prod, sending a jolt of electricity through him.

"You turned ten shades of red when the reporter asked if you wanted to take a walk on the wild side. Looked guilty as hell to me."

Her lashes fluttered and her gaze fell. "I did not."

"Did too." He'd learned from experience that the only way to deal with a problem was to confront it. Running didn't work. Ignoring it wouldn't either. He propped one arm on the post above her head and leaned in until only inches separated their faces. "Wanting to see if Nashville's bad boy can live up to his hell-raising reputation?"

"Of course not," she said too quickly. But her gaze shifted to his mouth and her breath puffed against his chin in shallow bursts. The tight points of her breasts pushed at her blouse.

She wanted him, and damned if the feeling wasn't mutual. He swallowed the sudden flood of moisture in his mouth and cursed the unwelcome response drumrolling through his veins. Kissing the bank owner's daughter would be a big mistake, but part of him wanted to forget common sense, taste her red lips and feel her slender length against him.

Go for it, his awakening libido urged. Then maybe the simmering sexual awareness between them would die a natural death and they could get on with the lessons. She wasn't his type and he sure wasn't hers.

He cupped her jaw with his right hand. The warm velvety texture of her skin surprised him. Tempted him. His fingertips teased her earlobe, her nape, and then closed around the cool satin of her hair. He tugged, tilting back her head and lifting her lips closer to his.

"Is this what you want, Juliana?" He cupped her jodhpurcovered bottom, pulling her closer, and lowered his head. In his hypersensitive state, her swiftly indrawn breath sounded as loud as a jet engine. Her fingers spread over his belly and dug into his waist, starting a fire he wasn't sure he could put out. But she didn't push him away. Her lashes drifted down and his lids grew heavy in response. His mouth hovered above hers, close enough that he could taste her sweet breath, and then sanity slapped him upside the head.

What in the hell are you doing, Tanner?

He hesitated, examining her flushed face, parted lips and the dark fan of her long lashes against her cheeks. Damn. The reporter had nailed Juliana's motive. The banking heiress was using him. And if he gave in to the urge to kiss her—hell, the urge to take her right here against the lamppost—he'd be using her, too.

Been there. Done that. Not going back.

He didn't want to be that selfish bastard again, and risking any kind of involvement with a woman whose family could pull the rug out from under his business could be career suicide. Because when the relationship ended—and it would end—there'd be hell to pay.

Swallowing a sobering lungful of air, he battled the need twisting through him like a tornado and shoved himself away. A sexy protest emerged from Juliana's mouth, but he ignored it.

"If a walk on the wild side is what you're after, Ms. Alden, find another sucker." Turning on his heel, he left temptation—and certain disaster—behind.

Thursday evening arrived long before Juliana could get a handle on her reaction to the near-miss kiss and the sting of Rex's rejection. But she wouldn't let a little discomfiture derail her agenda.

"Plan B. If the mountain won't come to Mohammed," she muttered as she turned her car into the stable's driveway.

Over the past two and a half days, she'd launched a full-scale fact-finding mission. By her calculations, she was as prepared for today's lesson as she possibly could be. She'd memorized the magazines recommended by her twenty- and thirty-something coworkers, bought clothing deemed appropriate by said magazines for casual dates with a hot guy and learned everything between the covers of the Department of Motor Vehicles booklet Rex had given her. To top it off, on her lunch hour yesterday she'd visited the local motorcycle dealership. The salesman had fitted her with the proper safety gear to the tune of several hundred dollars, and she'd spent a good part of last night curled up with a book—the Harley owner's manual.

She spotted Rex standing beside his motorcycle. The bees in her stomach buzzed into flight. Once again, he wore jeans and a Renegade T-shirt. His closed countenance brought heat to her cheeks. He hadn't forgotten their last encounter or her panting eagerness. Neither had she.

If he could disturb her that much without actually kissing her, then what kind of havoc could he wreak if—*when*—their lips connected? She trembled in her new biker boots at the possibility of exploring further.

She'd never had sex just for the sex's sake and wasn't totally comfortable with the idea now. In the past, each relationship she'd allowed to progress into intimacy had been one that she'd thought might eventually lead to love and marriage. None had, and she readily admitted that was mostly her fault. She'd never been head-over-heels in love or anywhere close to lust and that made it all too easy to get caught up in her job and forget her boyfriends. The guys eventually got tired of being neglected and dumped her.

Forget past failures. Focus on future successes. Wrapping herself in the knowledge that she looked young, hip and available, she took a deep breath for courage, parked and climbed from the car.

Come and get me, bad boy.

Rex's gaze lasered in on her clothing as she closed the distance between them, and he snapped to attention like a military man. His darkening expression looked more ominous than the storm clouds on the distant horizon.

Hold your ground. Don't let him rattle you.

"Good evening, Rex." Juliana's manufactured smile wobbled on her lips when he didn't return it. She extricated the hard rectangle of her motorcycle learner's permit from the pocket of her snug new jeans and handed it to him. "I'm ready for my driving lesson."

He took the permit, but his eyes examined her, not the card. She struggled with the urge to hitch up the low-riding stretch jeans and cross her arms over her close-fitting camisole top with its built-in push-up bra. At the moment, Juliana would have welcomed anything that would cover the two-inch wide band of bare skin around her midsection. Even the navel ring the sales clerk had tried but failed to talk her into sounded good since it would have covered part of her navel. These clothes were so not her, although she had to acknowledge the heady surge of power caused by Rex's widening pupils and devouring glance.

Rex blinked, handed back the license and abruptly pivoted toward the bike. "We'll start with ground work."

His voice sounded deeper than she remembered, but the stiff set of his shoulders looked familiar. How did he turn the charm on and off so easily? At the auction and with the reporter, he'd been Mr. Too-Hot-To-Handle, but with her, he was Mr. Don't-Mess-With-Me. Which was the real Rex Tanner and what was he thinking behind that blank expression?

Juliana wiggled her license back into her pocket and reached deep for the bravado to get through the next two hours. "I borrowed a manual and a video from the Harley dealership. I can name most of the parts of a motorcycle."

He grunted a nonanswer while he polished a spot off the fuel tank with the hem of his shirt. A glimpse of flat abdomen dusted with dark curls sucked the breath from her lungs.

Her studiousness obviously hadn't impressed him. But that was no surprise. She'd never met a guy who liked brainy women. She ought to know. She'd run off more than her share. *Take the initiative.* She cleared her throat. "Can I drive your motorcycle today?"

He shot her a hard look. "My bike is too heavy for a beginner to ride alone, and you're not wearing the proper gear."

"I wasn't wearing the proper gear Saturday night, either. I have a leather jacket and gloves in my car, if you insist, but it's a little hot for those, isn't it? Couldn't you ride behind me and help me keep the Harley upright?"

A muscle in the corner of Rex's jaw bunched. "Show me what you know."

Her heart *kaboomed* in her chest. *You can handle this.*

You're used to proving yourself, and you give presentations at work all the time. Her mental pep talk didn't keep her palms from dampening or her lungs from constricting. "Okay."

Juliana tried to block Rex's presence behind her from her mind as she circled the bike, naming the parts and regurgitating most of the salesman's spiel. She was out of breath by the time she finished and faced Rex again.

Was that a spark of approval lurking in his narrowed eyes? "That was today's lesson. Next week's, too. Did you memorize the entire manual?"

Her cheeks burned. She grimaced and hugged her waist. So data was her thing. Big deal. "Pretty much."

He smoothed a hand over his tied-back hair. Juliana curled her fingers against the need to test its texture. What was wrong with her? She'd never had the urge to stroke a man's hair before Rex, but she yearned to know if his was thick and springy or soft and silky. It was definitely well cared for, with bluntly trimmed ends and glossy sheen.

He exhaled long and slow. She caught a whiff of mint on his breath. "Put on the helmet and climb on."

The bottom dropped out of her stomach, and then she scrambled to do as he instructed before he changed his mind or she chickened out. Both very real possibilities. Her legs quivered as she mounted the bike, and her hands trembled when she reached for the rubber grips on the handlebars. The Harley felt bigger, broader than last time, but last time she'd been on the back and not in the driver's seat.

Rex donned his own helmet. He looked so sexy and rebellious dressed all in black from his boots to his helmet that her heart went wild. And then he climbed on behind her. Their bodies didn't touch, but his heat spanned the gap between them, and the fine hairs on her body rose as if magnetized toward him. His shoulders bracketed hers as his thickly muscled arms reached around her, and his hands flanked hers on the handgrips.

Juliana swallowed to relieve the sudden dryness of her mouth. Her pulse roared in her ears, nearly deafening her to his low-pitched instructions.

"When we're ready to roll, I want you to park your feet on top of my boots to get a feel for how I shift the gears. I'll cover your hands with mine to work the throttle and brakes." He suited words to action. His palms were hot and slightly rough against her skin. His fingers wove between hers.

Who knew the sides of her fingers could be so receptive?

Rex continued to rattle off safety tips and general info. Juliana struggled to focus on his words, but fear and an alien sensation intertwined low in her belly, interfering with her ability to process the instructions in a coherent manner. Good thing she'd picked up most of the info from the manual and driver's safety book.

"I'm going to start the engine, and then we'll take a slow lap around the farm."

She started trembling before the motor rumbled to life.

"Relax," he called over the motor's throaty growl.

Easier said than done. She wasn't sure which intimidated her more—the man behind her or the mechanical beast beneath her. The man, she decided, but by a narrow margin.

Rex rolled the bike forward to disengage the kickstand. His chest nudged her back and his breath teased the hair at the base of her neck beneath the round, bowl-shaped helmet. The insides of his thick biceps brushed the outsides of her arms and she shivered. This time there was no mistaking the cause. Sexual awareness. Good to know she wasn't incapable. She hoped the engine vibration concealed her response from Rex or she'd be in for another brush-off. Later, when she wasn't on the back of this monster, she'd scrutinize the budding sensations and the fact that she had erogenous zones in the oddest locations. That she had functioning erogenous zones at all was newsworthy in itself.

"Squeeze the clutch and put the bike in gear." His left hand manipulated hers over the mechanism on the handlebar and his left foot shifted the gears beneath hers. "And then you ease the clutch back out again," he said over her shoulder. "Slow and steady."

The bike sprang forward, thumping Juliana into Rex's chest. Her breaths shortened—not from fear of the bike, but because of the man curved against her spine. His warmth encircled her and her scanty camisole wasn't much of a barrier. She considered reestablishing the space between them, but the urge to stay burrowed against his chest was too strong to fight.

"Shift into second." His foot and hands moved and the bike picked up speed on the long gravel driveway. The power of the engine pulsated through her and each bump in the road chafed her body against Rex's like an all-over massage.

Hello! You can't learn two dangerous skills at once. Concentrate on learning to ride the motorcycle first or you'll get yourself killed. There will be time to work on the man-woman thing with Rex later.

Maintaining her focus wasn't as easy as it should have been, but Juliana concentrated on the changing engine sounds and tried to block out the rise and fall of Rex's chest against her shoulder blades.

Rex kept the bike on a steady course over the flat farm road for one lap around the property and then another and another. By the third circuit Juliana could anticipate when it was time to change gears and brace herself for the slide of Rex's thigh against hers before it happened. Her tense muscles slowly relaxed, allowing other sensations to penetrate the sensual haze fogging her brain.

The setting sun kissed her cheeks, and the sweet scent of honeysuckle filled her lungs. Warm, humid air caressed her arms and the narrow strip of bare skin at her waist.

I could get used to this. I could even like it.

Juliana Alden, biker chick. Her mother would have a stroke. A chuckle slipped from Juliana's lips, and then she sobered and said a prayer of thanks that her mother had decided to punish her with the silent treatment since the auction. She hadn't caught grief from her other family members, either, because her father had been out of town and her brother had been occupied with Holly.

Ick. Not a path she wanted to travel.

Rex downshifted and pulled the Harley to a stop. "Your turn."

Juliana's pulse, which had slowed to a steady thump over the last fifteen minutes, galloped once more. She twisted on the seat. Rex's face was so close she could see every pore, every individual blade of beard stubble, and each tiny crease at the corners of his eyes and on the surface of his lips. *Gulp.* "Already?"

She lifted her gaze to his. For several seconds, he didn't look away and then his dark chocolate eyes lowered to her mouth. Her breath lodged in her chest. She inhaled unsteadily. All she had to do was lean forward and—

Rex released the handlebars, slid back on the seat and fisted his hands on his thighs.

"You're ready to drive." His voice sounded an octave lower than usual. Rough. Rusty. *Sexy.*

Juliana wet her parched lips and batted down her disappointment. If she'd ever wanted a man to kiss her this badly, she couldn't remember the occasion. She'd certainly never experienced even a fraction of this much need for Wally.

Wally, she mentally cringed and faced forward again. How could she have forgotten about him? He was *nice* and steady and her parents liked him. According to her mother, his administrative assistant, a divorcée with three children, had bought him at the auction. How could Donna afford a bachelor at the obscene prices they'd brought Saturday night? A fifty-pound bag of guilt dropped on Juliana's shoulders. Wally had probably footed the bill. Had he been expecting Juliana to buy him? If so, she owed him an apology.

Perhaps by the end of the month marrying Wally wouldn't seem like selling out her dream of finding true desire. If she wasn't capable of heart-racing passion, then why hold out for it?

A cloud passed over the sun and she shivered. The rebel behind her would never understand the allure of a risk-free option or Juliana's fear that safe, sensible Wally might be the best she could do. "Are you sure I can handle the motorcycle?"

"Yeah. I'll be right here behind you if you need help." He kicked out the passenger foot pegs.

Juliana's palms dampened on the rubber grips. She missed the reassuring warmth of Rex against her back and the protective embrace of his arms and legs bracketing hers. She tested the clutch and throttle, and then lifted her foot to the gear pedal.

Rex's hands settled on her waist. The unexpected contact against her bare skin sent a shock wave through her. She released the clutch too quickly, and the bike jerked forward and choked off, slamming him against her back.

"Easy. Try again." His breath teased her ear.

How could she concentrate with his hands scorching her? As if he'd read her thoughts, he shifted them upward, away from her bare skin, but bringing them to rest on her rib cage just below her breasts. Not an improvement if clear thought was the goal. The thin fabric of her camisole did nothing to block the transfer of heat between his skin and hers.

Grinding her molars against the surprising need to cover his palms and slide them up a few inches, she put the bike back in neutral, fired the engine and tried again. The machine lurched and cut off. Her third and fourth tries weren't any more successful. Each hop smacked her against Rex, increasing her tension and frustration. "I can't do this."

"You can." His no-nonsense tone cut through her embarrassment. "Would it help if I put my hands back on the handlebars?"

"Yes." Heat rushed to her cheeks and steamed her scalp inside the helmet. She didn't dare turn to look at his face. "I'm having a bit of trouble concentrating when you…touch me."

His whistled breath sounded loud in the sudden silence.

"Drive." It sounded as if he'd forced the word through clenched teeth. His hands bracketed hers beside the controls.

Closing her eyes, Juliana tried to gather her scattered wits and visualized the required steps. The bike rolled forward. She quickly lifted her lids and fought to stay away from the white board fences. Changing into second gear went smoother. She wanted to pump her arms in triumph, but didn't dare release her stranglehold on the grips.

She'd just shifted into third gear when Rex moved his hands back to her waist. Each of his fingers sent a marching band of awareness parading across her skin. Her jaws clamped on a whimper. It took one hundred percent of her attention to keep from wrecking the motorcycle into a nearby apple tree.

And then it hit her. She was driving Rex's big, bad, black Harley. Sure, Rex was behind her, but *she* was in control of the machine. Adrenaline surged through her. She lifted her face to the wind and laughed out loud.

Her joy lasted all of five minutes. A fat raindrop landed on her cheek. Moments later the bottom fell out of the clouds and rain poured. Rex leaned forward and yelled in her ear. "Head for the barn. Park inside."

Juliana steered the motorcycle toward shelter and opened the throttle as much as she dared. She raced through raindrops pelting her arms and face like bee stings. Within seconds her clothing was saturated and goose bumps covered her skin. She downshifted and pulled through the open barn doors.

Rex reached around her to kill the engine, and then lowered the kickstand and climbed from the bike. Still high on her accomplishment, Juliana followed. She tugged off her helmet and set it beside Rex's on the seat. The rain hammered on the metal roof with deafening force, but the storm couldn't dampen her excitement, and she couldn't keep the grin off her face.

She—boring account auditor Juliana Alden—had driven a motorcycle and not just any motorcycle, but a *hog*…the most notorious machine on the road. If she could control this monster, then she could control anything—even her recently unsettled life.

She wanted to shout with joy, to laugh out loud and to celebrate her accomplishment. Instead, she threw her arms around Rex's neck and planted a kiss on his bristly cheek. "Thank you. Thank you. Thank you."

His hands fastened on her bare waist with scalding heat, but instead of pushing her away, Rex held her captive. His warmth penetrated her cold, saturated clothing, raising her temperature inside and out. Her breasts prodded his chest and his thighs laced with hers. Aroused male, encased in steaming wet denim, pressed against her belly. She shivered, but not from cold.

Juliana tilted her head back and met his gaze in the shadowy barn. Coffee-colored eyes burned into hers before tracing the rain trails across her face. A lone drop quivered on the corner of her lip. He bent and sipped up the droplet.

She gasped at the lightning force of the tiny caress and her heart slammed against her ribs. Her fingers curled into his shoulders, and then Rex's mouth took hers in a devouring kiss.

Hard. Urgent. His tongue tangled with hers and his hands splayed over her buttocks, yanking her closer. A dam burst. Shock receded and pleasure flooded Juliana's bloodstream.

She cradled his bristly cheeks and held on as unfamiliar but delicious sensations danced through her. His face and lips were damp from the rain, but hot, oh so hot. His evening beard abraded her palms and then her fingers reached his hair. She tugged the strip of leather free and twined the soft, springy strands around her fingers. The ends were damp and cool from the rain, a complete contrast to the fire flickering to life inside her.

His hands raked upward from her hips to her ribs. Her nipples tightened and her breath hitched in anticipation. One big hand cupped her breast and her knees quaked.

He stroked her tight nipple, stirring a swarm of need low in her belly. She'd never experienced anything so intense, so incredibly urgent. His hard thigh pressed the juncture of her thighs and Juliana shamelessly pushed back. Sparks ignited in her veins and a whimper of pleasure climbed her throat.

Rex jerked his head back, swore and set her away. He stalked across the barn to stare out the open door at the rain blowing almost horizontally. Wind whipped strands of his hair away from his rigid jaw.

Confused, Juliana blinked. Why had he stopped? Surely after that kiss, he had to know she was interested?

Maybe you're a lousy kisser. It's not as if you get much practice.

Her cheeks stung with a combination of embarrassment and beard burn, but her skin still prickled with need. Slowly, the rattle of the rain on the roof and the boom of thunder drowned out the roar of her pulse in her ears. Warmth seeped out of her wet clothing, leaving her chilled to the bone.

Examine the facts.

Rex Tanner wanted her. She'd seen the hunger in his deep, dark eyes, felt it in his kiss and in the brand of his tight-fitting jeans against her belly. But he wasn't happy about his desire. Why?

According to her online research, he'd been with dozens of other women. Juliana touched her lips. Was there something wrong with her? Some intrinsically feminine component she lacked?

Maybe he didn't like being with a woman who'd bought him any more than she liked the idea of buying a date.

Putting the embarrassment over the circumstances of their meeting aside, Juliana reveled in her discovery. For the first time in her life, she'd tasted the mind-melting passion other women whispered about. And if she wasn't completely incapable of desire, then what did that mean for her future with Wally?

She didn't have the answer, but one thing was certain. Her appetite for breaking the rules that had governed her life to this point had been whetted, and she couldn't wait until her next lesson.

Four

Could the day get any worse?

In answer to Rex's question, the rain switched over to hail. It struck the metal roof like drumsticks on a snare drum.

So much for the weather forecaster's twenty percent chance of scattered showers.

To get away from the temptation of the woman behind him, Rex considered stepping into the storm and letting the ice pelt his thick, horny hide, but he didn't have any dry clothes and he'd ridden over on his Harley. The temperature had dropped by at least twenty degrees in the past ten minutes. He'd be hypothermic before he could get home.

Lightning sliced the sky and thunder shook the ground. A frigid wind whipped through the open door, cooling his overheated skin and blowing his hair across his eyes. What had Juliana done with his leather string? He turned to ask but the question died on his lips.

Juliana hugged herself. Her teeth chattered and goose bumps covered her bare arms, shoulders and even the tantalizing strip of paler skin across her belly. His protective instincts kicked in. "Let me see if I can find something to cover your head, and we'll get you to your car."

"I'm n-not driv-ving in th-that."

He could barely hear her over the hail. "Your car has a heater."

"It's not worth g-getting hit by lightning to g-get to it."

Good point. She'd parked a hundred yards away across an open area. The afternoon heat had already escaped the building, but he rolled the barn door closed anyway. He had to get Juliana warm. All he had to offer was his damp T-shirt. That wouldn't help.

"C'mon." He led her into the tack room and shut the door. The temperature inside the eight-foot-square windowless room was marginally warmer. He searched the dim space hoping he'd somehow overlooked something in his cleaning binge that Juliana could wrap up in, but he found nothing. The barn had been a disaster when he'd leased it. Rats had taken over and made bedding out of any available material, so he'd scoured the place from corner to corner and thrown out everything. All that remained were a metal tack trunk, a steel drum for the feed and a rough cedar bench.

"Here." Dusky pink swept her cheekbones as she offered his strip of braided leather.

He tied his hair and tried to ignore her chattering teeth, but couldn't. His control dangled from a fraying rope and after that kiss the last thing he needed to do was touch her. Just his luck that his libido would emerge after months of hibernation for a woman he ought to avoid at all cost.

The fact that she was freezing her tail off without complaint got to him. Her silent shivers got to him. Even her damp flowers-and-spice scent got to him. In fact, everything about Juliana Alden knocked him sideways. "Turn around."

Eyes narrowing, she hesitated and then turned her back. He brushed her hands out of the way and briskly chafed the cool skin of her upper arms. Her quick gasp tugged his groin. The firmness of the muscles beneath his hands surprised him. He'd expected a desk jockey to be soft, but Juliana obviously kept in shape from her tight arms to her tight a—

Don't go there.

"I thought the weather back home was crazy." Home. Except for his parents' funeral, Rex hadn't been back to the ranch since the day he'd turned eighteen, and even though the property had been sold, he still thought of the ranch as home. But his place was here now. Near Kelly, Mike and the girls.

Juliana tilted her head and looked at him over her shoulder. Her hair glided over his fingers in a soft-as-silk caress. "The storm front sitting off the coast must have backed into the cold front coming from the northwest. Wilmington gets weird weather when that happens. In the winter, we get snow, which—trust me—is odd for the North Carolina coast."

Her shivers slowed then ceased. Her skin warmed and her muscles relaxed beneath his hands, but he didn't want to let her go. A jolt of pure hunger hit him low and hard. It had been too damned long since he'd stroked a woman's smooth, supple skin. Juliana leaned into him, and the desire to wrap his arms around her, bury his face against her neck and cradle her breasts in his palms grabbed him in a stranglehold.

He dropped his hands and stepped away, but there was nowhere to run in the confined space. Saddle racks jutted from the walls, forcing him to stand only inches from temptation. "We'll stay here until the hail stops and then you need to go home."

She faced him. "What about you?"

"I came on my bike. I'll wait until the rain lets up."

"And if it doesn't, you'll spend the night? Where? Here?" She gestured to the narrow four-foot bench.

"If I have to. I've slept on worse."

A stubborn glint entered her blue eyes and her chin lifted. The single, bare lightbulb revealed a reddened patch of beard burn along her jaw. Damn. He hadn't realized he'd been so rough. "I'm not leaving you here."

His pulse misfired. "There's no point in both of us being cold and uncomfortable."

"That's exactly why you'll be reasonable and accept my offer of a ride home. I have a jacket in the car, so once the hail and lightning stop and I can get to it, *I* won't be cold." Her gaze dropped to the points of his nipples clearly outlined by his damp, clingy T-shirt. "And I keep a quilt in my trunk. You can use that."

His reaction wasn't caused by cold, but he wouldn't correct her. If she looked lower, she'd figure it out by herself.

She tapped a finger to her swollen lips, and just like that, the memory of the kiss reignited the fire in his blood. Soft lips. Satiny tongue. He clamped his teeth, fisted his hands and fought to extinguish the blaze.

"Are you worried that someone will steal your motorcycle if you leave it here overnight?"

He should lie and say yes. It beat the hell out of admitting that he needed to put some distance between them before he pulled her back into his arms and put the strength of the bench behind her to the test. The flimsy thing probably wouldn't hold their combined weight.

Not something you need to be thinking about, bucko.

"No. The owner has a couple of dogs she lets loose after dark. They keep an eye on things."

"Then I'll give you a ride."

"There's no need—"

"I guess you could call for a pizza delivery and hitch a ride back with the driver if you're afraid to ride with me."

Afraid? He straightened at the insult to his pride. "I don't have a cell phone."

He'd given it up along with most of the other trappings of success. Besides, he didn't want his Nashville associates tracking him down. Not that he was hiding. He hadn't done anything illegal. But he had lost all respect for the man he'd become, so he'd cut those ties. Permanently.

"Mine's in the car. You can use it—if you insist on being impractical."

That set his teeth on edge. "I need to see to Jelly Bean. If the rain hasn't stopped by the time I finish then I'll take that ride."

He let himself out of the tack room and headed for the mare's stall. He hadn't prayed this hard for the weather to change since his first headlining concert in an outdoor venue. Twenty thousand fans had come to see him in the pouring rain. And they'd stayed despite the weather. He'd done his damnedest not to let them down, and from here on he'd do his best not to let himself down by crossing the line into temptation. But there were no guarantees of success. Juliana Alden had a way of getting around his common sense.

He had to get out of this auction package. He couldn't afford to repay her the thousands she'd bid on him, since most of his cash was tied up in Renegade, but he could afford the four hundred the local dealership charged for the motor-cycle driver-safety course. And the farm owner used to ride the horse-show circuit. He'd bet he could talk her into giving Juliana riding lessons in exchange for him doing a few more chores around here.

Yeah, that's it. Juliana would get her lessons—just not from him. As soon as he got her back to Renegade, he'd tell her goodbye.

* * *

"Let me buy you a drink."

Juliana's heart missed a beat at Rex's low-voiced invitation. She searched his face, but the streetlights didn't penetrate the shadowy interior of her car. Had she misread his stony silence during the drive back?

Her palms dampened and anticipation danced along her spine. Would he invite her upstairs? She wanted to be corrupted out of her Goody Two-shoes image. Really, she did, and she had a brand new box of condoms in her purse to prove it, but frankly, the idea of getting naked with Rex gave her heart palpitations, because she was starting to like him a little too much for this to be a wham-bam-thank-you-ma'am kind of encounter.

Last chance.

"Um…sure. I'd love a drink."

He circled the car, took the umbrella from her and guided her toward Renegade without touching her, but Juliana was highly conscious of his hand hovering at the small of her back.

The bartender looked up as soon as they entered. "Your sister's upstairs and, man, she's a mess."

"Give me a minute," Rex called to Juliana. He yanked open the door to his apartment and took the steps two at a time. Juliana eyed the crowd of construction workers leering at her from the bar. Unwilling to deal with the kind of attention her skimpy attire drew, she followed Rex upstairs.

As she entered his apartment, Juliana noted the suitcase beside the door and then the woman sobbing in Rex's arms. Unsure if she was intruding, Juliana hesitated.

"What's up, Kel?"

The petite brunette drew back. Her face was blotchy and red from crying. Fresh tears streamed from her dark eyes as she drew a ragged breath. "Mike's been hurt. He's in critical condition in Landstuhl, Germany."

"The military hospital?" Rex asked.

"Yes. He might—" Her voice broke. "They said he might not make it."

He gripped her shoulders. "What do you need me to do? Name it. I'll do it."

His tender tone vibrated through Juliana. What would it be like to have a man care that much?

"I need you to keep the girls."

"Whoa." He recoiled and then dragged a hand over his jaw. "Where are Becky and Liza now?"

"Asleep." She pointed toward a closed door. "I can't take them with me, Rex. I know you have to work, but I have to go. I *have* to see Mike."

"Yeah, you do, but Kelly, I'm not set up to watch the girls for more than a few hours. What about one of the other military wives?"

"You know I don't know them well enough to ask. Please, Rex. I don't have anybody else. And I have to get there be-fore…before…" A sob choked off her words.

The furrow between Rex's eyebrows deepened. Frustration and a touch of panic rolled off him in waves. "I can't close Renegade. I'm barely—" His gaze flashed to Juliana and then back to his sister. "I can't afford to close my doors and I don't have the staff to cover for me. The girls can't stay downstairs, and I can't leave them up here alone. I want to help, but I don't know how I can."

Juliana's heart squeezed in sympathy. The woman's hus-band was critically injured and thousands of miles away. If the situation was as grave as Kelly said, then there wasn't time to research alternative child care. Besides, from what Juliana's coworkers had said, good child-care centers had waiting lists.

And then the answer fell into place—an answer that could solve several problems at once. Irma, the lady who'd been more like a mother than a nanny to Juliana, had become increasingly lonely and unhappy since having to retire. Juliana worried about her. Helping Kelly meant helping Irma and there wasn't anything Juliana wouldn't do for Irma. And, Juliana admitted, she wouldn't mind having the opportunity to spend more time with Rex and uncover yet another layer of the complex man she'd bought.

"Perhaps I could help."

Both heads swiveled toward her.

"No," Rex barked.

"Who are you?" his sister asked simultaneously.

"I'm Juliana Alden. Rex's…friend. My evenings and weekends are free, and I suspect the lady who used to be my nanny would love to keep the girls for a few hours a day when either Rex or I can't be with them."

Hope flared in the eyes the same dark coffee shade as Rex's. "You like kids?"

"Yes, although I confess I don't have loads of experience. But I'm a fast learner and I don't give up easily."

"If you could cover the girls in the evenings then Rex could watch them in the mornings, and your nanny could cover midday."

Rex stepped between them. "We don't need to bother Juliana. I'll work something out. I'll call an employment agency or a local day care—"

Kelly looked horrified. "The girls are upset enough. They don't need that kind of upheaval."

"My town-house complex has a pool and a playground," Juliana added, earning a glare from Rex. "Irma could watch them at my place, and I grew up in Wilmington, so I know where all the parks and yummy ice-cream shops are located. How long do you think you'll be gone?"

Kelly gestured toward the suitcase. "I packed enough clothing for the girls for a week, but I don't know. It all depends on M-Mike."

"We don't want to inconvenience you." Rex didn't say *back off,* but it came through loud and clear in his clipped words.

Juliana ignored him. "It's no trouble at all. In fact, I'm sure Irma would love to have something to keep her occupied. She's recently retired and not enjoying it."

Kelly threw her arms around Juliana. "Thank you so much. I'm so worried about Mike. What if he—" Her voice cracked and a fresh wave of sobs racked her.

"I'm sure he's getting the best care possible." Juliana put an arm around Kelly's shoulder. "When does your flight leave?"

"Midnight."

Juliana glanced at her watch. "It's almost nine now. We need to get you to the airport. I'll drive you. Rex can stay here with the girls." She turned to Rex. "I'll be back as soon as I get Kelly checked in, and we'll work out the details."

Juliana's last glimpse of Rex as she led his sister out the door wasn't reassuring. His scowl and fisted hands didn't bode well for their week together.

Gentle, loving brother. Doting uncle. Rebel. And too proud to accept her assistance. The man's contradictions intrigued her more than a falsified account, and Juliana couldn't wait to figure him out.

Who'd have suspected the bean counter would be so difficult to shake loose?

Rex had invited Juliana in to buy her a drink and dump her, and here she was back in his apartment long after midnight. Worse, it looked as though he'd be stuck with her until Kelly returned. It wouldn't be a hardship if his body didn't hum like a generator when she was around, but that was one engine he couldn't afford to start.

What really pissed him off was that as much as he resented her help, he really didn't have a choice since he couldn't come up with another solution. Damn his sister for refusing to become a part of the support network on base. But Kelly had always been an ostrich who preferred ignoring a problem instead of dealing with it. She couldn't handle the tragedies of other husbands being killed in action, so she isolated herself from the wives and turned a blind eye to the possibility instead of preparing for it.

Reluctantly, he settled beside Juliana on the sofa. She looked slightly rumpled and incredibly sexy. With her lids at half-mast, she looked tired enough to nod off at any second. The urge to pull her head onto his shoulder wasn't a welcome one.

She covered a yawn with her hand. "I called Irma on the way to the airport and set everything up. She's thrilled about watching the girls, and Kelly's relieved that they'll be in experienced hands most of the time.

"Kelly, Irma and I worked out a schedule. The girls will spend the nights here with you. You'll deal with mornings and then drop them off at my town house. On weekdays, Irma will take over until I get home in the evenings. Becky and Liza will have dinner with me, and then I'll bring them back here for baths and bedtime. I'll stay until you can take over, and I'll watch them on the weekends."

Juliana had made plans, but she'd missed a few critical details. "Hold it. Most nights I don't get upstairs before two. That's too late for you to drive home, and I only have two bedrooms—the girls' and mine."

She sat up straighter. "Bedrooms aren't an issue because I'm leaving each night as soon as you get home." She rose, picked up her purse and took a step toward the door. "I'd like to stop by in the morning on my way to work so the girls can meet me. I think that would make them more comfortable with me tomorrow evening."

For a lady who was supposedly good with numbers, she wasn't adding them up very well. He rose and parked his hands on his hips. "How far do you live from here?"

"About twenty or thirty minutes, depending on traffic."

"And what time do you usually get up in the morning?"

"Six, but I'll rise earlier to come here."

"If you drive home, you'll get about three hours sleep before you have to get up and come back." As much as Rex hated to admit it, there was only one solution. "Starting tonight, you'll have to sleep here."

Juliana's mouth dropped open. She quickly snapped it shut again and backed toward the door. "That's not necessary."

"No way around it unless you can live without sleep. It's late. You're exhausted. Take my bed. The sheets are clean. I'll sleep on the sofa."

Her eyes rounded. "But I don't have clothes or…anything."

The idea of Juliana sliding naked between his sheets guaranteed he'd have a hard time sleeping—hard being the operative word. "I'll loan you a T-shirt. We can throw what you're wearing into the washer. We'll get the girls ready together in the morning, and then you can go home to dress for work. I'll follow you. You can show us around and introduce us to Irma."

A hand fluttered to her throat. Several silent seconds ticked past while she digested the new plan. "I…okay. But we could um…share the bed?"

Flames licked through his veins, singeing the edges of his common sense. He knew he shouldn't—*couldn't*—have her, but that didn't mean he'd be able to control himself if he had to lie beside her all night. "And then neither of us would sleep."

Her skin flushed and her lips parted on a ragged breath. "I'm sure we could figure something out."

Need throbbed insistently in his gut. "No."

He stalked past her, retrieved the largest T-shirt he owned—the more she covered the better—a new toothbrush and a bath towel. "Soap, shampoo, toothpaste are all in the bathroom. If you need anything else just yell."

After a moment's hesitation, she accepted the small stack. "Thank you."

He hesitated, but then forced himself to say what he had to. "No, thank you, Juliana. I didn't have a backup plan, and Kelly knew it. If you hadn't stepped in, I'm not sure what would have happened. I owe you."

And he wished like hell he didn't because those kinds of debts always came back to bite you.

Rex had been in the room while she'd slept.

Juliana raked her hair out of her face and stared at the neatly stacked pile of folded clothing—her panties on top—sitting on the edge of the dresser beside her purse. Her heart thumped out an irregular rhythm.

She shoved back the covers on the big leather platform bed and rose. Ten minutes later, after showering and dressing, she followed the smell of freshly-brewed coffee to the kitchen and stopped in her tracks.

Rex, wearing only jeans riding low on his hips, leaned against the counter clutching a mug and staring into it like it held the elixir of life. His hair was loose and rumpled, and beard stubble shadowed his jaw and upper lip. Long hair should lessen his manly impact, but if anything the soft strands drew attention to the rugged masculinity of his sharply angled jaw, square chin and his broad shoulders. Curls in the same dark shade dusted his powerfully built chest, and Juliana couldn't prevent her eyes from following the line of hair bisecting his well-defined abs to the button of his jeans.

"G'morning." His gravelly, sleep-roughened voice struck a match inside her, setting fire to her nerve endings as if they were fuses. She jerked her eyes upward and met his heavy-lidded gaze. He looked more like the big, bad wolf than ever and she wanted to be gobbled up by her reluctant rebel more with each passing day.

"Good morning."

She'd never spent an entire night in a man's bed—with or without him—and therefore, she'd never experienced a morning after. Was that why this felt so intimate and awkward? And yet she couldn't have left the room if she'd wanted to.

"Coffee?" He angled his head toward the pot on the counter.

"Please." Why couldn't she be one of those women who carried a makeup kit in her purse? She didn't even carry a comb or brush. She'd had to borrow his. Feeling unkempt and exposed, she dipped her head, swinging her hair over her cheek.

He filled a mug and passed it to her. "Milk? Sugar?"

She took it, being careful to avoid touching him. It was too early for that kind of shock to her system. "Just sugar."

He gestured toward the sugar bowl. "Help yourself."

"Thanks for um…washing my clothes." With the way her skin tingled, you'd think he'd handled her, not just her panties. The idea of becoming intimate with him was growing on her—almost enough to drown her remaining reservations about her crazy plan to break rules. Her hand shook as she sweetened the dark brew.

"You're welcome." He made no attempt to leave the kitchen. The room seemed to shrink and she had a hard time keeping her eyes off his body. If he'd lived a self-indulgent life before leaving Nashville as the tabloids claimed, then it didn't show. There wasn't an ounce of surplus flesh on his muscular torso.

She dragged her gaze from his pecs to his eyes. "Would you like for me to prepare breakfast?"

He scrubbed one hand across his nape. "I'm not sure what you'll find. I'm not a morning person. I usually don't eat until I go downstairs."

"May I search? The girls should eat before we head out. And honestly, there's not much food in my fridge either. I usually shop on Saturdays. Irma promised to bring lunch and snacks for the girls with her today."

"Go ahead." His assessing gaze slid over her, making her mouth dry and her palms dampen. She was out of her element and knew it. Not for the first time, she wished she had the sexual confidence of some of her coworkers, but the personal relationships in her past hadn't been the type to instill self-assurance. She opened the refrigerator and the cool air swept her hot cheeks.

She found eggs and butter in the fridge and then spotted bread on the counter. She located the pancake syrup in a cabinet. "French toast?"

"That'll work." His steady regard unnerved her. She tried to block him out as she mixed the batter, dunked the bread and laid it in the frying pan. What was he looking for?

He refilled his coffee cup. "You're not what I expected."

Ka-boom. Her heart pounded. She jerked up her chin. "Wh-why's that?"

"You dropped fifteen grand without batting an eyelash for lessons you could have bought for a fraction of that cost. I figured you had more money than sense."

Ouch. Talk about making a bad first impression.... "And now?"

"I was wrong."

The simple sentence filled her with an idiotic amount of pleasure. "Thank you."

"But that doesn't change the decision I made last night before Kelly showed up."

Uh-oh. She didn't like the sound of that. "Decision?"

"You need to take your lessons from someone else."

The bottom dropped out of her stomach. "Why?"

"Because I'm not looking for a short-term affair and you are."

Her lungs seized and mortification burned her face. "I *never* said that."

His mouth tilted in a skeptical slant. "Are you telling me you want to marry me?"

What! "No."

"But you're not averse to sleeping with me."

She gulped and focused intently on flipping the bread before meeting his gaze again. "What makes you think that?"

"Because you have a box of condoms in your purse."

Horrified, Juliana spun back to the stove. She prodded the French toast with the spatula even though it didn't need her immediate attention. "And how do you know that?"

"Because your purse was gaping open when I brought your clothes in this morning. The condoms were on top."

If she'd ever been more embarrassed, she couldn't recall the occasion, but she stood her ground. "You have quite an ego if you think they're for you."

Her snippy comment didn't faze him. Probably because it didn't come out in nearly as scathing a tone as she'd intended. How could it when he was right?

"That's what I thought, too, until I realized you're not the type of woman who picks up men."

"Don't be so sure," she blustered.

"You're an accountant."

"So?"

"So you like things neat, and you like to be prepared. The CDs in your car are arranged alphabetically. You memorize instruction manuals that most people don't even bother to read. You fasten your seat belt before putting the key in the ignition, and you check your mirrors three times before changing lanes. I'll bet you don't have a risk-taking bone in your body."

Boy did he have her pegged, and that annoyed her immensely. "I bought you, didn't I?"

"I'm guessing you researched my background before you did, because lady, you sure know a lot about me for someone who's not a country music fan."

Guilty as charged. If he'd noticed that her CDs were in alphabetical order then he'd probably also noticed she liked Broadway tunes. Little did he know she'd shoved his CDs under her seat before letting him into her car. "There's nothing wrong with being prepared."

"Never said there was. But the fact remains that what you want isn't available. I can't deny I need your help this week, but I'll arrange for you to take the rest of your lessons elsewhere."

She could concede to her embarrassment and his demands or she could stay the course she'd set. *Last chance. Last chance* echoed in her head. "Like you said, you owe me and I want my lessons from you. No substitutes."

Anger flared in his eyes and he opened his mouth—to argue probably—but snapped it shut again when the youngest of the girls toddled into the kitchen. She wordlessly held up her arms. Rex set down his coffee mug and scooped her up. "Hey, sweet pea."

The child popped a thumb in her mouth, laid her head on Rex's shoulder and then twirled a strand of his hair around the fingers of her opposite hand. The absolute trust in the gesture and the gentle kiss he planted on the child's crown brought a lump to Juliana's throat.

"Liza, this is Juliana. She's going to help me take care of you for a few days."

A pair of dark eyes briefly met Juliana's and then the child hid her face against Rex's neck. The tiny fingers tangled in Rex's hair wiggled in a wave and Juliana's heart melted. "Hi, Liza."

Juliana caught another peep from those shy eyes and smiled as she transferred the French toast onto plates. Kelly had told her Liza was three, Becky five and both girls adored their uncle. To hear Kelly talk last night, you'd think Rex was a big softie, but that wasn't the man Juliana had encountered.

"The girls must spend a lot of time with you."

He shrugged. "I try to help out when Mike's deployed."

An older girl bounced into the room and vaulted toward Rex. He caught her in his free arm so easily it was clear this was a common occurrence, and then he juggled a giggly girl on each hip. His smile nearly knocked Juliana's legs out from under her.

Seeing the obvious affection between Rex and his nieces turned her thoughts in a decidedly *un*temporary direction. She quickly squelched the unwelcome feelings. She'd never been one to listen for the ticking of her biological clock, and she didn't intend to start now. One month with the rebel was all she'd allow herself.

"This is Becky. Becky, Juliana is going to help out while Mom's away. You're going to spend the day at Juliana's house with her nanny."

"Hello, Becky."

The older girl studied Juliana suspiciously and then asked Rex, "Why? Why can't we stay here with you?"

"Because I have to work."

She might not have much experience with children, but Juliana could see the protests forming on that pouty lip and decided to head them off. "My town house has a pool and a playground, and Irma, the lady who took care of me when I was your age, is very excited about having young ladies to help her bake cookies."

Either the pool or the cookies did the trick. Both girls' eyes brightened. If only their uncle was as easy to bring around. Juliana stifled a sigh.

She had a plan and she would stick to it regardless of this slight detour. Despite Rex's avowed disinterest in a relationship, his kiss said otherwise, so her plan still had a chance. No one loved a tough case as much as she did, and she wasn't ready to throw in the towel yet.

She faced her reluctant seducer. "I need a key to your apartment."

And that, judging by Rex's balky expression, was the last thing he wanted to give her.

Five

Rex's life was spinning out of control—much like it had when he'd signed his first record deal, and others, his manager, his agent and the record company execs, had seized the wheel and started steering his life. He'd fought a long, hard battle to regain control, and he didn't like being knocked off track now.

Last night he'd been shanghaied by Kelly and Juliana. Today, Irma, as grandmotherly a woman as he'd ever met, had shooed him out of the way the moment he and the girls had arrived. She'd whisked Becky and Liza into the kitchen to help her unpack the groceries. Juliana had disappeared upstairs to dress for work, leaving him to prowl around her living room and wonder what in the hell he'd gotten into. Not that he'd had a choice. He wouldn't let Kelly down again.

Who was the real Juliana? The flirty siren who'd bought him at the auction, the innocent seductress who'd ridden his horse, the bold and sexy biker chick or the cautious woman who planned every detail and triple-checked everything? There were too many contradictions to count—contradictions that kept him off balance. He couldn't plan a defense if he didn't know his opponent.

Her living and dining rooms looked like something out of a magazine. Not fussy or cluttered, but decorated and comfortable. A soft toast-colored fabric covered the long sofa and matching chairs. The oversize furniture was the kind he could sink into and take a nap—which he sorely needed after tossing and turning on his shorter couch last night. A man could prop his boots on her wood-and-wrought-iron tables without worrying about scuffing the surface. The best part was that, other than a few colorful ceramic pieces on high shelves, Juliana didn't have valuable knickknacks all over the place that the girls could break.

A noise made him turn. He looked up and saw legs—amazing, long, sexy legs—coming down the stairs. And then the rest of Juliana came into view. In her gray body-skimming suit, twisted-up hair and low-heeled shoes, she bore little resemblance to any of the versions of Juliana he'd encountered thus far. This woman looked like a bank employee. Cool. Collected. In charge. The tap of her heels on the hardwood floor as she crossed to a cabinet drew his attention back to her killer legs.

Damned if he didn't find her sexy in a librarian kind of way. Not good. Not good at all.

She opened a drawer, withdrew something and then turned to face him. "Here's a key to my house."

Whoa. He backed up a step. Other than Kelly, he'd never given a woman keys to his place or even his truck. "Look, Juliana, I gave you my spare keys this morning because you and the girls need access to my apartment, but—"

"Yes, and it was clearly very painful for you," she said with a dose of sarcasm.

He shoved his hands in his pockets. "I don't need a key to your house."

"You will if you arrive before Irma in the mornings."

"I won't. I'll make sure of it. But if I do, you can let me in."

She shook her head and the tiny diamonds in her earlobes sparkled, drawing his attention to her delicate ears and the slender column of her neck above the collarless suit.

"That isn't practical. You live closer to the bank, so it makes more sense for me to go straight to work from Renegade. The earlier I can get to work, the sooner I can leave to be with the girls. Irma's thrilled to have them, but she's seventy, and she's worried that her stamina may not last a full day."

The skin between his shoulder blades prickled. No way out. Going into a woman's house without her... He suppressed a shudder. Swapping keys was *way* too intimate and smelled like a commitment. Commitments led to disappointments, and he'd already handed out more than his share of those. He wanted to unload Juliana and the unwelcome attraction for her, not add another loop to the rope temporarily binding them together.

Juliana reached out, grabbed his hand and pressed the key into his palm. She closed his fingers around the cool metal and squeezed. Her hands, wrapped securely around his, ignited desires he could not—would not—satisfy.

"Rex, it's a key ring not an engagement ring. There are no strings or expectations attached. Quit being such a *guy* and take it." She made being male sound like an insult. "I have to go. I'm running late."

But several seconds ticked past before her fingers loosened and her hands fell away. From the rapid flutter of her pulse at the base of her neck, he guessed he wasn't the only one feeling the heat generated by their exchange.

He cleared his throat. "I'll drop Becky and Liza off about 9:30 or 10:00 each morning."

She nodded. "I should be back by 6:00 at the latest. The girls and I will find you so you can tell them good night before I take them upstairs. You're welcome to stay here as long as you like. Irma makes great coffee."

This was so much like playing house, it gave him the willies. Knowing his past and his weakness, thinking about building a domestic relationship with someone was a luxury he couldn't afford. He backed up. "Right. See ya tonight."

And then he bolted for the kitchen like a damned coward. Running from what he couldn't have.

Wally Wilson was perfect for her on so many levels. So why couldn't Juliana be happy with him and forget this *last chance* nonsense?

She looked across the table at her companion. Handsome in an understated, preppy way, Wally was blond, blue-eyed and reasonably fit. He kept his skin evenly tanned with weekly visits to the tanning salon. Every hair stayed in place thanks to his skilled barber, and wrinkles didn't dare crease his suit.

No, women wouldn't get whiplash or have hormone surges when he walked through a room, but he was stable, responsible and unfailingly polite. He liked order and so did she. In fact, they had so much in common. Background, business, ambition…

As detail-oriented as Wally appeared to be about everything else in his life, he would probably be a conscientious lover. According to her friends, Juliana owed it to herself to find out before marrying him, but the idea didn't fill her with anticipation. Then again, she hated emotional displays. Life with Wally would be smooth sailing. No highs. No lows.

No fun?

She ignored that pesky inner voice and smiled at Wally. "Thank you for agreeing to switch our date from dinner to lunch on such short notice, Wally."

"I'm always happy to accommodate your schedule, Juli-ana. What did you say came up?"

She hadn't said and she didn't understand her hesitation in revealing the situation now, but if she was seriously consid-ering marrying him, then they shouldn't have secrets between them. "I'm babysitting this evening."

His brows lifted. "Babysitting? Have you ever babysat before?"

"Um…no. But the girls are three and five. I'm sure they can tell me if I do something wrong."

"I thought it might have something to do with your bach-elor."

Her chicken salad lodged halfway down her esophagus. She sipped her water. "It does indirectly. Rex—my bachelor—Rex's sister had to fly out of the country unexpectedly. Her husband's in the military, and he's been critically injured. She needed to be with him. Rex and I are watching their children."

"Couldn't she hire someone to do that?"

"Irma's helping."

"Ah, yes. Irma. I'd forgotten you still keep in touch with your nanny." He flashed a tolerant smile, displaying perfectly aligned teeth. Why did she get the impression he didn't really approve of her continued friendship with the woman who'd raised her while Margaret Alden had fought her way up the career ladder?

"Irma and I have lunch together at least once a month. I've been increasingly concerned about her lately. Retirement isn't working out." He nodded, but she had the impression he really didn't care about Irma. Juliana pleated her napkin in her lap. "Wally, my mother seems to think you expected me to buy you at the auction."

"Given the understanding between our families, I thought you might," he said in an expressionless tone. Come to think of it, Wally usually spoke without much inflection. His soothing voice would be an asset in dealing with upset customers.

"The understanding was that we'd date to see if we suited."

"Don't we?"

She concealed a wince. "I don't know yet, Wally, but please tell Donna I appreciate her stepping in. Although I confess I was a little surprised to see her at the club."

"Yes. There are those who can't forget Donna's humble beginnings."

Like his parents, Juliana suspected. Mrs. Wilson referred to Wally's administrative assistant as "trailer trash." His father called Donna worse. The Wilsons saw a gold digger out to sink her claws into the family fortune. Never mind that Donna had worked hard to get her GED and then had attended community college while raising a houseful of children single-handedly. Wally's mother couldn't see Donna's ambition or intelligence. Juliana, on the other hand, often teased Wally that she wanted to steal his assistant.

"Well, I apologize if I've made things difficult for you."

"No apologies are necessary, Juliana. In fact, this could work to our advantage."

"How so?"

"Because we're each being allowed to date outside our closed social circle without fear of repercussion."

That had to be the oddest comment she'd ever heard Wally make. Even stranger was the inkling that Wally—safe, sensible Wally—might have secrets.

Rex let himself into his apartment and stopped in his tracks when he spotted Juliana slumped in one corner of the sofa with her knees bent and her feet tucked beside her.

His heart thumped like a bass drum as he drew nearer. The lamp cast a soft glow over her sleep-flushed face. Dark lashes fanned her cheeks and her lips parted on a sigh of breath. She'd exchanged her suit for a pair of sleeveless pajamas. The black fabric reminded him of the satin sheets he'd had on his tour bus. Soft. Slippery. *Sexy.*

Shaking off the forbidden thought, he glanced down the hall. Through the open door, the soft glow of a night-light revealed the sleeping girls. Had they given Juliana a hard time? Was that why she'd planted herself out here like a sentry? Or had she fallen asleep waiting for him? The thought sent a streak of lightning sizzling through him. She'd made it clear that she wanted him with her insistence on the lessons and with that damned box of condoms. He'd thought of little else all day.

It would be so easy to take what she offered, to lead her to bed and lose himself in the spicy floral scent of her skin and the slick warmth of her body. For an hour or two she could make him feel like something more than a washed-up country singer who'd let his family down in all the ways that counted. Sure, he'd started sending money home as soon as he'd signed his first contract, but he'd never sent more than cold cash, and he'd never apologized for hurting the two people who'd loved him the most. Mindless sex could cure a lot of things—including guilt—for a while. He ought to know.

He fisted his hands against the urge to stroke Juliana into wakefulness. Oh yeah. It would be so easy to be that selfish SOB with her. And that was exactly why he had to keep his distance. He couldn't go back, couldn't risk letting Kelly and the girls down the way he'd let his folks down.

But Juliana being out here instead of in his bed could work to his advantage. He'd take a shower and wash away the temptation along with the food and bar smells, and then he'd wake Juliana and send her to his bed. Alone.

As quietly as possible, Rex entered his room to collect

fresh clothing. The sight of her suits lined up beside his jeans in the closet rattled him. He extracted what he needed and headed for the bathroom, only to receive another shock. Her toiletries neatly lined the counter and her shampoo stood next to his in the shower stall.

Yesterday, he'd wanted to get away from her. *Today, she'd moved in.* Oh yeah, his life was definitely veering out of control, but he'd learned the hard way how destructive that could be. It wasn't a mistake he'd repeat.

He stripped off his clothing, stepped into the shower and lathered briskly, valiantly fighting traitorous thoughts of Juliana's soap-slickened hands gliding over his skin, but he was too tired to maintain his mental barricades. In seconds, he had a painful hard-on begging for attention. He twisted the faucet to cold and shivered in the bone-jarring, frigid water while he rinsed off the soap and shampoo. After toweling off and pulling on clean jeans and a T-shirt, he set his shoulders. Time to put temptation to bed and try to catch some shut-eye before this merry-go-round started again tomorrow. Saturday. Juliana's day off. How would he concentrate on work knowing she was in his apartment all day?

He stopped beside the sofa and struggled with the bite of awareness. He couldn't forget the softness of her skin or the taste of her mouth. Dammit. He couldn't remember ever getting turned on so fast or having a woman haunt his thoughts day and night. Had to be the celibacy screwing with his head.

One week. He could hold out until Kelly returned home and then, debt or no debt, he'd dump Juliana.

"Juliana," he whispered. She didn't stir. He didn't want to raise his voice and risk waking the girls. "Juliana, wake up."

Nothing. Damn. He'd have to touch her. But where? The bare skin of her shoulder was too close to the shadowy area between her breasts. Too risky. He patted her kneecap. "Juliana."

She startled, inhaled a quick breath and jerked upright. "What? Oh, hello."

"Go to bed."

She blinked owlishly and scanned the room as if she couldn't remember where she was or how she'd gotten there. She looked flustered and adorable and kissable. Damn.

She shoved her hair out of her face. "The girls?"

"Asleep."

She yawned and her breasts lifted beneath her satiny shirt. "Becky had a nightmare. I guess I dozed off."

The quiet statement struck with the sudden impact of a rock hitting his truck's windshield. A crack slowly snaked through the resistance he fought so hard to maintain. "Nice of you to listen out for her."

What was it about her that fueled his engine like nobody else had? He'd met prettier women, women with bigger boobs and longer legs. But he couldn't remember one from his past who got to him this way, let alone one who'd have volunteered for the non-glamorous, tough job of babysitting somebody else's kids. Not that he'd ever known any of his past lovers that well.

Slowly, she unfolded and stood, and then she stumbled and fell against his chest. He caught her upper arms. Her fingers splayed over his heart. She couldn't miss the rapid-fire beat.

Her slumberous gaze lifted to his. "Sorry. My foot's asleep."

And not one single, sorry cell in his body was. His hands tightened. He wanted her so bad, he ached with it. Wanted to taste her damp lips. Wanted to caress her flushed skin. Wanted to bury his face in the valley between her breasts and make her as hungry for him as he was for her. Wanted to push her back on the sofa and bury himself between her long legs.

What would it hurt? It's what she wants prompted the selfish bastard lurking inside him.

Rex's jaw muscles protested his tooth-gritting abuse, and

he battled with the throbbing need he should have satisfied in the shower. No, it wouldn't have been as good as the real thing, but he could have taken the edge off his craving.

User. An icy drop of water from his wet hair snaked down his spine, shocking him into clearheadedness. He set her away, holding on only until he was sure she had her footing.

"Go to bed, Juliana."

All dressed up and no place to go.

Juliana paced Rex's bedroom. An early riser by habit, she'd awoken without an alarm. She needed coffee immediately and a newspaper soon. Today's edition should contain Octavia Jenkins's first installment about the auction. Juliana didn't want to wake Rex or the girls by running the sputtering coffee machine, and she didn't know if he subscribed to the local paper.

Clutching her key to the apartment and her wallet, she eased open the bedroom door. As silently as possible, she tiptoed into the den. Her heart stalled when she spotted Rex sprawled on the sofa and then raced as her gaze drank him in. His shiny hair spilled over the cappuccino-colored leather like bittersweet chocolate drizzled over milk chocolate. His bare feet hung over the opposite end. He'd shed his shirt and unbuttoned the top button on his jeans. The sheet he'd used lay puddled on the floor beside him. Her gaze returned to that unfastened brass button and the shadow of his navel behind it, and then raked over his bare chest to his bristly chin and parted lips.

Her mouth dried. He definitely knew how to use those lips. The question was how did she get him to use them again. On her. With each encounter, her desire to be held against that broad hair-spattered chest grew and her ambivalence over this crazy scheme faded, but she didn't appear to be getting any closer to her goal, so her uncertainty was a moot point.

What was she going to do to tempt him next, and how far could she go with the girls in the house?

She tiptoed to the girls' door and found them sleeping peacefully. Her heart twinged a little. She'd never expected to enjoy caring for them so much. They were sweet and funny and obviously adored their uncle. Unfortunately, Juliana was getting a bit too fond of their uncle as well. The idea of one month of naughty thrills and then a quick goodbye didn't sound nearly as attractive as it once had. In fact, she wondered if one month would be enough.

She wanted to know more about Rex Tanner than her online searches had revealed. Like what put those shadows in his dark eyes? And what had driven a man at the top of his career to self-destruct? Unfortunately, the girls couldn't tell her and Rex wouldn't.

Rex slept through her examination, but that was understandable since he'd only come upstairs four hours ago. Juliana eased through his apartment door—the one leading to the exterior stairs instead of through Renegade—aiming for the coffee shop she'd spotted down the street yesterday. The early morning humidity clung to her skin on the short walk. She purchased her caffeine fix and a newspaper and headed back to Rex's, where she settled at the picnic table on his upstairs deck overlooking the Cape Fear River.

The sun had risen high enough at 6:30 for her to read the newsprint, but not high enough to bake her skin. She wasn't one of those women who tanned well. She turned an unbecoming shade of boiled-shrimp pink, but she'd forgotten to pack her sunscreen. She'd have to retreat inside in a few minutes—back to the space dominated by Rex. And she didn't think she could handle him without a full load of caffeine in her system.

With her back to the house, she flipped straight to the Lifestyles section, found Octavia's byline and winced at the title of the article: Love at Any Price? She quickly scanned over the introductory info. Her eyes skidded to a halt when she found her name, and then she backtracked and began the paragraph again.

Bachelor nine. Rex Tanner and Juliana Alden each claim to have pure motives for participating in the auction. The former Nashville headliner says all he wants is publicity for Renegade, his new waterfront bar and grill. Ms. Alden declares her interests lie in the motorcycle lessons. But this reporter believes the relationship will yield more than improved revenues and riding skills. The sparks between the dashing biker and the proper banker nearly set the room ablaze.

Appalled, Juliana dropped the paper on the table and pressed cold hands to her hot cheeks. Was she so obvious? Everyone in Wilmington would know she was pursuing Rex. Everyone including her mother and Wally. The fallout from that would not be pleasant. Her mouth dried and panic made her heart palpitate erratically. She'd wanted a month of breaking rules, not a month of public embarrassment.

She dug her cell phone out of her pocket and hit speed dial. "H'lo," Andrea answered in a groggy voice.

"Andrea, I'm sorry if I woke you, but I've just read Octavia Jenkins's article. It's awful."

A groan carried over the phone line. "You didn't wake me. I've seen it. Oh my God. 'This romance is ready to be rekindled. Is Ms. Montgomery carrying the matches?' I am so *not* trying to win Clay back. I'm going to ask Octavia to print a retraction."

Juliana grimaced. She'd been so concerned with her own predicament she hadn't even read about Andrea or Holly. She scanned down the page and read the section Andrea had quoted. "I don't think you'll get a retraction. She hasn't really crossed the line."

"Says you."

"Did you see what she wrote about Rex and me? Now everyone knows what I'm doing. And if that's not humiliating enough, guess what? It's not working. You said he was such a womanizer that all I'd have to do was show up and keep breathing and he'd do the rest. Well, he's not doing it."

"What are you talking about?"

Juliana shot a quick, cautious glance over her shoulder and then whispered, "Getting Rex to seduce me."

"He's not interested?"

"He's interested…at least I think he is, but I… I wanted someone who would sweep me off my feet and overcome my doubts about this whole crazy scheme. He's not sweeping."

"Men are so obtuse. You're going to have to nudge him in the right direction. Let's meet for breakfast and plot our way out of this mess. I'll call Holly and tell her to meet us at Magnolia's Diner."

"I can't."

"Why?"

"Because I'm babysitting Rex's nieces today."

"Babysitting? No, no, no. Juliana, kids and sex don't mix. I'm coming over. We need to talk."

She took a fortifying gulp of coffee. "You can't come over because I'm not at home."

"Where are you?"

She hesitated and then confessed. "Staying at Rex's apartment above Renegade."

Silent seconds ticked past. "I'm sure there's a good explanation why you're living with him and not getting any? Besides the children, I mean."

Tapping drew Juliana's gaze to the girls' bedroom window. Two angelic faces grinned out at her. She smiled back and waved, and then pressed her finger to her lips in the universal Be quiet sign. "It's complicated, but I can't explain now. I have to go."

"You can't leave me hanging like that," Andrea squawked.

"Sorry. Have to. Bye." She disconnected over Andrea's protests, gathered her paper, coffee and keys and let herself inside.

"Man, you're driving me crazy, and your prowling is scaring off customers. Go away."

Rex frowned at Danny. "I thought I was the boss."

"Rex, I can handle this crowd. Go check on the girls or the chick or whoever's got your nuts in a knot."

Rex had never been more conscious of the empty apartment over his head. Dammit, it was supposed to be empty. He liked living alone. But he'd been out of sorts since yesterday morning when he'd awoken to silence. How had Juliana sneaked the girls out without waking him? Probably because sleep was next to impossible knowing he had a sexy *and willing* banker in his bed, and when he'd finally drifted off he'd dreamed of the bedroom door opening and Juliana beckoning him to join her. In his dreams, he hadn't refused her invitation. Heat pulsed through him.

He'd found a note from Juliana in the kitchen saying she'd taken the girls to her place, and that she'd like for them to spend Saturday night with her so they wouldn't disturb him. He was supposed to call her cell phone if he didn't like the idea. He hadn't liked the idea, but he couldn't explain why, so he hadn't called. One day less exposure to Juliana was one day he didn't have to fight the pull between them. No doubt the girls would love a sleepover. He should be grateful. But he wasn't.

The newspaper Juliana had left on his kitchen table hadn't improved his mood. Sure, the auction article had generated additional business as he'd hoped. They'd had the best weekend crowd yet, but too many customers had asked him about his romance with Juliana. They wanted a freaking fairy-tale ending and that wasn't going to happen. She might be a banking princess, but he'd proven he wasn't prince material.

He finished wiping down the bar and pitched his rag into the bucket of cleaning solution. "I didn't expect her to keep Becky and Liza at her place all weekend."

"What are you complaining about? You got your bed back, and she and the squirts aren't underfoot." Danny didn't have kids of his own, but he still lived at home and he had a gaggle of younger siblings whom he claimed were always in the way. "Go."

Rex glanced at his watch. Five o'clock. If he left now, he'd have time to take a quick shower and then play with the girls before dinner. "All right. I'm going. Call Juliana's if you need me. Number's by the phone."

Forty minutes later, he parked his truck in the driveway beside Juliana's sedan, climbed the stairs and rang her doorbell. No one responded to the bell or his knock, but using his key was too damned domesticated for him. He walked around to the back of the end-unit town house, but the girls weren't on the patio, and he couldn't see them through the French doors. Damn. He dug his key out of his pocket and let himself in. Using the key did *not* mean he and Juliana had a relationship beyond the girls and the lessons.

"Juliana? Becky? Liza?" Silence echoed back.

Bottles of nail polish stood like a line of candy-colored fence posts on the kitchen table, corralling a neat pile of hair ribbons and an assortment of other girlie stuff. Juliana's purse leaned against a stack of child-care and babysitting books on the hall table. That she cared enough to try to learn more about his nieces shouldn't get to him, but it did.

How could he have been so wrong in his initial assessment that she had more money than brains? He shrugged off his growing admiration. The last thing he needed was to soften up around her. Liking her and appreciating her generosity didn't change the fact that he was in debt up to his neck to her family, or that she was looking for a walk on the wild side and he wasn't. She wanted excitement and he wanted...

What did he want? Roots? Maybe. He scrubbed a hand over the back of his neck. One of these days, when the bar was on a firmer footing, he wouldn't mind having someone to come home to, but he'd made more than his share of mistakes and let a lot of people down. He shook his head. Even if he did decide to take a chance—one he was sure he'd blow—on something long-term, a banking heiress wouldn't be interested in anything permanent from a long-haired biker with a highway education and a wardrobe consisting of jeans and T-shirts with the Renegade logo on the back. She'd end up with a college-educated *GQ* guy in a suit. A man like the other bachelors at the charity auction.

Juliana and the girls couldn't be far if her purse and car were here. He locked up and headed for the playground. Excited, happy squeals made him detour toward the nearby pool. A couple of dozen folks populated the fenced area. Becky's rebel yell drew his gaze to the shallow end. She launched herself from the side of the pool and hit the water with a decent splash, but bobbed back to the surface thanks to a new hot-pink life jacket. Next, he spotted Liza, also sporting a new life jacket in smiley-face yellow, her favorite color. She dog-paddled toward a slender, dark-haired woman whose mostly bare back faced him.

Juliana. He didn't need to see her face to recognize her.

Every male hormone in his body pointed her out like a hunting dog signaled quail. The line of her naked spine and the curve of her waist in the hip-deep water brought a flood of moisture to his mouth and kicked his heart into a staccato beat. Her two-piece swimsuit wasn't skimpy by today's standards, but knowing only a few scraps of fabric separated him from her bare skin hit him with the blast of a spotlight. Sweat oozed from his pores. His black shirt and jeans magnified his reaction by absorbing every hot ray of the evening sunshine. Her low and husky laugh at Becky's antics only increased his discomfort.

Juliana ducked under the water, and Liza squealed and squirmed with joy and then cackled when Juliana shot out of the water, slicked back her hair and gently splashed Becky. Apparently, the banker had a playful side and the urge to play with her was getting damned hard for Rex to ignore. He gripped the white picket fence and struggled to corral his stampeding hormones.

"Uncle Rex!" Becky yelled.

Cover blown. He gritted a smile, ordered his body to behave and shoved open the gate. Juliana jerked around to face him and he nearly tripped over a seam in the sidewalk. Her breasts were round, pale, perfect and far too exposed in a blue top the exact shade of her eyes for his peace of mind.

"Wook, Unca Wex." Liza's voice drew his attention away from forbidden territory. "I swimmen."

"And doing a great job of it, sweet pea. Hey, Beck, killer cannonball." Becky responded by hauling herself out of the pool and launching another one, this one soaking him. He welcomed the cool water on his overheated skin.

"We've had a busy day." Juliana's quiet words forced him to look at her again—something he'd rather not do until she covered up from ears to ankles. "They should sleep well tonight."

At the sight of all that creamy, curvaceous flesh on display, words failed him. He grunted an affirmative.

"Is something wrong? You're supposed to be working." She folded her arms across her middle, which should have helped his concentration since it covered a lot of skin, but the move pushed her breasts farther out of her suit, resulting in a negative effect on his brain function. It took him a few seconds to weed her question out of his testosterone-induced fog.

"Danny's closing. I thought I'd take the girls out to dinner and then head back to my place. Tomorrow's my day off, so I'll keep 'em tonight and you can sleep in your own bed." He glanced at Becky and Liza in time to see their faces fall.

Juliana waded toward the pool steps. "We'd planned to grill kebabs tonight, and we've made homemade ice cream. Why don't you join us for dinner?"

Bad idea. How could he get out of it? "Kebabs?"

"We stuck 'em," Liza said in as bloodthirsty a tone as he'd ever heard from a three-year-old. He grabbed her upraised hands, lifted her from the pool and set her on the concrete.

Juliana bit her lip, but she couldn't hide the smile twitching on her mouth. The mischievous sparkle in her eyes slammed the breath right out of him. "The girls helped me assemble the kebabs. We bought the ice-cream freezer when we bought the life jackets. Cooking together seemed like a good activity."

"Right. Dinner sounds good." *Liar, liar, pants on fire.*

Becky vaulted out and gave him a soggy hug. He ruffled her wet hair with a surprisingly unsteady hand.

Juliana rose from the pool like a nymph in a wet dream. Rivulets of water cascaded over the peaks and valleys of a truly lust-worthy body. His throat closed and his skin ignited. The little flirty skirt of her bathing suit bottom stopped an inch below her navel, and the wet fabric clung to her hips like a second skin.

He exhaled slowly and turned his back on what he couldn't have to help the girls dry off. The week ahead yawned like an eternity.

"Wook." Liza lifted her hands. He blinked away the sensual haze clouding his vision, knelt beside Liza and focused on her tiny, pale pink-tipped nails. "Oo-liana painted dem."

"Pretty."

Juliana stopped beside them. Her toenails bore the same shade of polish. Rex fought the urge to trace the long, lean line of her legs with his gaze and lost. From his kneeling position on the concrete, the sight of those perfect breasts at eye level wreaked no end of havoc below his belt. Frustration and futility rose inside him.

Surrender man and be done with it.

No way. Too much to lose.

He stood and met the gaze of the woman determined to bring him to his knees. Damned if she didn't have him like a fish on the hook, and fighting the line wasn't getting him anywhere but reeled in and too tired to care. Unless he wanted to be left on the dock gasping for air, then he had to do something fast.

But he had a feeling it was too late.

Six

Rex prowled around Juliana's den like a caged animal. Examining an item here, looking out a window there, but never remaining still for more than a few seconds.

With her senses hyperaware of each shift of his muscular frame, Juliana sipped her favorite locally produced peach wine and tugged at the hem of the sundress she'd changed into after returning from the pool.

The fuchsia dress had hung in her closet unworn for years because the bodice dipped lower than she liked, and the hem was inches higher than comfortable. She'd bought it and the ridiculously high-heeled matching sandals for a cruise she, Andrea and Holly had scheduled to celebrate their twenty-seventh birthdays but had never taken due to Juliana's emergency appendectomy.

"I'll repay you for everything you've spent on Irma, the life jackets, the doll clothes, whatever. How much do I owe ya?" Rex's gaze raked her exposed skin for the third time. He glanced away and looked again, convincing Juliana that her sexy dress was worth every penny she'd paid for it even if she never wore it again.

She crossed her legs and then smoothed her hem. Rex's eyes tracked each movement. Hmm. Interesting. Leaning forward, she deposited her wineglass on the coffee table and hooked a finger beneath the thin gold chain at her neck. Rex's dark eyes fastened on the stroke of her fingers inside the V-neck of her bodice. His Adam's apple bobbed.

A sense of feminine power swelled inside her. He *was* attracted to her. What would it take to break through his restraint? *C'mon, bad boy, corrupt me.*

What had he said again? Oh, yes. "Your sister is covering Irma's salary. The rest…" She shrugged and gestured to where Becky and Liza played dress-up with their dolls in the corner. "It's my pleasure. The girls and I are having fun."

"I insist."

"Your sister said you would. The answer's still no, Rex." She kicked her ankle just a little, dangling the sandal from her toes just to see if he'd watch. He did. She bit the inside of her lip to stop a pleased smile.

His fists clenched and unclenched. "Kelly called this morning. Mike made it through surgery and he's stable. Now it's a wait-and-see game, but the doctors are optimistic."

She uncrossed her legs and shifted on the sofa. The move inched her hem higher—a bonus she hadn't anticipated. "For Kelly and the girls' sake I hope he pulls through."

"Yeah." The word was little more than a grunt. His gaze never left her legs.

"Are you sure you don't want some wine? I'm sorry I don't have beer." She leaned forward to retrieve her glass and savored the shift of his eyes to her cleavage. Her nipples tightened.

A femme fatale is born. The incongruity of the statement nearly made her laugh out loud. She loved the way Rex's hot glances made her feel all restless and warm. Parts of her body tingled that had never tingled before.

"No thanks."

Sometimes an account investigation led her in a surprising direction. She'd learned to trust her instincts and go with it. "Then could you stop pacing and sit down?" She patted the cushion beside her. "You're making the girls nervous."

A lie. The girls had quit watching him circle the room ten minutes ago, but each pass of those lean hips through her line of vision pushed her closer to sensory overload. My gosh, she was ogling him and his um…parts, and she really wanted to know if he lived up to the promise in those jeans. Her bold thoughts made her cheeks burn.

He lowered himself into a chair on the opposite side of the coffee table, rested his elbows on his knees and then propped his head in his hands. Juliana studied his thick hair, the tense line of his shoulders and tightened her fingers around the stem of her wineglass instead of reaching across the distance to touch him the way she wanted. She'd never considered herself a sensual or tactile person, but the better she got to know Rex, the harder it was to resist the urge to touch him. His sleek hair. His rough jaw. His hard muscles.

She didn't lack initiative in her professional life, but in her personal life she'd definitely be classified as a slow-starter. In light of Rex's reaction tonight, she almost looked forward to making a move. Almost.

He lifted his head suddenly and his coffee-colored eyes pinned her in place. "Why me? The truth this time."

The wine in her glass sloshed over her fingers. Stalling, she dabbed at the liquid with a tissue. He wouldn't accept an evasive answer this time, she'd bet, and she wasn't a gambling person. Her gaze flicked to the girls in the corner. How much did she dare explain? "Because I have a nice life."

"What?" He sounded as if he thought she'd lost her mind.

"I'm thirty years old. I have a nice car, a nice home and a nice job. *Nice* is bland and boring. Like me. I hoped your auction package might jar me out of my 'nice' rut. There has to be more to life than *nice,* and if there is I don't want to miss out."

Wary understanding softened his eyes and then he leaned back in the chair and clasped his hands over his flat belly— a relaxed pose, but the intense look in his eyes was anything but relaxed. "I used to want more, too. And then I realized that *more* wasn't as great as it sounded."

She savored the tiny insight into his thoughts. "Your music career?"

Seconds ticked past as he studied his knotted fingers. "Yeah. I couldn't wait to get off that ranch and be somebody besides Reed Tanner's boy. Then I was. And everybody wanted me to be somebody else."

"I don't understand."

"The record execs, my manager and my publicist signed me because I was different. And then they tried to turn me into a carbon copy of every other guy on the charts."

"But you made it to the top without sounding like everyone else." She wasn't a country music fan, so her comparison wasn't firsthand, but she'd read the online articles touting Rex's unique sound and fresh way with words, and she enjoyed his music.

"I made it because I fought 'em every step of the way. The point is, you don't have to try to be somebody you're not."

But who was she exactly? Until the pressure to marry Wally had come about, Juliana had been certain she knew. For as far back as she could remember, she'd been groomed to take her place in the Alden Bank executive offices. That goal had always taken precedence over anything and anyone else. And she'd been happy with that decision. A life without emotional ups and downs suited her. She'd had a ringside seat when Andrea had fallen head-over-heels in love and when her friend had crash-landed with a broken heart. Afterward, Juliana had considered guarding her heart and avoiding the same kind of pain a good idea.

But now she had her doubts. Look at Irma. Her former nanny had dedicated herself to a career of caring for other women's children. Now that age had forced Irma to retire from the job that had defined her, what did she have left? Nothing. No family. No hobbies. Juliana didn't want to be left with nothing, but she wasn't sure meekly falling in with her mother's plans was the answer.

The foundation she'd built her life on was shaking and she didn't know if it would settle or crumble beneath her.

She lifted her gaze to the man in front of her. "Was fighting for what you wanted worth it?"

If it had been, then why had he left his dreams behind?

He shot to his feet. "Becoming my own man was a journey I had to take, but I was selfish. I hurt people along the way. And I let 'em down. I shouldn't have."

Who had he let down? And how?

Before she could ask, he turned to Becky and Liza. "Girls, we gotta go. Get your stuff and say good night."

Juliana wanted to dig deeper, but in the hustle to gather the girls' belongings there wasn't time or opportunity for questions. She walked the trio to Rex's truck and helped buckle the girls into their car seats. First Liza and then Becky insisted on giving her a hug and kiss good-night, and the gestures tugged at Juliana's heart.

"Thanks for dinner," he said as he started the truck.

Juliana stepped back, folded her arms and watched them

drive out of sight. Would she ever have children? The odds didn't favor her chances. At thirty years old, she'd never come close to finding a man with whom she wanted to spend the rest of her life. Sure, she'd had relationships, but her dedication to her job had always outweighed her commitment to the man in question, and none of her dates had ever interested her enough to make her want to leave work early or take a day off. If not for Andrea and Holly, she'd probably never take a vacation.

If you marry Wally, you could have children. Yet another plus in the Wally column. So why couldn't she just agree to the engagement and be done with it? Why vacillate? Was she being unrealistic to want more than a good rapport with her spouse? Was true intimacy a fallacy perpetuated by romantic books and movies? And was she even capable of letting someone get that close?

Juliana's office door burst open Monday just before lunch. She marked her place on the ledger with a finger and glanced up. Her mother's scowl turned Juliana's stomach into a hornet's nest. Clearly, the avoidance punishment had ended. "Hello, Mother."

Margaret Alden slapped a newspaper onto Juliana's desk. "This is outrageous."

The Saturday edition lay open to Octavia Jenkins's column, "Love at Any Price?" Juliana masked a wince. So much for hoping her mother would miss the article. "Octavia is trying to sell papers, and she's supporting your pet charity. Did you notice she gave the address to which donations can be mailed?"

"Have you read this? Do you realize the damage she's done to your engagement?"

Juliana should have known her mother wouldn't ask her if she had feelings for Rex or if the column was off base. They'd never had that kind of relationship. No, Juliana had shared her confidences with Irma, Andrea and Holly.

"I'm not engaged yet, and if you read the entire article, then you'll see that Octavia has also implied a romantic entanglement between Wally and Donna and Eric and Holly."

Juliana had hated reading about her brother and her best friend, and she hoped Octavia had her facts wrong, and yet Juliana was afraid to call Holly and find out. "You know those aren't true."

"I certainly hope Eric isn't involved with Holly. She has disappointed her parents terribly by living out in that shack like a bohemian."

"It's not a shack. It's a restored farmhouse and her studio." She'd said the words so many times before they came out in a singsong chorus.

"And Wallace knows better. That woman is not one of us."

The snobbery offended Juliana. She should have been used to it by now since she'd heard it her entire life. "You mean she wasn't born wealthy and didn't have everything handed to her on a silver platter?"

Her mother's nose lifted. "You and Eric didn't have everything handed to you."

"Yes, we did, Mother. Everything except respect, which we've had to fight an uphill battle to earn." *And our parents' attention, which seemed connected to perfect behavior,* Juliana added silently. The friends she'd had in school who'd dared to disobey had been shipped off to boarding school. Juliana had always followed the rules for fear of being sent away from Irma, Andrea, Holly and home.

"I'm calling the newspaper to have Ms. Jenkins removed from this series."

Juliana sighed and pushed back an errant strand of hair. "Sex sells, Mother. Octavia is doing her job."

"Are you saying you're having sex with that…that man?"

A rush of heat swept Juliana's face. "No, but even if I were sleeping with Rex, it wouldn't be any of your business."

"Don't make it my business by ruining this merger. By this time next year, Alden-Wilson will be the largest privately held bank in the southeast, and I will be the CEO."

"Only if Mr. Wilson is willing to step aside, and from what Wally has said, his father's not all that interested in being second in command. Mother, you may not win this one." Juliana admired her mother's ambition. All her life, she'd heard tales of how Margaret Alden had had it all—husband, family and career. Juliana wanted it all, too.

A smug smile curved her mother's lips. "Let me worry about that. You worry about making amends with Wallace. And make sure this little hussy isn't encroaching on your territory. Don't let me down, Juliana. This merger is far too important for you to jeopardize it with an unsuitable fling. Are we clear?"

She stalked out of Juliana's office as abruptly as she'd entered it.

Juliana sat back in her chair. *Don't let me down.* The battle cry of her life. But this time the feeling that the merger might be more important to her mother than Juliana's life and happiness unsettled her.

The suffocating straitjacket feeling that had driven her to buying the baddest bachelor on the block closed in on her, squeezing her ribs and compressing her lungs.

Last chance. Last chance.

She had to get out of here. She closed the ledger, withdrew her purse from her desk drawer and locked up. On the way out, she paused by her administrative assistant's desk. "I'm leaving for the day."

And then she turned her back on the woman's gaping mouth, walked out into the afternoon sunshine, took a deep breath of the hot, humid air and tasted freedom.

Trapped in his own damned apartment.

Rex knew he could lie, claim he had business downstairs and escape, leaving Juliana to listen for the girls. But he wasn't a coward. In the past, his failure to face his mistakes had cost him. He wouldn't run again. He'd agreed to the auction, agreed to keep the girls. That meant any fallout from those choices was his and his alone.

But damn. A man could only take so much, and his resistance had been slipping since Juliana had surprised him and the girls at the barn this afternoon with a picnic lunch. She'd spent the next four hours laughing, teasing and playing with Liza and Becky, and he'd discovered yet another facet to the formerly uptight auditor. A side he liked too much.

Restless, edgy and as horny as hell, he paced his den. A beautiful woman wanted him. The feeling was mutual. Why did he keep fighting the hunger that chewed him from the inside out? Because sleeping with Juliana would be mixing business with pleasure. Always a bad idea. But more important was that giving in to the craving inside him would open the door to his biggest weakness.

But he ached for her. The smell of her. The taste of her. The feel of her. Wrapped around him. Just once.

Fool. Having a little sex with Juliana is about as safe as a recovering alcoholic taking just one drink. You'll be sucked back into the world that almost destroyed you so fast you'll never recover.

Juliana stepped out of the girls' bedroom and closed the door. Rex's stomach hit the soles of his boots.

She looked like a combination of angel and siren with her

sable hair hanging loose. The strands teased her bare shoulders and the cleavage revealed by a fragile, fluttery pale blue top that ended a couple of inches above low-rider jeans. A wide woven belt circled her hips with its tasseled ties swaying over no-man's-land with every hypnotizing stride she took toward him. Those tassels affected his libido like a flashing neon Come and Get It sign.

He dragged his gaze up to the half smile on her face. Trouble. Pure trouble. Sweat oozed from his pores, dampening his upper lip, chest and back. His heart drummed harder, faster. His breathing turned shallow.

"The girls are out for the night."

Her whisper sent a bead of sweat snaking down his spine. He suppressed a shiver. "You should turn in. Early start tomorrow."

"It's only nine. Why don't you put on some music?" She sank onto the sofa and crossed her legs. She'd removed her shoes at some point. Her pink-tipped toes wiggled, and the lamp reflected off a gold toe ring on her right second toe and glittered on an ankle bracelet.

Oh, man. He swallowed, but his mouth remained as dry as a dust bowl. "No stereo."

She blinked. "You don't own a stereo? Isn't that a little unusual given your previous occupation?"

"Music's no longer a part of my life."

"Why?"

For a lot of reasons, none of which he'd share. "No time."

"Was it hard to walk away from something you loved?"

Dammit. Why did she insist on getting inside his head? Every time they met, she peppered him with questions. "No."

Liar. There were times—like today, *like now*—when feelings bottled up inside him and his fingers twitched for his guitar so he could pour out those emotions. As a teen and later as an adult, he'd worked through his tangled thoughts with music, singing, writing lyrics or just playing melodies long into the night. Sometimes he'd thought music was the only thing that kept him sane.

The more time he spent with Juliana, the more his thoughts strayed to the old Fender in the back of his closet. But he wouldn't pull out the instrument, wouldn't let her force him back into that world. A world that had cost him his family, his home, his friends and his self-respect.

She rose and crossed to where he stood by the window overlooking the dark street below. He sucked in an unsteady breath and her spices-and-flowers scent filled his nostrils. "How did you do it? How did you find the courage to make your own life?"

The uncertainty in her eyes knocked him senseless. If she'd boldly come on to him, whispered naughty intentions in his ear or just planted those delicious red lips on his, he could have resisted her. Probably. But the doubts clouding her eyes shredded his defenses.

"What's wrong with your life?" From where he stood, her life looked pretty damned good.

She tipped her head back. Her breath swept across his lips and his pulse stalled. "Expectations. Theirs. Mine. Sometimes it feels like my life's not my own and what I want doesn't matter."

Sympathy softened his clenched muscles. This was the stuff she hadn't told the reporter, either, the first night or tonight. And he'd bet these were the demons that had driven her to buy him at the auction. He wanted to know more and yet he didn't. Knowing meant understanding. Understanding meant weakening. Weakening meant failing. Himself. Kelly. The girls. Juliana.

He didn't want to like Juliana, didn't want to respect her,

but if anybody could understand the pressure of others' expectations, he could.

He rolled his tense shoulders. "I know what you mean. For as far back as I can remember, my life was mapped out. Most kids get asked what they want to be when they grow up. Nobody ever asked me. I was born to take over the family ranch like my father and my grandfather before him."

"But that's not what you wanted?"

Just thinking about being tied to the ranch made his skin shrink. "I didn't want to spend year after year worrying about drought, disease or whether there would be enough money left to put food on the table after a rough winter. I didn't want to die young because I worked myself into an early grave like my grandfather. I wanted more. And I wanted out. Out of that one-stoplight town. Out from under my father's thumb."

Why hadn't he ever tried to explain his fears to his parents instead of hurling abuse at them? "I took off. But not without burning my bridges first. I followed my heart. That doesn't mean it didn't get me into trouble."

Her teeth worried her bottom lip. He fisted his hands against the urge to free the soft swell from assault. "So you do understand. And all I need is the courage to follow my heart?"

"Something like that, but there are always consequences for the choices you make, Juliana. And sometimes by the time you realize the price you've paid is too high, it's too late to fix it."

All she needed was courage, but courage was the one thing Juliana lacked most at the moment.

If this had been a face-off with the top dog at the FDIC, she'd have been rock steady, but all she wanted was to feel like a woman instead of a pawn in a banking merger. The passion in Rex's kiss could give her that.

His heat and masculine scent ensnared her. Juliana's legs trembled and she felt slightly dizzy from an adrenaline rush. Couldn't he tell how much she needed his touch? Why wouldn't he kiss her?

Why don't you kiss him?

A novel idea. And a scary one. But taking an active role wasn't nearly as scary as it once had been because she liked and trusted Rex.

But what if he rebuffed her again? Would she have to give up and admit her tepid romance with Wally was all she deserved? A touch of panic quickened her pulse.

"What is it you want so badly?" he asked.

"I want to take control of my life, to do something just because I want to not because it's expected or because it's the wisest course of action." She swallowed and dampened her lips. "I want you, Rex Tanner."

His eyes slammed shut and his jaw muscles bunched. "Bad idea."

"I think it's a great idea." Faking moxie she didn't possess, she rose on tiptoe and pressed her lips to his. He stiffened and remained as rigid as a sun-baked brick wall while she brushed her lips over his once, twice, a third time. If not for the rapid hammering of his heart beneath the palms she'd braced on his chest, she'd think him unaffected. Encouraged by that telling sign, she licked his bottom lip. A groan rumbled from deep in his throat.

Slowly, she settled back on her feet. "Show me how to take control, Rex."

A battle raged in his eyes. Just when she'd convinced herself she'd played her cards and lost, and her hopes began to sink, he snatched her upper arms, yanked her close and slammed his mouth over hers in a hard, unrestrained kiss.

Shock lasted scant seconds and then a myriad of sensations

engulfed her. The inferno of his tongue as it sliced through the seam of her lips to tangle with hers, the heat of his hands as they splayed over her hips and pulled her against the branding iron of his erection combined with his taste and scent to overwhelm and arouse her beyond her wildest expectations. The infusion of pure, undiluted passion made Juliana drunk with desire and doubly glad she'd never been exposed to this level of arousal before, because without a doubt, the rush was addictive.

His hands skated upward until his thumbs reached the bare skin above her jeans. He drew circles on either side of her navel. She broke the kiss to gasp for air. The simple caress made her a lover of low-rider jeans for life. Her gaze lifted from his beard-shadowed jaw to kiss-dampened lips and then to his dark, hungry eyes.

His unblinking gaze held hers as one big hand coiled in the dangling end of her belt, holding her captive. The other raked upward, sweeping beneath her voile camisole and over her waist and ribs to cup her breast. Her fragile bra was no barrier to the back-and-forth motion of his thumb over the sensitive tip. A knot of need tightened in her belly, pulling tauter with each slow pass until every thought centered on quenching the fire he'd ignited. Her lids grew heavy. She fought to stay focused on Rex's face.

No man had ever looked at her that way, as if he would strip her bare and take her where she stood or die trying.

She liked it. Liked knowing she'd reached the limits of his control. And hers.

A shiver chased over her skin. She'd always dreamed of a man who wanted her—*her*—not the Alden heiress. And she'd found him. Too bad forever wasn't in the cards. Even if she wasn't a boring bank auditor who calculated the odds of every endeavor, she could never hold the attention of a man who thrived on taking risks, a man who had the courage to confront his fears.

But she wouldn't think about that. Not now.

He worked magic with his fingers, teasing her, tantalizing her. Her nails curled and unfurled against his chest, but his T-shirt was in the way. She wanted to touch his skin. Before she could pull the hem of his shirt from his waistband, he'd released the front catch of her bra and palmed her. Rational thought evaporated the moment his hot fingers enclosed her. She dug her nails into his waist, fisting cotton and tugging him closer.

His mouth slanted over hers, softer this time, but still ravenous. He suckled her bottom lip, bit it gently and then soothed her with his tongue.

One of them was trembling. Her? Him? Who cared?

He removed his hand, and she whimpered a protest at the loss of warmth, but then he whisked her top over her head and crushed the fragile fabric in his hand. He lifted it to his face and inhaled deeply as if drawing in her essence. Wow. So sexy. And then Rex backed toward the bedroom, leading her by the leash of her macramé belt. Her heart raced, yet her feet seemed to move in slow motion.

Inside the bedroom he stopped. "You're a smart lady. Tell me to get out."

She gulped air and responded by closing and locking the door. He dropped her blouse and flicked her bra straps over her shoulders with one finger. Juliana shrugged and the lacy garment fell to the floor. Rex traced the curves of her breasts with his eyes and then with long fingers. He grazed her tight nipples with his short nails and her breath shuddered in and out again. Dragging her by her belt, he backed toward the bed and sat, pulling her between his splayed legs to take her nipple into his hot mouth.

Her head fell back on a moan. She slapped her fingers over her mouth. With the girls next door, she had to be quiet. And for the first time in her life, being quiet during sex might be a challenge.

Rex untied her belt, but held both ends, holding her hostage—not that she intended going anywhere now that he was finally doing what she'd hoped for all along. He ravaged her breasts with gentle scrapes of his raspy evening beard, soft tugs from his seductive lips and silken swipes from his hot, wet tongue, and then he drew her deep into his mouth. Her knees wobbled. She dug her fingers into his shoulders and then tangled them in his hair. His leather tie was in the way. She pulled it free and combed her fingers through the long, soft strands.

Rex plucked at the button and zip of her jeans. His knuckles brushed her navel and her stomach muscles rippled involuntarily. His big palm scorched a path from one hip to the other as he eased the snug denim down one inch at a time. By the time he got the fabric to her knees, she was ready to rip her jeans off, throw them across the room and beg him to fill the empty ache expanding inside her. She braced herself on his shoulders and stepped out of the pants. Eager, impatient, she burned with an unfamiliar urgency.

Rex drew back to examine her itty-bitty panties with an appreciative gaze. Had she ever felt this desirable in her life? No. *Bless the lingerie store at the mall.*

His fingers hooked under the lace, raking her panties down her legs and discarding them, and then he lifted her jeans from the floor, pulled the belt free of the loops and stretched it between his hands. With slow, deliberate movements he wound the ends around each wrist. Her heart missed a beat.

"Close your eyes and turn around, Juliana." The rough order made her quiver.

The time for her walk on the wild side had arrived. The question was did she have the courage to follow through?

Seven

Last chance. Last chance.

With her pulse thumping a deafening beat in her ears, Juliana lowered her lids and turned her back to Rex. The air around her stirred, sweeping over her skin as Rex shifted behind her. A second later, something alternately cool and rough crossed her breasts. Startled, she peeked. Her belt.

He dragged the braided strands left, right and back again and again. Each of the glass beads woven into the pattern teased her like a cool fingertip, while the cording, similar to the mild calluses on Rex's palms, lightly abraded her skin. The heat of his breath between her shoulder blades was her only warning before he nuzzled her hair aside and placed an open-mouthed kiss on her nape followed by another on her neck and her shoulder, her back…

Nipping. Kissing. Grazing.

His teeth. His lips. The belt.

She thought she'd implode as each new sensation built upon the last. A shudder shook her.

The belt slid lower, gliding over her waist, hips and curls. She gasped as the beads bumped over her highly sensitized flesh. And then he took the belt on a return trip, raking her nerve endings into a combustible pile and turning her legs to rubber.

"Turn around."

She forced her uncooperative muscles into obedience. The belt tightened beneath the curve of her bottom. Her nails bit into her palms and her teeth clenched on a moan as the beaded strands slid to her calves, ankles and back again. Rex pulled her closer. She braced her hands on his chest and then lowered them to his belly and bunched his T-shirt in her hands. She had to feel his skin on hers.

This couldn't possibly get better. Could it? She had to find out. She tugged upward and opened her eyes, reveling in the hunger she found in his. "Rex, please, I need to feel you against me."

He pitched the belt onto the bed behind him and helped her remove his shirt. She flexed her fingers, anticipating touching him. And then she did, burying her fingers in the dark curls on his chest, but reality far exceeded fantasy. Supple hot satin rippled below her fingertips. The tickle of his wiry hairs teased her palms. And then she cupped his face and kissed him. She couldn't possibly find the words to express how good he made her feel, but she could show him by pouring it into her kiss.

Rex's arms banded around her, fusing her to the length of his hot torso as he consumed her mouth roughly, greedily. It wasn't enough. Juliana wanted more, needed more, ached for more. As if he read her thoughts, he shifted her until she straddled one muscled thigh. The position left her open and vulnerable, a situation he took advantage of by easing his fingers between them to comb through her curls, find her wetness and caress her with deft strokes until she weaved unsteadily on her trembling legs. He pressed deeper, stroked faster and the tension inside her twisted into an almost unbearable knot.

She broke the kiss to gulp for air and alternately tangled her fingers in his hair and clenched his shoulders. His bristly jaw abraded the tender underside of her breast and then he caught her nipple with his lips, his teeth and gently tormented her right over the edge of reason. Release arced through her, scattering sparks clear down to her toes.

She forced her heavy lids open and smiled into his dark eyes. She traced a finger over his tight jaw. "Wow."

"Condoms. Get 'em," he rasped.

She turned to do as he bid, opening the purse she'd left on the dresser and retrieving the box with trembling hands. By the time she turned around he'd removed his boots and socks and stood towering over her. Juliana's heart pounded out a nervous rhythm as he shed his jeans and briefs with one sharp shove. His hair was wild and disheveled from her handiwork, and he looked every inch the rebel with the stubble on his jaw and upper lip and an untamed look in his eyes.

Her gaze skated over his broad chest to the erection jutting from a bed of dense dark curls. Thick. Hard. Hers. At least for now. Her mouth dried and her pulse blipped hummingbird fast.

Rex wanted her. *Her.* His desire was there plain to see. No man had ever been so blatantly aroused by just pleasuring her. In fact, few had ever taken the time to make sure she enjoyed the encounter.

He ripped back the comforter and held out his hand. She laid hers in his big palm and he drew her closer. The impact of his hot arousal against her belly sent her breath shuddering from her lungs and then his mouth took hers in a deep, soul-robbing kiss. The condoms fell from her fingers as she gave in to her need to stroke his supple skin, test his thick muscles and cup the derriere she'd shamelessly ogled when no one was looking.

He tipped her toward the mattress. The cool glide of his hair over her shoulder and then her breast had to be the most sensual thing Juliana had ever experienced. No wonder so many men liked long hair. Rex's dragged like cool satin over her heated skin as he feasted on her breasts, her belly. His tongue dipped into her navel and then swirled a path from hip bone to hip bone. It was simultaneously too much and not enough.

When he *finally* parted her curls and found her with his mouth, she had to shove her fist against her mouth to quiet her cries. She'd wanted to experience passion, and boy, was she. All too quickly, release undulated through her. Never had she felt anything this intense and at the same time frightening. Frightening because she was out of control, a slave to her desires, and because she had a feeling Rex Tanner was more man that she—or any woman for that matter—could handle. He'd be a rocket ride to heartbreak for any woman foolish enough to expect more than short-term thrills.

Good thing that temporary was all she wanted.

Wasn't it?

Doubts nipped at her conscience. Could she be happy with *nice* after this?

The self-indulgent beast rode Rex's back, clawing for sexual satisfaction the way it used to after a concert—only worse. The fangs of need sank deeper into his flesh than ever before.

Give, you selfish SOB. For once in your life give. Don't take.

He fought to leash his raging hunger and let Juliana drag him up her body one excruciating inch at a time, and then he grabbed the discarded box of condoms and shoved it in her hand. His entire body quaked with the effort it took to restrain himself from taking her—using her—to slake his hunger.

"You want control? Take it." His voice came out raspy and rough, as if he'd played in too many gigs in smoke-filled bars.

Surprise flashed in Juliana's passion-glazed eyes. Her breasts jiggled as her breath shuddered in and then out again, fueling his desire. He cradled her, marveling in the softness of the pale skin filling his palms and the sexy little sounds she made when he rolled her nipples between his fingers and thumbs. Those whimpers almost did him in.

Her hands trembled as she carefully slid a fingernail beneath the flap, opened the box and selected a condom. He'd given her the task because he wanted her so badly he was beyond finesse. He'd have shredded the damned box like an overly enthusiastic teen. Juliana gently tore the plastic wrapper with her fingers. He'd have ripped it open with his teeth. And then she slowly and carefully withdrew the protection.

He'd bet she was the kind who never tore wrapping paper. If he weren't about to burst out of his skin, he might have appreciated her diligence and savored the anticipation of having her hands on him, but right now he was too busy losing his mind to appreciate anything. Fisting his hands, he braced himself, but nothing could prepare him for her light, delicate touch as she smoothed the latex over him.

He ground his teeth and concentrated on a complicated riff. The soft, downward sweep of her fingers came close to stopping his heart and melting his brain, and then her fingers tightened around him. She stroked him from base to tip once, twice, a third time. Too good. Too intense. But he'd promised her control and, dammit, he'd let her have it if it killed him. Which it just might. His breath whistled in through gritted teeth, and he shook with the effort to hold on, but he couldn't stop the groan boiling from his chest.

The glow of feminine power radiated from her blue eyes, darkened her cheekbones and curved her damp red lips. She knelt over him, straddling his thighs, and he prayed she'd put him out of his misery. The faster the better.

She reached over his shoulder for her belt and his pulse stuttered. *Bondage?* The banker didn't seem the type. Not that he couldn't learn to like sex games if this affair continued. Which it shouldn't. Couldn't.

Wouldn't.

He couldn't bring her down to his sewer-rat level.

But instead of winding the belt around his wrists, she trailed the knotted ends across his chest and then over his belly like a dozen caressing fingers. The cool beads swept over his skin, electrifying him like a shorted-out microphone. She snaked the belt around his erection and slowly slithered it free. Holy spit. She *would* kill him. He bowed off the bed, pitching her forward until her soft breasts seared his chest. Fisting his hand in her hair, he drew her mouth to his and kissed her until his lungs burned.

"Stop torturing me," he warned against her mouth.

He felt her smile against his lips, and then she drew back a few inches and he saw laughter in her eyes. He teetered closer to the edge of reason. "Am I torturing you?"

"You know it." He grasped her hips and dragged her forward until her hot, wet body covered his, urging her to take him where he needed to be—inside. But she didn't. She rocked, sliding slick and hot along his length and ripping a hoarse groan straight from his gut. He fisted his hands in the sheet. Wild and impatient, the selfish demon inside him roared. He could give into the clawing hunger and become the self-absorbed SOB who used women or fight it and let Juliana have her way.

He'd fight. But *damn,* it was hard.

And then he decided two could play this seductive torment-ing game. He raked his palms up Juliana's thighs, found her moisture with his fingers and plied her sensitive flesh until her back arched and she writhed with pleasure. Her gaze locked with his and his heart slammed against his chest.

Take her. Take her. Do it. Now.

She splayed her fingers over his chest and paused with him poised at heaven's gate. His muscles bunched. He was a split second away from tossing her on her back, ramming home and selfishly taking his pleasure, when Juliana took him with a slow slide deep into the blistering, wet glove of her body.

His lungs emptied in a rush. Stars flashed behind his eyelids. He forced his eyes open and the pleasure magnified. He'd never seen a more seductive sight than Juliana riding him. With her skin flushed and her swollen lips parted, she gasped for breath and then she opened her eyes and met his gaze with a blaze of white-hot passion. Never mind that every deliberate swivel of her hips destroyed dozens of his brain cells, he liked seeing her this way, liked watching Juliana come unglued.

He stroked her, pushing her toward another release, and then her breath hitched and she clenched him tight. Rex lost it. He grasped her waist and held her as he thrust deep and hard and fast as one explosion after another detonated in his body, rocking him with pleasure more intense than any he'd ever experienced.

Juliana collapsed against him and his arms encircled her automatically as if they'd done that before. They hadn't. He'd never held a woman after he'd used her. But he wanted to hold Juliana, wanted to keep her close.

Trouble. Damn, he was in trouble.

He stared at the ceiling in numb silence as Juliana slipped off him and into the crook of his shoulder. His heart slowed, but his muscles didn't relax. He couldn't get a word past the anger and self-disgust choking him as Juliana curled her fingers on his chest. Moments later, her body went slack as sleep took her. She wouldn't rest as easily and she sure as hell wouldn't be wearing that satisfied smile if she knew what kind of man she'd shared her body with.

He was clean, disease free. He made damned sure of that by getting tested often. But Juliana deserved better than him. Hell, any woman deserved better than a guy who couldn't remember the names or faces of more than a handful of his past lovers.

It had been so easy to believe the hype and the media, too easy to believe the world owed him and not the other way around. He'd taken the female fans who'd wanted to show their appreciation in a sexual way as his due. Physical release had been his drug of choice, and now that he had a hit of pure ecstasy coursing through his veins, he wasn't sure he'd be able to resist the lure again.

He didn't know how to have a healthy sexual relationship. Sure, he'd tried a few times, but monogamy hadn't worked. He'd never stuck with one woman long because he couldn't. He lacked the gene or the moral fiber or whatever it was that made a man capable of committing. He was flawed.

Loving Juliana—no, not loving—*sex* with Juliana had unleashed the beast that used women, the jackass who'd disgraced his family and himself.

His parents had never attended his concerts. The demands of the ranch had made getting away for a weekend almost impossible. Then one night, his family had surprised him after a big show. Rex hadn't known they were there until the roadie had opened the dressing-room door to show them in.

His mother, father and sister had stopped in horrified silence on the threshold, their wide eyes going from Rex to the half-naked groupie coiled around him. Rex had quickly zipped his pants and tucked in his shirttails. But the damage had been done.

Hell, he'd been inside the woman, but he hadn't known her name and couldn't introduce her to his family. He'd watched realization dawn on his mother's face quickly followed by embarrassment and shame. He'd turned to his father, expecting a guy to understand—boys will be boys and all that—but he'd seen disappointment and disgust. And then he'd looked at Kelly's flushed face. The pride he'd always seen in his sister's big brown eyes hadn't been there.

Rex hadn't been raised that way. He'd been taught since he was knee-high to respect others—especially women. And here he was doing the opposite. Using. Discarding. He'd never forget the awkward tension filling the room as the groupie had straightened her clothing, collected an autograph—because they never left without one—and then she'd squeezed out the door. His family had left right behind her without saying a word.

One sad, disapproving glance over his mother's shoulder had said it all. Rex had become a man not even a mother could love.

He'd been ashamed of his behavior. But had he learned his lesson? No, he'd defiantly kept right on carousing right up until the day his parents had died.

Self-disgust rolled over him. Tonight he'd begun the cycle of self-destruction again. Without a doubt, he'd made a mistake in getting physical with Juliana Alden.

The question was could he undo the damage?

Or was it too late?

Juliana awoke to limbs weighted with satisfaction, a smile she couldn't suppress and an empty bed. The latter niggled like an account entry that didn't belong, but she brushed aside her misgivings. Last night had been amazing. Rex was the most unselfish lover she'd ever had, and he'd brought out a sensual side of her that she hadn't known existed.

How had she made it to the age of thirty without experiencing such wonderful, levitating, delectable passion? Had to be the man. Self-service orgasms and the partners from her past just couldn't measure up to Rex Tanner. But then he reportedly had a lot of experience pleasing women.

She cast off the strangely disturbing thought and glanced at the bedside clock. It was far too early for Rex or the girls to be up, but late enough that Juliana should consider getting ready for work soon. She didn't want to. For the first time ever, she wanted to call in sick so she and Rex could replay last night's passionate encounter.

Passionate. Her. Yes, *her.* Bubbles of anticipation floated through her bloodstream. Reality quickly and brutally popped them. This was only lust, wasn't it? She wouldn't have slept with Rex if she hadn't liked him, but she'd never intended their month together to be more than a last fling and an opportunity to prove to Andrea and Holly that she wasn't missing out on anything by following her mother's suggestion to marry Wally.

No, this heady feeling couldn't be more than lust. She wasn't an impulsive person, and she never made important decisions without thoroughly researching her options. Logic always triumphed over emotion, and logic said Wally was proper husband material. She couldn't afford to fall for Rex, so she wouldn't. It was as simple as that. She had two and a half weeks to enjoy his company, and then she'd fulfill her obligations.

Last chance. Last chance.

The straitjacket of expectations tightened around her, making it difficult to take a breath. Goose bumps rose on her skin and her stomach churned. Swallowing her rising anxiety, Juliana sat up and shoved her hair off her face with an unsteady hand. The ceiling fan overhead whirled, cooling her naked skin. She could handle a purely physical relationship. Couldn't she?

Certainly. Other women did it all the time.

Rising from the bed, she listened for Rex in the adjoining bathroom, but heard nothing. Where could he be? And then she caught sight of her face in the mirror over his dresser and grimaced. Her hair looked like she'd been through a hurricane, and she had mascara smudges beneath her eyes. Vanity forced her to take a quick shower, brush her teeth and apply a touch of makeup. She combed her damp hair, shrugged into her bathrobe and then eased open the bedroom door and jerked to a halt.

Déjà vu. Rex slept on the sofa, wearing only unbuttoned jeans. Her smile faded and a sinking feeling settled in the pit of her stomach. Why would he sleep out here when he had a perfectly good bed—and her—in his room?

Doubt crept over her like an incoming fog. Hadn't he enjoyed last night as much as she had? Her achy well-loved muscles and the love bites and beard burn he'd left on her skin indicated he had. But maybe she hadn't measured up to Rex's other lovers.

Horrified, she pressed a hand to her chest. Had he been faking it? With her vast experience at faking it, surely she would have recognized pretense?

Maybe he was trying to shelter the girls from the adult side of his and Juliana's relationship. She liked that idea better than thinking he might prefer the too-short sofa to sleeping with her.

Part of her wanted to shake him awake and pepper him with questions until she had her answers. Her more cautious side feared what she'd hear. Confrontation wasn't a problem for her at work where she knew her subject and often had the supporting data in front of her, but in her personal life, she sucked at it and this morning… She bit her lip and tightened the belt of her robe. Why wasn't there a manual for mornings after?

She tiptoed into the kitchen and flipped the switch on the coffeepot. Within seconds, the appliance gurgled to life. Juliana watched Rex, half hoping the machine's noisy hisses and coughs would rouse him. From where she stood, she could see the top of his head, his shoulders and chest. The sudden change in the cadence of his breathing made her pulse quicken. In moments, she'd have her answers. Like them or not.

Rex lifted his left wrist, checking his watch, she guessed, and then he swiped his hand over his face. She wished she could see his expression. Was he smiling as she'd been when she'd first awakened? Or did he have regrets?

He inhaled deeply, and then sat up and shoved his hair back with both hands. His head turned abruptly and he spotted her. She saw the exact second he recalled the intimacy they'd shared. Tension stiffened his features and his spine straightened. Not a good sign when she'd hoped for a smile and a hello-babe-let's-go-back-to-bed-before-the-girls-awake kiss.

Clinging to his earlier declaration that he wasn't a morning person and hoping that was the only cause of his less than happy-to-see-her reaction, Juliana swallowed to ease the dryness in her mouth. "Good morning."

"'Morning." He slowly rose and faced her with a dark, inscrutable gaze.

The blatant masculinity in his beard-roughened face, broad chest and the unbuttoned jeans sent adrenaline and estrogen pulsing through her system. "You didn't have to sleep out here."

"Yeah, I did."

"Because you didn't want the girls to find us in bed together?" If she were a superstitious person, she'd cross her fingers.

"Because last night shouldn't have happened. It won't happen again."

The arousal simmering in her stomach turned cold and hard like cooling candle wax. Last night she'd had the best sex of her life and he was willing to dismiss it? "I'm sorry to hear that. Do you mind if I ask why?"

"Yes."

She waited for him to elaborate. When he didn't, she asked, "Yes what?"

"Yes, I mind if you ask."

"That was a rhetorical question. Why can't we make love again?"

A nerve in his jaw twitched. "Look, Juliana, you're an attractive woman. It's been a while since I... It's been a while for me. I should have controlled myself last night."

This grew worse by the second. "Are you saying you were just scratching an itch and any woman would have done?"

He hesitated and those silent seconds crushed her heart in a vise. Breathless with pain, Juliana turned back to the coffeepot and filled a mug with unsteady hands. She didn't want the fragrant brew, didn't even know if she could keep it in her churning stomach, but she couldn't face him right now.

And then an even more painful realization hit. Lust wouldn't hurt this much. That meant that her feelings for Rex might be more than simple physical desire. Was she falling for him? Her heart pounded. No, she couldn't be. He didn't fit in with her life plan or her career goals.

"Juliana, I'm sorry."

She straightened her spine, lifted her chin and met his solemn gaze. She tightened her fingers around the mug in a grip that would break more fragile china. "I'm not sorry."

She wasn't. Taking control of their relationship, her sexual pleasure and her life was—what had he said?—oh, yes, a journey she had to take. But she wasn't the auditor with the highest success rate at Alden Bank and Trust for nothing. When she wanted something, she didn't give up without a fight. And she wanted more of the passion Rex Tanner had shown her. More of her reluctant rebel. She wanted— needed—to store up memories for later.

Did he want the same? She didn't know, but she'd learned early on that if you wanted something and didn't speak up, then you got exactly what you asked for. Nothing. And if that meant she had to become the seducer instead of the seducee then she'd willingly take on the role.

Rex exhaled harshly. "You don't get it. I can't be the man you need. You're hearts and flowers and forever. I'm not. I let people down, Juliana. It's what I do best."

Forever? Her mind snagged on the word. "I didn't ask for forever, Rex. All I'm asking for are the two and a half weeks remaining in your auction package."

His jaw muscles bunched.

She closed the gap between them and opened her hand over his chest. His heart beat frantically beneath her palm. "Seventeen days, Rex. That's all I want."

Now that you've tasted passion, can you live without it?

Of course she could. She had her life mapped out and if she wanted to make it to the top, the way her mother had, then Juliana couldn't afford detours. Especially not the kind that made her think of taking days off to laze in bed with a lover.

Eight

Apparently his momma had raised a fool, Rex told himself as he stopped outside his open bedroom door.

Otherwise Juliana's offer of a no-strings-attached relationship wouldn't have his mouth salivating and his heart palpitating at the sight of her lying on his bed in a puddle of moonlight and tangled sheets. Obviously he'd learned nothing from his past.

He wanted her as badly as he wanted his next breath. If her alarm hadn't sounded this morning immediately after she'd dropped her offer on the table, then—right or wrong—he probably would have dragged her back to bed, shoved her robe from her shoulders and buried himself deep inside her.

Forget the bed. He would have taken her in the kitchen. He'd been that hot, that eager, and it hadn't taken giving a performance in front of tens of thousands of screaming fans to get him harder than a steel rod. Juliana had managed that feat all by herself, which meant she had the power to take him lower than he'd been when he'd hit rock bottom. Not good.

But damn, he craved her. Craved her like an addict needing a fix.

Quit thinking with your balls, Tanner.

His eyes adjusted to the darkness of the apartment. In the silence at two in the morning, he could hear the whisper of Juliana's breath. She lay on her side with her dark hair spread across his pillow just the way she'd been last night when he'd forced himself to leave her.

His heart thumped hard and fast, like a beater against a bass drum in an up-tempo song.

Head for the sofa. But his feet didn't move and his unblinking gaze remained fixed on the woman who'd dominated his thoughts all day. The ceiling fan stirred the air, surrounding him in her scent.

Accepting her offer isn't the same as using her.

Wasn't it? Would he be backsliding into that selfish SOB mindset if he gave her what she wanted? Hell, he'd never intended to live the rest of his life like a monk.

If not celibacy, then what do you have planned, bucko?

Nothing. The answer surprised him. All his life, he'd worked toward a goal. First on getting off the ranch, second, on landing a record contract, and then on making it to the top of the charts. He'd accomplished all three, leaving a trail of casualties in his selfish, self-destructive wake. After his parents' deaths, he'd set his sights on getting out of Nashville. Once he'd managed that, he'd focused on getting Renegade open and making himself available to Kelly and the girls. Once again, mission accomplished, but this time he had no intention of hurting or disappointing anyone.

His personal life hadn't figured anywhere in the equation. Now what? He pinched his knotted neck muscles. If one-night stands were out of the question, then was he looking for something more? Something permanent? Was he marriage material? Probably not. But maybe after he had the bank note paid off, he could be for someone willing to take a chance on a rough-off-the-ranch guy who was trying to get his priorities straight. Someone strong enough to yank him back in line when he tried to take what he wanted without giving back.

Someone like Juliana.

Whoa. Back up.

As much as he liked and desired Juliana and appreciated her stepping in to help out with the girls, he couldn't see the banking heiress settling for an almost broke high-school dropout who'd burned all his bridges. Even if she did want him, her dragon lady of a mother wouldn't accept him into the family, and he refused to come between Juliana and her folks. One of these days, she'd realize what he cost her, and she'd hate him for it the way he hated himself for letting his selfishness ruin his relationship with his family.

But a relationship—even a temporary one—with Juliana wouldn't be another nameless, faceless encounter like the ones from his past, the devil's advocate in his head argued. He not only knew her name and where she lived, he knew her favorite flavor of ice cream—peach—and a dozen other details about her, like her cautious nature, the way she weighed the risks before making a move, the sarcasm that sneaked out when she was nervous and her tendency to research everything from him to motorcycle manuals to child care. As for her face, he'd never forget it.

Go for it.

He took a step toward the bed, but stopped. Juliana had not only resurrected his libido, she'd made him think about music, and that scared the hell out of him. He'd had that damned song—the one he'd been writing the day his parents had died—in his head all day. Music had been his salvation once, but it had also become his damnation, his path to ruin. He couldn't let music back into his life. Too risky.

Juliana shifted, rolled on to her back. "Rex, is that you?"

He swallowed. "Yeah."

She threw back the sheet and sat up. Moonlight danced over her bare skin. "Lock the door and come to bed."

His fists clenched and his chest burned. He sucked in a forgotten breath.

What the hell. You're damned anyway.

His fingers turned the lock and his feet carried him forward. He stopped beside the mattress and prayed for the strength to turn around before it was too late. And then Juliana rose on her knees, and any chance he had of saving his damned soul vanished when her cheek pressed his chest over his hammering heart.

He peeled his shirt over his head and joined her in the bed. And he hoped like hell he wouldn't hate himself more than he already did in the morning.

Juliana looked across the sun-dappled playground to where Rex crouched beside Becky and Liza in the sandbox and saw something she hadn't even known she'd missed.

Neither of her parents would have played hooky from work to waste a day building sand castles that afternoon storms would wash away or let their little girl cup their face with sandy hands to plant sticky kisses on their cheeks the way Liza did to Rex. In Juliana's world, hugs had been allowed only when she was neat and tidy. Irma had dealt with the messy side of life, the sticky kisses, the dirty hands, the skinned knees and the difficult questions of a teenage girl trying to understand her changing body and the rascally boys at school.

A few yards from Rex and the girls, a woman blew bubbles.

Her children chased them, squealing and laughing and falling down to roll in the sand. At a picnic table farther down the park, a gathering of preschoolers and their mothers celebrated a birthday with songs and games. The joy on all those faces, young and old, opened an aching void in Juliana's chest. If she followed in her mother's footsteps, would she ever have moments like these?

Liza's laughter drew Juliana's gaze back to the sandbox. Rex lifted his head and their gazes met. He spoke to the girls, and then rose and stalked toward her, wearing a sexy, melt-her-bones smile. He could make her heart pound with nothing more than a look. Did she have a similar effect on him? If so, he concealed it well. Not that he hadn't been an amazing and generous lover the past two nights, but she had a feeling she was the only one losing control in bed. Her work had taught her to recognize the signs when someone was concealing information. Rex was holding something back and she wanted to know what.

The T-shirt he'd pulled on over his swim trunks after climbing from the pool hugged his powerful chest. An afternoon breeze fluttered the hem over his flat stomach. Her gaze skimmed down to his hairy legs. Her palms tingled. She adored the rough texture of his legs against her skin when they made love, and making love with Rex… Warmth washed over her. Suffice to say she'd never doubt her capacity for passion again.

"Glad you took the day off?" Rex sat down beside her on the picnic-table bench, straddling the wood so he faced her with his splayed knees bracketing her. One of his big hands swept up and down her spine and the other landed on her thigh beneath the picnic table.

"Yes." And more than a little surprised. Shirking work wasn't like her. Her pulse skipped erratically as Rex's long, lightly calloused fingers inched beneath the hem of her shorts to trace the elastic leg opening of her panties. She glanced around quickly, but no one could see his mischief beneath the table. Arousal coiled hot and low in her belly, shortening her breath and moistening her mouth.

He played her body as well as he played his guitar on the CDs she and the girls secretly listened to in the car. Juliana struggled against her thought-numbing response. She'd never understand what made Rex tick if she kept letting him distract her. "What did you mean when you said you let people down?"

Rex's spine stiffened and his smile faded. He removed his hands and turned on the bench to face the girls. Instantly, Juliana missed the warmth of his touch.

"I meant I let people down."

"Yes, I got that part. But who? How?"

He exhaled heavily. "Juliana—"

His none-of-your-business tone told her he was going to brush aside her curiosity again the way he'd done each time she'd asked personal questions. She didn't intend to let him avoid answering this time.

"Please, Rex, I've read so much conflicting information about you online that I'd like to know the truth."

Silent seconds ticked past. The girls giggled and added another leaning tower to their sand castle. Birds chirped. None of the other park visitors seemed to be sharing her knife-edge of tension.

"I already told you that I hated the ranch." He hesitated, bracing his elbows on his knees and lacing his fingers. To anyone else, he probably looked relaxed, but Juliana saw the whiteness of his knuckles. "What I didn't tell you was that my folks tried to talk me out of going to Nashville. They didn't want me to chase a dream that was more likely to die than come true. Their intentions were good. They didn't want me to be hurt. But I didn't see it that way. Before I left, I said some obnoxious stuff to them about being ignorant hayseeds who had no ambition to better themselves."

"How old were you?"

"Eighteen."

"You were just a kid. Everybody knows kids—especially teens—aren't known for making the wisest choices." Except for her. She'd always done the right thing for fear of the consequences.

His head swiveled toward her. "I was old enough to know better. I should have shown more respect. But I didn't. I really let 'er rip. I can't remember half of the garbage I spewed."

"Should I quote the cliché about hindsight being clearer?"

He stared at the girls and his Adam's apple bobbed as he swallowed. "I had a couple of rough years in Nashville. Mom sent money I knew they couldn't spare. I didn't ask for it, but I took it. I was broke enough to humble myself that much, but not enough to apologize. I *never* apologized. Dad wrote and told me I could come home. I told him I'd live in the streets first."

The pain and regret in his voice made her heart ache. Juliana curled her fingers around the tensed muscles of his biceps and squeezed in a silent show of support.

"When I was twenty-two I lucked out. I was hanging out in a seedy bar. I couldn't even afford a beer, so I just sat in a back corner and listened to the music. The singer onstage was pretty bad. The crowd got rowdy. Somebody threw a beer bottle at him. It caught the guy upside the head and knocked him out. It looked like hell was gonna break loose and I was a long way from the exit. So I went the other way. I climbed on the stage, grabbed the man's guitar and started belting out songs as hard and fast as I could, hoping to head off something ugly while his bandmates tried to revive him. The crowd settled. The singer came to. I got off the stage and headed for the door. A guy from the audience followed me and offered me a record deal right there on Second Avenue. Turns out he was a bigwig at one of the labels. And the rest…" He shrugged.

"The rest is history. But I want to hear the part I can't read on the Internet. Who did you let down and how?"

"You ever let folks down?" His dark gaze pinned her to the bench.

Only recently, but she hoped her mother would get over Juliana buying Rex. "I've always been the rule-following type. I toed the line because I was paralyzed by the idea of disappointing my parents."

"Thought so."

That stung. But she didn't want to talk about her coward-ice or the difficult conversations that lay ahead, because it had taken her thirty years to find the nerve that Rex had possessed at eighteen. "I admire your courage in following your dreams. What happened after the record deal?"

"I started making money. I sent some home. I guess I wanted to make amends for being a jackass, but I couldn't swallow my pride enough to show up and apologize in person. Hell, I didn't even have the guts to call and say it over the phone.

"And then it was too late. A couple of years ago, Mom and Dad were killed in a tornado. I never thanked them for sup-porting me. And I never said I'm sorry. They died thinking their son was an ungrateful, selfish son of a bitch. And they were right."

Juliana slid her arm around his waist. "I don't think you're selfish."

"That's because you don't know me. I had a concert sched-uled the day of the funeral. Would you believe I actually had to stop and think about where I wanted to be? Where I *ought* to be? In the end, I asked Kelly to reschedule the funeral for an earlier time and then I chartered a private jet so I could do both—the funeral and later, the concert. I went onstage that night and performed like nothing had happened. Like I hadn't just laid my parents in the ground.

"The next morning, I looked in the mirror and I realized I didn't like the man I'd become. I tried to get out of my contracts, but they were airtight. So I self-destructed, once again thinking about my sorry ass instead of the sixty-three people in my band and road crew who depended on me for a living."

"You were grieving, Rex, and some people deal with grief by ignoring it until they have a little distance."

He shot to his feet and looked down on her with tormented eyes. "Don't try to turn me into one of the good guys, Juliana. I'm not the man for you. What we have is good *for now,* but I won't be around for the long haul. Don't count on me."

And then he pivoted on his heel and returned to the girls. Juliana pressed a hand over the ache consuming her chest. Her heart was breaking not for herself, but for Rex.

She was no Beauty, but there was no doubt in her mind that Rex was a wounded Beast who needed someone to show him that he wasn't a monster.

That someone was her.

"Rex, visitor for you," Danny called out on Saturday afternoon.

Rex set the spreadsheets on his desk in the Renegade office and swore. Probably another customer wanting to needle him about the newspaper article. Octavia Jenkins's second installment had appeared in the paper this morning. She'd spouted more of the same fairy-tale nonsense, this time comparing his and Juliana's relationship to the Disney movie the girls had been watching on TV during Octavia's last interview.

He rose and made his way out front. Before Juliana had left for work yesterday, she'd offered—no, she'd insisted—on taking a look at his books to see if she could come up with any ideas for increasing his revenues and decreasing his overhead. He wasn't crazy about letting her see the gravity of his financial situation, but numbers were her thing. She had the fancy degree and credentials to prove it. All he had were scars from the school of hard knocks.

He glanced over the thinning lunch crowd before following Danny's pointing finger to the man sitting at the far end of the bar. Rex's muscles locked.

"Long time no see, Rex. What's up?" his former manager called out.

Rex ignored John Lee's outstretched hand. "How'd you find me?"

"What happened to 'Hello, John Lee, great to see you after all this time?'" When Rex didn't respond he continued, "My clipping service picked up that piece on you and the bachelor auction. Had to come and see for myself if it was really you. The long hair…now that's a good look on you."

Damn. Rex had known the risk of discovery going into the auction, but he'd figured after the way he'd left Nashville nobody would be interested in looking him up. "What do you want, John Lee?"

"You. You left before the label or the fans got tired of you. I read about your bar and your publicity efforts for the place. I know of a better way to draw a crowd. Say the word and I'll have a contract in front of you before happy hour starts."

"Not interested. I'd rather lose Renegade than go back to that life."

In the blink of an eye, John Lee dropped his good ol' boy facade and the sharp-as-a-new-scalpel businessman who'd taken Rex to the top of the charts took its place. "Look, Tanner, you can't walk away when you're still at the top."

Rex ground his teeth. "Newsflash. I already did."

"I know you gotta miss the women."

Strangely, Rex didn't. God knows he'd had his share of come-ons from bar patrons, but none had tempted him. Until Juliana. But his weakness with her was a sign that he wasn't cured of his addiction. "Nope."

John Lee smoothed a hand over his hundred-dollar haircut. "I know I rode you hard after your parents passed, but I was trying to help you keep your mind off their deaths. Now you've had time to get over it. C'mon back. Let's make music and money, son."

"No, thanks." He turned and strode toward his office.

"You owe a lot of folks, Rex."

The words stopped Rex cold. He slowly pivoted. "I don't owe anybody. I cleared my debts."

"What about your band? They were counting on you for another ten-year ride."

"I found jobs for every one of the guys and the roadies, too."

"But not with a headliner raking in your kind of dough. There's only one Rex Tanner."

"Yeah. And he runs a bar and grill. Have a safe trip home, John Lee."

"I'll be down the street at the Hilton for a couple of days. Think over my offer. Call me when you see the light. Cell number's the same, but here it is in case you misplaced it." He pulled a business card from the pocket of his custom-tailored western suit and offered it to Rex. Rex ignored it. John Lee laid it on the bar and then headed out the door.

Rex snatched up the card and crushed it in his fist, and then he stalked back into his office and dropped into his chair. He pitched the crumpled card on his desk. It landed on the spread-sheets. His gaze dropped to the bottom line and his gut knotted. Without a doubt he needed cash. The auction had increased business, but not enough. Unless a miracle happened, then Rex would very likely default on his loan in another forty-five days.

He missed music. No doubt about it. But could he live with himself if he accepted John Lee's offer? Rex had learned the hard way that the money's not worth jack if you can't live with the decisions you're making.

But if you were headlining again then you could afford to give Juliana the kinds of things she deserves.

Whoa. That thought blindsided him. Did he want more than great sex and a short-term affair with Juliana? He rubbed his jaw. Maybe. He'd never had a more responsive lover. God knows she lit up his light bar like nobody else ever had. He liked her, liked her cautious nature, her sarcasm, her generosity and her damned-near insatiable curiosity. She'd weaseled stuff out of him that nobody else had and done it so smoothly that he hadn't even realized what she was doing until he'd spewed his guts out.

Each day he spent with her and the girls made him wonder what it would be like to have a family. With someone like Juliana, who gave as good as she got.

He scrubbed a hand across the back of his neck. He couldn't support a family on Renegade's current earnings. If he were headlining again he could, but then Juliana wouldn't want anything to do with the kind of louse he'd become. He didn't think for one second that he was strong enough to keep the selfish monster inside him under control. Look how quickly he'd caved with Juliana.

But he had to admit, he was tempted to try. Tempted for Juliana's sake. But if he let her down, he wouldn't be able to live with himself.

A no-win situation.

And happiness… Hell, he didn't deserve it.

A noise jolted Juliana from a deep sleep. She pried open her eyes and listened. Heat blanketed her back from shoulders to knees and a heavy arm draped across her waist. She turned her head on the pillow. Rex hadn't woken her tonight.

Before she could decide what that meant, another whimper made her jerk upright. The sound came from the girls' room. She jumped from the bed and tugged on her robe.

"What's wrong?" Rex's husky whisper called through the darkness.

"One of the girls is upset." She wanted to ask him why he hadn't made love to her when he'd come to bed tonight, the way he had each night since they'd become lovers, but the cries from the other room grew louder. She dashed into the hall and then into the girls' room. Becky sobbed into her pillow.

Juliana sat on the bed, brushed back Becky's dark hair and whispered, "Bad dream?"

"Daddy," Becky wailed. "I want my daddy."

Juliana felt Rex behind her before she heard him. Heat radiated off his bare chest, drawing her like a magnet. "Remember what Mom said when she called earlier? They'll be here in the morning, Beck."

But Becky wouldn't be consoled. Rex reached past Juliana and scooped his niece into his arms. He headed for the den, but not fast enough. Liza sat up. "Whassa matter?"

Juliana kissed her brow. "Becky had a bad dream. She's okay. Go back to sleep."

"Me up, too." Liza lifted her arms. Juliana couldn't resist. She carried Liza into the darkened den and sat down on the opposite end of the sofa from Rex and Becky.

"Mommy said Daddy was h-hurt really, really b-bad and that he almost went to h-heaven," Becky choked out between sobs. "Is he…okay?"

Rex tucked her head beneath his chin and nuzzled a kiss into her hair. "He got banged up, but the doctors have fixed him. He might be slow as a snail for a while, and he'll probably need your help with some stuff, but he'll be okay. I know he's going to be happy to see his girls."

"Will he have to go back to that bad place?"

Sympathy squeezed the air from Juliana's lungs. She had no idea how to answer Becky's question. The girls were far too young to understand the importance of their father's job.

"Not for a long time. Maybe never, Beck," Rex replied.

"I don't want him to go back. Ever. And I don't want him to go to heaven and leave me here." Becky's sobs turned into gasps and hiccups.

Liza's lips began to quiver as her sister's distress agitated her. Juliana feared the children might never settle. Her gaze landed on the guitar in a corner. She'd noticed the guitar case in the back of the closet when she'd moved into Rex's home and then she'd spotted the instrument in the corner when she'd brought the girls home earlier tonight. What had made Rex drag it out? He'd claimed music was no longer part of his life. Had that changed?

"Why don't you sing to her?"

Rex's head jerked toward her. "What?"

"Sing for her. It might calm her down. I've been playing your CDs in the car and she likes your music."

In the dim illumination from the streetlights streaming through the front window, she could see his jaw muscles bunching and shifting. He swallowed hard and grimaced as if he were in pain. Finally, he exhaled. "You want that, Beck?"

Becky nodded.

"Me, too. Me, too," Liza added.

Rex sat Becky on the sofa and crossed the room with a stiff stride. Every muscle in his bare back above his hastily pulled on jeans looked knotted. Juliana wondered if she'd misread the significance of the guitar coming out of the closet. Moments later, he returned with the instrument, settled on the ottoman and hesitated.

Becky scooted against Juliana's side. Liza burrowed deeper into Juliana's lap. The sweet smell of the girls' strawberry-scented bubble bath encircled her and she felt a twinge of sadness. Her mother had missed moments like this. Soothing nighttime fears had been Irma's job.

"Do you need a lamp on?" Juliana asked as she tucked Becky beneath her arm.

"No." His voice sounded rough, raw. He strummed a few chords, stopped and started again. And then he sang, low and husky, gaining strength as the song progressed. The girls settled. Rex lifted his eyes and his gaze locked with Juliana's as he transitioned into a song she hadn't heard before, one about a man wanting to put the past behind him and live again.

There was something so inherently sexy about a bare-chested, barefoot man cradling a guitar in the near-darkness and singing about starting over that Juliana's insides melted.

Rex's up-tempo songs kept her toes tapping on her daily commute, but his ballads often brought tears to her eyes as this one did tonight. For a man who didn't talk much, Rex's magical way with words entranced her. What would it be like to be serenaded by the man she loved, to hear his deepest feelings expressed in lyrics and music? She'd never know.

Several songs later, Rex drew to a close and set the guitar aside. It was only then that the mesmerizing spell he'd cast over her broke and Juliana realized both girls had fallen back to sleep.

"Let's get them to bed." Rex rose. His hands brushed her hip and thigh, electrifying her, as he lifted Becky.

After they tucked the girls in and returned to their room, Juliana faced Rex in the moonlight. "That was beautiful. I don't know how you gave it up."

He shoved his hands in his pockets. "I walked away because I didn't like the person I'd become."

"I don't understand."

His hands fisted and his rigid body language warned Juliana she might not like whatever he said next. "On the night we met, you asked me if I had jealous husbands chasing me. I said not anymore. But I used to. After a show, I'd indiscriminately screw any woman that my manager brought into my dressing room. I don't remember their names or their faces. I used them and discarded them like paper cups. Like they were worthless."

Shocked into silence, Juliana could only stare at him. So the Internet stories had been true.

"I didn't care if they were married or single. All I cared about was letting off steam, coming down from my post-concert high. Other folks used drugs. I used sex. I used *people*."

The man she'd come to know over the past three weeks bore no resemblance to the self-absorbed person he described. But there was more than sordid truth in Rex's confession. Juliana heard pain and self-loathing in his voice.

He shoved a hand through his tangled hair. "My behavior shamed and disgusted my family. Hell, I probably even broke up a few marriages."

His wounded gaze lasered in on hers. He expected his revelation to repulse her. "Now you know why you need to stay the hell away from me. I'm a selfish jerk who doesn't know how to have a healthy relationship with a woman. I'm not good enough for you, Juliana, and if you're half as smart as I think you are then you'll pack your stuff, get out and forget you ever met me."

And she knew in an instant that she couldn't do as he asked. She wasn't just in lust with Rex Tanner. She was falling in love with him.

Nine

Why didn't Juliana tell him to go to hell?

Why didn't she flee his apartment in disgust?

Wasn't that what he expected? What he wanted? Yeah, because the sooner she dumped him, the sooner he could quit waiting for it to happen.

But instead of revulsion in Juliana's beautiful blue eyes, Rex found understanding and a tangle of emotions he couldn't decipher on her moonlit face. She closed the distance between them and lifted her palms to blaze a path across his chest, and then she cradled his face in her hands, tugged him down and peppered soft kisses over his face and finally on his mouth.

His pulse drummed in the triple digits. The blood drained from his head to pool with an insistent throb behind his zipper.

He covered her hands and drew back. "What are you doing?"

Her soft, sexy gaze met his and a tender smile trembled on her lips. "Loving you."

His heart stalled and then slammed against his ribs like automatic gunfire. "Me? Or the guy with the guitar?"

Her thumbs rasped over his bristly jaw. "The guy who just sang his nieces to sleep. The one who gets inside me with his words and melts me with his touch. The man who taught me to take control of his Harley and my life. You, Rex Tanner."

He couldn't comprehend half of what she said, but couldn't string the words together to ask her to explain. A knot formed in his throat. He gulped it down. "Bad idea."

"I can't think of a better one." And then her tongue coasted across his bottom lip, igniting the fuse of desire in his veins.

Her fingers threaded through his hair and Rex struggled to recall the reasons why this shouldn't happen. Music was part of it. He didn't want to go back on the road, but as far as he could see, he only had two options. Tour or lose the bar.

In the first case, he'd hurt Juliana by reverting to his previous bad habits. He'd like to believe he wouldn't, but he had ten years of proof that he probably would. But even if he could control the selfish beast inside him, he'd still be on the road nine months out of the year. A beautiful woman like Juliana wouldn't sit at home alone waiting for him. He'd seen the marriages of his band and crew members disintegrate for exactly that reason. Lonely wives were unhappy wives.

In the latter case, he'd cause a rift between her and her family. Juliana's mother had barely tolerated him at the auction. She wouldn't accept a washed-up country star or a bar owner—especially a broke one who owed her bank money—as a son-in-law.

Son-in-law.

Whoa. He rocked back on his heels. His gaze hungrily devoured Juliana's damp lips and flushed cheeks.

Was he thinking marriage? With Juliana.

Hell, yes. But how could he make it work? He couldn't.

Juliana's teeth nipped his jaw and her palm stroked over the hard ridge beneath his jeans, making thought impossible. Later. He'd try to figure out how to make this relationship work *later.* Right now he needed her, ached for her, and it had nothing to do with pent-up excitement from playing music. This was all about her. Her scent. Her taste. Her acceptance of him, warts and all.

He banded his arms around her, holding her as tightly against himself as he could get her, and seized her mouth, pouring his feelings into the kiss, showing what he couldn't say. He raked his palms up and down her spine, savoring her shiver, and then he cupped her butt and buried his erection in the heat of her belly. Nothing had ever felt this good.

He bunched her robe in his fists, lifting an inch at a time until the fabric was out of the way and he could stroke smooth, bare bottom. Her gasp incited him. Still it wasn't enough. He wanted to hear her whimper and cry out as orgasm rocked her. The sounds she made when he pleasured her were almost enough to get him off.

Naked. He needed her naked. *Now.* He shucked her robe and palmed her breasts, teasing the tight, beaded tips. Her head fell back, exposing her throat to his lips. He sucked and nipped her fragrant skin and laved the fluttering pulse at the base of her neck. Still not enough. He eased his hand between them and found her curls, her moisture. He devoured her mouth, gulping down her moans as he stroked her until she squirmed and then quaked against him.

Her nails scraped over his back, making him shake all over, and then she fumbled with the opening of his jeans and shoved his pants and briefs down his thighs. Urgent and hurried, her soft fingers skated over his butt, his waist, his hips, and then she wrapped her hand around him and caressed him from base to tip, damn near blowing off the top of his head in an ecstatic shower of sparks. He yanked his head back to gasp and groan.

She dropped to her knees to help him out of his jeans and then her dangerous hands made the return trip, feathering his legs with a light touch until she reached the tops of his thighs. Juliana tipped her head back and met his gaze as she took him into her mouth.

Holy spit. He didn't deserve this. Didn't deserve *her*.

His hands fisted in her hair and every muscle in his body clenched as he fought to hold on, but the silken swirl of her tongue nearly undid him. Fire roared through him and he nearly let go, but more than his own satisfaction, he wanted to give Juliana pleasure. He yanked her to her feet, nudged her backward until she fell on the bed and then he hit his knees and loved her with his mouth—something he'd never done for the groupies. She tasted hot and wet and sweet and uniquely Juliana.

Her moans and pleas sounded like music to his ears as he played her into one release and then another. And then he rose above her, parted her legs and sank into her in one long, deep stroke.

Heaven.

No doubt about it, he could learn to love it here. Hell, he already did. He withdrew and sank back in. Again. Again. Her silky legs encircled his hips and her heels dug into his buttocks. She wiggled beneath until he thought he'd go insane. He swallowed her cries as he pounded out a rhythm guaranteed to drive them both over the edge. His lungs burned. His heart raced. His skin dampened, melding with hers.

Her wandering hands wreaked havoc on his self-control. She stroked, scraped, brushed and squeezed. And he knew he was going to lose it. *Hold on, hold on.* He bowed his back to sip one tight pearly nipple and then release rippled through Juliana. Rex said a prayer of thanks as her cry filled his ears and then he let go. A series of explosions began at the base of his spine and detonated upward.

He collapsed. Boneless. Totally wiped out.

Totally in love.

Oh hell.

"I'm in love with her." The words erupted from Rex's chest like a volcano that had built up so much pressure it had no choice but to blow.

Kelly blinked and then turned to her husband, who'd stretched out on a lawn chair in their backyard. The girls danced around him in the grass, raining kisses and questions. Other than being ten shades too pale, Rex thought his brother-in-law was a damned fine sight. His broken bones would mend and the bruises would fade. Whether or not he could return to active duty remained to be determined.

"Mike, Rex and I are going inside to get some cold drinks." She pointed at Rex. "You. Kitchen. Now."

Rex followed her inside, already regretting his outburst, but the words had been expanding inside him since last night. He hadn't said anything to Juliana because he'd needed to digest them and to plan first. The right thing to do would be to let her go. He wasn't a prize and she sure as hell deserved better. But how could he walk away?

Kelly handed him a beer. "Spill it."

Rex passed the bottle back. "It's 10:30. Too early for drinking."

"I want to loosen your tongue." But she put the beer back in the fridge. "Start talking or I'll pour the beer down your throat."

He swiped a hand over his hair. "I'm in love with Juliana Alden. She's a banking heiress, for crying out loud. Too good for a high-school dropout like me. And I'm thinking about going back on the road."

Wariness clouded Kelly's face. "Okay. One thing at a time. Do you want to tour again?"

"No."

"Then don't."

"I think I want to marry Juliana."

Kelly growled in frustration. "I'm trying to follow your train of thought here, Rex, but you're not making it easy. What's stopping you from marrying Juliana? The girls adore her, by the way."

He paced the confines of the tiny kitchen. "I need the money. The bar's not making it, Kel. It might in time, but I don't have time. The note's coming due."

She slapped his arm. "You have money, moron."

"If I did, we wouldn't be having this conversation. And if I ask Juliana to marry me when I'm about to default on a loan to her family's bank, then she and her folks will think I'm doing it because of the money."

"You have your part of Mom and Dad's estate."

He balked. "That's not mine. When I left the ranch I forfeited my share."

"Dang it, Rex, you sent money home every year for ten years—money Dad used to keep the ranch going. I tried to discuss this with you after the funeral, but you tuned me out and the lawyer says his letters came back unopened. In fact..." She held up one finger. "Wait here."

She left the room and returned a moment later to hand him a file. "Here's all the account info. See if it's enough to tide you over until Renegade's in the black."

He opened the file and surprise punched the air from his lungs. It wasn't a fortune, but it was more than enough to pay off his loan. But it wasn't his.

"I remember telling you to save this for you and the girls in case something happened to Mike." He didn't need to mention the close call they'd just had. "You keep it."

He tried to give her the file, but she put her hands behind

her back. "It's not mine. It's yours. Mike has life insurance. Don't let your pride screw up your future."

Pain crushed his chest. "Kelly, I don't deserve this. I was an ass."

"I know. I was there. But Mom and Dad loved you, Rex. They always loved you, and they understood your need for your songs to be heard. They were so proud of you. We all were. We weren't crazy about your lifestyle…." She shrugged. "But that was because we were afraid you'd kill yourself."

He grimaced. "You can't say I didn't try."

"Rex, you've never been afraid to fight for what you wanted. So why aren't you fighting now?"

Good question.

"Pride has always been your biggest problem, big brother. So…swallow your pride, take the money and go get the girl."

"She deserves better than me, Kel."

"That's what being in love is all about—trying to be the person the one you love deserves." She hooked her arms around his waist and hugged him. "And stop punishing yourself for the past by denying yourself the music you love. There's bound to be a way you can have music in your life without doing concerts."

She lifted a hand and tugged on his hair. "And quit hiding that handsome mug from the world under all this. Let me give you a real haircut. I've been dying to do more than trim your ends for ages."

Hiding. Yeah. That's what he'd been doing. And Juliana had dragged him out of his cave and back into the light.

The question was did he have the guts to lay his heart on the line?

If Emily Post covered guidelines on how to end an almost-engagement, then none of the etiquette lessons Juliana had endured during her formative years had included them.

As far as she was concerned, no matter what she served, lunch would be hard to swallow. She put the finishing touches on the lemon chicken and roasted asparagus she'd picked up from Wally's favorite restaurant and then brightened the chandelier in her dining room. Intimacy wasn't her goal for this private meeting.

She loved Rex Tanner. In that blinding moment of discovery last night, Juliana's past mistakes had become clear. She'd never taken a chance on love because she'd been afraid of letting emotion overrule logic, but playing it safe hadn't made her stronger or smarter than her friends and colleagues who'd nursed numerous broken hearts over the years. Playing it safe had made her an emotional coward.

She didn't fool herself into believing her decision wouldn't have repercussions—difficult ones. First and foremost, she'd disappoint her mother—never a pleasant experience, but Juliana wasn't a child who feared being shipped away to boarding school anymore. She might even lose her job at Alden's, but despite the fact that she'd never wanted to work anywhere else, she'd rather lose her job than lose Rex.

And, yes, saying goodbye to Wally could jeopardize the merger that Alden's needed to stay competitive with the conglomerate banks, because Mr. Wilson was the type to hold grudges. But this wasn't the Middle Ages. Businesses could merge without families doing the same.

Beginning today, she would make new plans for her future—a future she hoped to spend with Rex. He hadn't said he loved her, but no man could be as tender, as devoted to her pleasure or as concerned about hurting her as he was unless he had deep feelings for her. If he didn't care for her, then he would have used and discarded her as he had the groupies in his past. Instead, her reluctant rebel had tried to scare her off with words while his eyes had begged for understanding.

Tonight she'd tell him she loved him. And tomorrow… Her mouth dried and her pulse fluttered. Tomorrow she'd deal with the consequences of her decision.

The doorbell rang and Juliana's stomach plunged to her pumps. Her guest had arrived. Pulling a painful breath into her tight chest, she prayed for the courage to take a huge risk. With her future. With her heart.

She opened the door. "Hello, Wally. Thanks for agreeing to come over for lunch."

He revealed a practiced smile and pulled a bouquet of red roses from behind his back. "As always, I'm happy to accommodate you, Juliana."

Why hadn't she noticed how smooth he was before? Too smooth, too polished, too pleasant. His smile didn't even crinkle the corners of his eyes. Not that Wally wasn't handsome. He was in a catalogue-model kind of way—good-looking enough to catch a woman's eye, but not enough to threaten a man.

Safe. That's it. Wally was safe, she realized with a flash of insight. No wonder she'd agreed to consider marrying him.

She accepted the flowers. "Thank you. Please come in. I'll put these in water. Would you care for a drink before lunch?"

"No, thank you. I have a meeting later. You have to return to work as well, don't you?"

"Yes." Although she probably wouldn't be able to focus any better than she had this morning. "Have a seat in the dining room. I'll bring out lunch."

Five minutes later, she had the meal on the table, the flowers in a Waterford vase and a swarm of angry hornets ricocheting around her stomach. She doubted she'd be able to swallow a single bite.

Wally launched into a discussion about his latest work project—a project that would have fascinated Juliana a few weeks ago. Andrea was right. She and Wally never discussed anything but work. Her lack of participation must have finally dawned on him. "So, Juliana what's this impromptu lunch really about?"

Soften the rejection. But her mind emptied of anything except the unpleasant task ahead. She folded her napkin and laid it beside her plate. "Are you and Donna enjoying your Saturday suppers?"

"Yes, as a matter of fact, we are. And are you enjoying your riding lessons?"

She couldn't remember seeing that sparkle in Wally's eyes before. "Yes. Even more than the lessons, I've enjoyed baby-sitting for Rex's nieces. Spending time with the girls has made me eager to have children of my own. That's not something I've ever dwelled upon. It seemed like a vague possibility for the very distant future."

"Not so distant. You're already thirty. And I'm forty." His soft hand covered hers on the table and she felt nothing except a strong urge to move away. "We need to get started. We'll make beautiful children together, Juliana."

Anxiety closed her throat. Juliana withdrew her hand, sipped—gulped, actually—her water and took a bracing breath. "I appreciate the time you've spent with me and your patience while waiting for me to come to a decision about us, but I'm sorry, Wally. I can't marry you."

Panic flashed in his eyes and then his expression turned placid, albeit a little flushed. "Of course you can. We're perfectly suited."

His refusal to accept her rejection surprised her. "I don't love you."

"I don't love you, either, but I expect our feelings will change over time."

Why did his blunt confession take her aback? She'd

been thinking the same way until recently. "Wally, I love someone else."

His brows dipped. "Your bachelor?"

"Yes. Rex Tanner."

"Your mother is no more likely to accept him into the bosom of the family than mine is to welcome Donna."

Juliana gaped. "Donna? You love Donna?"

Wally lowered his gaze and fidgeted with his silverware. "I've been in love with Donna since the first day she set foot in my office, but I never acted on my feelings until the auction forced them into the open." A tender smile flickered on his lips—the kind Juliana had never seen directed at her. "I don't know whether to bless you or curse you for that. But the fact remains, the Donnas and Rexes of this world would never be accepted into our social circle."

"That's a risk I'm willing to take."

His chin set in a stubborn line and his eyes hardened. "Then you're being foolish. Look at what you stand to lose. My father would disown me if I married Donna. Your mother is likely to do the same if you marry your bar owner."

"I know." The weight of that knowledge sat heavily in her stomach. "Wally, I've spent my entire life trying not to disappoint my mother, but by playing it safe I also insulated myself from the real world. I've been watching from the sidelines instead of experiencing life firsthand. I don't want to do that anymore."

He leaned back in his seat. "Then we'll compromise. We'll marry. Our families and our businesses will benefit. I'll turn a blind eye to any *hobbies* you might have if you'll do the same. We will of course need to present a grandchild or two relatively soon to make our parents happy, but beyond that, you may live your life in any way you see fit as long as you're discreet."

Dumbfounded, Juliana could only stare at Wally. He couldn't possibly be suggesting what she thought he was. Could he?

He reached into his pocket and pulled out a small, square blue box. *A ring box.*

Someone knocked at the front door, but Juliana's muscles wouldn't obey the order to get up and answer it. *Was he out of his mind?* A proposal followed in the same breath as a statement of his intentions to commit adultery and permission granting her the same freedom. This was a side of Wally—a distasteful side—Juliana had never seen before.

Wally opened the box, revealing the largest, gaudiest diamond Juliana had ever seen about the same time a key grated in the lock and her front door swung open. Rex stepped inside. His gaze sought and quickly found hers, and then one dark sweeping glance took in the meal, the flowers and the ostentatious boulder in Wally's extended hand.

Rex's jaw tightened and his eyes turned hard and cold.

Horrified, Juliana bolted to her feet. "Rex, it's not what you think."

And then she saw what he'd done. "Your hair. You cut your hair."

The windblown, carefree style wasn't banker short by any means. The long layers covered his ears and brushed his collar, accentuating his square jaw. If anything, he looked even more handsome than before.

She took a step toward him but Wally rose, blocked her path and faced Rex. "I'm Wallace Wilson, Juliana's fiancé. And you are her bachelor, correct?"

Rex's gaze shifted from her to Wally and back again. Every muscle in his body looked knotted.

"You're not my fiancé, Wally," Juliana corrected.

"That's only because we were interrupted before I put my ring on your finger." He held the ring where Rex couldn't miss it. "We've been unofficially engaged for months. Your mother has already booked the church and the caterers and set the date. On October twenty-first you'll be my bride."

That sounded like her mother. When all else failed, bulldoze. But Wally? Wally had never been the bulldozer type.

"I don't want to marry you, Wally. I'm sorry, but I don't and I won't." She pushed her way around him and approached Rex. "I wasn't going to accept his proposal."

Rex's nostrils flared and his lips flattened into a straight line. "How long have you been dating him?"

"Six months, but—"

"And you've been seeing him—*engaged to him*—while you've been sleeping with me?"

Juliana always, *always* trusted facts, but she had to admit the facts did not look good at the moment. "Not exactly, we—"

"So what was I? A walk on the wild side like the reporter said?"

"Yes. *No!*" How could she explain? "Rex, it started out that way, but then I fell in love with you."

He'd wanted to hear those words. God, he'd wanted to hear them, but Rex couldn't believe them now.

He should have trusted his gut. What they had was too good to be true. He'd never been faithful to a woman before Juliana. Why had he expected fidelity? What in the hell made him think he deserved it?

Juliana had told him about the pressure of her family's expectations and her dissatisfaction with her "nice" life, but she'd deliberately kept quiet about the perfect fiancé waiting in the wings. She'd used Rex—*used him*—to scratch her restless itch.

The pain shredding his insides was indescribable. He never would have expected his—*not his, dammit*—rule-following banker to lie. He had to get out of here. He pitched Juliana's house key onto the hall table, pivoted on his heel and headed out the door.

"Rex, wait." Juliana followed him outside and down the sidewalk. She planted herself between him and his truck in the driveway. "Please, let me explain."

"If he's your fiancé, then you've said enough."

"He's not. Not officially."

Not officially. What in the hell did that mean? Forget it. He didn't want to know.

"My parents want me to marry Wally to cement a merger between his family's bank and Alden's. I agreed to see if Wally and I suited. That's all. I never agreed to marry him. And I invited him here today to tell him that I couldn't marry him. I had no idea he'd bring a ring."

Yeah, right. A man didn't spend that kind of money without some encouragement. The damned ring probably cost more than Rex had borrowed from the bank to start up Renegade.

"Juliana, you run from your parents rather than speak your mind. Were you hoping he'd refuse to take my cast-offs and save you having to find the guts to tell your mother no?"

He hardened himself to the pallor of her face and the quiver of her painted lips.

"No. No, it was never that. But you're right. I never had the courage to defy my parents before. Not until I bought your auction package. I'm not good at defiance and I hate confrontation unless I have the facts to back up my arguments. But I don't love Wally and I won't marry him, no matter how much my mother wishes otherwise. I love *you*, Rex, and I will do anything—*anything*—to be with you."

She was one hell of an actress. The pain in her eyes and the sincerity in her voice looked and sounded real.

"You used me for a cheap thrill. You're no better than a

groupie." No better than he'd been when he'd used and discarded women. His chest tightened until he could barely draw a breath, and he hurt all over as if he'd been run over by a tour bus. If this is how the women he'd used felt, then he ought to be shot. Another wave of self-disgust washed over him.

"Rex, I love you. You have to believe me." She lifted a hand to cup his jaw. He intercepted it, lowered it back to her side and released her. He would not allow her touch to confuse the issue because when she touched him, he couldn't think straight.

He'd been a fool to think a rich, educated *heiress* could be happy with a guy like him. Juliana belonged with the kind of guy who could buy her a skating rink of a ring. A guy who wouldn't drive a wedge between her and her family.

That guy wasn't him.

"That's the problem, Juliana. I can't believe anything you say anymore."

He clasped her upper arms, moved her aside and climbed in his truck. He shot one last glance at her as he put the vehicle in motion and wished he hadn't.

Damn, those tears looked real.

Life on the road and out of Wilmington looked better every minute.

Ten

"Why did you call this meeting, Juliana?" Margaret Alden glanced at the mantel clock of the Alden living room as if she had somewhere she'd rather be. It had always been that way.

Irma had filled in for Margaret at Juliana's school functions, and the nanny had been the one who'd played dolls with Juliana, taught her to cook, how to apply makeup and do her hair. Irma had been the mother Juliana's mother had been too busy to be. Juliana didn't want to be that kind of mother to her own children—if she ever had any. Her pulse stuttered and her mouth dried. Her chance might come sooner than expected.

She swallowed, but her nausea refused to subside, and then she glanced at her father and brother. She wanted to go home, climb under the covers and cry her eyes out over the disastrous encounter with Rex. But that would only lead to another headache.

Her lack of courage was what had led her here. It was time

to stand up for herself. She took a deep breath. "I'm not marrying Wally. I had lunch with him Monday and told him the engagement is off."

Her mother set her wineglass down so abruptly it was a wonder the base didn't snap. "Are you out of your mind? Do you realize what this could do to the Alden-Wilson merger?"

Be strong. Mother goes for the jugular at any sign of weakness. "The banks can merge without a marriage. I am not a stock option or an asset to be traded in the deal. I'm your daughter. And I'm in love with someone else."

"The biker?" High-pitched horror raised her mother's voice.

"Rex Tanner, the bachelor I bought at your auction."

"He's totally unsuitable."

"For you maybe, but not for me."

"Eric, talk some sense into your sister."

"I can't do that, Mother. If Juliana's in love, then she needs to follow her heart. You tried to barter me in the deal and I was stupid enough to go along with it. The best thing that ever happened to me was having Priscilla run off."

Juliana turned toward Eric so quickly she nearly gave herself whiplash. What had changed his mind? No, she didn't want to know. Not if Holly was involved. Her brother went through women like most men went through neckties. She couldn't handle her best friend becoming one of his cast-offs.

Yes, she could. And she'd be there to pick up the pieces and help Holly through it. That's what friends were for.

"Richard," her mother screeched at Juliana's father.

"I agree with Eric. Juliana needs to follow her heart. The bank is strong enough to survive with or without the merger if Wilson turns pigheaded. When do I get to meet this Reg, Juliana?"

Another surprise. Juliana could count on one hand the times her father had gone against her mother's wishes and still have the majority of her fingers left over. Juliana wanted to kiss him.

"His name is Rex. And you won't get to meet him unless I can make him understand this convoluted situation. He found out about Wally and he's angry. Right now he won't accept my phone calls. But I love him, so I'm not giving up yet."

She'd phoned and left messages for two days, but Rex hadn't returned her calls. Today his message machine hadn't picked up, so she'd driven to Renegade during her lunch hour to talk to him, but it was his day off and Danny, the bartender, had said Rex was out.

She had to find him and make him understand. Especially now. Her period was late. Juliana couldn't remember one single time in her life when her body hadn't run like a well-organized calendar.

Was she pregnant? Her pulse jigged erratically and panic threatened to choke her. They'd used protection every single time except the night Becky's cries had woken them. She'd known since junior-high health class that once was enough.

Did she want to be pregnant? She touched a hand to her agitated stomach and took in a slow, calming breath. Thoughts of having Rex's baby excited and worried her. She wanted a man who loved her, not a man who married her because of a misplaced sense of duty. She wouldn't force Rex to be with her for the sake of a baby.

Then there would be the fallout from this conversation to deal with. Her mother's pinched expression didn't bode well. If her mother couldn't forgive her, then Juliana might find herself alone, pregnant and out of a job. Certainly, she had her savings account, the remainder of her trust fund and investments to fall back on, but those wouldn't last indefinitely. She'd have to get another job, and she wanted more for her child than a single parent who worked sixty-hour weeks. Rex had shown her what she'd missed as a child and no baby of hers would take second place to a career.

Her mother's sharp gaze landed on Juliana's hand. Juliana faked smoothing a wrinkle from her linen skirt. No need to raise a panic before she knew for sure. The first pregnancy-test result had been negative, but the instructions warned of the possibility of a false negative if the test were run too soon and suggested waiting a few days to run a second test. She had a second kit waiting in her bathroom at home. She'd never been an impatient person, but waiting until the weekend was excruciating.

She licked her dry lips. "That's all I had to say, but I wanted you to have the facts before going into the meeting with the Wilsons tomorrow. I hope you understand."

Her mother looked as inflexible as ever. "Juliana, you have never been the type to make illogical and impulsive decisions. For the good of the bank, you *will* rethink this matter."

"Mother, Wally's in love with someone else, too. I'm not going to ruin four lives for the sake of the bank. If you can't accept that then—" she swallowed the panic clawing her throat "—then I'll have to tender my resignation."

She didn't wait to hear the response to her ultimatum and probably couldn't have heard it anyway over her thundering pulse. Juliana picked up her purse and left.

"Visitor for you," Danny said from the office door Thursday evening.

Danny had told him about Juliana's earlier visit. "It's my day off. I'm not here."

"It's not Juliana."

And it wouldn't be John Lee. Rex had formally turned down his former manager's offer and driven him to the airport. Kelly and the girls needed Rex now more than ever while Mike was on the mend. Rex couldn't go back on the road and he couldn't spend the rest of his life running and hiding. Eventually, he'd have to come out of his office.

Danny waited by the door. "All right. I'm coming."

He rose and followed Danny out front. An attractive blonde waited at the end of the bar. He didn't know her. At least he didn't think he did. What if the women from his past saw Octavia's articles the way John Lee had and looked him up? He'd be apologizing for the rest of his life.

"Can I help you?"

"Rex?"

"Yeah. Do I know you?"

"No, we've never met."

Good, not a woman from his past. The knot between his shoulder blades eased.

"Excuse me a sec." She opened her cell phone and pushed a button, but didn't speak into the phone. "But I did see you at the bachelor auction. Nice haircut."

The front door opened. He glanced up and Juliana, looking like a slice of summer sky in a blue dress the color of her eyes, walked in. His stomach dropped and his pulse rate tripled. Adrenaline flooded his veins, but he tamped down the feeling. He was *not* happy to see her. She'd lied to him and betrayed him.

"Nice meeting you, Rex, and I hope to see more of you in the future, but I'm out of here." The blonde slid off the bar stool and then headed for the exit. "He's all yours. Call me," she said as she passed Juliana.

He could add being devious to Juliana's sins. She approached cautiously. With her pale skin and the dark bruise-like circles beneath her eyes, she looked as bad as he felt. He hardened his heart. Her conscience probably wouldn't let her sleep at night. "What do you want?"

"We need to talk."

"Nothing left to say."

"Rex." She looked over her shoulders and then met his gaze again. Agony and worry filled her eyes. "I'm late."

It took five seconds for her meaning to kick in. His legs threatened to give out. "Follow me."

He led her to the office with his mind and stomach competing in a back-flip competition. "Sit."

Her flowers-and-spice scent filled his lungs as she passed and his blood pooled behind his zipper. Dammit. How could she still get to him when he knew she'd lied to him?

He shut the door. "How late?"

"Just a few days."

"Have you done a test?"

"Yes. It's negative. But Rex, I've never been late. Ever. I'll run another test this weekend, but I thought…I thought you should know."

"So if slumming didn't get you out of the marriage you didn't want, you figured getting knocked up with my kid would?"

She stiffened. "I didn't get pregnant on purpose."

"Don't jump the gun. You might not be pregnant." He folded his arms across his chest. "Why didn't you have the balls to just say no to the marriage?"

Juliana dipped her head and knotted her fingers in her lap. "All my life I…I felt like my parents only loved me when I was perfect. The straight-A student, the ribbon-winning horseback rider, the most graceful debutante. Whenever I stepped out of line, my mother threatened to send me to school out of state. And I knew she'd do it. By the time I turned sixteen, several of my schoolmates had been exiled to boarding school."

The pencil snapped in his fingers. He pitched it in the trash. Did she expect him to buy that poor-little-rich-girl crap? "That has nothing to do with me."

"It does. When I bought you at the auction, I was rebelling. Yes, I know, thirty is a little late to get started, but it took me being backed into a corner to find my nerve. My mother cooked up her scheme for me to marry Wally to cement the Alden-Wilson merger. I felt like a commodity instead of a daughter. Worse, all the facts, all the logic pointed to the marriage being the sensible choice. I've always trusted facts more than emotions and the facts said to say yes."

Her eyes begged for understanding. "But I didn't want to. For once in my life, I wanted to experience the passion other women whisper about, even though I seriously doubted that I could since I've never…" Her cheeks flushed. "I figured that if I couldn't find what I was looking for with a man as blatantly sexy as you, then I was a lost cause, and I may as well marry Wally because I had nothing to lose."

He bit his tongue. The dragon lady couldn't be as bad as Juliana painted her, and if Juliana expected him to believe she'd never had good sex before him, then she probably expected him to believe in the tooth fairy.

"You bought me because you wanted to get laid? What made you think I'd be so easy?"

Pink tinged her pale cheeks. "You were right when you accused me of researching your past. From everything I'd read, you sounded like a guy who would get the job done and move on without thinking twice."

Damn. Didn't that just make his day?

"But then you weren't the rebel I'd read about. You weren't interested in corrupting me and you were a softie with Becky and Liza. But strangely, that made me want to be corrupted more than ever. I was physically attracted to you in a way that I'd never been to any other man, Rex. And I liked you."

Liked him. Why didn't she just stick a pin in his ego and deflate it?

"I have never chased a man in my life, and I chased you. I bought clothing that would give my father a heart attack, and I acted like…like a hussy."

Juliana wouldn't recognize a hussy if she passed one standing under a red light on the street corner. "That doesn't excuse what you did."

"No, it doesn't. I bought you with the intention of using you and walking away at the end of the month. And that's unforgivable. But if anyone can understand how much I regret that, then you should."

Whoa. Low blow. The woman fought dirty.

"Rex, my life was boring and empty until I met you. I don't want to give up what we have. And even though the facts say a boring, rule-following bean counter is not the right woman for you, my heart tells me I can be and that I will be if you'll give me a chance. I love you, Rex."

His molars clamped together. Why did his heart blip every time she said that? He still couldn't believe her. A woman who had everything couldn't fall for a guy like him. And then there was the poor-little-rich girl, *Mommy Dearest* mother and no-passion thing. Juliana was laying it on too thick even for a country bumpkin like him to believe.

"That doesn't change the facts. I'll do my part for this kid—if there is one. But that's it."

"But—"

"No buts. We're through. And if you're pregnant then I'll want a paternity test as soon as possible. I won't pay child support for Wilson's kid."

She flinched and pressed a hand to her chest. "I've never slept with Wally."

"Tell it to someone who cares."

The problem was that someone was him. But he'd get over it. "You know your way out."

As soon as the office door closed behind her, he spun in his office chair and picked up his guitar.

"What is this?"

Juliana picked up her briefcase and looked at her mother. Her heart skipped a few beats then raced. "A pregnancy test."

"I can see that. Why do you have it?"

Her mother hadn't fired her for dumping Wally, but this might be the final straw. "Mom, you came over to give me a ride to work while my car's in the shop, not to paw through my trash or put me through an inquisition."

"I did not paw through your trash. This was in the bathroom wastebasket. On top. Are you expecting that man's baby?"

That man, said in that contemptuous tone, rubbed Juliana the wrong way. "Rex. His name is Rex. And I don't know yet."

"And what will you do if you are?"

Was it too early in the day to develop a stress headache? And did she dare take anything for it if she was pregnant? She needed to buy a pregnancy book. Just in case. "I don't know. Rex and I will work out something."

If he'd ever speak to her again.

"I know a discreet doctor—"

"I'm not having an abortion!"

"You'd rather disgrace your family by having a child out of wedlock?"

"Single women have children all the time these days, Mother. It's no big deal anymore." But it was to Juliana. If there was a baby, then she wanted her child to have two loving parents.

"I will not have a bastard grandchild."

The words were a true wake-up call. Her own passivity had led her mother to believe she had the right to make Juliana's decisions. "Mother, *you* will not have a choice. This is my decision and only my decision."

"One you will live to regret." Her mother marched out of the town house. Juliana followed. The ride to work passed in icy silence. She hated the tension between them, but none of this would have happened if her mother had ever opened the lines of communication or if Juliana had dared to assert her independence a decade ago.

She climbed from the car and stopped her mother outside the bank by touching her hand. "Mother, believe it or not, I didn't go into that auction with the intention of hurting you. And I would like to have your support in whatever choices I make about my future."

The pinched look around Margaret's mouth wasn't new, but the concern in her eyes was. Her fingers briefly squeezed Juliana's. "You have no idea what you're getting yourself into, and you're fooling yourself if you think illegitimacy won't have negative repercussions for you or the child."

Two hours later, Juliana sat at her desk with her third cup of decaf coffee at her elbow. It just didn't pack the same eye-opening punch as caffeinated brew. She'd finally managed to make sense of the spreadsheet in front of her when Eric strode in looking furious.

"Tell me she's wrong."

"Who and wrong about what?"

"Mother says that bastard knocked you up."

Beyond Eric, she could see her administrative assistant's eyes widen. "Could you close the door, please?"

He did and then he turned back to her desk with fury in every stiff line of his body. What was up with Eric? Her brother was usually cool and calm no matter what the circumstances.

"I don't know if I'm pregnant yet."

"Is he going to marry you?"

"He says he's not."

"Son of a bitch. I'll kill him."

"Eric, there are extenuating circumstances you don't understa—"

But her brother turned and stormed out without waiting for Juliana's explanation. The hornets in her belly took flight. This was *so* not good. She yanked open her desk drawer, grabbed her purse and raced out of her office. No time for the elevator. She ran down two flights of stairs and made it to the lobby before remembering she didn't have a car. Flustered and in a panic, Juliana sprinted back upstairs to her office.

"Heather, can I borrow your car?" she huffed to her assistant.

Since this wasn't a request Juliana had ever made before, Heather looked suitably confused.

"My brother is going to kill my—" Her what? What was Rex exactly? "—my lover if I don't stop him," Juliana explained. That sounded melodramatic, but she was too frazzled to search for saner words at the moment.

Heather dug out her keys and tossed them across the desk. "Good luck. Blue Honda. Third row."

Juliana blessed the traffic gods for their favors as she sped through town, catching all green lights and driving well over the speed limit for the first time in her life. Eric's SUV was the only car parked in front of Renegade—not surprising since the bar hadn't opened for the lunch crowd yet. Juliana parked, leaped from Heather's car and ran inside. The place was empty. She heard a thud and a grunt coming from the direction of Rex's office and darted in that direction.

She skidded to a stop at the end of the hall in time to see Rex block Eric's right fist. Eric quickly swung his left and again Rex intercepted.

"Stop it!" she screamed.

Her cry distracted Rex for a split second. His gaze met hers. Eric landed a blow, snapping Rex's head back. Rex staggered a few steps and then righted himself. Blood oozed from his split bottom lip.

"Eric, *stop.*" Eric ignored her and took another swing, which Rex deflected. Juliana sprang forward, putting herself between her brother and Rex. "I said stop."

As badly as she wanted to check on Rex and assess his

injuries, she didn't dare look away from Eric in case he tried to hit Rex again. Had her brother gone crazy?

"I will break you, you sorry son—"

"Then you'll break me, too, Eric. I love him. And I won't stand by while you or Mother or anyone else tries to harm Rex for something that's my fault. Yes, *my* fault," she added when Eric's eyes narrowed. "Get the whole story before you go off half-cocked again."

Eric's fists unclenched. The men acted like two wolves ready to fight over territory. Juliana risked a glance at Rex. His bottom lip was already swelling. She dug in her purse for a tissue and pressed it to the trickle of blood. He jerked his head out of her reach but accepted the tissue.

He didn't even trust her to touch him. That hurt. "I'm sorry. This is my fault. It's entirely my fault."

Eric snorted. "How in the hell do you figure that? This bastard used you."

"No Eric, I used him. I bought Rex and I seduced him."

Her brother choked a sound of disbelief. "Like I'd believe that."

His incredulity insulted her. "Well you should. It's the truth. And you owe Rex an apology."

"Like hell. If he's innocent, then why didn't he fight back?"

Rex pitched the bloody tissue into the trash. "Because my daddy always said if you do the crime, then you'd better be man enough to take your punishment. I slept with your sister and if she's pregnant, I may be the father of her child. And no, I won't marry her. I deserve your anger. Bring it on."

She spun to face him. "Are you insane?"

"Not anymore."

His acerbic tone implied he had been insane to be with her. The verbal jab slipped between her ribs with lethal stealth.

"I'm sorry, Rex. I am truly sorry that I hurt you. That was never my intention. Go back to work, Eric," she said without turning.

"Not without you."

She sighed. "Go. I'm right behind you."

After a pause, Eric's footsteps departed. Silence descended on the small office like a dense cloud of suffocating smoke.

"I'm sorry. I don't know what's wrong with Eric today. He's usually very even-tempered. I'll call you as soon as I know…as soon as I know whether or not I'm pregnant."

"I won't come between you and your family, Juliana. No matter what. I'll close Renegade and go back on the road first."

"Back on tour?"

"My former manager made me an offer this week."

Loss welled inside her. If he left, she'd never have a chance to change his mind. "You have to do what makes you happy, Rex. And if selling is what it takes…then I have contacts through the bank. I'll try to help you find a buyer."

Tears pricked the back of her eyes and a sob blocked her throat. She swallowed to subdue it, but it refused to disappear.

"But you're the one who told me that running never solves anything. If you can find it in your heart to forgive me, to give me a chance to prove my love, then I'll follow you anywhere. I'll quit my job—if I still have one—and live on a tour bus or wherever else you want. I don't care what my family thinks. I want you—" Her voice broke. She closed her eyes, struggled for composure and then met his gaze again. "I want you to be happy," she repeated, "even if it's not with me."

And then she left as quickly and quietly and with as much dignity as possible considering her world had just collapsed.

Nobody could act that well. Even an Oscar winner couldn't fake the pain Rex had seen in Juliana's eyes and heard in her voice.

She wanted him to be happy when she clearly wasn't.

She'd leave her family for him when pleasing them had ruled her life.

Doubt crushed him like a concert light bar falling from the stage scaffolding. Had Juliana been telling the truth? About her childhood, her mother, all of it? And if she was, then what next?

He flexed his fingers and the tight skin on his right hand pulled, making him wince. The pain came not from the punches he'd blocked, but from the blisters on his fingertips. Music had poured out of him since he'd caught Juliana with the *GQ* jerk. He'd barely been able to eat or sleep for the words and melodies playing in his head.

Writing songs had been his favorite part of the business, and if the past four days were anything to go by, then he hadn't lost the songwriting gift that had sold so many records. Hell, the stuff he'd written since losing Juliana was ten times better than anything he'd previously penned because his guts were all over the sheet music.

Maybe Kelly was right. Maybe he could have his music without touring.

Could he also have Juliana?

She claimed she loved him. Did she?

His heart kicked into a faster tempo.

Could a sophisticated debutante be happy with a high-school dropout? What did he have to offer a woman who had everything?

"You have a visitor," Danny said from the office door on Saturday afternoon.

Not again. The game was one Rex didn't want to replay. "I'm not here."

"It's not Juliana."

"Yeah. That's what you said last time."

"It's an older lady. She looks mean enough to flatten nails into sheet metal with her teeth. C'mon, man, she's scaring the customers."

Rex rose from behind the desk and followed Danny out front. The lunch crowd had ebbed, and the dinner crowd had yet to arrive. The third newspaper article had come out today. Because he and Juliana had canceled their appointment last Monday with Octavia, she'd left them out of her story this week, focusing instead on some of the other couples. If he had any luck at all, he wouldn't be harassed about riding a black motorcycle instead of a white horse today.

He heard his manager's voice say, "He'll be right out," about the same time he recognized his visitor. The dragon lady. Juliana's mother. Hell. He'd rather hear about the damned white horse.

Her eagle eyes—the same blue as Juliana's, but without the softness—beaded on him and her haughty posture turned rigid. Regal. He'd yet to figure out how these society women managed to look down their noses at somebody a foot taller than they were.

"Mrs. Alden."

"Mr. Tanner. Might I speak with you privately." It wasn't a question. It was a demand.

"My office is this way." He led her the short distance. "Have a seat."

The costly leather chairs, expensive desk and bookcases were relics from his Nashville days, and he had a feeling Mrs. Alden appraised each item within seconds of crossing the threshold.

She lowered herself into the visitor's seat. "I'll pay off your note if you'll stop seeing my daughter."

She didn't beat around the bush. Rex sat down and rocked back in his chair. "I've already stopped seeing Juliana, and I pay my own debts."

"I've taken the liberty of checking into your accounts. I don't see the reserves you'll need to make the payment on time."

"That's because my 'reserves' are not in your bank. In fact, I'll be closing all of my accounts with Alden's, beginning with the loan." He opened his desk drawer and withdrew the cashier's check he'd drawn this morning for the amount due on his note. Thanks to his inheritance, he could pay off his debts. He'd also set up college funds for Becky and Liza. He slid the check across the desk. "You've saved me a trip."

She didn't pick up the check. "I'll cancel your debt if you promise me you won't contact Juliana again."

"And what if she's carrying my kid?"

"That need not concern you. We'll handle it."

He sucked a sharp breath. How would they *handle* it if Juliana carried his baby? Would the dragon lady pressure Juliana into a decision they'd both regret? Anger, never far from the surface these past few days, boiled over. The fact that Mrs. Alden was every bit as overbearing as Juliana had described doubled his ire. Juliana hadn't lied about her mother. Did that mean she hadn't lied about anything else?

"Mrs. Alden, you can take your money and shov—"

"*Mr. Tanner,* don't say something you might regret. I will only make this offer once."

He rose and leaned over the desk, bracing himself on his fists. "Lady, you tried to sell your daughter, and now you're trying to buy me off. My opinion of you couldn't get any lower. If you have half a brain in your head, then you'd better start thinking about your daughter instead of your damned bank."

"I beg your pardon." He'd never seen a spine that stiff.

"It's not my pardon you need to be begging. It's Juliana's. Your actions are pushing her away and you're going to lose her if you don't wise up. The woman who bought me is one who's been stuck under your thumb for thirty years. It was only a matter of time before she got tired of your dictatorship and rebelled."

"I want what's best for Juliana."

"And you're damned sure I'm not it." He circled the desk and stretched to his full height, towering over the dragon lady. "What could be better for her than a man who worships her and would lay his heart at her feet? Because that's what you and your scheme have cost her."

Mrs. Alden rose stiffly, but Rex took satisfaction in taking a little starch out of her spine.

"You haven't heard the last from me, Mr. Tanner."

"No, ma'am, I probably haven't, but I have a news flash for you. If Juliana's carrying my baby, then you're not going to crush my child under your thumb like you did your daughter. I'll see you in hell first. And *that* is a promise you can take to the bank."

He snatched up the check and forced it into her hand, and then yanked open his office door.

Eleven

Another unpalatable meal.

Juliana wished she were anywhere except the exclusive waterfront restaurant with her mother. She'd awoken cranky and achy this morning, and to top it off she'd run the second pregnancy test with another negative result. She didn't know whether to be disappointed or relieved or to buy a third test on the way home. She wanted to know before she got her hopes up more than she had already.

She and her mother had never had the Sunday-brunch-meeting type of relationship—unless they were meeting for business. If her mother was going to fire her, then Juliana wished she'd get it over with. After almost an hour of meaningless chitchat Juliana just wanted to go home and crawl into her Whirlpool tub.

"Mother, why are we here?"

Her mother seemed more uncomfortable, more uncertain than Juliana had ever seen her before. "I realize I've not always been there for you, and I don't always understand your determination to do things the hard way, but I don't want to lose you, Juliana. Mr. Tanner seems to think I might."

Juliana blinked. "Excuse me? What does Rex have to do with this?"

"You're so like me. You're completely absorbed with your career and—"

"But I'm not you and I don't want to be you. I always thought I did, but recently, I realized how much you missed out on life." Juliana pressed her lips together and wished the words back. "I'm sorry. That was rude."

"And deserved, I'm afraid. I did miss much of yours and Eric's childhoods."

"We had Irma. But it would have been nice to have you, too."

"Yes, maybe, but I had so much to prove. Back in those days a woman had to work twice as hard as a man to make it to the top in the corporate world."

"Things have changed."

"In some ways, but you're still as naive about men as I was, Juliana."

"I don't understand."

"I was also a wealthy young woman. I had men vying for my attention. It quite turned my head. I fell in love. Twice. And each time, I eventually realized I wasn't the main attraction and my heart was broken. The men were after my daddy's money." She folded her napkin and laid it beside her plate, then lifted her gaze to Juliana's. "I didn't want that to happen to you."

Her mother had never discussed her past relationships. It seemed odd to hear these confidences now. "Maybe you should give me credit for being able to recognize the guys looking for an easy ride. I've dated and dumped my share. But that doesn't explain why you're so determined to push me into marriage with Wally."

"I wanted you to have a stable marriage based on compatibility in jobs and backgrounds. My father arranged a suitable marriage for me. I was trying to do the same for you and your brother to protect you from the pain I'd experienced."

Surprise stole her breath. "You didn't love Daddy when you married him? Not even a little?"

"I respected him and we had many common interests."

It sounded familiar and so sad. The relationship her mother described was exactly the kind of match Juliana and Wally had contemplated, and if Juliana hadn't met Rex, she'd probably be picking out china and silver patterns and settling for a life without love. Close call. Too close.

"If you don't love him, then why have you stayed with him for thirty-eight years?"

"Because I grew to love him. Not as ardently as you appear to love Mr. Tanner, but comfortably. We're like a matched pair of shoes. We function best together."

"Shoes?" How depressing. "As much as I like shoes, Mother, I don't want to live like one. I want more than that."

"Juliana, you could get hurt."

"I already hurt. I can't imagine the pain getting any worse. But you know what? I'd do it all again." Even knowing the outcome would be a broken heart, Juliana realized, she would risk loving Rex again. Gambling with a guaranteed bad result. A first for her. But then Rex had given her so many firsts.

"When did you talk to Rex?" If her mother had talked to him recently, then maybe he hadn't left town.

Juliana had never seen her mother squirm before today. Her cheeks darkened. "Yesterday. I tried to buy him off."

"You what?" Juliana squeaked in horror.

"My father tried to buy off each of the men who broke my heart and they took the money. That's how I knew they didn't love me. Your Mr. Tanner told me exactly where I could put my offer to cancel his business loan. Quite inappropriate, really."

Conflicting emotions battled inside her. Her mother had tried to get rid of Rex. And he'd refused. She pressed fingers to the smile trembling on her lips. Simultaneously, her eyes stung. "You shouldn't have done that."

"I've gone about this awkwardly, but I want what's best for you, my dear, and I thought I knew what that was. However, I was wrong. I suspect the right man for you might be Mr. Tanner. *Rex.*"

"It may be too late."

Her mother reached across the table and covered Juliana's hand. "It's never too late. And you are my daughter. If you're sure he's the man you want, then you'll find a way to win him."

"It's not that easy."

"Nothing worth having ever is. And if there is a baby, then we'll adjust. With or without a marriage. Shall we go? I imagine you need to contact Mr.—Rex."

"Mother, Rex hasn't even said he loves me."

"Then I imagine getting him to do so is your top priority."

The entire conversation seemed surreal. Juliana robotically followed her mother out to the car. Tomorrow was Monday, Rex's day off. Did she dare try one more time? Could she make him understand when the facts were stacked against her?

There were times when Juliana wished politeness hadn't been instilled into her from birth. This was one of those times. She wanted to ignore the doorbell and stay curled up on the sofa with her Swiss-chocolate-almond-flavored coffee.

Comfort coffee.

She wasn't pregnant.

She'd called in sick to work because she didn't know what to make of the aching disappointment when she'd made her discovery after lunch with her mother. She needed to discuss her confusing feelings with Andrea and Holly, and she'd called each of them earlier, but neither was at home. Just as well. What could she say? How could she explain her conflicting emotions?

The bell rang again, followed by a hard pounding on the wood. Reluctantly, she set down her mug, rose and shuffled on bare feet to the door. It was probably Eric or her father checking to see if she was all right. She looked through the peephole and her breath caught.

Rex.

Her heart thumped harder and her palms dampened. She smoothed them over her shorts. What did he want?

You'll never know if you don't open the door.

She glanced in the mirror over the hall table and winced. Her hair was tangled and her skin pale. She hadn't bothered with makeup. Even her nail polish was chipped because she'd been nibbling her nails. *You're a wreck.*

No time for repairs now.

She fumbled the lock and then turned the knob and opened the door. Air whooshed out of her lungs. Rex looked wonderful, tall and tanned with his jaw gleaming from a fresh morning shave. His lip was still a little swollen from Eric's punch. He wore his usual jeans and black boots, but today he'd pulled on a white western-style dress shirt with black onyx snaps—the kind he'd worn on his CD covers.

She couldn't read the expression in his dark eyes as they swept slowly over her face, breasts, belly and legs, and then back up again. Her skin tingled in the wake of his visual caress and she gulped.

"Good morning, Rex." So formal, when what she wanted to do was thread her fingers through his shorn hair and kiss him until they were both dizzy from lack of oxygen.

"'Morning." He shifted on his booted feet. "Can I come in?"

"Certainly." She stepped away from the door. His cologne teased her nose as he passed. She glanced out at her driveway because she hadn't heard the growl of his Harley and saw his pickup truck parked beside her sedan. Two motorcycles stood side by side in the truck bed.

Her pulse accelerated. Two bikes? What did that mean?

She closed the door and followed him into the den. The width of the room separated them. The distance seemed as vast as an ocean. *No use stalling. Say what you must. And then if he leaves... You'll deal with it.* "You didn't have to come over. I would have called later today. I'm not pregnant."

He inhaled sharply. "I'm sorry."

Confused, Juliana frowned. "Sorry I'm not pregnant?"

"Yeah. No." He swiped a hand through his hair, ruffling the strands the way she longed to. "Yeah."

He shook his head, looking as perplexed by his answer as she was. "I'd love to see you pregnant with my baby."

And that made absolutely no sense since he'd dumped her. Her heart fluttered as fast as a hummingbird's wings. The fact that he hadn't jumped for joy when she'd shared the news had to be a good sign, didn't it?

"How do you feel about it? About not being pregnant?" he asked with narrowed eyes.

Should she lie? No. She hugged her arms over her chest. "Disappointed."

"Why?"

"What do you mean, why?"

He closed the distance between them, stopping only inches away. The temptation to burrow into his broad chest and to wind her arms around his middle pulled at her.

"Do you want to have a baby? *My* baby?"

He shouldn't tease her like this. "Does it matter?"

"It does to me." His voice was low and quiet, barely a rumble of sound.

She scrubbed her upper arms, glanced away and then back again. "Yes. Yes, I'd like to have your baby."

His lips twitched and some of the stiffness left his shoulders as he exhaled. She hadn't even noticed his tension until she saw it drain away.

"Let's take a ride." He nodded toward her front door.

"Why?"

"I want to show you something. And I thought you might want to try soloing on the motorcycle. I have a bike for you in the back of the truck."

She wanted to go. Did that make her a glutton for punishment? Or could she take this opportunity to explain one more time that she loved him and had never intended to hurt him? She lifted her chin. She would not give up without a fight. "I need to change clothes."

"I'll wait."

Ten minutes later, she sat beside him in his truck wearing her low-rider jeans—because they were the only jeans she owned—and an untucked poplin shirt. The shirttails covered her belly. She hadn't dressed to seduce him. He needed to understand that he wasn't getting the sexy siren she'd pretended to be.

Miles passed before he spoke. "Your mother came to see me."

Juliana grimaced. "I know. I'm sorry. She didn't mean to insult you. She actually thought she was doing the right thing."

"Yeah." He sounded more amused than angry.

"And you won her over when you refused the money. Rex, I can't apologize enough. You've seen the absolute worst of my family this week. They—"

"Love you," he interrupted.

She considered the strange events over the past few days

and nodded. They never said so, but actions spoke louder than words. "Yes, I guess so. But still…"

"You're lucky to have them."

The sadness in his voice tugged at her heart. She reached across the space between them and covered his fist on the bench seat. He turned his hand over and opened it, lacing his fingers between hers. That simple gesture gave her hope. She clung to the feeling as they drove out of town.

He turned at a familiar fruit stand and she sat up straighter. "Are we going to the farm?"

"Yeah."

When they arrived, Rex rolled his motorcycle down a narrow metal ramp from the truck bed to the gravel driveway first and then repeated the action with a smaller bright blue bike. He reached into the saddlebag and withdrew an owner's manual. "Need to read it before we go for a ride?"

Her cheeks heated, but the tender smile on his lips curled her toes. "No."

He tucked the book away and handed her a set of keys and a helmet the same color as the bike. "This one works the same way as my bike, but weighs about half as much. Give 'er a try. We'll take a few slow laps around the farm."

Fear and excitement raced through her veins as she buckled the helmet and climbed on the motorcycle. Her hands trembled as she grasped the rubber handgrips and fired the engine. She had no idea what kind of game Rex was playing, but she'd play along just for the opportunity to be with him.

He led her around the perimeter of the land, glancing back frequently to check her progress. A sense of freedom filled Juliana as the wind whipped her shirttails and caressed her cheeks. No matter what happened after today, she would buy herself a motorcycle, and she would not revert back to the woman who'd let fear of disappointing her parents rule her life. It was *her* life and she intended to live every second of it from this moment forward.

She followed Rex through an open gate, and drove down a path and up a shallow rise. The freshly mowed grass smelled heavenly. When he stopped and killed the engine, she pulled alongside him and did the same. He removed his helmet and climbed from his machine. She mimicked his actions.

Why had he stopped here in the middle of this pasture?

"This is a good place for a house," he said.

"It's a beautiful site." Insects buzzed and not one single cloud marred the blue sky. A hundred yards away, fish splashed and ducks quacked in a small pond. Cattails waved in the breeze and lily pads dotted the water's surface.

"I'm buying the farm and I'm going to build right here." He pointed to the ground at his feet.

She jerked her gaze to his and found him watching her carefully. "You're not going back on tour?"

"No. Everyone I love is here."

"I'm sure Kelly and the girls will be thrilled."

"Will you?"

Her breath hitched. "Me?"

Rex cupped her shoulders. The look in his eyes weakened her knees and made her heart pound. Hope brought a lump to her throat.

"I love you, Juliana. I want to marry you and build a home with you. Right here." His spread his hand below her navel and then he rubbed in a slow circle. Desire curled beneath his palm. "I want to make babies with you."

She mashed her lips together and blinked furiously while she tried to make sense of his words. "Me?" she repeated.

"Yeah, you. I have a thing for good girls who want to be bad." His be-bad-with-me grin made her absolutely giddy with delight.

"I like being bad with you."

"Good. Because I feel like being bad right now and for the next fifty years or so." His hands tangled in her hair and then he took her mouth in a deep, soul-robbing kiss.

Juliana savored his taste, the slickness of his tongue and the heat of his breath on her cheek. She wriggled closer, winding her arms around his middle and fusing herself to the hot length of his body.

He lifted his head and tenderly stroked her cheeks. "I should have believed you when you told me about your mother and your childhood. But I'll never buy your story about being an unresponsive lover. Babe, you are the hottest woman I've ever known."

Pleasure percolated through her and a smart-aleck grin stretched her lips. "And you should know."

He winced. "I'm sorry for all the women who weren't you. And I swear to you that none of them excited me the way you do."

She cradled his jaw. "Don't be sorry, Rex. Your past is what made you the man I love."

He inhaled deeply and closed his eyes. His jaw muscles bunched. "Say it again."

The deep timber of his voice sent a tidal wave of longing through her. "I love you. *You,* my reluctant rebel."

He brushed back her hair. "And in case you're afraid your mother is right about me wanting your money—"

"I'm not."

"You don't have to be. My share of my inheritance from my parents was enough to pay off my loan and make a big down payment on this land. If I need to show your folks a financial statement—"

"You won't have to do that. You've already won my mother over. She was the tough sell."

She rose on her tiptoes and pressed her lips to his. His big hands cupped her buttocks, lifting and pressing her tightly against the solid ridge of his arousal. The kiss was long and slow and deep. She wanted to weep from the sheer eroticism of the way he made love to her mouth. And then his hands swept beneath her shirt. Rough skin abraded her waist.

She gasped, drew back and clasped his right hand in hers. Blisters in various stages of healing covered his fingertips. "What happened?"

He shrugged. "Loving you has filled me with music. I can't play as fast as my brain forms the lyrics and melodies."

His words touched her profoundly. Juliana pressed a hand to her heart. "I would never ask you to give that up. I meant what I said in your office. If you want to go back on the road, I'll quit my job and follow you anywhere."

He lifted her hand and kissed her knuckles. "You love your job. I don't want you to quit. I realized it's the songwriting I love. Not being onstage. Not the fans. Not the traveling. I can stay here with you, run Renegade and write songs for other people to sing. According to John Lee, my manager, I should make enough money to take care of you and any babies we make." His hand smoothed over her belly, stirring up a whirlpool of need.

He dropped to one knee in the grass and reached into his pocket. The diamond solitaire he pulled out flashed fire in the sunlight. It wasn't nearly as flashy as Wally's ring but it was ten times more beautiful. "Marry me, Juliana Alden. Let me love you forever."

Winding her arms around his neck, she slid down his body an inch at a time until she knelt with him in the grass and then she kissed him, pouring all of her love into the caress. His arms banded around her, holding her close. She lifted her lips a fraction of an inch and looked into the eyes of the man she loved.

"On one condition. You get rid of that crazy notion that you have to support me. I make good money, and I'm good at what I do. One of these days I may cut my hours to spend more time with our children, but this will always be a partnership. We'll take care of each other."

"Deal."

"Then yes, Rex Tanner, I'll marry you and spend forever with you. I can't think of anything more perfect than making music and babies with you."

Rex slid the ring onto her finger and Juliana grinned through happy tears. Forget nice. Forget boring. The adventure of a lifetime had just begun. She'd get to be bad whenever she wanted and it would be so good.

* * * * *

EXPOSING THE EXECUTIVE'S SECRETS

BY
EMILIE ROSE

Kira,
Your words are magical.
Thanks for putting me in the gondola.

One

"This one's going to come back to bite you, Andrea. Please choose another bachelor."

Andrea Montgomery's heart bumped along faster than a roller coaster. Her stomach alternated between the rise of anticipation and the plunge of trepidation. She sipped her complimentary champagne, tucked her numbered bidding paddle beneath her arm and then reached for her dearest friend's hand and squeezed.

"Holly, I can't. You know I have to do this."

"Buying him is a mistake. Remember how torn up you were when he left?"

As if I could forget that kind of pain.

"That was then. I'm *totally* over him now." And she was. Absolutely. Without a doubt. How could she not be over a man who'd led her on for years and then dumped her without giving her a believable reason?

Andrea released Holly's fingers and then plucked at the black silk charmeuse of her gown. What little fabric there was in the garment clung to her like a second skin. The neckline plunged almost to her navel, and if the slit in the ankle-length skirt were an inch higher no one would have to wonder whether or not she wore panties.

She shifted on her stiletto heels—the only part of the outfit she liked—and scanned the crowd of overexcited, expensively attired women consuming free champagne and bidding on bachelors. No one in this affluent, conservative country club crowd suffered from the same overexposure as her.

"What were you and Juliana thinking when you chose this dress? As much as I love sexy clothing, this gown is too obvious and over the top. Couldn't you have chosen something more subtle? Subtle is sexy. Obvious is tacky. I feel like a high-priced call girl. No wait. Even a working girl would leave a little mystery and cover more skin."

Holly didn't even crack a smile. "When seduction's the name of the game you bring out the big guns. You're planning to bring Clayton Dean to his knees. Juliana and I thought you should dress the part of femme fatale."

Clayton Dean. Hearing his name wound Andrea's nerves tighter. "You've miscast me. A femme fatale seduces the man in question. I have no intention of revisiting the sheets with Clay. He had his chance eight years ago and blew it. And how many times do I have to tell you? I'm not out for revenge. All I want to do is show him that there are no hard feelings."

"Uh-huh." Holly didn't attempt to hide her skepticism.

Her friend knew her too well. "Okay, so I won't mind if he eats his heart out just a little over what he could have had. But that's all. I'd be a fool to hand him my heart again."

"I agree. That's why I'm going to keep repeating, *this is a bad idea* like a broken record until you get it."

"Holly, I've lived through the humiliation of Clay dumping me once. My coworkers' pity was hard enough to swallow the first time. And according to Mrs. Dean, Clay's staying in Wilmington only until his father is well enough to return to the helm at Dean Yachts, and then Clay will sail back to Florida. I promise I won't forget this is temporary."

"You're trying awfully hard to sell yourself on a bad idea, Ms. Marketing Director."

"Cut it out. Remember this is not just about me. Without Clay the business might have to temporarily shut its doors, putting me and a thousand other employees out of work. Joseph Dean has been like a second father to me. I've been worried about his mood since his stroke three weeks ago. He and Clay need to work this out before it's too late." The possibility of losing her mentor put a lump in her throat.

Holly's frown deepened. "What if father and son do kiss and make up and Clay returns for good? He'll be your boss. Will you still love your job then?"

Andrea winced. Good point. Darn it. As if she didn't have a boatload of doubts already about working with Clay. "I need to move forward. I can't do that until I put the past behind me. I'm a loser magnet, Holly. I have to break the cycle, and to do that I need to know what's so wrong with me that Clay and every guy I've dated in the past eight years dumps me just when I start to believe there might be something to the relationship."

Holly stamped her foot in irritation. "I could smack you. How many times do I have to tell you there's nothing wrong with you?"

"Says you."

Holly's attention shifted to something beyond Andrea's shoulder. "I hope you're right about being over him, because Clay looks good. Really, really good."

Andrea choked on her champagne. After catching her breath she discarded the flute on a passing waiter's tray and braced herself before following Holly's gaze to the other side of the opulent Caliber Club ballroom. Her first glimpse of her former lover knocked the wind right back out of her.

Clay did look good. Amazing, in fact. Damn him. The last thing she wanted or needed was to still find him attractive. His shoulders were broader than she remembered, and his tuxedo hinted at muscles he hadn't possessed as a lanky twenty-three-year-old. A nostalgic smile tugged her lips. He may look more sophisticated, but he still hadn't learned to tame his beaver-brown hair. The longer strands on top curled in disarray just as they had after she'd rumpled them when they made lo—

She severed the thought instantly. No need to travel that heavily rutted dead end road again.

She didn't think he'd spotted her yet, and she wanted to keep it that way—right up until she bought him. A combination of anticipation and unease traversed her spine.

"Putting the past to bed will be worth every penny I have to bid on bachelor number thirteen tonight."

One of Holly's eyebrows lifted. "Bed? Freudian slip?"

Andrea scowled at her friend. "You know what I mean. I want this over and done with. Final. Finished. Forgotten."

"If you say so." The doubt in Holly's voice didn't instill confidence. "We knew our trust funds would come in handy one day, but I don't think our granddaddies intended us to buy men—even if it is for a charitable cause. Juliana certainly dropped a bundle on her rebel."

Juliana had been the first in their close-knit trio to buy her man. Andrea hoped her straight-laced friend could handle the rebellious biker bar owner. "I hope that goes well."

"Amen. I hope none of us regret tonight's nonsense."

"Holly, we agreed—"

"No, you and Juliana agreed. My arm was twisted, but I'm in for better or worse."

The gavel sounded like a starter's pistol. Andrea nearly jumped out of her skimpy dress. Bachelor twelve left the stage to meet his date, and the women in the audience went wild in anticipation of the next offering. She covered her ears as the decibel level rose and wondered if she should chalk this foolish plan up to too many margaritas and walk away.

No. She couldn't. She wanted a life and that meant dealing with her messy, painful past. The band's drum roll rattled in tandem with her rapidly thumping pulse as the emcee announced the next bachelor.

Her bachelor. Clayton Dean.

Andrea pushed the tousled mass of her hair—the style another contribution from her friends—away from her face. Sure, she talked a good game by pretending that buying and confronting the man who'd shattered her heart and her confidence eight years ago was going to be a piece of cake, but her insides quivered and her knees knocked beneath her trampy dress. She'd loved Clay, had planned to marry him, have his children and run Dean Yachts by his side. His abrupt departure had nearly destroyed her.

What if her plan went terribly wrong?

She squared her shoulders and squashed her doubts. It wouldn't. At thirty years old she was more than mature enough to face a former lover without making a fool of herself. Besides, she'd strategized every last detail—the same way she would an extensive marketing campaign.

Buy him, thereby obligating him to seven dates and giving her seven opportunities to:

Impress him with her acquired business savvy.

Tempt him, but keep her distance.

Question him to find out why she was so easy to leave.

Dismiss him from her heart and her head.

The women surrounding her screamed maniacally as Clay took his place center stage. Who wouldn't want a series of dates with a handsome naval architect and award-winning yacht designer? But she was determined that Clay would be hers. *Temporarily.* Andrea clenched her numbered fan so tightly the wooden handle cracked.

An omen? Goose bumps raced over her skin.

Holly leaned closer and spoke directly into Andrea's ear to be heard above the din. "Are you sure you can handle Seven Seductive Sunsets with Clay?"

"Of course." She waved away Holly's concern, but tucked her free hand behind her back when she realized her fingers trembled.

And then she lifted her paddle and cast the first bid on her former lover—the man who would soon be her boss.

If he didn't love her, he'd kill her. Clay glared at his mother as he took the stage.

Smile, she mouthed and pointed to her own curving lips.

He turned a big, phony smile to the crowd. His mother could have warned him about the bachelor auction for charity, but no, she'd planned the date package, put his picture in the auction program and then shanghaied him the moment he'd docked today. He'd tried to buy his way out of this fiasco with a hefty donation, but nobody bulldozed Patricia Dean once she set her mind to something, and she'd set her mind toward making a fool of her only son.

But he owed her, so he let her get away with it.

As if he didn't have enough on his plate running his own company, he had to take control of Dean Yachts until he could hire an interim CEO. That meant working with Andrea, Dean's marketing manager, on a daily basis. Regret tightened like a fist around his heart.

He did not want to be here—not back in his hometown or up on this stage being auctioned off like a repossessed yacht. There was too much flotsam under the bridge, and there were too many disappointments, too many broken promises.

The women—tipsy from the sounds of it—called out lewd suggestions, but he'd be damned if he'd shake his wares or prance around like a male striper for his audience. If the other bachelors wanted to act like fools fine, but he wouldn't. Being stuck babysitting some bubble-headed socialite was already beyond the call of duty.

Clay stood in the hot lights as stiff as a mast. One spotlight baked his skin. Another panned the crowd as the emcee rattled off Clay's vital statistics. Staring out at the hysterical women, he mentally dared any one of them to buy him.

And then he saw her—*Andrea*—in the crowd. His lungs deflated like a sail without a breeze and his stomach shriveled into a hot lump of coal. Damn. What was she doing here? He'd thought he had until Monday to prepare himself for seeing her again.

He'd loved her—almost enough to turn a blind eye to the discovery that had knocked his foundations out from under him.

The spotlight shifted back to the stage, blinding him. The bid climbed higher, *embarrassingly high* compared to the last two saps. He should be proud he wasn't going as low as a junked schooner, but he wasn't. He wanted off the stage. The sooner, the better. The bidders used numbered paddles instead of calling out bids, and he couldn't see who wielded the numbers because of the damned lights, so he didn't have a clue who bid what.

The gavel hit the podium. "Sold," the emcee shouted. "Come and collect your prize, number two-twenty-one."

Good. Finally over—at least the first part of his torture. Clay gladly vacated the stage. His eyes adjusted to the dimness at the bottom of the stairs in time to see Andrea hand a check to the woman behind the desk. Shock locked his muscles.

Andrea had bought him!

He caught a glimpse of her wavy blond hair and caramel-colored eyes a split second before the visual impact of her black dress nearly knocked him to his knees. Her pale breasts poised on the brink of spilling from the gashing deep neckline, and a slit cut nearly to her crotch displayed one long, satiny leg. His breath lodged in his throat and he almost swallowed his tongue. Heat exploded in his groin.

Mayday. Mayday.

She strolled in his direction, smiling at him with a cool confidence he didn't recall her having when she'd been his lover. "Hello, Clay. Shall we find a quiet corner and make our arrangements?"

Her voice slid through him like smooth, aged whiskey. How could he have forgotten her soft, southern drawl or the temperature-raising effect it had on him?

"Hold it," a thirtyish African American woman called out. A tall, pale guy holding a camera stood beside her. The woman made a squeezing motion with her hands. Clay moved closer to Andrea. "Arms around each other, please, and smile."

Clay gritted his teeth into a smile and put his arm around Andrea. His palm found bare skin. Damnation. The back of her dress was as bare as the front. Her body heat seared his palm and penetrated his tux jacket. Fire streaked through him. Fire he had to extinguish. Right now.

Andrea gasped, nearly expelling her breasts from the shiny black fabric. Clay couldn't help himself. His gaze shifted to her creamy skin. And the camera flashed. Oh hell. Caught looking. Before he could ask the reporter to take another shot Andrea pulled free, pivoted on her very sexy heels and strolled away with a mind-altering sway to her hips.

Whoa. That was not the same woman he'd left behind. The Andrea he'd known would never have worn a dress guaranteed to make a man forget his manners and his name.

Reeling from the unwelcome slam of desire, he shook his head and caught sight of his mother's smug smile. She was up to something—something he was certain would make him regret coming home more than he already did.

Clay followed Andrea toward the door. After the way he'd left her he'd expected her to want him dead.

Why would she come to his rescue tonight?

And what would it cost him?

"What game are you playing, Andrea?" Clay's voice rumbled over her, deep and familiar, but with a rough edge Andrea didn't remember.

Her heart raced and her breath came in short bursts—not caused solely by her hasty retreat from the prying eyes inside. She reached the deserted gazebo at the end of the dock jutting into the Cape Fear River and wished she could keep on walking. Despite two weeks of planning, she wasn't ready for this confrontation, but she braced herself and turned.

With the lights of the Caliber Club behind him, shadow concealed most of Clay's face. His cheeks appeared leaner and his jaw more sharply defined than eight years ago. Jagged streaks of moonlight reflected off the water in wavering beams. One slashed across his eyes making them a more intense blue than she recalled.

"I don't have time for games, Clay."

"Then what's this about?" He jerked a thumb, indicating the club. "A trip down memory lane?"

"Can't a woman rescue an old friend from the money-hungry masses without complaint?"

"Old friends. Is that what we are?"

Could they ever be friends again? Doubtful. But she could fake it long enough to get the closure she needed. "I hope so."

"So this is you being self-sacrificing?"

His sarcasm stiffened her spine and heated her cheeks with a not-so-subtle reminder that she'd been something of a pampered princess when he left town. But that had changed. She'd learned the hard way not to take anything for granted—like happiness, promises or loved ones. "You have a problem with that?"

"You never could lie worth a damn. You get a quiver in your voice. C'mon. Spill it, Andrea. Why are we really here?"

She cursed the telling sign of her agitation and cleared her throat. "We have to work together. So anything that makes your life easier makes my life easier. Saving you from that—" she gestured toward the club "—seemed like a nice thing to do."

"You're claiming this is about work?" More sarcasm. He clearly didn't buy her story. She couldn't blame him.

Pursing her lips, she exhaled in resignation. This wasn't going as well as she'd anticipated. She'd expected him to be grateful, not suspicious. "I need to know that I can count on you not to bail before Joseph's back on his feet."

His breath hissed. "I have my own business to run. I'll stay until the headhunting firm I've hired locates an interim CEO, and then I'm out of here."

She gaped and then snapped her mouth closed. "You can't hand Dean Yachts over to a stranger. Your father would—"

"My father has nothing so say about it," he interrupted in a flat don't-argue-with-me tone.

Reeling, she scrambled to make him understand. "The doctors expect Joseph to make an eighty to ninety percent recovery from the stroke. His mental faculties are clear, but his stamina isn't what it used to be. Knowing you'd be here is the only reason he agreed to stay out of the office while he recuperates."

A balmy June breeze whipped her hair across her face and ruffled the edges of her gown, nearly baring her breasts. Clay's gaze lowered to her cleavage. Her nipples peaked and an ache started deep inside her. Damn. It.

"I didn't ask for an update." Clay shifted deeper into the shadows. In the darkness she couldn't read his expression. Did he like what he saw? Did he have even one moment's regret for walking away from what they'd had? Had he thought about her at all since he'd left?

Stop it. It doesn't matter.

But it did. Andrea clenched her fingers around the long chain strap of her sequined evening bag.

"You should have. He's your father. In a couple of months he'll be back on the job unless you rush him and he ends up endangering his health. Give him time to heal, Clay."

He shoved his hands into his pockets and turned away, presenting her with his back—a broad, unyielding wall of resistance.

The creaking of the dock boards and the clang of the sailboat lines in the slips broke the silence, but the familiar sounds didn't have their usual calming effect.

Ask him why he left.

But she couldn't. Not yet. Because she wasn't sure she was ready to hear his answer. What if he told her something hideous and then she had to face him daily for the next few months? But she would get the information out of him before he left.

Andrea sighed and plucked a strand of hair from her overly glossy—thanks to her friends—lips. She joined Clay at the rail, and the citrus and spice scent of his cologne wafted to her on the breeze. Memories washed over her, tugging at her like a strong riptide. Memories of a night very like this one. High school graduation night. The tiny cabin of his sailboat. Making love for the first time. Learning his body as he learned hers.

Stop.

She shifted restlessly and pushed away the past. Okay, so she still found Clay physically appealing. Big deal. That didn't mean she'd let the current of attraction pull her under. He'd hurt her too badly for her to ever trust him again.

Stick to the agenda, Andrea. Focus on what you're good at—your job. And the rest will follow.

She took a deep breath and launched into her practiced spiel. "Dean Yachts has a backlog of pending orders. You'll have to plunge into the deep end if we're to keep up with our production schedule. Your father will tell you whatever you need to know to stay afloat."

His jaw hardened. "I don't need his help."

She bit her lip and battled frustration. Mending the breach between the men might be harder than she'd anticipated. "You may not need it, but Joseph needs you to ask for it. He's depressed and more than a little shaken up by his brush with mortality. He's looking forward to having you at home."

He turned his head and met her gaze. She'd never considered Clay inflexible or implacable in the past, but his face wore both traits now. His square jaw jutted forward. "I docked my boat at Dean's. I'm berthing there."

"Security didn't notify me."

"Mom cleared it before I arrived."

Neither Mrs. Dean nor security had informed Andrea, which was odd since Andrea was unofficially in charge at the moment. But then Mrs. Dean had been acting strangely since she'd let it slip that Clay would be coming home and arriving just in time to participate in the auction. But Andrea would worry about that later.

"You will go by the house to see your father, won't you?"

"No."

Another wave of frustration crashed over Andrea's head. "Clay, Joseph needs his family around him."

"It's a little late for him to start thinking about his family." Bitterness tightened his voice.

"What does that mean?" He remained silent and Andrea's irritation and curiosity mounted. What had happened eight years ago to cause this rift? "It's never too late to say you're sorry."

He pivoted sharply. Moonlight illuminated the flattened line of his mouth and his narrowed eyes. "Is that what you want? An apology?"

She gasped. As if an apology would be enough to fix what he'd done. "I wasn't talking about me. I meant you and Joseph. He's your father, Clay. *Wake up.* You could have lost him. Take this opportunity to fix things between you before it's too late. You might not get another chance."

"You don't know what you're talking about."

"Then explain it to me." She crushed her evening bag in her fingers, half hoping, half fearing his answer.

He made a scoffing sound. "You couldn't handle it."

"Try me." A minute dragged past. Two.

"It's over, Andrea. Let it go."

If only she could, but even now Clay's nearness stirred

things best left undisturbed. She traveled a few shaky steps down the dock being careful to keep her heels from getting caught between the boards. "Just in case you're worried, I'm not interested in picking up where we left off. But we have to work together, Clay. I need your support in front of the staff."

"You'll have it." He shadowed her down the dock. "Mother says you've single-handedly run the company for the past three weeks."

Was that grudging respect in his voice? "I've done what I could, but we have over a thousand employees. It's been a true team effort."

"Why can't you continue without me?"

"Because people expect a Dean to be at the helm of Dean Yachts, and we need someone capable of coordinating all the teams involved in production. I can't do that." She paused and turned. "About these dates…I'm not expecting, nor do I want, the romance promised in your auction package."

"My mother's auction package," he corrected. "I had nothing to do with it. She planned the entire thing. I'm just her damned puppet."

Why didn't that surprise her? "Whatever. I want us to be civil, to show folks that there are no hard feelings. Reputation is everything in yacht building, and I don't want any rumors of dissention inside the company spreading or Dean's will lose business. If you have any problems with me or my work, then I'd prefer you keep them to yourself until we're away from prying eyes."

He swore. A muscle in his jaw twitched. "I'm sorry if I hurt you. If we could go back—"

If he'd hurt her? She choked a humorless laugh at the absurdity of his comment and held up a hand, halting his words. "Would you still leave?"

He raked his fingers through his hair, stared across the water. Ten seconds ticked past and then he exhaled. "Yes."

Somehow she managed not to stagger under the impact of his reply. Clay couldn't possibly know how badly he'd hurt and humiliated her eight years ago. She would never give him—or any other man for that matter—the power to do so again. Never.

"That's all I need to know. I'll see you Monday, Clay."

Two

Traversing the wide sidewalk leading from the docks to Dean Yachts on Monday morning felt like coming home. But home was somewhere Clay no longer belonged.

Perched high on a grassy knoll overlooking the Cape Fear River, the sales and marketing division looked more like an expensive beach house than the main offices of Dean Yachts. When he reached the front doors Clay turned. From this vantage point he could see the entire operation.

A series of pale blue metal buildings in a range of shapes and sizes spread along a half-mile section of the riverfront property. Each building housed a specific stage of production, and Clay had worked in every one of them in one capacity or another beginning in his early teens. Both his grandfather and his father believed in learning the business from the ground up.

During Clay's absence murals of various Dean Yachts'

models had been painted on the waterfront sides of the structures giving the impression of a life-size parade of boats heading into port.

Docks, some covered, some not, jutted from the shoreline. The slips held yachts nearing completion. Unless things had changed in eight years, the dock located directly behind the sales office was reserved for finished vessels awaiting delivery. His and one other occupied the slips.

Clay let his gaze run over the complex again and sadness weighted him like ballast. He'd once taken pride in knowing that one day all this would be his. But not anymore. He'd forfeited everything when he'd run from the truth.

Shaking off the bitter memory and the resulting sense of anger, betrayal and disappointment, he shoved open the wide glass door, stepped inside the reception area and jerked to a halt. Nothing looked the same. What once had been a dim, utilitarian entrance now looked as classy as the stateroom of a fine yacht. Sunlight streamed through the windows and skylights onto a gleaming teak floor. A gracefully curved reception counter had replaced the old metal desk, and beyond that a glass wall blocked the wide hall leading to the offices.

The young woman seated behind the desk looked up and flashed him a smile that could sell toothpaste. "Good morning, sir. May I help you?"

"I'm Clayton Dean."

Her smile dimmed a few watts and she sat up straighter. "One moment please. I'll let Ms. Montgomery know you're here. You're welcome to have a seat while you wait."

A flip of her hand indicated the leather seating group against the wall. Another change. "No need. I'll find her."

The woman sprang from her chair and blocked his path. "I'm sorry, Mr. Dean, you'll have to wait until Ms. Montgomery gives you clearance."

What? "Clearance?"

"You'll need a security pass." She punched a button on the gadget clipped to her belt and spoke quietly into her nearly invisible headset receiver. "Mr. Dean has arrived."

Had he stepped into the *Twilight Zone?* When he'd left eight years ago Dean's hadn't had any security other than locking the buildings at night and occasional drive-by from the sheriff's department. This morning the back door closest to the dock—the entrance Clay had used since he was a kid—had been locked, and yesterday he'd had a sticky encounter with several members of the security crew when he'd taken his motorcycle out for supplies and to arrange for delivery of a rental car. They'd called his mother before letting him pass back through the gate.

"She'll be right with you, Mr. Dean." The receptionist punctuated her words with another high-wattage smile.

Clay couldn't sit. This building held too many memories. Good ones. Bad ones. A flicker of movement drew his attention to the glass wall. Andrea strode down the hall. Her figure-skimming sage-green suit was as professional as Saturday night's black dress had been drop-dead sexy. She'd twisted her thick blond hair up onto her head revealing the long, pale line of her throat. The polished woman before him was the antithesis of the unsure girl he'd left behind.

A section of the glass glided open. "Thanks, Eve. I'll take it from here. Good morning, Clay. Please come with me."

Andrea's gaze briefly hit his and then she headed back the way she'd come before he had a chance to reply. His gaze automatically shifted to the curve of her hips as he followed her down the hall. She'd always had a killer walk. Her perfume tantalized him. It wasn't the sweet flowery scent he remembered. This fragrance had a spicy and alluring kick to it.

He cursed his response. Rekindling the old flame was out of the question. He could not stay in Wilmington and face the lie that continued to erode his pilings on a daily basis.

Had his father kept his word? Clay couldn't ask and doubted he'd get an honest answer if he did. How could he trust anything his father said anymore? How could he trust himself with that DNA?

His muscles dragged like metal against rust-covered metal as they approached his father's office. Struggling to get a handle on the emotions welling inside him, Clay paused in the corridor. He clenched and unclenched his hands as memories assailed him.

The last time he'd taken this walk he'd been on top of the world. He'd come home from the University of New Orleans a day early to ask his father to go with him to buy Andrea's engagement ring, and then he'd opened the door without knocking and his world had crashed.

Determined to face yet another specter from his past Clay forced himself forward. Every stick of the old office furniture—including the damned couch where Clay had found his father screwing Andrea's mother—had been replaced with expensive-looking classic pieces.

He caught Andrea's guarded gaze and noted her pinched expression. Did she know what had happened right here under her nose? She and her mother had always had an enviably close relationship, the kind of link he'd never shared with his father. If Andrea didn't know about the affair, she'd be just as disillusioned by her mother's behavior as he had been by his father's. He wouldn't do that to her.

He jerked his head toward the door. "What's with all the new security?"

"We're protecting our assets. Our base-price yachts cost

a million dollars. Most of the models we build far exceed that. We can't risk vandalism or theft." She gestured for him to take a seat behind the cherry desk and tapped on a sheaf of papers waiting on the blotter with a pale pink—not red like Saturday night—fingernail. "I need you to read and sign these."

He remained standing, but lifted the pages and read a few paragraphs. Surprise forced his head up. "What is this?"

"A noncompete clause. Nothing you see or learn here can be used to compete against Dean designs."

"You're joking."

"No, I'm not. You're a naval architect with your own design firm, but temporarily you're an employee here. We have to take precautions against our ideas being pirated."

Fury boiled in his veins at the insult to his ethics. He fought to contain it. "You expect me to run the place, but this," he rattled the sheets, "says you don't trust me."

Her lips firmed and her chin lifted. "It's a business decision, Clay. Emotion doesn't enter into it."

Bitterness filled his mouth. *He* wasn't the cheat in his family. "My father's idea?"

A defiant glint entered her eyes and a flush rose in her pale cheeks. "No. Mine."

That doused his anger like nothing else could. He had no right to complain. He'd earned Andrea's distrust. He skimmed the pages, scratched his name across the line at the bottom of the page and passed the document to her.

She nodded acceptance. "I've left the current order summary and a packet of info to reacquaint you with the company in your in-box. You'll need to familiarize yourself with our existing client roster since they're allowed to drop in at anytime to check the status of their project. I'd suggest you look through those documents until Fran, your administrative assistant arrives. She comes in at nine. Her office is through here." She shoved open a door on the starboard side of the room.

Andrea acted like a car show model—gesturing stiffly here and there, making minimal eye contact, but he noticed the slight tremor of the pages she held. Another needle of regret stabbed him. He and Andrea had once been as comfortable together as two lovers could be.

"When Fran arrives she'll make your security ID and fit you with the necessary safety equipment. You'll need to swipe the ID card to access the controlled areas and the front gate. We have one delivery tomorrow and another next week. Both are noted on your calendar. There's quite a bit of hoopla attached to delivery celebrations. Again, Fran will fill you in.

"I've scheduled a production walk-through at three this afternoon for you. My office is still where it used to be if you need anything." She headed for the door.

"Andrea." He waited until she turned. "I won't work in here. My office is out there." He pointed toward the wide window overlooking the water. *The Expatriate,* one of his own designs, rocked beside the dock to the rear of the sales office.

Her eyebrows dipped. "You expect me to trot out to the dock every time I need to speak to you?"

"Either that or call my cell phone." He extracted a business card from his wallet and wrote his cell number on it. He passed it to her and their fingers brushed. The contact hit him like a bolt of lightning.

Strictly business, Dean.

"I'll see if I can have maintenance run a phone line to your boat."

"You said my assistant's name is Fran. Your mother changed positions?"

"No. Mom doesn't work here anymore. She left years ago."

Good. One less ghost he'd have to face.

Day One. Six hours successfully behind her, and three more, including Clay's tour, to get through before Andrea could call it a day.

As she made her way down the dock to Clay's "office" after lunch she ran an assessing gaze over the sleek lines of the fifty-foot sport-fishing vessel. Nice. Habit and just plain good manners forced her to remove her heels before ascending the ramp to Clay's boat rather than risk damaging his deck.

Andrea usually reserved her finer suits for delivery celebrations. When a customer accepted ownership of their new yacht the Dean's sales staff wined and dined them with a champagne feast. There wasn't an event today, but she'd had an attack of vanity this morning knowing this was Clay's first day on the job.

Before she entered the production buildings later this afternoon to reintroduce Clay to the area managers she'd have to dig her rubber-soled deck shoes out from under her desk. It wouldn't be the first time she'd worn a designer suit with her Docksides. If she'd been less vain she'd be wearing the boat shoes now instead of carrying her heels.

She spotted Clay through the glass-topped door leading to the salon. His laptop sat open and ignored on one end of the galley table he'd turned into a desk while he flipped through a stack of familiar brochures—brochures she'd designed.

A combination of anxiety and pride eddied through her.

Dean Yachts had come a long way since he'd left, and Andrea was proud to have been instrumental in the change. Old school practices still reigned over modern technology in the production department, but that was because hand-crafted workmanship was part of Dean's appeal. No mass production here. But Joseph had allowed her to update the way they interacted with the public. She'd poured her heart into the Web page, the reception area, the offices and the brochures in Clay's hands.

She tapped on the glass and Clay looked up. His cobalt-blue gaze locked with hers, momentarily impeding her ability to breathe. *Damn. It. Control yourself.*

He rose and crossed the room. Ignoring the stretch of his white short-sleeved polo shirt over his wide shoulders and muscular chest should have been easy, considering what he'd put her through, but it wasn't. Nor could she overlook the way his pants fit his lean hips and long legs. It wasn't fair that she still found him attractive after all the time and heartache she'd wasted on him. But she'd get over it.

The door opened, jarring her back to the present with a waft of cool air-conditioned air. Until then she'd been too antsy to notice the cloying June heat and humidity. Both were a fact of life on the Wilmington waterfront.

She cleared her throat. "May I come in? We need to discuss the image we intend to convey to the reporter. I realize this is work time and we shouldn't discuss personal issues, but I have plans for this evening."

Plans that included a pint of death by chocolate ice cream and a strategy phone call to Juliana and Holly, her partners in the auction scheme. She also needed to make sure Holly—who'd been reluctant about the whole bachelor auction idea—had bought the firefighter Andrea and Juliana had chosen from the program for her.

She didn't know how Clay did it, but without moving a muscle he seemed more alert, more wary. "What reporter?"

"Didn't you know the local paper is chronicling each auction couple for the duration of the dating package?"

He shoved a hand through his already disheveled hair and moved away from the door. She stepped through and closed it behind her.

"No. My mother shanghaied me as soon as I docked. I spent Saturday afternoon being fitted for a tux and arrived at the club minutes before I hit the stage—too late to read the hype and the fine print. Mom didn't tell me about the reporter or even what my date package involves. All I know about it is what I could hear of the emcee's spiel to the crowd."

Glancing around the cabin, Andrea took in the smoky gray leather seating and the rich cherry wood. Nice. Elegant, but masculine. She gestured to his laptop computer. "Do you have Internet access?"

"Yes. Wireless."

"May I?" At his nod she typed in a Web address. A few clicks later she read aloud, "The lucky lady who wins bachelor thirteen will be treated to Seven Seductive Sunsets, including an old-fashioned carriage ride through the historic section of town, horseback riding on a local beach, a riverboat dinner cruise, a hot air balloon ride, dinner and dancing at Devil's Shoals Steakhouse, a daylong sailing adventure and a private bonfire on the beach."

Was Clay swearing under his breath? She couldn't be certain because he turned and marched into the galley. A second later he returned and shoved a bottle of water in her direction.

"Are you willing to skip the dates? I'll reimburse you what you paid for the package."

"Try explaining that to the reporter. Bad press."

His jaw muscles flexed. "There's no way out of this?"

"Dating me didn't used to be a hardship." Andrea mentally kicked herself. Nothing like showing your damaged ego.

"No. It wasn't."

Her gaze bounced back to Clay's and her heart missed a beat at the intensity in his eyes. *Don't do it. Don't get sucked under. Tempt him, but keep your distance.* She dampened her lips and belatedly accepted the water from him. The chilled bottle helped her regain her focus.

"But that was then. Now we're two professionals who stand to gain quite a bit of publicity for our respective businesses if we conduct ourselves appropriately."

His lips thinned. "That's what this is to you? A publicity stunt?"

"That and an opportunity for us to put the past behind us and move on." She gestured to the salon and galley. "This looks quite…homey."

He leaned his hip against the galley counter and crossed his ankles, drawing her attention to his leather deck shoes worn without socks, and the sprinkling of dark hair peeking out from beneath the hem of his pants. "That's because it is home."

"For now, you mean."

He shook his head. "I live on *The Expatriate*."

"Permanently?" She couldn't conceal her surprise.

"Yes."

She curled her bare toes into the lush cream-colored carpeting and shifted her weight from one foot to the other as she scanned the interior again looking for signs of a feminine occupant. "Will we need a gate pass for anyone else on board?"

"I live alone."

Relief rushed over her—relief she had no business feeling. "Have you ever owned a home? Besides a boat, I mean."

They'd once talked of buying a house on the beach with a long expanse of sand on which their dogs and children could run. She'd bought the house, but lacked the children and pets. Having recently turned thirty she'd decided that if she wanted those factors to change—and she did—then she had to get the ball rolling.

His jaw hardened. "I had an apartment over a marina when I first moved to Miami. After I designed and commissioned my first yacht I moved on board. I've been living on the water ever since."

"That certainly makes it easy to move." She bit her imprudent tongue when his eyes hardened.

"Easy to leave, you mean?"

Be nice. Do not pick a fight. "That's not what I said."

"You want to take off the gloves?"

"I beg your pardon?"

His gaze drifted from the V-neck of her pantsuit to her bare feet and back to her eyes. Sensation rippled in the wake of his thorough inspection and ended up tangling in a knot behind her naval. "You're clenching your fingers and even your toes. Are you spoiling for a fight, Andrea?"

"Of course not," she answered quickly—too quickly, judging by his raised eyebrow. She hated that he could read her so easily. Exhaling slowly, she made a conscious effort to loosen her grip on the water bottle and her shoes.

When did you lose control of this meeting? Make your point and leave.

"We need a strategy for our interviews. It's important to hide any tension between us from Octavia Jenkins. She's a small-town reporter with big-city aspirations, and she's willing to dig up dirt when necessary."

His eyes narrowed. "You have dirt?"

Other than a long list of loser dates and an on again, off again relationship with a Dean's client? "Me? No. My life's an open book. You?"

He hesitated. "Not personally."

What did that mean? For the first time she wondered if something or someone besides her had driven Clay from Wilmington. But no. She had to go with the facts as she knew them. Clay's mother might buy the story that he'd left home because he couldn't get along with his father, but Andrea didn't believe it for one second. The Dean men had argued hard and often. Everyone claimed it was because they were too much alike. But their bond had been strong despite the bickering.

Clay drank from his bottle and then wiped the back of his hand over his mouth. "Andrea, we were lovers. If Jenkins is as ambitious as you said, she's not going to have to do much digging to uncover that."

"No. But it's not like that's news to anyone who matters."

Pensive furrows carved his brow and a nerve twitched beside his mouth. "How aggressive is she?"

"I don't know. Why?" What kind of secrets did he have?

A shake of his head was her only reply.

Andrea moved away from the computer and glanced down the companionway. Clay's bedroom. Her steps faltered, her pulse quickened and her knees weakened. Why did being ten paces from Clay's berth still get to her? She had no intention of tumbling back into his bed. But an old familiar ache filled her belly.

Nostalgia. That's all it is. Ignore it.

She had to get out of here even though they hadn't settled on a story to feed Octavia Jenkins yet.

"We'll talk later about the reporter. I have a conference call in a few minutes. I'll see you in an hour for the production walk-through."

Clay snapped his cell phone closed and dragged a hand over his face. The pushy journalist had laid waste to his plan to delay the dates as long as possible. If the Miami headhunters found an interim CEO quickly, then he'd have been able to return home without fulfilling his end of the auction bargain.

Cowardly? Probably. But he didn't know if he could date Andrea, spend hours with her by candlelight and firelight and walk away again. No, he wasn't still in love with her, but he was far too attracted to her for his peace of mind. Falling for her again would be too easy. But nothing had changed. In fact, his inability to stick with one woman more than a few months since leaving Andrea reinforced the fact that he might be like his father and incapable of fidelity.

He checked his watch. Damn. Late for his meeting with Andrea. He snatched up the safety glasses required anywhere on the property other than this dock and the sales building and left his yacht behind. Andrea met him at the end of the sidewalk.

How could a woman look attractive in bulky safety glasses and rubber-soled shoes? And yet Andrea did.

Clay shoved on his glasses and cursed his errant hormones. "Sorry to keep you waiting. Phone call. Can you change your plans for tonight?"

Eyes wide, her head whipped toward him. "Why?"

He accompanied her through the security gate and across the pavement toward the first metal building. "Because the reporter is demanding an interview to discuss our first date. That means we need to have one unless you want to blow her off."

"We can't do that." She dipped her head and tugged at her earlobe. Years ago that had been a sign that she was uncomfortable. Was it still?

"I suppose I could." She looked about as excited as she would if he'd invited her to spend the evening in a mosquito-infested swamp without bug repellant.

"The dinner cruise has an opening tonight. Where do you live?"

"I have a house on Wrightsville Beach."

Regret needled him. Eight years ago they'd discussed buying a house on the beach together. "I'll pick you up at seven. The boat sails at seven-thirty. I'll need directions to your place before you leave."

"I'd rather meet you there. That will give both of us more time to get ready."

The door to the building opened before he could reply. Andrea greeted the man and then turned to Clay.

"You remember Peter Stark, don't you? He's our production manager now."

"Good to see you again, Peter." Clay offered his hand. The man hesitated long enough before shaking Clay's hand to make his lack of welcome known without being flagrantly rude.

The cold shoulder shouldn't have surprised Clay but it did. Peter had been Clay's mentor-slash-babysitter from the first day Clay had set foot on Dean's soil. The man's allegiance clearly belonged to Andrea now.

"How's it going, Peter?" Andrea asked.

"Right on schedule except for those cabinets." Peter addressed Andrea. "The fancy wood the owner requested isn't in."

"I'll make a—" Andrea stopped and glanced at Clay as if realizing that would be his job now. "Clay can call the distributor to check status when we get back to the office."

"We could make do with mahogany," Pete insisted.

"My grandfather always said, 'The customer's not paying us to make do. He's paying us to make what he ordered.'" Clay lived by the quote since his clients often made illogical design requests.

"Yeah, well the wood's holding up everything else in line."

"I'll get on it before I leave today. If all else fails, we'll cancel the order and go with my suppliers."

"Your daddy won't like that," Peter challenged. "We've dealt with this company for twenty years."

"My father's not running the show right now. I am. If a company can't deliver, then we'll find one that can—just like our customers will if we don't give them what they've asked for. If the holdup is a problem, then shift the line. Bump the next order in front of this one. I'll make sure the client understands the delay."

The scene repeated itself as they circled the facility and Clay reacquainted himself with familiar faces. Employees addressed Andrea. She redirected them to Clay. By the time they left the building Clay wondered why his mother had begged him to come home. The employees trusted Andrea. They didn't trust him.

Considering he'd left town rather than live a lie or risk failing Andrea the way his father had failed his mother, the lack of trust rubbed salt in an open wound.

Three

If they had to date, then Clay had decided he'd choose the least romantic in the package first. How intimate could a three-hour cruise on a riverboat carrying four hundred people be?

He gave himself a proverbial pat on the back as he followed Andrea and the hostess the length of the brightly lit main salon of the *Georgina* past a laden buffet and tables crowded with families, including boisterous children. Treating this date like a client dinner would be a piece of cake in this setting. They'd probably even have to share a table with strangers.

But instead of showing them to one of the eight-person tables, the hostess stopped in front of a glass-and-brass elevator located at the stern of the ship. They entered the cubicle. Clay caught a glimpse of the second floor as the clear box drifted upward. The lighting on the second level was a little dimmer. A DJ occupied a small stage. Most of the patrons looked like college kids. Nothing he couldn't handle even though he'd given up keg parties years ago.

But the elevator kept rising until it reached the third floor. Clay's stomach sank faster than an anchor. He'd congratulated himself too soon.

The setting sun on the western horizon cast a peachy glow over the upper deck's glass-domed atrium. No more than a dozen widely spaced tables for two occupied the area surrounding a parquet dance floor. At the far end of the enclosure a trio of musicians occupied a small stage.

The doors opened with a ding, and the wail of the sax greeted them. Clay had learned to like jazz during his years at the University of New Orleans, but sultry jazz combined with Andrea in a sexy black dress jeopardized his plan to keep the date on a business footing.

"Mr. Dean?" The hostess held open the doors. Her tone and expression implied it wasn't the first time she'd called him. "I need to seat you. We'll be underway in five minutes."

With a growing sense of unease Clay followed Andrea and the hostess to a table tucked into the far corner. No buffet. No crowds. No noisy kids. No distractions.

Too intimate. He seated Andrea and then himself. The linen-draped table was small enough for him to reach across and hold her hand if he wanted. Which he didn't.

A waitress filled their water goblets, promised to return with champagne and departed.

"Not what you were expecting?" Andrea asked.

How could she still read him after eight years? "I didn't know what to expect. My mother made the arrangements for each date. All I do is choose a day and time." He sipped his water, but the cool liquid stopped short of the burn low in his gut. "The riverboat wasn't here when I left."

"No. She's only been here a few years. The owners brought her in as part of the downtown renewal project."

"There have been a lot of changes." And not just in his hometown.

It should have been impossible for Andrea to look more beautiful tonight than she had in the siren's dress at the auction, but she did. Sunlight sparkled on her loose honey-colored hair, and she'd smudged her eye makeup, giving her a just-out-of bed look that played havoc with his memories. Her silky black wraparound dress swished just above her knees and dipped low between her breasts, hinting at the curves beneath, but revealing nothing except the fact that she wasn't wearing a bra.

He swallowed another gulp of water and wished he hadn't noticed the slight sway beneath the fabric when she'd greeted him at the bottom of the gangplank. But hell, he was a man, and there were some things a guy just couldn't miss. Unrestrained breasts ranked high on that list. His list anyway.

The powerful engines of the riverboat rumbled to life. Clay relished the slight vibration. Some liked the silent glide of sailboats, but he preferred the leashed power and throaty growl of an engine. The boat maneuvered away from the dock and headed up river.

Clay focused on the safe view of the shore rather than the more dangerous one of the woman across from him. The tall pines on the bank were a far cry from the sand, palms and towering waterfront buildings of Miami. He'd become so accustomed to glass, brick and modern construction that he'd forgotten how impressive raw nature could be. The dark green of the treetops and the layers of red and yellow in the riverbank resembled a painting.

The waitress returned, poured the champagne and vanished, leaving a silver ice bucket behind.

Andrea sipped from her flute and stared through the glass at the passing scenery as the sun sank lower. "Wilmington will never be as cosmopolitan as Miami, but it is modernizing."

Clay ignored his champagne. If he hoped to get through tonight without regrets, then he had to keep a clear head. The last thing he needed was alcohol. He rated his chances of avoiding the dance floor and body contact as slim to none. Andrea used to love dancing. She'd even taken ballroom dancing as a physical education class in college.

"Why did you attend the auction?" He forced the question through a constricting throat.

She blinked at his question and hesitated before answering. "Besides the fact that your mother and Juliana's were the event organizers and Holly, Juliana and I were informed that our attendance was mandatory?"

He'd suspected his mother's part in this fiasco would come up eventually. Had she put Andrea up to this? It seemed likely. His mother had adored Andrea, but if Mom was matchmaking, then she was doomed to disappointment. "Yes. Besides that."

Andrea shrugged, drawing his attention to her bare, lightly tanned arms and shoulders. The pencil-thin straps of her dress didn't cover nearly enough skin. "Holly, Juliana and I each turn thirty this year, and we gain control of our trust funds. We don't need the money because we all work and we're well paid, so we decided to invest some and donate the rest to a good cause. The charity auction seemed like a fun idea."

She'd hung with the same crowd since high school. He'd severed his friendships when he'd left town because he hadn't wanted anyone telling him who Andrea had chosen to replace him. Any one of his buddies would have been eager to fill his shoes. "Your friends bought men, too?"

"Yes. Tell me about your company," she said after the waitress served the salads and departed.

"Seascape recruited me during college. Rod Forrester, the owner and an established yacht designer, wanted someone who could buy him out when he was ready to retire. I signed on as an intern, and he taught me the practical side of the business the University of New Orleans couldn't. Rod retired last year."

Andrea's foot bumped his ankle beneath the tiny table. A spark of need ignited and spiraled up Clay's thigh. "Excuse me. Seascape is doing well?"

"Very. Rod was more open-minded than Dad. I never would have won the awards for innovative design working at Dean Yachts." Bitterness crept into his tone.

For several seconds Andrea's caramel-colored gaze studied him. "Your father's not as close-minded as he used to be."

"I like the changes I've seen. Who should I credit for prying him loose from the tar gluing his feet in the past?"

She shrugged. "Me. I told him we either moved forward or we'd be left behind. It helped when business increased along with our marketing expenditures and in doing so validated my push for change."

His opinion of Andrea climbed another notch—something he couldn't afford. She'd managed to change his father's stubborn mind, something Clay hadn't been able to do. Clay and his father had battled over Clay's "newfangled" ideas and every suggestion for improvement Clay had made had been dismissed.

The band launched into an up-tempo song and other couples took the floor. Clay did his best to ignore them. He couldn't ignore the subtle sway of Andrea's body as she moved her shoulders to the music. Her gaze drifted toward the dancers several times as she finished her salad.

He felt like a heel. He might resent being forced to participate in the auction, but Andrea had paid big bucks for these dates, and he had no right to cheat her. She deserved to get something for her money. Dancing with her would be tough, but he could handle it. He squared his shoulders and stood.

"Shall we?"

Andrea's head tipped back and her hair cascaded over her shoulders. Eyes wide, she dampened her parted lips. Heat unfurled in Clay's belly, and he regretted his invitation, but it was too late to retract it. Andrea's fingers curled around his. Awareness traveled up his arm like a mild electric current.

He led her toward the small parquet square and then he turned, rested one hand on her waist and laced the fingers of his other hand through hers. She stepped into his arms, and *damn,* she fit as if she'd never left.

Her palm burned against his and the heat of her skin permeated the fabric of her dress. He'd forgotten how good she felt in his arms. And he didn't want to remember now. He searched his mind for a diversion. "Tell me about the delivery tomorrow."

"The caterers will arrive to set up at eleven. A champagne luncheon will be served at noon. The party lasts as long as it lasts. At that point the customer calls the shots. Sometimes they board the boat and leave immediately. Sometimes they hang around hours or days while they familiarize themselves with how everything works. Wear a suit tomorrow."

"I remember." He twirled her under his arm. She stepped back into his embrace without missing a beat. Just like old times. Her scent filled his lungs. A strand of her hair snagged on his evening beard. He jerked his head back.

Focus. On. Work. "I haven't had a chance to look at the schedule yet. Who's the client?"

A smile glimmered in her eyes and danced on her lips. "Toby Haynes."

Clay frowned. "The race car driver?"

"Yes. This is his third Dean yacht."

The news that NASCAR's most notorious playboy would be onsite tomorrow distracted Clay from the brush of Andrea's thighs against his, but not enough to stem his reaction to holding her close and knowing only a couple of inches and a few thin pieces of fabric separated him from Andrea's bare skin. He blamed his reaction on abstinence.

He'd broken up with Rena five months ago after she'd thrown a tantrum when he'd given her a sapphire necklace instead of an engagement ring for Christmas. He hadn't misled her because he'd told her up front that he wasn't looking for marriage, but the nasty breakup had left a bitter taste in his mouth. He hadn't dated since. A waiting list of design requests kept his evenings busy. Work was a demanding, but reliable mistress.

Clay glanced at the table. The food—and his excuse for escape—hadn't arrived. "Repeat customers are good."

Andrea's tender smile unsettled him. "Yes and Toby's always fun. He's very hands-on through every stage of production, and since each yacht takes almost a year to complete we see a lot of him. The staff looks forward to his visits."

Had he been hands-on with Andrea? Did she look forward to his visits? An ember in Clay's gut smoldered. *Don't go there, man. You gave up your claim eight years ago.* But he couldn't deny the flicker of jealousy and that pissed him off.

He twirled her again, but Clay wasn't concentrating on his footwork. This time he stepped forward when he should have gone backward. He collided with Andrea. He banded his arms around her to steady her and her soft curves molded against him. His lungs and heart stalled. Every cell in his body snapped to attention. It would be so easy to temporarily forget the demons that had driven him away.

Andrea gasped. Her golden gaze locked with his. Her breath swept his chin. The music played on, but Clay couldn't break free of the magnetic pull to resume the dance. Holding Andrea in his arms felt like coming home.

His lips found hers without him consciously making the decision to kiss her. Sensation sparkled through his veins like a shaken magnum of champagne and his fingers tightened on her waist. His tongue swept over her bottom lip and into the warmth of her mouth. She tasted familiar. How could he remember her flavor after all this time?

She melted into him, meeting him halfway, testing and tangling, stroking. His tongue. His back. His memory. She matched him kiss for passionate kiss, and damn, she tasted good. Silky, sweet and hot, with a hint of champagne. A groan rumbled from his chest as hunger overpowered him.

Her palms splayed on his back under his jacket. The rasp of her nails hit him like a match to dry kindling, inflaming him. He cupped her hips, pulling her even closer. A roar filled his ears. His pulse? The wind?

Applause.

Clay jerked back. The couples around them clapped as the band finished a song, but several diners aimed their indulgent smiles in Clay and Andrea's direction.

Dammit. Dammit. Dammit. Coming home was a

mistake. He couldn't erase the past, and he sure as hell didn't want to revisit it.

He'd never survive ripping his heart out a second time.

Oh God, I'm not over him.

Yes, you are. Andrea silently argued with the voice in her head. Her hormones remembered. That's all.

She was *over* Clayton Dean.

Totally.

She stepped back, mentally and physically separating herself from the man and the memories swamping her. At the same time she filed away the information that her libido had only been hibernating. Good to know since she'd feared that switch had been permanently flipped into the off position.

Battling light-headedness and a racing pulse, she took a shaky breath and fought the urge to cover her hot cheeks. Instead, she hid her clenched fists in the full skirt of her dress. "Our dinner is waiting."

Clay's closed expression revealed nothing. He gestured for her to precede him to the table. Andrea crossed the room on unsteady legs.

One day. One blasted day and already her plan had sprung a leak. Where had she gone wrong? She condemned her traitorous body for ignoring her carefully mapped out plans. She was supposed to make Clay want her not vice versa, but there was no denying the fizz in her blood or the flush on her skin, and her reaction had nothing to do with the champagne in her glass.

Falling for Clay was a dead end street she refused to travel again. If he expected to temporarily resume the physical relationship they'd shared eight years ago, then he was ringing the wrong bell. *Temporary* had been excised from her vocabulary. She wanted forever this time. But not with Clay. She'd never trust his promises again.

As she slid into her chair she blinked in surprise. When had the tiny white lights outlining the frame of the atrium been turned on? She'd been too caught up in Clay to notice. The twinkling bulbs gave the impression of dining beneath a starlit sky. Romantic. Too romantic. But escape from the boat was impossible since they were somewhere in the middle of the Cape Fear River, and hurling herself overboard wouldn't be wise.

She surreptitiously checked her watch. Two more hours to get through. Determined to devote her full attention to her prime rib, she draped her napkin across her lap.

"Should I apologize?"

The huskily voiced question made her heart stumble. She lifted her head with a jerk. Regret filled Clay's deep blue eyes, and for some stupid reason that stung.

Had she expected him to suddenly realize he'd made a mistake by leaving her and declare his undying love? Of course not. She wanted closure, not a new beginning. She needed a man she could count on, one who wouldn't let her down. Clay had abandoned his responsibilities *and her* without looking back.

She forced a smile to her lips and a lightness she didn't feel into her voice. "Apologize for a kiss? Heavens no, Clay. We've shared hundreds of those in the past. But we work together now, so no more of that, okay?"

Clay excelled at running. And he hated himself for it. Not the physical sport which kept him in shape, but the mental gymnastics of avoiding a confrontation that could lead to nothing but trouble.

His feet pounded the pavement as his brain hammered

out the issue. This morning he'd run from Dean Yachts, from Andrea standing alone on the back deck of the sales office with a mug in her hands and her face turned toward the sunrise. He'd run from memories of the countless sunrises they'd shared on the deck of his old sloop and an aching need to spend more with her. He'd run from her casual dismissal of a kiss that had capsized him.

His burning lungs and the sweat pouring from his body told him he'd pushed himself too hard. Circling back, he made it halfway up the Dean driveway before the *thwump, thwump* of an approaching helicopter broke the morning silence. The craft swept over his head, aiming for the helipad beside the sales building—another new addition in the past eight years. Who could it be? Their customer wasn't due for four more hours.

Clay reached the parking lot as three male passengers, each carrying duffel bags, jumped from the helicopter. One waved and Andrea, still on the deck of the sales building, waved back. Even from a hundred yards Clay couldn't miss the smile covering her face. She used to smile that way for him. The thought sucker punched him.

"Andi!" the waving visitor called loud enough to be heard over the rotors and Clay grimaced. The guy must not know how much she hated the nickname, but Andrea's grin widened and she headed toward the helipad.

Clay picked up his pace.

Andrea met the visitors halfway across the lawn. The man leading the pack dropped his bag, snatched her into a hug and swung her off the ground, and then he planted a kiss right on Andrea's smiling lips.

Clay's steps faltered. His lungs weren't the only thing burning. His stomach joined in the party with jealousy he had no right to feel. Andrea wasn't his. Could never be his again.

And then he recognized their guests and the blowtorch in his gut intensified. Toby Haynes and his entourage.

With the NASCAR pretty boy's arm still looped around her waist, Andrea greeted each of the other men and then turned toward the offices. She spotted Clay and her smile faded.

Clay closed the distance between them as the helicopter lifted off. Once the noise and wind died down Andrea said, "Clay, meet Toby Haynes, Bill Riley, his captain, and Stu Cane, his first mate. Gentlemen, this is Clayton Dean. He'll be filling in for his father today."

Haynes sized him up and offered a handshake. "Hey, man. How is your dad?"

Clay's stiffening muscles had nothing to do with his run. He didn't like the guy coiled around Andrea like a boa constrictor. And he didn't know the answer to Haynes's question.

Andrea filled the breach. "Joseph is recovering nicely. He's sorry he can't make it today, but he'll call later if Patricia will let him near a phone. She's trying to keep him from getting entangled with work. He's only allowed one phone call per day."

Clay's belly sank lower. His father had called every day since Clay arrived, and Clay had refused to take his calls.

"I look forward to hearing from Joe," Haynes said. "Won't be the same without him here."

What was with this guy and nicknames? No one called his father Joe.

"You're early." Clay ground out the words. Where had his famed diplomacy gone? Rod had sworn Clay had the coolest head in a crisis of anyone he'd ever worked with. The cool head wasn't in evidence today.

Haynes's smile didn't waver. "Couldn't stay away. Had to see my lady. Lucky I didn't come a'knockin' last night when we got in." He punctuated the statement by squeezing Andrea.

His lady? Did Haynes mean the boat or Andrea? Could be either since boats were referred to as female.

The driver nodded toward the dock. "So whose sweet baby is that in the slip behind *Checkered Flag 3?*"

"Mine," Clay replied through a clenched jaw.

"She's a beaut. Wanna show her off?"

Like he wanted a case of jock itch, but Clay's designs were his business. Personal likes and dislikes didn't enter into it. "Let me take a shower first."

"No need to pretty up on my account, Dean."

Andrea stood between them, her head following the byplay like a fan at a tennis match. Wariness and something Clay couldn't identify filled her eyes. "Toby, I still have loads to do. You guys can wait inside, or I can call Peter to give you a tour of *Checkered Flag 3*."

Clay would be damned if he'd let Haynes slobber over Andrea for the next four hours. "I'll take care of our customers."

Had he stressed the word *customer* too much?

"See there, angel. Dean junior has us covered. Do your thing, but don't you pretty up either. My eyes couldn't handle it if you were any more gorgeous."

Clay's jaw ached from gritting his teeth. Surely Andrea didn't buy this good ol' boy garbage?

"I'd love a tour, Dean. Starting with your boat. Then mine."

Clay swallowed the emotions boiling inside him. *He's a client.* "You look like a man who'd appreciate a high-performance yacht. Come on board."

Haynes kept pace beside him. His flunkies followed like ducks in a row. "Good lookin' lady."

Clay suspected Haynes meant Andrea—not a discussion

he intended to have. Not until he figured out what in the hell he was going to do with his gut-knotting reaction to Haynes touching her, kissing her. "My best design yet. She was built by a firm in Key West."

He rattled off the boat's specs as he gave his unwanted visitors a guided tour of the inside and then the outside. When they reached the bow Haynes tapped the waist-high fiberglass housing. "What's this?"

"My bike." Clay rocked back the white domed cover to reveal his Harley. He'd bought the motorcycle to celebrate buying out Rod. "I use a hydraulic davit to put her ashore."

Haynes ran his hands over the housing, the wench and motorcycle, caressing each like he would a woman. Not a thought Clay wanted to entertain. "Hot damn. Can my boat be outfitted for one of these?"

"Sure."

"How fast?"

"I'd have to check with the production team, and we'd need the specs for your bike. It's a custom-fitted housing."

"I have a couple of weeks. I scheduled to take that time off to be with Andi anyway." Clay's muscles seized. "I want you on the design team of my next boat. Your design and Dean's quality will make for one sweet baby."

Clay wouldn't be here, but there wasn't any point in revealing that detail. He secured his bike. He wanted this racing redneck off his boat before he knocked him over the rails. "Make yourself at home and help yourself to whatever's in the galley. After I shower I'll call Pete to see if we can accommodate your schedule."

Haynes waited for the other men to circle the starboard and then he turned and stopped, blocking Clay's path. "She's a special lady."

"I'm happy with *The Expatriate*."

"I meant Andrea."

Clay remained silent. It wasn't easy.

"But some bozo hurt her a while back, so she's gun-shy."

An iron first crushed Clay's heart. "That bozo was me."

Haynes smirked. "I know. Most of your employees have been here a *l-o-n-g* time. They saw how you hurt her and they're real protective of her. None of 'em is shy about warning a fella off." The race car driver's smile turned predatory. "Don't set your heart on taking up where you left off, Dean. I've been coaxing Andi for three years, and I don't aim to lose this race. She will be mine."

Clay's hackles rose at the challenge, but at the same time regret weighted him like ballast for the embarrassment he'd caused Andrea. She'd been working at Dean for a year when he'd left her, and they'd made no secret of their love before that. The employees knew he'd planned to marry her and that he hadn't.

But what in the hell was he supposed to do? He couldn't stand in the front of a church and promise to keep only unto Andrea till death do us part knowing that in the pews behind him sat two people who'd made a mockery of those vows and everything he believed in. If his parents' "perfect" marriage was a lie, then in what could he trust?

Staying in Wilmington had meant either lying for his father and concealing the affair, or revealing the sordid truth and breaking the hearts of the two women he loved the most— his mother and Andrea. So he'd run, because taking the dirty secret and leaving town would hurt both women less in the long run than his father's and her mother's betrayal would.

No, Clay realized, he couldn't have Andrea, but he'd be damned if he'd let this race car Romeo hurt her. From what he'd read in his sports magazines Haynes didn't park his car in anybody's garage long-term. He only made pit stops.

Andrea deserved a man who'd love her forever.

"If you haven't won her by now, Haynes, then you don't have what it takes. It's time for you to haul your car to another track."

Four

Sandwiched between the man she'd once loved and the man she thought she could love, Andrea struggled to keep her hands and voice steady.

This was her first yacht delivery without Joseph, and her mentor was counting on her to get it right. She wouldn't let him down. Thank heavens most of the work had been done ahead of time, because concentrating on the details of the celebration was nearly impossible under the circumstances.

How could she focus on her speech or the presentation of the flag signed by every employee who'd worked on Toby's boat with Clay glued to her side? Could he possibly stand any closer? Moving away didn't work because he shadowed her. His cologne, a refreshing blend of lime and sandalwood, permeated every breath she took. Their hands and hips bumped *again,* and her pulse stuttered just as it had the last dozen times.

And how could she help but compare the two men when Toby seemed determined to shoehorn himself between her and Clay? Both men were lean, muscular and just over six feet tall, but there the similarities ended. Clay's beaver-brown hair and blue eyes were shades darker than Toby's sandy hair and silvery eyes.

Toby was serious about his driving, but little else. He was always good for a laugh and a good time. Whereas Clay—the new Clay—seemed serious about everything. Where had his easy and seductive smiles gone? Not that she wanted to be seduced, but the intense way he looked at her now made her skin feel dry and other places…well, the opposite.

Damn. It. Attraction toward Clay was not part of her plan.

Her feelings for each of the men were so different. She'd loved Clay blindly and without reservation—the way only the young can. Her feelings for Toby on the other hand were more mature, more cautious. She accepted that he wasn't perfect, and he seemed willing to accept what she was willing to give. Not that she'd given him much yet.

While both Clay and Toby smiled and sounded courteous as they discussed elements of the yacht and the features Toby wanted Clay to add, there was an underlying tension crackling between them. They clearly didn't like each other, but why? Andrea looked from one man to the other, searching for clues.

As if he took her scrutiny as a sign of encouragement, Toby hooked an arm around her hip, pulling her away from Clay. He clinked his champagne flute against hers and then leaned closer.

"With Junior here to handle the company you can take your vacation after all, Andi." He didn't speak as quietly or intimately as she would have expected considering their foreheads touched. "I'm leaving the boat here so your boys can add a few more toys to it, but you and I can fly down to the Bahamas, party all night and stay in bed all day."

Andrea's mouth dried and her heart raced, but not with the anticipation she'd expected to feel. She didn't dare look over her shoulder to see what Clay thought of Toby's invitation. He had to have heard it as did everyone else in the vicinity.

A confusing swirl of emotions whipped through her. Toby was attractive, the poster boy of the NASCAR circuit, and when he kissed her she felt…*something*. Not explosions, but his kisses were pleasantly stimulating. Months ago she'd accepted his invitation to spend the two weeks after he took possession of his yacht cruising with him because she thought they could have a future together. They weren't lovers yet, but if Joseph hadn't had a stroke that would have changed tonight.

"Andrea is needed here," Clay said in an authoritative tone that rubbed Andrea like coarse grit sandpaper and snapped her to rigid attention.

She had no intention of leaving town. In fact, as soon as she'd heard Joseph's prognosis she'd called Toby and informed him that she needed to cancel because she couldn't leave Dean in limbo. But to have Clay demand she stay… Indignation flushed her skin. Couldn't he have asked?

She considered arguing just for the sake of arguing, but she wasn't going to leave, so what was the point? With her mind in turmoil over Clay's return and the lingering attraction she felt for him, she didn't want to commit to an intimate relationship with Toby at the moment. She refused to go to bed with one man when another monopolized most of her waking and sleeping thoughts.

She had to exorcise Clay before she could move

forward. Besides, she'd yet to accomplish any of the tasks she'd set for herself when she decided to buy him.

"Would you excuse us a moment, Toby?" She grabbed Clay's bicep, and his muscles flexed beneath her fingers. His body heat burned her palm through his silk shirt. It took an inordinate amount of concentration on her footing to lead him to the far corner of the reception hall without mishap because her leg muscles wanted to turn mushy. The moment she arrived she removed her hand and shifted her cool champagne glass to her hot palm. "My vacation has been scheduled for months. If I wanted to take it, I could."

"I would think your priorities have changed. Where's your allegiance to my father?"

"Where's yours?" How dare *he* question her dedication?

Anger darkened Clay's eyes and flattened his lips. "I'm here, aren't I?"

And eager to leave as soon as possible. The perfect solution popped into her brain. She leaned back on her heels and smiled. "I'll postpone my vacation if you'll call off your headhunters. Stay until Joseph's back on his feet and I'll do the same."

A nerve in Clay's jaw jumped. His nostrils flared. "You didn't used to be manipulative."

"I didn't have to be. Everything I wanted was mine for the asking." And now it wasn't. Not that she wanted to go back to being the spoiled girl she used to be. She'd found immense satisfaction in earning her rewards instead of having everything handed to her.

Clay's gaze swept the room and then seemingly focused on Toby. "You have yourself a deal. I'll stay, but don't forget we have the interview with that reporter you want to impress Thursday night and six more dates. Make sure you're available."

"I will be. Excuse me." Andrea returned to Toby. She could feel Clay right behind her. "I'm needed here while Joseph's out of commission, but I'll hold you to the rain check you promised."

Toby winked. "Gonna let me bunk at your place since you were gonna be bunking in mine?"

Clay stepped into her line of vision—one long, lean line of tense male. Disapproval radiated off him in waves. Why? There were no rules in the employee handbook prohibiting fraternization between staff and customers. She frowned at him and then, forcing a smile to her lips, turned back to Toby.

"And have you miss spending the first night on your new yacht? I wouldn't dream of it. Besides, *Checkered Flag 3* is stocked and ready to go. You and the guys can stay on board and eat some of that food. The Dean's crew will work around you."

Toby touched her cheek. "Then at least let me take you to dinner."

Clay's hand settled on her waist, startling her. "You can have her tonight, but tomorrow night she's mine. I guess Andrea forgot to mention she bought me and seven dates with me at a bachelor auction. We have another date tomorrow night."

And that's when understanding clicked into place. She was a bone and she'd just been pitched into a dog fight. But that made absolutely no sense because Clay didn't want her, a fact his eagerness to leave town made clear. So what was his problem?

Grouchier than hell from a lack of sleep, Clay paused his warm-up stretches the moment Andrea stepped out on the back deck of the sales building with a mug in her hand.

Her morning ritual, he'd discovered, included arriving an hour before the gates opened and sitting on the deck to enjoy the sunrise.

The sense of relief he felt that she hadn't spent the night on Haynes's boat only worsened Clay's foul mood. He had no business caring where she slept or with whom. But he did care, dammit. He wanted her to be happy, and a race car driver with a short attention span and a bad track record wasn't going to do the job.

He grabbed his water bottle and his shirt, and then vaulted from his deck to the dock and headed in her direction. His unrested muscles protested the move. He'd spent half the night tossing and turning, involuntarily listening for Haynes to return from his dinner date and wondering if Andrea would be "bunking" with the cocky jackass.

Each slap of the windswept waves against the bulkhead had reminded Clay of the days and nights he and Andrea had spent in the narrow berth of his sloop. Because both of them lived at home when they weren't sharing university dorm rooms with other students, privacy had been scarce and most of their lovemaking had taken place in the tiny airless cabin of his sailboat.

Did she ever think about the hot summer days and nights when they'd made love until sweat puddled on their skin?

Last night he couldn't think about anything else, and when he'd fallen asleep Technicolor reruns had streamed through his dreams.

"How's the view from your place?" he called out.

She spun abruptly in his direction. Another one of those curve-hugging suits outlined her figure, this one in a pale pink color that brought out the flush on her cheeks. The above the knee length of her skirt combined with a pair of dangerously high heels made her legs look seriously sexy. His pulse slapped like a flag in a gale force wind.

"Pardon me?"

Andrea had always had a thing about killer shoes. From what he'd observed that hadn't changed. With Herculean effort he winched his gaze upward over her legs, hips, narrow waist, breasts, raspberry lips and eventually reached her golden brown eyes.

"You're still hooked on sunrises. I'm guessing you bought your beach house for the view."

She sipped from her mug. Coffee, he guessed, from the scent mingling with her perfume on the morning air. "Good guess. And it's lovely, but not as peaceful as here."

The sweep of her hand encompassed a fish jumping, an egret taking flight from the opposite bank and a family of otters playing nearby. Her gaze coasted over his bare chest, down his torso and then his legs, making him damned glad he'd installed a home gym on *The Expatriate*. He tightened his fingers on the T-shirt he carried and hoped his thin running shorts would conceal his body's instantaneous reaction to her proximity. He'd been hard all night with no relief. Was it any surprise he'd spring eagerly back into action?

"Late night?" Haynes hadn't returned until two. Had he been with Andrea the entire time?

"That's none of your business, Clay, unless it affects my work."

"It is if you fall asleep on me. I've set up another date for this evening. We're going horseback riding on Holden Beach before meeting with Octavia Jenkins. I'll pick you up at six."

"No need. We can leave from here."

"What? You don't want me in your house?"

She hesitated a beat too long. "Not at all. My house

would be out of the way. I keep a set of casual clothes in my office."

He wanted to see her house, wanted to know if she'd built the one she'd planned so many years ago. He opened his mouth to insist on picking her up, but a wolf whistle from the dock interrupted. Clay didn't have to turn to know Haynes was awake.

"Don't let me keep you from your run, Clay," Andrea said, but her gaze and smile were directed at the car jockey.

Dismissed and pissed. Wasn't that a great way to start his day?

One more date down and her heart none the worse off, Andrea congratulated herself on Wednesday evening as she approached the parking area beside the stable where she and Clay had borrowed horses for their sunset ride on Holden Beach.

Screeching gulls, crashing surf and thundering hooves had made talking difficult, and since each of them had their own mounts there had been no touching and no sparks. Well, relatively no sparks.

She'd experienced a few flickers when a sexy motorcyclist wearing low-slung jeans, a snug white T-shirt and boots had pulled up beside her car in the gravel lot. She couldn't help checking out his wide-shouldered, lean-hipped, tight-butted form as he climbed from his bike, but then he'd removed his helmet and her stomach had hit rock bottom. Clay.

Because of Toby's upgrade request she'd known Clay owned a motorcycle, but she hadn't seen Clay's bike and her brain hadn't merged the pictures of Clay and a Harley. It was a sexy visual she could live very well without.

He'd breached her defenses twice today. This morning

he'd gotten to her with his bare, hair-dusted chest, six pack abs and skimpy running shorts. Not good. Not good at all. But this evening's sparks didn't count, did they, since she hadn't known who caused them until it was too late to douse them?

She spotted Octavia Jenkins waiting at the head of the trail and slowed her steps.

"Evening, folks," the reporter said. "I thought we'd do the interview right over there at the picnic table. I've already lit a couple of citronella candles to keep the mosquitoes away."

This is where they would find out how much of the past the reporter intended to rake up. Hoping Octavia would keep her article light and entertaining, Andrea crossed the wiry grass with dread weighting her feet. She sat at the table and Clay settled across from her. Their feet bumped beneath the scarred wood and her heart hiccupped.

No more of that.

Octavia flipped open her notebook and then turned to Andrea. "Is it difficult to work for a man you once thought you'd marry?"

Andrea froze with her hand midsweep through her tangled hair. So much for light and fun. She fought the urge to squirm on the bench of the picnic table, and she didn't dare look at Clay. "Th-that was a long time ago. Both Clay and I are more concerned with Joseph's rehabilitation and maintaining Dean's production schedule than we are with our former relationship."

"Any chance of fanning those old embers back to life?"

"No," Andrea and Clay answered quickly and simultaneously.

Andrea sought his gaze across the table, but his narrowed gaze focused on the reporter. She knew *she* was lying about the unexpected remnants of attraction, but was Clay? Had he been completely unmoved by Monday night's kiss?

And what about this morning? He'd practically undressed her with his eyes—a pulse pounding event for her. Damn. It. Had it had any effect on him?

"You're barking up the wrong tree," Clay added as if he'd guessed her question, and Andrea's cheeks burned.

"I could swear I've seen a few smoke signals." Octavia paused to write something in her notebook. Andrea wished she could read what it said, but the flickering candle didn't provide enough light in the shadowy dusk to make it possible to read anything from her side of the table.

"You started dating your senior year in high school. According to your yearbook, your class voted you most inseparable couple, most likely to have a dozen kids and most likely to celebrate your fiftieth wedding anniversary together. The fact that you dated for five years after graduation despite attending universities a thousand miles apart supports your schoolmates' predictions. How could they be so wrong?"

Ohgodohgodohgod. Andrea's gaze found Clay's. *Please don't reveal my biggest flaw—whatever it is—to this reporter.*

"People and circumstances change," Clay said quietly with his gaze locked on Andrea's.

His answer both relieved and frustrated her. She wanted to know why he'd left, but she didn't want *the world*, or even the readers of the Wilmington newspaper, to know.

Octavia wrote and then looked up. "How does it feel to return to the job that was destined to be yours, Clay?"

"My life and my design firm are in Florida now. This is temporary." Tension clipped his words.

"Do you like your new company better than being part of a sixty-year-old family business your grandfather founded?"

Andrea didn't envy Clay being on the hot seat, but she secretly applauded Octavia for asking the very questions that had run through her own mind.

"It's neither better nor worse. I saw an opportunity and took it."

The reporter persisted. "I'm just trying to understand what made you decide to chuck a guaranteed future. You are the only heir to the Dean Yachts' fortune. What will happen to the company and its employees once your father's gone? Will the company fold, be sold or will you take over?"

The shift of Clay's jaw and the tightening of his fist on the table signaled his uneasiness. Andrea found herself feeling sympathy for Clay instead of the antipathy she should be feeling. She should relish his discomfort, but instead she wanted to reach out to him. Since the reporter would definitely get the wrong idea if she did, Andrea stretched her leg beneath the table and brushed her foot against Clay's booted ankle. It was something they used to do at family dinners, a way to stay connected when circumstances demanded otherwise.

Other than a flicker of his eyelids Clay didn't acknowledge her touch, but warmth tingled up Andrea's leg.

Get a grip. Your shoe touched his boot.

Maybe she didn't have any effect on him anymore. If that were the case, then making him regret what he'd given up would be a lost cause. No. She couldn't believe a relationship that had turned her life inside out had left him totally unscathed. She'd continue to wear her sexiest suits and her look-at-me shoes.

Eat your heart out, Clayton Dean.

She faced Octavia. "That decision is years down the road. Joseph's stroke was minor. He's on medications to prevent another one and he should be fine. Certainly, he'd like for Clay to come home, but he understands Clay's need to prove himself."

Clay's gaze found and searched hers as though asking if what she said was true. Andrea gave a slight nod.

If Joseph Dean knew why Clay had left town, he had never said. But one thing Andrea knew for certain was that Joseph, although saddened by Clay's abrupt departure, had never condemned his son. His lack of anger convinced Andrea beyond a shadow of doubt that the problem that had driven Clay from town was her. Otherwise, Joseph, who liked to vent, would have spouted off long and hard over Clay's desertion.

"Your father is on line two," Fran said Friday morning through the wireless intercom-slash-phone system the crew had rigged up for Clay to use in his dockside office.

Clay's heart slammed against his chest like a boat hitting a sandbar at full throttle. For the past two days the reporter's question had echoed in his head. "What will happen once your father's gone? Will the company fold, be sold or will you take over?"

How could he walk away from the dream his grandfather had worked so hard to make a reality—a dream Clay had shared for many years? How could he not?

Hell, he couldn't even face going into the offices. Since Wednesday night he'd avoided Andrea whenever possible and used the phone or e-mail to communicate instead of walking the short distance up the dock to the offices. Seeing the sympathy in her eyes after the way he'd treated her had hit him hard.

From the safety of Miami nearly eight hundred miles away he'd underestimated the difficulty of being near her and not touching her. The physical attraction hadn't died.

If anything, he found the mature and confident Andrea more potent than the girl he'd left behind.

"Mr. Dean?"

Clay reached for the button to tell Fran he wasn't available—the way he had every other time his father called. But that wouldn't stop the calls. "I'll take it," he said and lifted the receiver.

"You need to stop wasting your one phone call a day on me. I have nothing to say to you," he said to his father without preamble.

"Clayton. Son. We need to talk."

He hadn't heard his father's voice in eight years. It didn't resonate like it used to. The words sounded slow and measured. A trick of his memory or a result of the stroke? Clay hardened his heart.

"You said all you needed to say when you asked me to lie for you."

"I regret that. I was wrong."

"No kidding." Sarcasm sharpened his tone. "And there were two of you. Two of you who swore that you had perfect marriages. Marriages between high school sweethearts. Just like Andrea and me. It was a lie."

"I never cheated before or since, son. I swear it."

Acid burned Clay's throat. "You expect me to believe you?"

"I told your mother I'd been unfaithful. She forgave me, Clay. Can't you?"

"Did you tell her you cheated with her best friend? With a woman she loved like a sister?"

Silence stretched between them. "No. I risked a twenty-five-year marriage by coming clean. I didn't want to ruin her lifetime friendship with Elaine. There were extenuating circumstances—"

"So you're still living a lie."

"I've accepted responsibility for my actions. Now you need to take responsibility for yours. You shouldn't have made Andrea suffer for my mistake. You had no right to hurt that girl, Clay. My weakness had nothing to do with her."

A familiar stab of pain hit him. No, his father's weakness had nothing to do with Andrea and everything to do with Clay. Everyone called Clay a chip off the old block. Was his father's inability to be faithful a flaw Clay had inherited? He hadn't wanted to risk it. Hell, he'd been afraid to.

"You have no business telling me what's right."

"Clay, there's something you need to know."

"I don't want to hear any more of your confessions or your excuses."

"And I'm not offering them. Please, son, I wouldn't ask if it weren't important. Give me a few minutes of your time."

"I'm giving you and Dean Yachts two months of my life. Don't get greedy and don't call again." And then he replaced the receiver.

"What are you doing on board?"

Andrea gasped and pivoted toward the door of the stateroom. She hadn't heard Clay approach over the sound of the yacht's engine, the clap of water against the hull and the crew members bellowing back and forth above deck as they tested various mechanics of the yacht they were about to put through its paces. If all went well, the craft would be ready for pickup next week.

"I'm helping with the sea trial. Why are you here?"

"Overseeing the trial. You don't need to come along."

"Your father asked me to."

Clay folded his arms across his chest, straining his butter-colored polo shirt at the shoulder seams. The color picked up the sun-bleached highlights in his hair. His khaki-covered legs splayed in the doorway. "I'll handle it."

"Will you call Joseph and report back? He'll want to hear every detail."

"Stark will call him."

"If all your father wanted was Peter's report, I'd fax it to him. Joseph wants to be here. He's never missed a trial. And since he can't be here he wants a firsthand accounting. From me. So you can go back to your office and do whatever it is you do when you hide in there all day."

"I'm not hiding. I'm avoiding the nauseating cow eyes you're making at Haynes."

"Cow eyes! I'm doing no such thing. I go to lunch and dinner with Toby. That's it. I do not make stupid faces." How could she when she was totally conscious of Clay acting like a wet-blanket chaperone just one slip down the dock?

"If you leave now, you can have lunch with him today."

"Forget it, Clay. I'm not getting off this boat. I made a promise and I keep *my* promises."

Clay's lips tightened and his nostrils flared. His hands fell to his side and he clenched his fists. From the hard glint in his eyes she guessed he wasn't thinking about her promise to his father, but the promise Clay had broken eight years ago.

She wished the words back. This wasn't a discussion she wanted to have when any of the three crew members aloft could and probably would interrupt them at any moment since the boat had to be inspected from bow to stern.

"If you'll excuse me, I need a copy of the checklist." She tried to brush past him, but he remained planted like a bulkhead in her path. The horn sounded, signaling that they were pulling away from the dock, and then the boat moved beneath her feet.

"Andrea, I had to leave."

She checked the companionway past his shoulder. Empty.

"Really? And you couldn't have taken the time to say goodbye in person? You had to leave a message on my home phone at a time when you knew I'd be sitting at my desk at work? 'Andrea, I'm sorry, but I can't marry you. I'm leaving town and I won't be back. Forget about me.'" She mimicked his voice and hated that hers cracked over the last phrase. She hated even more that she could still remember the exact words he'd used to dump her.

He grimaced and swallowed, looking very much like a man in pain, but if he felt pain or anything else over breaking her heart, he'd erased it from his eyes by the time he lifted his lids. "It's the best I could do at the time."

Aggravation gurgled in her throat. "If you want me to understand why you were such an inconsiderate ass, then you're going to have to do better than that, Clay."

"I'm sorry."

"I don't want an apology. I want an explanation."

He held her gaze and then shook his head. "An apology is all I'm offering."

"That's not good enough." She tried to step around him, but he caught her upper arms, pushed her back a step and kicked the door closed.

Oh hell. Ready or not, it looked like they were going to duke this out now.

Five

Clay's thumbs stroked the sensitive skin on the insides of Andrea's arms and a telling shiver rushed over her. Damn. It. She did not want him to know he could still get to her.

"Do you think I didn't hate hurting you? Leaving you?"

"Then why did you?"

His silence cut deep. "I couldn't… I couldn't stay."

His hoarse words cut deeper. She gathered her damaged dignity and tried in vain to shake off his tight, but not painful grip. "I'm glad you found it so easy to move on with your life and forget about us. Now let me out of this cabin."

"Listen."

"Let me go, Clay. The crew—"

"Do you hear that?"

All she heard were the sounds of a boat underway and her pulse hammering in her ears. "Hear what?"

"The waves breaking against the hull. Every time I

hear it I think about us on *Sea Scout*. Hot. Sweaty. Naked."

Not fair. Desire exploded inside her, radiating outward until Andrea's skin flushed with the memory of making love on Clay's boat. The fight drained out of her. "Don't you dare bring up that."

"I didn't forget, Andrea." His hands slid upward, over her shoulders and her neck until he cupped her jaw. Andrea stood frozen in his grasp and yet something deep inside her melted. This was so not part of her pla—

His lips touched hers and her objections sputtered into silence. Soft sips turned into hungry, consuming, tongue-entwining kisses as he coaxed her into responding. His fingers threaded through her hair, tilting her head back and holding her as his lips slanted left and then right, always delving deeper.

Her fists bunched by her side and then she lifted them and clutched his waist. She meant to push him away. Really, she did. But she needed to hold on. For balance. Either the boat had hit turbulence or she had.

He shifted his stance and her breasts brushed his chest. Daggers of desire slashed through her, carving a trail to her womb. She'd forgotten how marvelous the tightening coil of arousal felt. Forgotten the steam of Clay's breath against her cheek, the rasp of his afternoon beard on her chin and the bite of hunger so strong she could barely think.

Why could no other man do this to her?

His hands raked down her spine to splay over her bottom, caressing, heating, arousing, and then he drew her closer and the rigid press of his erection burned her belly.

He wasn't unaffected by this *thing* between them. Good to know. She rose on her toes, wound her arms around him and leaned against him, fusing her body to the length of his. He traced her hip, her waist, her ribs and then one big hand opened over her breast, molding her. The lightweight fabric of her sleeveless sheath dress offered no protection from the warmth of his touch. His thumb grazed her nipple, circling, scraping until a needy sound squeaked past her lips and into his mouth. She broke the kiss to gasp for breath.

His mouth found her throat. Nipped. Suckled. Laved. He urged her backward until the berth hit the back of her legs and his thigh wedged between hers. Sweet pressure. Agonizing friction. Her nails dragged down his back and his groan rattled against her.

So delicious. So not part of her plan.

The sound of footsteps penetrated the steamy windows of her brain. She jerked out of Clay's arms and swiped a hand across her mouth a split second before the stateroom door opened.

Peter jolted to a stop, his narrowed eyes taking in the cabin's two heavy breathing occupants. His lips turned down. "We've reached the inlet. I brought copies of the checklist. Clay, we need you above deck. Start in the galley. Sir," he added belatedly.

Andrea's face and neck stung—not only from what she suspected would be a bad case of beard burn.

Clay shot her a look she couldn't decipher, snatched a checklist from Peter's hand and then left.

Andrea exhaled slowly and met the gaze of the man who'd been her staunchest ally at Dean's besides Joseph. The disappointment in Peter's eyes hit hard, but not as harshly as she condemned herself.

Are you out of your mind?
Closure, dummy. That's what you want.
Nothing more. Nothing less.

* * *

What in the hell was he thinking? Clay raked a hand through his hair and leaned against the bulkhead.

Kissing Andrea, holding her had been amazing, but then he'd known it would be. No lover over the past eight years had excited or fulfilled him the way Andrea had. But he couldn't start something with her because he couldn't finish it.

So why torture himself?

Because sitting in his boat every evening and listening to her laughter as she and the car jockey sat on the other yacht's back deck sipping cocktails was torturing him. The only thing worse than their laughter was the silence when they retired inside. Being staked to an anthill would be easier to endure than the silence and wondering if they were in Haynes's hot tub or spread across his king-size bed.

Andrea had called Clay an ass for not dumping her in person, and he couldn't change her opinion by explaining why he'd run from the Dean offices, climbed into his car and driven until an empty gas tank made him pull over. He'd sat on the side of the highway for hours thinking about the repercussions of his discovery and searching for understanding. He'd stayed there until a passing state trooper had pulled in behind him and called a tow truck.

God knows Clay had needed to talk to someone, but who could he have called? He'd trusted no one the way he did Andrea, and he couldn't tell her. He'd left the phone message because he hadn't trusted himself to look her in the eyes or even hear her voice without blurting out the painful truth about their parents and his own doubts.

Could he have committed to one woman forever—the long-distance lover he'd only seen during summers and school vacations for the past five years? Or would he be as weak as his father? Clay would never know. He'd made his choice and he had to live with it.

He checked off the last item on his list and located Andrea and the crew in the salon. "Done."

His pulse accelerated the moment his gaze found hers. He could still feel the heat of her kiss on his lips and the throb of need in his blood. She quickly looked away but not before he saw regret in her eyes.

What if he told her why he'd left? He'd asked himself that question a thousand times. Could she forgive him for spoiling her illusions about her mother and her mentor? Or would she hate him for selfishly ripping the blinders off so they could be together?

And did he even want another chance with her? Giving her up the first time had damned near destroyed him, and he wasn't sure he could go through that again and stay sane. Best to keep his distance as he'd originally planned. No matter how much he wanted her.

"Come about and open her up," Stark told the captain. "Andrea has plans tonight. We don't want to make her late."

Clay's gut muscles clenched. "With Haynes?"

Andrea's chin lifted. "No. With my mother. Not that it's any of your business, but Friday night is girls' night. It's tradition."

A tradition she'd started back in her college days when she'd moved into the dorm room she'd shared with Holly and Juliana, he recalled. She was still close to her mother. That meant Clay definitely had to keep the secret. Better for her to think ill of him. She could find another lover, not one who'd love her as completely as he had, but she couldn't find another mother.

As long as that lover wasn't Haynes.

Clay turned to Stark. "How long before we get that housing built for Haynes's motorcycle?"

"Another week. Had to fabricate a mold." The production manager's disapproval was hard to miss.

"Put a rush on it. We have another delivery next Friday. We need to get his yacht away from the dock ASAP."

"We can move it to another dock. Or you can move yours," Stark said with just a touch of belligerence. Clay almost called him on it, but firing the production manager would only lengthen his stay in Wilmington.

"Get the job done, Peter. Ask for volunteers for extra shifts if you have to."

And in the meantime, Clay decided, he'd keep Andrea occupied by scheduling as many of the auction dates as he could while Haynes was in town.

Both the prodigal son, Clayton Dean, and Andrea Montgomery, the former love of his life, swear the ashes of their past are cold, but this reporter believes this romance is ready to be rekindled. Is Ms. Montgomery carrying the matches? And will Dean Yachts survive the heat when this dynamic duo reignites?

"Oh my God." Andrea groaned, dropped the Saturday newspaper on the kitchen table and buried her face in her hands. Octavia Jenkins's first installment in the Wilmington paper embarrassed Andrea beyond words and made her sick to her stomach. That was nausea twisting her stomach in knots, wasn't it? Of course it was. How would she hold her head up at work?

She lifted her head to peek again at the black-and-white picture of her and Clay sharing a liplock on the *Georgina*.

Who had taken that picture and when? She'd hadn't seen the reporter or photographer on the boat, but then Holly had warned her that Octavia had a sneaky side.

This was all Clay's fault.

Anger propelled her through showering and dressing. She drove like a mad woman to Dean's and practically scorched a trail down the dock past Toby's darkened boat to board Clay's. Lifting her fist, she hammered on the glass upper portion of Clay's door. When Clay didn't respond she pounded harder until she saw a light come on inside and then he emerged from his stateroom. Her stomach flip-flopped. She must have woken him.

Clay jogged up the stairs and across the salon. By the time he unlocked and slid open the door Andrea had worked up a good head of steam. How dare he look so damned sexy with his stubble-shadowed jaw. He also looked rumpled. And bare. And aroused. His wrinkled boxers couldn't conceal his morning erection even in the dim light cast by the lampposts on the dock.

Her entire body warmed. Which only angered her more.

"What's wrong?" he asked.

Andrea blinked away her unwanted response and slapped the newspaper against his chest.

"Read it. Worse, look at the picture. I will not be a pity case again when you leave. Been there. Done that. Didn't like the T-shirt."

Clay wrestled the wrinkled newspaper from her hands, flipped on the overhead light and scanned the article.

Andrea mashed her lips together and fumed. "You have got to stop kissing me."

Clay lifted his gaze. "Stop kissing me back."

"You— I—" she sputtered with fury. Any second now

she was going to shriek like a boiling tea kettle. "How dare you try to blame this on me."

"Aren't you the one wearing figure-hugging suits and do-me heels to work everyday?"

Guilty. Her cheeks caught fire. "I dress to please myself."

"Yeah. Right. Either you're trolling your bait for me or Haynes. Which is it?"

Speechless with rage she glared at him.

He dragged a hand over his bristly chin and her fingers prickled. Damn. It. "Do you know what time it is, Andrea?"

"I—" In her rush to confront Clay she'd forgotten her watch, but the sun had barely begun to lighten the horizon. "No."

"It's 5:20 a.m. Too early to stand in the cockpit and have a screaming match. Come inside. I'll make coffee."

He pivoted and headed for the galley, slinging the paper onto the table as he passed and flicking on lamps. Andrea stood on the deck and debated the intelligence of following him.

For one, Clay wasn't dressed. She risked a peek at his tight tush and then wished she hadn't when her pulse skipped.

For two, he looked too delicious with all that tanned, hair-dusted skin on display. Damn. It.

For three, she hated that she was still attracted to him— so attracted that even Octavia Jenkins could see it. If the reporter could, then who else could? And what would it do to the relationship she planned to have with Toby?

And last, Dean's employees would read this article and think her a fool for falling for him again. She'd lose the respect she'd fought so hard to win.

"Shut the door. You're letting in mosquitoes."

Against her better judgment Andrea stepped over the threshold and closed the door, sealing herself into the intimacy of Clay's salon. It was one thing to conduct business with him when they were both fully dressed, but another when he had pillow creases on his cheek and shoulder.

"This is not the kind of publicity we want, Clay."

"Nope, but what can you do about it? She's writing the story."

"We can stop giving her anything to write about."

Clay punched the on switch and his coffeemaker gurgled to life. "You're the one who insisted we had to go on the dates."

But that was when she had a fail-safe agenda. Now she wasn't so sure her success was guaranteed. But backing out of the auction package would only cause more speculation. "We have to go on the dates. She'd have a field day if we didn't."

"Speaking of dates, I planned to call you today. I've scheduled the hot air balloon ride for five tomorrow morning if you're available." He leaned against the counter and Andrea fought to ignore his nakedness. They'd had countless talks in their past wearing less. Why did the breadth of his shoulders, his six-pack abs, lean hips and long legs still mesmerize her? It wasn't fair. But at least his erection had subsided. Otherwise she wasn't sure she'd be able to locate a functioning brain cell.

Her gaze skimmed back up the dark line of hair dividing his torso and slammed smack dab into Clay's narrowed eyes. He'd caught her checking out his package. Embarrassment heated her like a sauna, making her skin hot and tight.

"I'm available. For the balloon ride. Could you put on some clothes?"

He held her gaze for ten full seconds, and then he pushed off the counter and descended the stairs, but he didn't close his bedroom door. Andrea tried to look away, but her unimpeded view of his stateroom and the corner of his bed covered in tangled sheets captivated her. Coming on the heels of yesterday's kiss and Clay's confession that the sound of water against the hull made him think of her and sex made the air-conditioned interior suddenly feel twenty degrees hotter.

How stupid was she that she couldn't see a train wreck coming and step off the tracks? But she couldn't abandon her mission. She hadn't gotten Clay out of her system, found out why he'd left her, or reunited him with his father. Her job wasn't anywhere near finished. No matter how much she wanted it to be.

"I can't believe I let you talk me into this," Andrea grumbled as she climbed from Clay's rental car in an open field Sunday morning. "Of all the auction dates *this* is the one I dreaded the most."

Clay's smile flashed white in the predawn hours of Sunday morning. "Afraid of heights?"

Andrea looked across the field to where the huge hot air balloon waited like a hulking shadow. There wasn't enough light to make out the colors. The headlights of a van illuminated four people clustered around the balloon basket sitting on the ground. Soon she and Clay would be up— way up—in that. "Maybe. A little. And your package promised sun*sets* not sun*rises*."

"You prefer sunrises."

It touched her that he'd considered her preferences, but a sunrise ascent was too romantic for words, and she didn't want romance from Clay. Especially not after the newspaper article and seeing him practically naked. It was bad enough that his kisses still made her blood simmer. Okay, boil, she admitted, but no more of that.

Her hiking boots and jean clad legs swished in the tall, dew-covered grass as they neared the balloon team's van. She shoved her hands into the pockets of her sweatshirt jacket. "There's no steering wheel and no parachute."

"Hot air balloons have been around since the seventeen hundreds, and our pilot is a licensed twenty-year veteran."

"His experience is the only reason I agreed to this." She'd been asking herself if she was crazy ever since Clay told her about the date yesterday morning.

"Good morning," a man in a flight suit called out. "I'm Owen, your pilot, and these folks are Denise, Larry and Hank, our ground crew. They'll pick us up on the other end and return you to your vehicle. If you're ready to see the world from a bird's-eye view, then climb aboard."

He entered the basket first and then turned to lend Andrea a hand. On unsteady legs she mounted the portable steps the crew provided, climbed inside and clutched the basket's rim. Clay followed. The first thing Andrea noticed was the lack of space. The three foot by four foot basket was crowded with the three of them, a cooler and a couple of metal air tanks. If you weren't friendly with your fellow passengers before you took off, you would be before you landed. The second thing she noted was the proliferation of ropes and cables connecting the basket and balloon and who knew what else. She quickly scanned each line, looking for frays, and thankfully, found none.

"Ready to cast off?" Owen asked.

As tense as an anchor line in a strong current, Andrea nodded. Her heart raced with a combination of fear and excitement. The ground crew hustled around and then the basket rocked beneath her feet. She gulped and closed her eyes. The roar of the propane burners firing startled her into opening them again. The burners hadn't sounded this loud from across the field. The balloon slowly lifted off.

Andrea's pulse pounded. She wanted to inch closer to Clay, but she didn't dare move and rock the basket. Besides, Clay had already accused her—and rightly so—of trying to tempt him. She wouldn't give him the satisfaction of clinging to him. Clutching the four-foot high sides tighter, she watched her feet and concentrated on breathing normally.

"We'll fly at somewhere between five hundred and fifteen hundred feet off the ground, depending on the wind direction," Owen said.

High. Very, very high. Not good to know.

Clay covered her hand with one big warm palm and coward that she was, she soaked up his silent support. Countless minutes passed.

"Look," Clay spoke directly into her ear so that he could be heard over the noisy gas burner.

Andrea's racing heart stuttered. She forced herself to look over the edge of the basket and strangely, it didn't make her feel dizzy or sick. They'd cleared the tree line. The sun squatted like a big peach semicircle on the horizon, streaking the ocean with color. Dawn twinkled on the white, sandy beach. Fear loosened its stranglehold on her throat.

"See your house yet?" His breath stirred her hair and Clay's warmth spooned her back. Every molecule in her hummed with awareness of his proximity. When she shook her head he braced one arm on the side of the basket and reached around her with the other to point.

She swallowed the rush of moisture in her mouth and squeezed her thighs together in an effort to stop the tingle between them. How could she be getting turned on with a stranger standing within touching distance? She searched the direction Clay indicated until she found her robin's egg-blue cottage. Five years ago she'd bought an older home. It had taken years to totally renovate it from the garage at ground level to the widow's walk on the third floor. "Yes."

A radio transmission from the ground crew gave wind speeds and directions, but Andrea barely paid attention to the pilot's reply as she gazed in wonder at Wilmington and the southern North Carolina coastline blossoming beneath her. And then Owen turned off the burner and the silence overwhelmed her.

"It's beautiful." She loosened her grip, flexed her cramped fingers and looked over her shoulder at Clay. His warm, minty breath swept her cheek and his big body cradled hers. She stomped hard on the memories trying to crowd forward.

She turned and that left them kissing-close in the cramped basket. Clay looked totally relaxed. "You've done this before."

"Rod, my former boss, is into balloon racing. I've crewed for him a few times. There's nothing like the silence and the sensation of drifting on an air current."

Andrea blinked in surprise. This was a side of Clay she hadn't seen before. When they'd dated he'd been something of a control freak—not in a bad way as in wanting to control her. He just wanted things the way he wanted them. Precise. Logical. Orderly. He'd always been a black-and-white guy. Shades of gray hadn't been part of his color palette. What had caused the change?

"I would never have imagined you riding in a basket and letting the wind blow you wherever it dared."

His gaze locked with hers. "People change, Andrea. And you have more control over direction up here than you'd expect. Air currents at different levels travel in different directions. You choose your path."

Conscious of Owen standing just inches away, she nodded. Clay had changed and so had she. She'd gone from naive and trusting to sophisticated and guarded. She no longer believed in fairy tales and white knights, and while she wanted a happily ever after, she was more than willing to create that for herself instead of relying on a man to provide it.

That was what this bachelor auction deal was about. Choosing her path… Taking control, pointing her life in the right direction and going full speed ahead, and she would succeed no matter what the cost.

"Can you come in for a minute?" Andrea asked when Clay turned into her driveway.

"Sure." He'd barely seen her house in the predawn light when he'd picked her up. Like most beachfront homes hers had been built on pilings to keep it above the water-line in the event of a hurricane. The parking area beneath it had been enclosed. A three story windowed octagonal tower stood sentry on the left front corner. Soaring arched windows fronted the opposite side. The panes sparkled in the noonday sun. Clay followed Andrea up the curving stairs to her front door.

"Come in and have a seat. Can I get you something to drink?" She led him from the entry to the spacious living room overlooking the dunes and beach below.

"No. I'm good."

"Excuse me a minute." She jogged up the staircase, leaving Clay standing by the window with his hands fisted in his pockets and regret squeezing his chest. Sand-colored tile covered her floor and cool blue ocean colors dominated the upholstery. The glass-topped tables looked as if they'd been formed from driftwood. Splashes of orange, peach and yellow brightened the space, reminiscent of the beach at sunrise.

This was the dream house Andrea had described during those nights on his sloop, the house they'd planned to share.

She returned moments later, approached him and extended her hand. "I think it's time I returned this. I'm sorry I didn't send it sooner, but I didn't have your Florida mailing address."

Curious, Clay held out his hand. She opened her fingers and something small and light dropped into his palm. A tiny diamond winked in the sunlight streaming through the wall of windows. Surprise sucker punched the breath right out of him. His promise ring. The one he'd given her the night they'd graduated from high school—the night they'd made love for the first time and promised to spend the rest of their lives together.

The ring symbolized a broken promise and everything he'd lost. Because two people had lied. And because he hadn't had the guts to stay and see if he was made of stronger stuff than his father.

Even if he could have thought of an appropriate response, he probably couldn't have forced the words past the knot in his throat. He closed his fingers around the cool metal and swallowed.

"We need to put the past behind us, Clay." Andrea's eyes darkened with pain—pain he'd inflicted.

"Yeah. But you can keep this."

She put her hands behind her back. "I don't want it. I don't want to remember anymore."

He didn't want to remember either. But he couldn't forget.

Six

"I don't get in a race car unless I have a good chance of winning the race," Haynes called out as Clay passed the *Checkered Flag 3* early Thursday morning.

Grudgingly, Clay halted on the dock. Haynes's crew had left the day after they'd arrived, but the driver had remained behind like a splinter being shoved a little deeper beneath Clay's fingernail with each passing day.

"I study the other cars and the other drivers, and I gotta admit, Dean, you're giving me a run for my money that I didn't see coming."

Clay clenched his teeth. The man was a customer, so no matter how badly Clay wanted to tell him to go to hell and take his boat with him, he'd keep it polite. "There is no competition."

"Junior, you don't believe that any more than I do."

Three days had passed since the hot air balloon ride.

Three days of Andrea lunching on Haynes's boat and going out with him each evening. Three days of the promise ring burning a hole in Clay's pocket.

The man's presence had gnawed at Clay this past week until he had to face one indisputable fact. This wasn't a case of sour grapes—him not wanting Andrea, but not wanting anyone else to have her either. He was jealous. *Jealous.* He wanted Andrea for himself and after seeing her home—the home they could have shared—he realized the roots of his feelings ran deeper than he'd expected. He might even still love her.

"Think whatever you want, Haynes. Your motorcycle housing should be installed by this afternoon. You'll be free to go." He resumed walking toward his boat, his refuge.

"My money says I'll get her into the sack before you do, Dean."

Clay's muscles locked. Everything in him urged him to board the yacht and chase a few teeth down the jack-ass's throat with his fist, but Clay walked on, savoring one small victory.

Andrea hadn't slept with Toby Haynes. And Clay would do whatever he must to keep it that way.

The tingle was gone from Toby's kisses, Andrea fumed. And it was Clay's fault.

How could she think about a future with Toby—or any man for that matter—when her past with Clay kept slapping her in the face? Every touch and glance reminded her how good it had been between them before it ended. But her memories had been skewed by youth and blind love, hadn't they? He wouldn't pack the same punch now. Would he? Of course not.

She turned her head and looked at Clay across the front

seat of his rental car. He looked Miami-debonair in his pale sand-colored linen suit. He'd left the top two buttons of a shirt in the same shade of cobalt-blue as his eyes unbuttoned.

"For someone who wanted to buy his way out of these dates a few days ago you seem eager to get through them all."

Clay turned into the parking lot and turned off the engine. "Aren't you enjoying yourself?"

"Yes." So much, unfortunately, she'd neglected her agenda. Tonight she'd get it back on track. Come hell or high water, she would eradicate Clayton Dean from her thoughts. "But we don't have to rush to get through them."

"You'd rather I stayed on board and played solitaire every night while you're out with Haynes?"

She hadn't been out with Toby *every* night, but she didn't mind if Clay thought so. "No. You could visit your parents. Your father asks about you every day. You've been home thirteen days, Clay, and you haven't even called him."

Clay's expression hardened. He shoved open his door and rounded the car to help her out. The heat of his palm on hers addled her. She tried to pull free, but Clay wouldn't let go. Short of making a scene by struggling she was stuck walking so close beside him down the cobblestone sidewalk that their legs swished against their joined hands. Sparks traveled upward from each impact. Not good. Not good at all.

They passed the Renegade Bar and Grill owned by the bachelor Juliana had bought. For a moment Andrea considered dropping in to see if her friend and the rebel were together, but decided against it. Juliana had to work this out for herself, but Andrea sincerely hoped the biker would show her uptight friend a little of the excitement she'd been missing before it was too late.

A white flower-bedecked carriage, the kind used in

fairy-tale weddings, waited at the end of the block. Unlike the sleepy carriage horses Andrea usually encountered in tourist spots, the glossy white gelding in the harness looked alert and eager to go. The driver tipped his top hat. "Evenin', Ms. Montgomery, Mr. Dean. Climb aboard."

Andrea climbed into the carriage and stopped. A single peach rose lay on the seat. That particular shade—the color of sunrise—had always been her favorite. Had Clay bought the rose? Or was it part of the carriage ride package and the color choice coincidental? And what about the champagne bucket on the opposite bench? Clay's doing? Or had his mother arranged that, too? She preferred to credit Patricia because Andrea didn't want Clay doing nice things for her.

She lifted the flower and settled on the leather seat facing the horse. Clay sat beside her—too close for comfort. He stretched his arm behind her. She hugged her wrap closer, but the open weave of the crocheted fabric didn't protect her from his touch against her bare back. Clearly, the sexy halter dress had been a mistake.

The driver snagged the champagne bottle, popped the cork without spilling a drop and filled two flutes. He handed one to each of them and then stepped aboard and clucked to the horse. The sudden movement threw Andrea against Clay's arm. She quickly sat forward again.

Clay touched his glass to hers. "To the past and the future."

The carriage, flower and toast, combined with the clip-clop of the horse's hooves, tugged Andrea's heart like a riptide. She couldn't—*wouldn't*—be swept under Clay's spell again.

What better way to spoil the romantic mood than to find out why he dumped her? It took a second glass of champagne and fifty minutes of silent pep talk for Andrea to work up her courage. Even then, she couldn't force the words out until they rounded a corner and the carriage depot came into view.

"What did I do to make you leave?" she blurted with scant minutes left in their ride.

Clay whipped his head to face her and his eyes narrowed. "Nothing."

"Come on, Clay, we both know better than that."

Shutters slammed in his eyes. "Andrea, it wasn't you."

Was he lying? He had to be. "Then what?"

"Let it go."

"I can't." She wouldn't tell him about all the guys who had dumped her since he left. Her pride couldn't take it and she didn't want his pity. "If you'd messed up or had another one of your arguments with your father, then I would have heard about it. Joseph is known for verbally letting off steam."

Clay, with his back and shoulders stiffer than she'd ever seen them, looked away. "He never said anything?"

"Not one word. Which is why I know I was the cause."

The hand not holding his champagne flute fisted and a nerve beside his mouth twitched. "Dammit, you weren't."

"Then tell me who or what was. I didn't even know you'd returned from New Orleans that day until the receptionist stopped me on my way out to ask why you'd cut your visit short." Andrea twisted toward him on the bench seat. "Clay, why would you walk right past my office without bothering to say hello or goodbye when we hadn't seen each other in months?"

His jaw locked into rigid lines, but he didn't look at her. "I can't explain."

She'd had no idea this conversation would hurt so much or that once she worked up the nerve to ask her questions he'd refuse to answer them. "You just woke up that morning and decided to start over somewhere else?"

His gaze met hers and Andrea gasped at the agony in his eyes. Agony and secrets. Whatever the reason he'd left her it must be too horrible to share.

What was wrong with her? Did she lack some essentially feminine component?

"Andrea, it wasn't you. If you never believe another word I say, believe that."

She wanted to believe him. Really she did. But she had years of disastrous relationships and Joseph's silence as evidence that Clay was lying. "You used to trust me, Clay."

A disgusted sound erupted from his throat. He stared at the driver's back. "I used to trust myself."

His barely audible words staggered her. He'd found someone else. He'd moved on and left her stuck in the past.

The pain in Andrea's eyes gutted Clay. She'd been reticent since the carriage ride despite several attempts on his part to initiate conversation.

He followed her into her home. A single light glowed on an end table in her great room. She shed the white crochet stole she'd worn over her black-and-white halter-necked sundress and draped it over a chair.

The back of her dress left her bare to the waist. She wasn't wearing a bra and no tan lines marred her honey-toned skin. The front of her dress resembled a bathing suit with its gathered fabric cupping her breasts like a plump, mouthwatering offering. Knowing a single knot at her nape was all that kept him from cupping the soft swells had kept Clay at half-mast throughout the evening.

Andrea closed the blinds, blocking out the inky darkness of the ocean at night and the lights of a shrimp boat offshore. She faced him, knotted her fingers and bit her lip. "Was she better in bed than me?"

Shock stalled his heart. "What?"

"You said you used to trust yourself. That means you must have met someone in New Orleans. Someone who tempted you and turned you on more than I did. Someone who offered you more than what we had."

"Where in the hell did you get that crazy idea? There wasn't another woman, Andrea."

"Of course there was. Otherwise you would never have walked away from Dean Yachts. I know how much the company meant to you. But you're not the type to rub another woman in my face, and Joseph wouldn't have fired me or asked me to leave. So you left. You didn't have to do that, Clay. I could have taken it if you'd told me the truth."

How could she possibly believe he could love another woman more than he'd loved her? Clay crossed the room, clasped her upper arms. Her soft skin seared him. Knowing he shouldn't, but unable to help himself, he caressed her from her shoulders to her wrists and back.

"You're wrong. Dead wrong. What we had was good. Damned good. But it wasn't enough for me to forget—" For him to forget his father's infidelity or the fear that he was his father's son. He couldn't explain without saying something that would hurt her more. "It wasn't enough for me to stay."

She flinched. "Obviously."

She tried to pull free, but Clay held fast. He couldn't find the words to convince her that the problem hadn't been her, so he used only the weapon he did have, the passion simmering between them, and he started with the one thing he'd wanted to do since picking her up three hours ago. Hell, what he'd wanted every single day since she'd bought him two weeks ago. He kissed her.

Her lips remained unresponsive beneath his through the

first kiss. By the second she'd softened, and by the fourth she'd arched into him, wound her hands around his waist and welcomed his tongue in her mouth. The press of her soft flesh against him squeezed the air from his lungs. Gasping, reeling, he lifted his head.

Arousal flushed her skin and quickened her breath. The pulse at the base of her throat fluttered wildly. He pulled first one then the other chopstick-type things from her hair and the golden strands cascaded over the backs of his hands like cool silk. He dropped the hair sticks onto a nearby table.

His heart slammed into his ribs and his pulse nearly deafened him. How could the hunger be stronger now than it had been when he'd been head over heels in love with her? But it was. It swelled in him until he wanted to forget finesse and foreplay. He wanted to toss her back on the sofa and ravage her like a pirate storming a ship. He wanted to touch her, taste her and lose himself inside her until they were both too weak to move.

He stroked her lush bottom lip with his thumb and then dragged his hands from her shoulders down her satiny back to her waist and back again. She shivered against him and sighed a sweet breath against his skin. Desire expanded her pupils and darkened her eyes. Her high heels brought her forehead level with his chin. All he had to do was lean in to nuzzle her temple and pull her scent into his lungs. And then he had to kiss her again and again.

Common sense warned Clay to slow down and consider the consequences of his actions, but he couldn't. Years of denying himself what—who—he really wanted pulsed in his veins. He cupped Andrea's breasts and teased her beaded nipples, savoring her whimpers of pleasure. He traced the top of her dress, his fingertip meandering a drunken trail between cool fabric and warm smooth skin.

And then he discovered the zip at the back of her waist and eased it down. His hands dipped beneath the fabric to find silky panties and even softer skin. He cupped her buttocks and pulled her hips flush against his.

Andrea's breasts rubbed against him as she panted for breath. Her nails dug into his waist and then she tugged his shirttail free. Her touch on his back nearly brought him to his knees.

This wasn't about Haynes or his damned challenge. This was about making love to a woman Clay had never forgotten. If his feelings for Andrea hadn't diminished after eight years' absence, then maybe they never would. Maybe he hadn't inherited his father's weakness. Without a doubt she deserved better than him, but he knew for damned sure he had more staying power than Toby Haynes.

Her teeth nipped his neck and Clay shuddered. If he made love with Andrea tonight, he couldn't walk away from her again. What would it take to persuade her to give him a second chance? And if he succeeded would she be willing to pay the price? They couldn't live here and couldn't run Dean together the way they'd once planned. He'd have to convince her to come with him to Florida without telling her why they couldn't stay in North Carolina.

That might be his hardest job yet.

Revisiting the past was always a mistake. Tonight Andrea was counting on the fact that nothing was ever as grand through the eyes of maturity as the rose-colored memories of youth portrayed it, and if going to bed with Clay was the only way to prove that time had exaggerated his magic, then so be it.

Holly's warning slithered into her subconscious. Was she trying too hard to justify a bad decision? Was this a mistake?

No. Clay was like a hangover Andrea couldn't seem to shake, and the men at Dean swore the only cure for a hangover was the hair of the dog that bit you.

She linked her fingers through his and led him toward the stairs.

He halted at the bottom. "Andrea, are you sure?"

Sure that she wanted to be over him? Absolutely.

Sure that this was the way to go about it. Not so much. But nothing she'd tried in the past eight years had banished him, so what choice did she have other than to play this last card? "We have to do this if we're going to put the past behind us."

A frown puckered his brow. "Have to?"

"Have to." She released his hand and pushed his suit coat over his shoulders. Pulling it from his arms, she hung it on the newel post, and then moving quickly before she talked herself out of this, she released the buttons of his shirt. Once his shirt hung open, she stroked her fingers down the center of his chest, over his zipper and the rigid erection beneath it.

His breath whistled through clenched teeth. He caught her hand and dragged it upward. The dark line of hair bisecting his belly tickled her palm and then his hard, tiny nipple bumped beneath her fingertips. She could feel his heart pounding and then he lifted her hand and kissed her knuckles, her wrist, the inside of her elbow.

Dizzy with need, Andrea dragged in a much needed breath and backed up the stairs, leading Clay to her cathedral-ceilinged sanctuary. Moonlight streamed through the tall windows, illuminating her bed. She'd never shared her room with another man.

Not even Toby.

Toby. Her future. Maybe. Toby, who'd been amazingly

understanding about her preoccupation with work—meaning her temporary boss—and with her refusal to become intimate. Although his patience seemed to be wearing thin these last few days.

And then Clay's hands stroked from her waist to her underarms and back again. His thumbs swept beneath the bodice of her dress to brush the sides of her breasts and then beneath them. Thoughts of Toby evaporated.

Andrea's nipples tightened until they ached. She wanted—no needed—Clay to touch her. "Please."

"Please what?" he rumbled huskily against her neck. "This?" His thumbnails scraped over her nipples. "Or this?" He rolled the taut tips between his fingers.

"B-both." She bit her lip on a moan. He caressed her breasts and nuzzled her neck until her knees weakened.

When he removed his hands she opened her mouth to protest, but he captured her face in his palms and caught her words with his mouth. The passionate kiss dug deep, excavating memories and emotions she'd thought long since buried.

No, no, no. Sex with Clay wasn't supposed to be this good.

But it was. Desire smoldered in her belly, scattering embers of heat in all directions. She shifted restlessly, trying to stop the tingle between her legs, but the movement only exacerbated the situation because her wiggling brushed her breasts against his chest.

There was nothing familiar about the hot, supple skin of Clay's waist and back. Muscles she didn't recall undulated beneath her fingertips. His chest was the same. *Different.* But his taste… That she remembered.

He caressed her with a surety now, a single-minded determination to drive her absolutely witless that she didn't think she could have forgotten. Even if she'd tried.

His fingers tangled in her hair and then teased her nape. He released her and stepped back, putting scant inches between them. Cool air swept her hot skin. She forced her heavy lids open and realized he'd untied her halter dress. It fluttered to the floor, dragging over her sensitized skin like a caress to land beside the shirt he'd discarded.

When she stepped into his arms again the heat of his bare skin fused to hers. Breast to chest. Belly to groin. She struggled to recall her agenda.

Look for flaws. What is he doing wrong?

Nothing, absolutely nothing.

Look harder.

She reached for his waistband, released his belt and the hook of his pants and then glided the zipper down. His slacks and boxers slid over his hips and down his thighs with almost no effort, and then she caught her breath. The length and breadth of him hadn't been a rose-colored memory embellished by time and distance. The few lovers she'd had since Clay had not measured up. Damn. It.

Her fingers curled around him, stroking burning hot flesh and coaxing a slick droplet from the tip.

Clay groaned, caught her hand, stilling her. "Condom."

The enormity of what she was about to do hit her and she hesitated. Either sleeping with Clay was the right thing to do or it was very, *very* wrong. Did she dare risk it? She had to. The rest of her life was at stake. She couldn't continue living in limbo.

"Top drawer. Right bedside table." The reasons she'd bought the condoms nicked her pleasurable haze, but she blocked it.

He kicked his shoes and clothing aside, and she stepped out of her dress and heels. The sudden loss of height made her feel small and delicate. The top of her head barely reached his chin. Her mouth dried and her pulse pounded.

Cupping her buttocks, he bent his head and devoured her mouth and then shuffled her backward until the mattress bumped her legs. He released her only long enough to rip back her comforter. And then he stood and looked at her.

Moonlight flooded the room but shadowed his face. Did he like what he saw? She worked hard to stay in shape. She wanted him to drool. Wanted him to be sorry he'd walked away. Andrea thrust back her shoulders and his gaze immediately fell to her breasts. Clay had always been a breast man. Heaven knows he'd spent countless hours worshipping hers with his hands and mouth. The memory sent SOS flares through her bloodstream.

"Beautiful." He circled one areola with a fingertip, making her gulp back a whimper of need. And then his finger coasted down her breast bone, over her navel and along the elastic of her bikini panties. Her skin rippled in the wake of his touch and a shock of sensation whipped through her. His fingertip dipped behind satin, teased her curls, found her wetness and her pleasure point with accuracy that belied the passing of eight years. Unbearable tension blossomed at her core, making her shift restlessly. But he only allowed her a taste of what was to come before removing his hand. She nearly cried in frustration.

Clay knelt in front of her, rubbed his cheek against the triangle of fabric and inhaled deeply. She squeezed her eyes shut against the memories of him doing the same years ago. His palms opened over her hips and then stoked downward, easing her panties over her thighs, knees, ankles.

If this was a mistake, it was too late to turn back. Every cell in her body begged for more. She braced her hands on his shoulders and lifted one foot and then the other free of the fabric. From his kneeling position on the floor Clay rocked back and looked up at her. Her heart stuttered at the tension straining his face, but she couldn't see his eyes, and she needed to, needed to if he was half as aroused as she.

Impatiently, she reached out and flicked on the bedside lamp. A peachy glow filled the room, but before she could read his expression Clay lowered his gaze to her tangled curls, lifted his hands to her hips and nudged her to sit on the bed. Andrea sat, because her legs were ready to collapse anyway. He outlined her dark blond triangle and then stroked her damp center with a lightly callused fingertip. She cried out at the potency of his touch. Need tightened inside her. His breath warmed her thigh and then he found her with his mouth. His passion-darkened gaze held hers as he tasted her, and every cell in her body turned traitor.

It wasn't supposed to be this good. Her fingers clutched the sheets and her head fell back. Her heels pressed the floor as she lifted her hips, silently begging him to give her the release she craved.

Clay's hands skated over her belly, her ribs and found her breasts. Trouble. Oh, was she ever in trouble. Good. Too good. Close. So close. She teetered on the edge of climax, her spine arching, her breath locking in her chest. And then he lifted his head. Frustrated and disappointed, Andrea sagged against the mattress with a muffled groan.

Clay yanked open the drawer, found and applied a condom. He rose over her, cupped her knees and pushed them upward, exposing her. His thick tip found her entrance and then he slid home in one deep, penetrating thrust. She banded her arms around him and tangled her legs with his, holding him close to savor the familiar sensations as they rushed over her.

She hadn't forgotten how well he filled her, how deep

he touched her or how perfectly they fit together. He withdrew only to plunge again and again, driving deeper, faster and harder with each thrust. Her body greedily lapped up every drop of sensation and hungered for more. Tension spiraled. Time hadn't exaggerated how swiftly he could propel her up and over the peak. Orgasm crashed over her with category five hurricane force. She muffled her scream against his shoulder and clutched his back, digging in her nails.

But Clay wasn't done. His mouth found her breast, sucking hard and drawing another gale of desire from deep within. His hips ground against hers, and then he kissed as if he couldn't get enough of her. She met him kiss for kiss. And then his face tightened and he groaned her name as he lunged once. Twice. The third time pulled Andrea into another vortex of passion she didn't have the strength to resist.

Clay braced himself on his elbows above her. Their bodies remained fused from ankle to chest, and the warmth of his breath steamed her sweat-dampened skin.

As Andrea struggled to regulate her own breathing a sobering thought crashed her back to dry land.

Clay hadn't disappointed her. Not even close.

Damn.

It.

Seven

A chime woke Clay from a sound sleep. He opened his eyes to unfamiliar terrain. Not his yacht. Andrea's bedroom. Last night flashed through his mind, and desire jolted his body like a lightning strike. For the first time in eight years he was right where he belonged. In Andrea's bed.

He turned his head and found her flushed face on the pillow beside him. Rolling to his side, he snuggled closer to her warm body, palmed her breast, nuzzled her soft hair and inhaled her scent. No perfume. Just pure woman with a hint of her coconut shampoo. A smile stretched his lips.

She stiffened and cursed, wiping his smile away as quickly as it had appeared. After one panicked look over her shoulder at him, she jerked upright in the tangled sheets and then flung back the covers and bolted into the bathroom chanting, *"Ohmygoshohmygoshohmygosh."*

He watched her adorable tush disappear around the

door with unease prickling the back of his neck. "Everything okay?"

She reemerged, hastily tying her robe and wearing a strained look on her face that didn't bode well for his morning appetite. "You're here. I overslept. No, everything is not okay."

The doorbell rang again—twice in rapid succession this time—and she winced. "Not good. Not good at all."

She hustled out of the room and down the stairs. He heard the front door open and then hushed voices carried up the stairwell.

Clay sat up, raked his hands through his hair and swung his legs to the floor. It was a good thing he and Andrea had taken a quick shower at 3:00 a.m. after making love that last time, because it didn't look like a leisurely shared bath would be on the agenda this morning. Even without the early morning visitor they had less than an hour to get to work.

Damn. He'd wanted to join her in that big whirlpool tub, lather every inch of her smooth skin and feel the jets swirling water around them while he buried himself deep inside her.

Next time.

He searched for his clothes and tugged them on. If he was lucky he could slip onto his yacht, shave and change without anyone at Dean noticing his wrinkled suit. He didn't want to make Andrea the object of gossip and speculation again, but sooner or later Dean employees would find out they were back together. From her less than lusty reaction this morning he gathered she needed a little time to get used to the idea.

He opened the cabinet over the bathroom sink, took a swig of her mouthwash and mulled over his last night's discovery. He'd fallen in love with Andrea again. Maybe he'd never stopped loving her. Whichever, he didn't intend to let her go this time. All he had to do was convince her to move to Miami.

He borrowed her hairbrush and then headed down the stairs. Who had the balls to drop in on her this early in the morning? It damned well better not be Haynes.

The voices—one too high-pitched to be the race car driver—led him through the den and into the kitchen. A boy with light brown hair sat on a barstool with his back to Clay. A backpack occupied the stool beside him. Who was the kid and why had he shown up at Andrea's door so early in the morning?

Andrea turned from the refrigerator, spotted Clay and froze midstep with an orange juice container clutched in her hand. Her mouth opened and closed, but no sound emerged and then her cheeks turned crimson. Her panicked gaze bounced from him to the kid and back again. The boy swiveled on the barstool.

Clay opened his mouth to say hello, but the words vanished. He stared at a picture of himself as a kid. Same sun-bleached hair, although the boy's was a few shades lighter. Same blue eyes. Same straight nose. His face and chin were a little rounder than Clay's had been. And that was Andrea's mouth, her full pouty lips.

"Clay, you should have waited upstairs," Andrea said.

He didn't even look at her. Couldn't pry his gaze off the boy. "What's your name, son?"

"Tim Montgomery. Who're you?"

Possibly your father. His lungs squeezed. "Clayton Dean."

The kid's eyes lit up. "Uncle Joseph's Clay?"

Uncle? "Yeah. How old are you, Tim?"

"Seven."

Clay's heart and lungs stalled. He'd fled Wilmington

eight years ago without once looking back to see what re-percussions he'd left in his wake. He'd left a big one.

He had a son.

Why hadn't Andrea told him? How could she have kept his child a secret? How could his mother? Patricia Dean had known how to reach him. The old anger and betrayal reared up inside him, but he tamped them down. He didn't want his son's first impression of his father to be that of a raving lunatic. But Clay was furious. More furious than he'd ever been in his life.

And he was scared. Damnation. He had a son and he knew nothing about kids.

Tim swiveled back and forth on the stool. "Andrea's taking me to work today 'cuz of school. Maybe I can work some with you, too?"

Andrea? He called his mother by her first name? He looked up to see a tender smile on Andrea's face. She filled the boy's glass and ruffled his hair. Tenderly. Lovingly. As a mother would.

Another wave of anger broadsided Clay. She'd denied him the opportunity to love his son. His jaw and fists clenched. He deliberately made himself relax one knotted muscle at a time. "It's June. Why aren't you on summer vacation?"

"Tim's in the year-round program," Andrea answered for the boy. "Today is take-your-child-to-work day, but since my mother is retired and my father is out of town on a weeklong business trip I volunteered to let Tim shadow me."

Her father and mother? "What do your parents have to do with this?"

Andrea put away the juice and then stared at him for several heartbeats. Confusion puckered her brow. "Tim is my brother."

Brother? Like hell. The kid was the perfect combination of Clay and Andrea. How could she deny her own child? Why had none of the gossipy workers at Dean told him Andrea had borne his son? Because they protected her. Because they remembered the way Clay had hurt her.

"Andrea, could I speak to you upstairs?" He barely managed to force the words out past the fury crushing his windpipe.

Wariness entered her eyes. She clutched her robe tighter. "Sure. I need to get ready anyway. Finish your cereal, Tim. I'll be right back and then we'll go."

Clay took another lingering look at his son, trying to absorb every detail, from the cowlick on the back of his head to the missing front top teeth, scraped knee and double-knotted sneakers. A lump rose in his throat. He'd missed so damned much.

He turned and gestured for Andrea to precede him and then followed her upstairs and into her bedroom. He closed and locked the door. "What in the hell do you mean, *your brother?* That boy's mine."

Shock slackened her features. "He is not."

"You're lying."

"Do I look like I've had a baby? You were certainly close enough last night *all three times* to see any stretch marks or scars." She sounded insulted, indignant.

If she'd had any signs of pregnancy, he'd been too busy making up for lost time and reeling from the discovery that he still loved her to notice. "He's mine," he repeated. "Why else would you look panicked when I saw him?"

"Because my little brother can't keep a secret. He'll blab to anyone who'll listen that you were here this morning and I wasn't dressed. I do not need that broadcast all over Dean."

What she said made sense, but it was still a lie. It had

to be. "He looks like me. How in the hell could you deny me my child?"

The confusion in her eyes turned into sympathy. She touched his arm. He yanked away, unwilling to let her dilute his anger with passion. "Clay, Tim couldn't possibly be yours. For one, I would know if I'd given birth. Two, he was born in February. The last time we slept together was New Year's Day before you graduated in May."

February. Was she lying? You couldn't fudge a birth date by six months. And then it hit him, knocking the strength from his legs and sucking the air from the room. He sank down on the rumpled bed and dropped his head into his hands. *February*.

He'd caught his father and Andrea's mother in May. He did the math and came up with nine months. Damnation. Tim wasn't his son. He was his half brother, a product of his father's adulterous affair with Andrea's mother. He had to be. Both of Andrea's parents were blondes, and the kid had brown hair. While Andrea's father had blue eyes they weren't *that* shade of blue—the blue Clay saw in the mirror each morning. And Clay… Clay was a chip off the old block. No wonder the boy looked like him.

"I can't believe you think so little of me that you'd believe I'd hide your child from you. Or that your mother or father would let me." She picked up a pillow and whacked him across the back with it. Anger, not embarrassment caused the redness in her cheeks. He could hear it in her clipped words, see it in her mast-straight posture, but most of all, he saw honesty in her eyes.

His heart rate slowly returned to normal, but his mind and stomach churned. He pinched the bridge of his nose. He wasn't a father. He was a brother. A half brother to Andrea's half brother. How damn twisted was that?

Did his father know? Did his mother? Did Andrea's father?

She crossed to the bedroom door, unlocked and opened it. "Please go, Clay. I have to get dressed. I'm running late and we have a delivery today. I have loads to do."

Once more her mother and his father had capsized Clay's world. Tim was a living, breathing reminder of his father's infidelity. And Clay couldn't tell Andrea. He rose. There was so much to say and none of it could be said. Last time he'd run. This time he couldn't. He wouldn't walk away from her again.

He wasn't his father. If he still loved Andrea after all these years apart, then he would love her until he took his last breath.

But this wasn't just about him and Andrea anymore. An innocent boy could be hurt. Clay had to find out who knew the truth about Tim's parentage. That meant he'd have to talk to Andrea's mother, and even though he'd rather swim through an alligator-infested swamp, he'd have to talk to his father.

He paused in the open door inches from Andrea, close enough to feel her heat and inhale her scent. Even his shocking discovery this morning wasn't enough to stop the rush of hunger through his veins. "We'll talk tonight."

He lifted a finger to brush her cheek and bent to kiss her, but she flinched out of reach. "There won't be a tonight, Clay. Last night was a mistake. Blame it on nostalgia or hormones or whatever you want. I won't sleep with you again. I have my future planned and it doesn't include you."

Her words hit him with a staggering blow, but he didn't go down. He had his work cut out for him. He would change her mind.

* * *

Considering the incredible night Clay'd had, this was turning into one lousy morning.

The first person he saw after passing through the Dean's gate was Toby Haynes. The race car driver sat on his yacht's back deck sipping from a mug, and while Clay would rather ignore him, courtesy demanded otherwise. "Morning, Haynes."

"Dean." The man's eyes traveled from Clay's unshaven face to his rumpled suit and back. "Wild night?"

As much as Clay would love to tell the jerk exactly where he'd been, what he'd been doing and who he'd been with, he wouldn't. "You're up earlier than usual."

"Waiting for Andrea. Thought we'd share coffee this morning. But she's late."

Clay hesitated. "She'll be here soon and she has Tim with her. It's take-your-kid-to-work day."

"Not surprising. She's nuts about that kid. And you know this how?"

Clay ignored the question. He wouldn't lie. "Enjoy your coffee."

He walked toward *The Expatriate*. Toby's laugh made him turn back.

"Son of a bitch. Never let it be said I'm a poor sport." The race car driver lifted his mug in salute. "This round to you, pal. But don't get cocky. I'll be back to give you another run for your money. Andrea's worth the effort and I mean to have her."

Clay's competitive hackles rose. Not for the first time he wanted to knock the jackass over the rails. "By all means, come back when you're ready to order *Checkered Flag 4,* but Andrea and I won't be here."

"Why's that?"

"My business is in Miami."

A smartass smile played about Haynes lips. "If you think she's going to leave this and go with you, then I gave you too much credit in the smarts department. Andrea won't leave Wilmington or Dean."

"You're wrong."

"Want to put money on that wager, junior? Because this looks like a sure-fired winner for me."

Pressure built in Andrea's chest until she was ready to scream.

At the rate she was going she'd never be ready for the delivery celebration in time. She took a deep breath, tried to concentrate on the multitude of details yet to be handled and tried even harder to block out the Technicolor flashbacks of last night that kept blindsiding her. It wasn't easy when each movement, each shift of her suit over her supersensitized breasts made her remember.

The sex had been incredible. Otherwise, she would have booted Clay out of her bed after the first time. But after a long drought of delicious partner-induced orgasms she'd greedily indulged in every morsel of satiation Clay had offered.

Peter, bless him, had come after Tim, claiming he needed "help" that only the seven-year-old could provide. Andrea hoped the pleas she'd made on the drive to work would keep Tim's lips zipped about Clay being at her house so early in the morning.

Clay, damn him, had been in and out of her office half a dozen times in the three hours since she'd arrived. Add in a surprise visit from Octavia Jenkins and the last thing Andrea's frayed nerves needed was to hear a helicopter approaching.

Please, please, please don't let the new clients arrive early. Their yacht isn't even at the dock yet.

She hadn't had time for a cup of coffee and caffeine withdrawal was kicking in. She pressed a hand to her throbbing head. A tap on her door drew her gaze away from the window and an entirely new tension squeezed her temples.

Guilt swamped her. "Toby. Good morning."

"Morning, angel." He crossed the room, but stopped on the opposite side of her desk. No good morning kiss. And that worried her less than it should have. She wasn't the type who could kiss one man and then kiss another only hours later. "I'm heading out today."

She blinked in surprise. "But you have another week left in your vacation."

He shrugged. "I'm gonna head back to the track. I shouldn't have taken time off midseason anyway. My relief driver is struggling. The boys will take the yacht."

That was not relief coursing through her veins. Was it? Damn Clayton Dean for confusing her. "I'm sorry to see you go."

"I'll be back. Count on it." He winked.

Behind her, the *thwump, thwump* of the helicopter setting down shook the windows and rattled her aching head.

"That's my ride and my crew. Don't go giving your heart to somebody else while I'm gone, Andi." He tugged on the brim of his racing cap, pivoted and left. Without a kiss goodbye.

Andrea sank into her desk chair, propped her elbows on her desk and dropped her head in her hands. Her future had just walked out the door while her past resided at the end of the dock like a blot on her personal landscape. She'd counted on this week clearing the decks. Instead, the past several days had made her more confused and depressed than ever before.

She didn't love Clay. And she never would again.

But she seriously doubted she'd ever be able to love anyone else.

Damn. It. Damn. Him.

No sooner did the helicopter lift off than Clay walked in again carrying a mug of coffee. She was almost grouchy enough to wrestle it from him.

"What now?" She winced at her bitchy tone.

Clay took one look at her face and passed her the mug. "Careful. It's a New Orleans brew. Stronger than you're used to."

How did he know she needed a caffeine fix? And then she mentally smacked her forehead. They'd shared enough mornings on his old sailboat for him to know she couldn't start her day without coffee. She wrapped her fingers around the warm mug, inhaled and then took a sip. Bliss. "Thank you."

"You're welcome. Mind if I show Tim *The Expatriate?*"

Mind? She could kiss him. No. She couldn't. No more of that. "I'm sure he'd like that."

"I can keep him occupied until the party if it would help."

Why did he have to be nice? She didn't want him to be nice. "That would be great."

She wanted him to be the selfish bastard who'd broken her heart. The selfish *forgettable* bastard who'd broken her heart. Because then it wouldn't be hard to let him go. Again.

On the back deck of the Dean sales office Andrea glanced furtively around and then dialed her friend's number on her cell phone. The new owners were due within the hour and her nerves were shot. She took a moment while the caterer set up the champagne lunch to escape.

"Rainbow Glass. This is Holly."

"I messed up," Andrea whispered.

"Oh, Andrea. What did you do?"

"I slept with Clay." Silence greeted her confession. "Go ahead and say it."

"I'm too good of a friend to say I told you so. So why did you? Sleep with him, I mean."

Andrea raked a hand through her hair. "My reasoning seemed logical at the time. Sex was supposed to be anticlimactic, disappointing."

"And it wasn't."

"No. It was good. Better than I remembered." Her skin flushed. "Damn. It."

"Do you still love him?"

"No. For heaven's sake, *no*. Are you crazy?" She darted a glance toward the dock. "How could I love a man who'd hurt me that way? I'd have to be an idiot to go back for more."

"What about Toby?"

"He's gone. He left an hour ago, and even though he said he'd be back, I get the feeling he won't. He didn't even kiss me goodbye." Andrea bowed her head. "Holly, I've done it again. I've killed another promising relationship."

"I know you don't want to hear this, but good riddance. Juliana and I both think Toby was only after the conquest. Once you'd slept with him we think he would have sailed off into the sunset."

Were her friends right? No, they couldn't be. They hadn't spent hours with Toby, hadn't witnessed his gallantry or the way he treated her like she was the most important thing in his life…next to racing.

"I think you're wrong, Holly. This thing with Toby has been going on for years." And her heart could learn to pitter-patter at his touch with a little practice. She was sure of it.

"You mean he's been toying with you—like a cat does a mouse—for years."

The blast of an air horn startled her and she almost dropped the phone. Andrea spun toward the dock as the crew maneuvered the newest yacht into the slip recently vacated by the *Checkered Flag 3* to ready it for the delivery celebration. Tim manned the horn on the fly bridge. She could see his elated grin from a hundred yards away. She waved and then Clay climbed to the top deck and stood beside him.

Andrea's stomach dropped like an anchor. Tim did resemble Clay. The startling thought stole her breath. But how could that be? It couldn't. It was simply coincidence.

"Holly, can we do lunch really soon? I want to hear about you and Eric. I still think you cheated by buying Juliana's brother instead of that gorgeous firefighter, but Octavia could be right. Eric might be the right guy for you. Opposites attract and all that."

"Shut up, Andrea Montgomery. That article was inexcusable, and you can bet I'm going to strangle Octavia for writing such dribble. Eric is a friend. That's it. No matter how good-looking he is."

"So you admit he's handsome." Holly sputtered, but a signal from the receptionist caught Andrea's eye. "Look, Holly, I have to go—the new owners are here and I have Tim today. Crazy day."

"After a crazy night. Andrea, stay out of trouble and out of Clay's bed until you figure out where you want this to go. He's not staying. Remember that."

How could she forget? He'd leave her just like last time. And she still didn't know why she was so dumpable.

Elaine Montgomery looked stylish and far younger than her age with her blond hair upswept and her pantsuit skimming her slender curves. Heads had turned as she crossed the restaurant, heading for the table where Andrea waited. But as usual, Andrea realized, her mother didn't notice the attention. Andrea could only hope she'd look as good when she reached her fifties.

"Aren't Holly and Juliana joining us tonight?" her mother asked as she slid into the booth across from Andrea at the trendy new restaurant on Market Street.

"No. They're busy with their bachelors. What about Patricia?"

"She's stuck to Joseph like a stamp on an envelope. She hasn't left his side since the stroke except for the day of the bachelor auction, and then she hired a nurse. I had hoped Clay would stay with Joseph some and give Patricia a break. I don't think she would agree to leave Joseph with anyone else again. Heaven knows, your father and I as well as most of the Caliber Club members have offered."

The diamond eternity band Andrea's father had given her mother for their thirtieth anniversary several years back sparkled in the overhead light and Andrea felt a twinge. At the rate she was going she'd never get a wedding ring let alone another piece of jewelry to celebrate reaching a marriage milestone.

"I'm working on Clay, but he still refuses to speak to his father and he won't tell me why. So it's just the two of us again this week." Andrea welcomed the waiter's arrival because it gave her time to organize her thoughts. After he took their drink and appetizer orders and left she noticed the tension around her mother's mouth. "Is everything okay?"

Her mother's smile looked forced. "Of course. And before I forget, Timmy had a wonderful time today. Thank you for taking him. You know how much he loves spending time at Dean. I left him chattering nonstop to your father about his day and Clay. I think he has a new hero."

Andrea concealed her wince and hoped Tim would keep her secret.

"How is working with Clay going?"

Her mother had no idea what a loaded question she'd asked. "He handles the details of Dean like a pro. Joseph will be pleased."

"But?"

Where should she start? With her mistake last night or with Clay's odd accusation? Normally, she and her mother were as close as sisters, but Andrea wasn't ready to share her blunder because she didn't understand it. In her head she knew sleeping with Clay had been a stupid and stupendous mistake—one she couldn't repeat no matter how loudly her body clamored for his. But each time he'd touched her today—and he'd done so often during the delivery celebration—her hormones had thrown a party worthy of Mardi Gras. She'd felt as drunk and dizzy as if she'd partied on Bourbon Street all night even though she hadn't touched a drop of the champagne they'd served.

In a way, she had partied all night. Her skin flushed at the scorching memory of how many times and how noisily she'd partied. She grabbed her ice water and sipped. "Who in our family has dark hair?"

Her mother looked up abruptly. "Why?"

"Because Clay thought Tim was his son." She snorted in disgust. "As if I'd keep something like that from him. But he said Tim looked like him. And I guess Tim does a little. I think it's mostly because of the hair and the eye color. Daddy has blue eyes, but I couldn't figure out where the hair came from."

The waiter arrived with their drinks and salads and then took their entrée orders and departed.

The ice in her mother's glass tinkled as she lifted her

Tom Collins to her lips. "Your great-grandfather, my grand-father, had dark hair, and I'm sure there are other relatives on your father's side, but at the moment I can't recall who."

"Then I guess Tim's a throwback." Andrea speared a cherry tomato.

"Yes." Her mother lowered her drink and reached for her salad fork. "Tim said that was Clay's car I saw in your driveway this morning when I dropped him off."

Andrea's appetite vanished. She toyed with her salad. So much for secrets. "Yes."

"Do you think it's wise to become involved with him again?"

"I'm not."

"Andrea, his car had dew and sea spray all over it and the hood was cool. He hadn't arrived recently."

Andrea cringed. "I just want to get over him, Mom. I thought sleeping with him would do the trick."

Her mother covered her hand. "Oh honey, that never works."

"How would you know? You met Daddy in high school and you've been together ever since. Why can't I find a perfect love like that?"

Elaine lowered her gaze, but not before Andrea caught a glimpse of deep sadness. "Love is never perfect and I did have a life before your father, you know."

Andrea blinked in surprise. "I thought Daddy was your first love."

"Harrison was my first lover and he's the love of my life. I count my blessings every day for him."

First lover?

Her mother and father had been high school sweet-hearts. They'd married right after college—just like Andrea and Clay had planned. When had her mother had time to take another lover? If she and Andrea's father had broken up at some point and then reunited, they'd never mentioned it. Had her mother's word choice been a slip of the tongue?

As close as she and her mother were, Andrea was certain she didn't want to hear about her mother's intimate life. So she let the subject drop, but that didn't stop the questions from tumbling through her brain.

Eight

Clay paused in his morning run long enough to buy a Saturday newspaper from the local convenience store. After checking the score for the Marlins game he turned to Octavia Jenkins's second installment.

Clayton Dean seems eager to monopolize Andrea Montgomery. Sources say the former lovers have completed four of their seven dates in only two weeks. Is that because Clay fears the sexy contender vying for Andrea's affections or because the old ashes aren't as cold as they claim? This reporter has learned that it's not only Andrea's sunsets Clay's after. The couple has shared a few sunrises, too.

Damnation. It's a wonder Andrea hadn't hammered on his door before dawn again this morning to chew him out.

She'd like this installment even less than the last one. Clay folded the paper and jogged back toward Dean.

His pulse kicked up a notch and it had nothing to do with his pace. He wanted to see Andrea again. The sooner, the better. They had three dates left, and he would use them to convince her to come with him to Miami. No matter what the car jockey said, Clay knew he would succeed. Failure wasn't an option.

Clay turned up Dean's mile-long driveway. He'd been stymied in learning more about Tim's parentage. Last night he'd invited his mother to dinner to quiz her to see what she knew. She'd countered by issuing an open invitation for him to eat with her and his father. Clay had refused. He wasn't ready to face Joseph Dean yet.

That left Elaine Montgomery. Clay intended to corner her as soon as possible and he had the perfect excuse. Tim had left his hand-held video game on Clay's yacht yesterday.

Two hours later Clay rang the Montgomery's bell. Elaine opened the door. Her eyes, the same caramel-brown as Andrea's, widened with surprise and a hint of fear.

"Clayton. How n-nice to see you." She lied politely, but not well.

"May I come in?" Surprisingly his voice didn't reflect his inner turmoil even though betrayal burned like acid in his throat.

Her reluctance couldn't have been clearer. Last night had been girls' night. Had Andrea told her mother about Clay's reaction to meeting Tim?

"I have Tim's video game." He dangled the canvas carrying case from his fingertips.

"Tim and his father have gone fishing. I'll give it to him when he returns. Thank you for bringing it." She reached for the bag. Clay moved it out of reach.

"His father?" This time the sarcasm seeped out.

Elaine's face paled and tensed. "Come in."

She led him to the living room. It looked the same as it had eight years ago. He and Andrea had made out on that couch too many times to count. "May I get you a drink?"

He couldn't pretend this was a social call. "Does my father know?"

"Know what?" she asked, feigning ignorance, but the woman would never make it as an actress. The way she twisted her wedding ring around on her finger and the slight quiver of her lips gave her agitation away.

"Don't play games with me, Elaine. Tim is my father's son."

She drew herself up, lifting her chin in the same way Andrea did when preparing for battle. "You are mistaken. Harrison is Tim's father in every way. His name is on the birth certificate."

"That may make him responsible in the eyes of the law, but that boy carries Dean DNA."

She opened her mouth, but Clay cut her off. "Don't waste my time with lies. I want to know who knows, and if my father does, then why didn't the bastard do something?"

"And what would you have him do? Force me to have an abortion? Divorce your mother, the woman he loved more than life, and destroy two families on the possibility that Tim *might* be his?" She hurled the words in a burst of temper.

What right did *she* have to be angry? She'd ruined his life not the other way around, and if he were as selfish as his father, he'd consider returning the favor. But taking Elaine Montgomery and Joseph Dean down meant taking Clay's mother and Andrea down, too. "If he loved her, he wouldn't have cheated on her."

"We're not perfect, Clay. None of us. And that includes

you." Shoulders drooping, she sank into a chair. "We all make mistakes." She wrung her hands, looked away and then met his gaze. "Don't blame your father for this. It was my fault."

"It takes two."

"You don't understand."

"Then explain it to me. How could you betray your husband and your best friend? And how long was the affair going on?"

She hesitated long enough that Clay thought she wouldn't answer, and then she lifted her head and met his gaze. "It was only that one time. Your father and I both regretted our lapse immediately. We knew how much our selfishness could cost us and the ones we loved, and we vowed it would never happen again. And it didn't. When Joseph realized you'd left and you weren't coming back it hit him hard. And I felt doubly guilty for having been a part of what drove you away. What you saw that day should never have happened."

"If you loved your husband so much, why risk an affair?"

Sadness and regret filled her eyes. "Because a long time ago I was in love with your father, and then he met my best friend. From that moment on Joseph didn't have eyes for anyone else. Patricia became his world."

Surprised, Clay lowered himself to the sofa. In all the stories his parents and Andrea's had told about being high school sweethearts, they'd never shared this part. "You married another man."

"Yes, and I love Harrison, but it wasn't the same as the love I felt for your father. You never forget your first love. That's why you'll never forget Andrea or she you.

"When I hit forty I started wondering what I'd missed by marrying so young and not seeing the world, and in not becoming your father's lover when I had the chance. Stupid of me to yearn for the what-could-have-beens when I had everything. A husband who pampered me. A beautiful, talented daughter. A million-dollar home. And I…" She paused, closed her eyes and took a deep breath. When she lifted her lids he saw strength and resignation on her face. "I seduced your father, Clay. Not deliberately or maliciously. But the result was the same.

"I was forty-seven years old. It never occurred to me that I could get pregnant. Harrison and I had tried for years after Andrea was born to conceive another baby. We'd always wanted a large family. As soon as the doctor told me I was expecting I was overjoyed. It wasn't until later that the doubts and the fears crept in, and I realized I didn't know who the father was. And it could have been either of them."

He flinched. Too much information.

"I had a difficult pregnancy from the very beginning, so I quit my job. And honestly, I was relieved because then I didn't have to face Joseph or the shame on his face every day. Because of my age I was more concerned with whether or not my baby would be healthy than I was with whose DNA he carried. Either way, Tim was a blessing. He was born as bald as a cue ball. His baby hair came in the same dark blond Andrea's is now and his eyes were blue like my husband's. It wasn't until Tim approached his third birthday that both darkened. We do have some dark-haired relatives."

He didn't want to feel sympathy for her, dammit, but the fire of hatred he'd fanned for eight years cooled a little.

"Does my father know?" he repeated.

"He's never asked and I've never volunteered the information. The same goes for Harrison and your mother."

"How could she look at Tim and not see me?"

"Tim takes after me in many ways, and Clay, love is a powerful thing. It can make you overlook what you don't want to know. In fact, none of us truly knows who Tim's father is. We've had no reason to have DNA testing done. And the blood types are inconclusive."

"Does your husband know you cheated? Does Andrea?"

"No. It was over. It couldn't be changed. And it wasn't going to happen again. Telling them would only upset them and cause pain. So I didn't. Harrison adores Tim. I would never do anything to drive them apart."

Her confession confirmed that Clay couldn't tell Andrea why he'd left without hurting her or Tim. So where did he go from here? "I love your daughter."

"Do you?" She sounded skeptical.

"I won't leave Wilmington without her this time."

"If you'd loved her enough, you wouldn't have left her the last time."

Clay sucked a sharp breath at the unexpected attack.

"And if you truly loved your father, you'd forgive him for not being perfect, and you'd quit punishing your mother for something that wasn't her fault."

He'd be damned if he'd be lectured to by the woman who'd almost wrecked his family and still could if this news got out. He stood and stalked toward the door. His hand closed around the knob.

Elaine pressed a hand to the door, holding it closed. "You were the most important thing in Patricia's life, Clay. You can hate me if you want to, but she didn't deserve what you did to her. And neither did Andrea."

Clay glared at Elaine Montgomery, jerked the door open and left.

The truth stung.

Andrea used to love Mondays, the promise of a new week, the excitement of what she could accomplish in the next five days and interacting with the employees as they gave shape to customers' dreams with fiberglass and wood. But her love of Mondays had turned to dread since Clay's return.

These days she stayed as tense as a flag pole, waiting for Clay to walk in or worse, summon her to his "office" as he had this morning.

She gathered the necessary files and made her way down the dock in her rubber-soled Docksides and a pantsuit. No more sexy shoes or short skirts. Mission accomplished. She'd made Clay want her. But her goal had backfired because the reverse was also true. He'd made her want him.

The sun beat down, promising another scorching June day with suffocating humidity, but today, thanks to Olivia's article, Andrea's temper rivaled the weather. She boarded Clay's yacht and spotted him at his desk/galley table and then knocked on his door with more force than necessary.

He lifted his gaze from the documents in front of him and the impact of those blue-blue eyes hit her like too many caramel apple martinis on an empty stomach. *Toughen up, girl.*

With a jerk of his chin he motioned for her to enter. The door glided open easily beneath Andrea's fingers, and the air-conditioning swept over her, cooling her skin but doing nothing for her temper or the warmth settling in the pit of her stomach.

"Sit down. Did you bring the prospective client list?"

She deposited the files in front of him and slid into the seat farthest away from him. Unfortunately, that gave her an unobstructed view of the companionway leading to his stateroom.

Tim had chattered incessantly about the cool gadgets on Clay's boat, piquing Andrea's curiosity, but she didn't dare ask for a tour. If she went below decks and heard the slap of the waves on the hull, her resolution to keep her distance would probably crumble under the weight of her memories of his tongue stroking her mouth, his hands on her breasts and his hips grinding against hers.

Blinking away her distraction she focused on her notes. "The Langfords are visiting tomorrow to order a seventy-foot sport-fishing craft. The Richardsons will be here on Friday. They're not sure exactly what model they want, but they can afford almost anything we build. I've also included two new appointments that aren't on your calendar. All four couples have been financially prescreened."

He glanced at the paperwork and then pushed it aside. "I've made reservations at Devil's Shoals Steakhouse for us tomorrow evening."

Alarm skittered over her. Devil's Shoals was the most romantic and exclusive restaurant in the area. "No."

"What do you mean, 'no'?"

"I'm getting pitying looks from the staff because of Octavia's story. I will not go out with you and have them think I'm stupid enough to fall for you again. From here on you'll see me at work and nowhere else."

A line formed between Clay's eyebrows. "We have three dates left."

"As the one who purchased your auction package I have the right to cancel the dates. I'm exercising that option."

"What about the publicity?"

"Forget it. I'd rather not have it than have this…bilge."

He rolled his pen between his fingers—the same way he'd rolled her nipples. Heat filled her cheeks and her panties, and her traitorous nipples tightened. Andrea looked away and ended up staring at the corner of his bed. Damn. It. Why couldn't the sex have been lousy? And why couldn't she forget how *un*lousy it had been?

"My mother invited me to dinner," Clay said quietly.

"That's wonderful."

"I won't go alone."

Every muscle in Andrea's body tensed with dread. *Don't ask. Oh please, don't ask.* "I'm sure you can find a date."

"I'll go only if you'll come with me."

"Don't be ridiculous. Your parents want to see you not me."

"Fine. I'll send my regrets."

Andrea fisted her hands beneath the table. She'd promised to do whatever it took to get Clay and Joseph together. Going to dinner would accomplish that goal. If she was lucky, this goal wouldn't backfire on her the way the other one had. Sleeping with Clay had been a rotten idea. How had she talked herself into it?

"All right. But this isn't a date. I'll meet you there."

"No deal. I'd show up and you wouldn't. I'll pick you up at six and we'll go together or not at all."

He had her and he knew it. She wanted to scream. Instead, she forced herself to nod. "I'll be ready."

A whirlpool of emotion twisted in Clay's belly. Anger. Resentment. Betrayal. Guilt.

His hand shook as he extracted the keys from the ignition and stared at the large Colonial house where he'd grown up. A smarter man would put the car in gear and drive away. Even with Andrea looking beautiful and sexy in a flirty yellow sundress by his side this wouldn't be a pleasant night.

"Clay?"

He blinked. Andrea stood beside his car in the semicircular driveway. He hadn't even heard her get out of the vehicle.

The front door opened and his mother stepped out onto the deeply shaded, two-storied, columned porch. As a kid

Clay had shimmied up those columns like a monkey does a tree much to his mother's dismay and his father's amusement. But it had been years since he'd felt so carefree.

No backing out now. He'd come this far. And dammit, he wasn't a coward. Years of anger, acrimony and accusations bubbled like lava inside him waiting for release. Tonight he'd confront his cheating father with the facts the minute he got him alone.

He shoved open his door, joined Andrea and walked beside her up the wide brick walk.

"Hello, dear." His mother greeted Andrea, kissing her cheek, and then she turned to Clay. Her arms banded around his middle and she hugged him tight enough to squeeze the breath from his lungs. When she drew back tears glistened in her eyes. "Welcome home."

Guilt burned him like battery acid as Elaine's words replayed in his head. *She didn't deserve what you did to her.* "Mom, it's good to see you."

What else could he say? It *wasn't* good to be home. Clay examined her carefully made-up face, noticing the lines of strain he'd been too angry to see the day of the auction. His mother looked older, tired, nervous.

"Come in, come in. I've been cooking all day. I made all of your favorites, Clay." Clay followed the women inside.

"Where was Dora when you invaded her kitchen?" The cook and housekeeper had been with them since Clay's teens.

"She played cards with your father and the occupational therapist while I cooked, and tonight is her bingo night."

Occupational therapist? Clay looked to Andrea for explanation. Sadness tinged her smile. "Is poker still the only way to get Joseph to do his exercises?"

Exercises? His mother had said his father's stroke had been a mild one, that he'd be as good as new in no time.

She turned toward the living room which surprised Clay. His family had always preferred the sunken den at the back of the house with its view of the Intracoastal Waterway to the rarely used formal room on the street side. The living room furniture had been pushed apart and the coffee table removed.

And then he saw his father and Clay's world stopped. The slam of his heartbeat in his ears drowned out his mother and Andrea's conversation. The stooped man in the chair bore little resemblance to the robust man Clay had cursed for eight years.

A lopsided smile lifted the right corner of his father's lips, drawing attention to the drooping muscles on the left side of Joseph Dean's face. He tried to stand and immediately Clay's mother rushed to his side to help him because he couldn't do it alone.

He couldn't do it alone.

Andrea, in the guise of giving Joseph a hug, pulled him to his feet and steadied him. "Hi, handsome. I hear you're beating the pants off the therapist again."

"I'm trying. Have to get even for what she puts me through." His father's voice sounded weak, more like the voice on the phone than the forceful tone Clay remembered. It was only then that Clay noticed the metal walker to the right of his wingback chair.

Andrea stepped aside, but Clay noticed she didn't go far. One of her hands rested on his father's waist, tightening when Joseph lifted his right hand and wobbled on his feet.

Clay's shoes seemed leaded. With great effort he forced his feet forward to accept his father's handshake.

"Good to have you home, son." His father's voice broke and tears filled his eyes.

"Dad." Shocked by his father's weakness, Clay looked away. Why hadn't anyone warned him? And then Clay realized Andrea had tried and he'd refused to listen. In the past two weeks he'd cut her off each time she'd mentioned his father.

And then it hit him why they were in the living room. His father probably couldn't manage the three stairs down into the den.

"Why don't you two sit down and catch up," his mother said, gesturing for Clay to take the wing chair beside his father's. She and Andrea tried to help Joseph sit, but he irritably waved them away and slowly, awkwardly worked himself back into his seat.

His mother touched Andrea's arm. "Honey, I could use your help in the kitchen."

Clay's gaze met Andrea's as she passed. He found sympathy and understanding in her eyes. Her hand caught and squeezed his and then she let go before more than a spark could ignite.

The door between the dining room and the kitchen swung closed behind the women. Alone at last. Clay fisted his hands and took a deep breath and faced his father. This was it. The opportunity he'd been waiting for to tell his father exactly what he thought of him. To tell him about Tim.

But Clay couldn't do it. He couldn't verbally strike the weakened man in front of him.

But he would. Later. When his father was stronger Clay would tell him how badly he'd screwed up his life. For now he'd stick to a relatively safe topic—business.

Concerned by Clay's silence, Andrea turned on her front mat after unlocking her door. He hadn't spoken since leaving his parents' home. "Clay, are you all right?"

Her porch light illuminated the strain in his strong face,

the down-turned corners of his lips and the crease between his eyebrows. "I didn't know he was this bad."

Where was the satisfaction she'd expected to feel? She'd wanted Clay to be shocked, wanted him to feel guilty for not rushing to Joseph's bedside immediately following the stroke and for refusing to see his father since coming home. And yes, as petty as it now seemed, she'd wanted to scare Clay into acknowledging that he could have lost his father without healing the breach between them.

But instead of gloating over the success of the evening, she felt Clay's pain, remembered the shock of seeing a man she revered brought to his knees—literally and figuratively. She'd had five weeks to come to terms with the changes in Joseph Dean. Clay had had mere hours.

"His prognosis is good."

"He can barely walk. His left hand is practically useless."

"The physical challenges will improve with continued therapy. He's already made great strides since it happened."

He swallowed visibly and raked a hand through his hair, ruffling it the way she had Thursday night. Her fingers curled around the memory and her pulse stuttered. Damn. It.

"He was worse than this?"

She nodded. "The doctors say he'll make most of his recovery in the first few months and then continue at a slower rate for the rest of the first year afterward."

He blinked and straightened, but his eyes still looked shell-shocked. "Thanks for going with me."

"You're welcome. Are you going back to your yacht now?"

He shook his head. "I need...to think. I'm going to drive around awhile."

As distracted as he seemed, driving wouldn't be safe. The road was loaded with summer tourists who had no idea where they were going. It took full concentration to avoid an accident.

Without a doubt Clay needed comfort, but Andrea feared that if she invited him inside she'd give in to her overzealous hormones and comfort him in bed. Despite changing the sheets and spraying perfume on her mattress, her bedroom still smelled of Clay. He inhabited her dreams every night as surely as if he lay beside her in the bed. Instead of erasing the memories, sleeping with him had apparently refreshed and reinforced them. She couldn't stop thinking about him, about his touch, the warmth of his breath on her skin or the surge of him deep inside her.

A shiver started in the pit of her stomach and worked its way to her extremities in the form of goose bumps. She rubbed her hands along her upper arms. "Want to take a walk on the beach?"

He shoved his hands in his pockets, looked at his car and down the street and then his gaze returned to hers. "Sure."

She led him through the den, pausing to shed her sandals and drop her purse in a chair while he kicked off his leather deck shoes and rolled the legs of his khaki pants to midcalf. He followed her out the back door and down the steep steps to the beach. The moon whitewashed the water and the day's warmth lingered in the sand sifting between her toes. A balmy breeze blew off the ocean, rippling the hem of her sundress against her knees and tossing her hair.

They walked a half mile in silence, side by side like the old days, but back then they would have been wound around each other or at the very least, holding hands. Andrea realized Clay was no longer beside her. He'd had stopped a few yards down the beach while she was lost in the past. She backtracked and stood beside him.

He exhaled and shoved his hands in his pockets. "Tell me what happened."

She'd expected him to ask during dinner. Instead he'd turned into the man who'd cohosted the delivery celebration with her Friday afternoon. He'd been polite, but distant, keeping the conversation impersonal and treating his mother and father more like clients than family.

"Joseph had an embolic stroke. That's caused by a clot that travels through the bloodstream and lodges in the brain, cutting off blood flow and damaging the affected cells."

"Who found him?"

A weight settled on her chest. Andrea stared at the undulating water. "I did. We were due to go on a sea trial after lunch. Joseph was late, but I thought he might still be on the phone with one of our more demanding clients, so I kept working. When I finally went looking for him, I found him on his hands and knees in the middle of his office." Guilt closed her throat. "If I'd gone sooner—"

Clay caught her arm and pulled her around to face him and then he released her just as quickly, but the heat of his touch remained imprinted on her skin. "There's no way you can blame yourself for this."

"Joseph is never late for anything. I should have checked on him earlier."

"Why didn't he call for help?"

"He couldn't. His speech was affected. Luckily, the medicines they gave him at the hospital reversed that. You probably noticed he's still a little slow to find the words, but he does find them, and his thought processes are clear."

"He's very…emotional."

Clay's embarrassment over his father's tears had been obvious. "Another side effect of the stroke is having trouble controlling emotions. That, too, should improve."

Clay tipped his head back and swiped his face with his hand. "He won't be able to return to work in two months."

"The doctors said he might be, but in a reduced capacity. He needs your help, Clay, for as long as you can give it."

The moon blanched all color from his face. "Dammit, I have my own company to manage. I can't stay here."

"Could you relocate Seascape?" She wanted the words back the moment they left her mouth.

What are you saying? Do you want him to move back home?

No. Definitely not. She couldn't face him and the hunger she felt for him on a daily basis, because she could never trust him not to hurt her again. If he returned she'd have to leave Dean and leaving Dean would break her heart. She'd invested the love in the company that she couldn't find in her personal life. The staff was like an extended family.

He stalked toward the waterline, stopping only when an incoming wave lapped at his ankles. "I am returning to Miami. I can't…stay here."

Andrea dampened her dry lips. Her heart thudded heavily and her palms moistened. She loved Patricia and Joseph Dean almost as much as she did her own parents, and the Deans would be overjoyed if Clay returned to Wilmington and took his rightful place at Dean Yachts. She had to do everything in her power to make that happen.

Inhaling deeply, she braced herself to ask the question she'd known all along she would have to ask. "Would you stay if I resigned?"

Fists clenched, Clay rounded on her and splashed back in her direction, stopping only inches from her. "Dammit, Andrea, I told you you're not the reason I left."

She lifted her chin to meet his gaze. "But you won't

explain why you did, so until you level with me, Clay, I have to go with what the facts tell me. And the facts tell me I'm the reason you and your father aren't speaking."

His jaw muscles bunched. His brow creased and his lips compressed. For several seconds he held her gaze and she thought he might actually tell her what she desperately needed to know. She tensed in anticipation, in dread. *What is wrong with me? Why does every man I care about dump me?*

"I want to talk to his doctor."

She blinked at the abrupt change of subject and her lungs deflated. "I'm sure that can be arranged. Ask your mother to set it up. And while you're at it, you might want to consider offering to watch your father once in a while. Patricia has barely left his side since this began, and she needs a break before she collapses."

"I'll talk to her about hiring some help."

But he wouldn't offer to stay with his father. Andrea sighed. Her job was far from done.

Nine

Would you stay if I left?

Clay focused on Andrea's words as they retraced their path. Her question proved she was willing to leave North Carolina. Haynes was wrong.

He didn't want to think about watching his father sip from a straw because Joseph couldn't drink from a glass without dribbling down his shirt. Clay didn't want to think about his father's lasagna being served in child-sized bites because he couldn't manage a knife. Clay didn't want to think about what would happen to Dean when he returned to Miami.

He didn't want to think. Period.

What he wanted—*needed*—was a night of hot, sweaty sex to distract him from the ache in his chest dinner had left behind. Heartburn. That's all it was. The pain had nothing to do with the shock of seeing his father tonight and everything to do with the spicy meal—even if Italian food had never bothered him before.

He'd had a setback in his plans, but that didn't mean he couldn't keep moving forward in his quest to convince Andrea to go back to Florida with him.

On the concrete pad at the base of her steps Andrea turned on the spigot to rinse the sand from her feet. Clay eased his foot between hers underneath the gushing faucet. He brushed his toes over her ankle, around her heel and stroked the gritty sand away from her instep. He heard her breath catch and bit back a satisfied smile. Andrea had always loved a foot massage and he'd give her a good one. Upstairs. Preferably naked.

She gripped the banister and lifted a suspicious gaze to his. "What are you doing?"

He rested his hand beside hers on the wood, fingers parallel and touching hers. Only inches separated their bodies and an ocean breeze lifted strands of her hair to his cheek, snagging the silken threads in his evening beard. "Washing my feet. And yours."

He shifted his leg, dragging the inside of his thigh against hers, but stopping his knee short of her panties. The cool water rushing over his feet did nothing to cool his quickly rising libido.

Her lids lowered and she swallowed. "Don't, Clay."

"Don't what?"

The look she aimed at him said she was wise to his strategy. "Don't try to tempt me back into bed."

Guilty and totally unrepentant, Clay felt a smile twitch on his lips. "Is that what I'm doing?"

She backed up the bottom step, putting distance between them but raising her eyes level with his. "I know you're upset. Tonight must have been hard for you, but I'm not interested in a temporary fling."

He turned off the water and straightened. "Who said anything about temporary?"

"You did when you said you were leaving."

Cupping her jaw he looked deep into her eyes. "Come back to Miami with me."

Her eyes widened and her lips parted on a gasp. Before she could voice the objections he saw chasing across her expressive face, Clay covered her mouth with his. At the touch of her soft lips, desire, hot and instantaneous, flared in his blood. He climbed the step, crowding their bodies together on the narrow tread, and then banded his hand around her waist to pull her soft, warm curves closer.

She couldn't possibly miss his erection against her stomach. He wanted her. Bad. No other woman had ever been able to draw such an immediate response from him. If that wasn't love, then what was it?

Her palm flattened against his belly as if to push him away, but she didn't. Good thing. He'd have tumbled backward onto the concrete at the bottom of the steps. For safety's sake he shifted sideways and nudged her back against the railing which freed his hands to comb through her hair, down her spine and over her hips to tease the small of her back with his fingertips. He coaxed her mouth with his, twining his tongue with hers and nipping at her bottom lip until his head spun.

Andrea's nails scraped over his waist and a shiver shook him. He cupped her breast, flicking his thumbnail over the hardened tip. She moaned into his mouth and then tore her lips away from his and turned her head aside, granting him access to the pulse fluttering wildly at the base of her throat. She tasted good, smelled good, felt so damned good in his arms. How had he lived without her for eight years?

Her breasts shuddered against his chest and then her fingers tightened, pushing him away this time. "Stop."

"Stop what? This?" He caught her earlobe in his teeth and gently tugged a gasp from her. "Or this?" He rolled her nipple between his fingers.

"B-both." Arousal flushed her cheeks.

Clay lifted his head and lowered his hands to her waist. Her panted breaths and expanded pupils told him she wanted him as much as he wanted her. "Let me make you feel good, Andrea."

She stiffened and frowned. "Why? So you can hurt me again later?"

"I won't hurt you, babe. Trust me."

She wrenched from his arms and raced up the steps. At the top she turned to watch his slower ascent. "That's the problem, Clay. I don't trust you anymore and I never will again."

Whoa. Her words set him back.

She unlocked the back door and stepped inside, scooped up his shoes and then stabbed them against his chest. "Go."

He searched for a way to salvage the evening, a way to get his plans back on track. If he could get her into bed, he could remind her why they belonged together. He dragged a fingertip down her arm. "Andrea—"

She turned on her heel, crossed the den and yanked open the front door. "Get out, Clay."

All right, so maybe he was moving too fast for her. He had six weeks left to change her mind. He could afford to be patient. "I'll see you in the morning."

"Not if I see you first," he heard her grumble a split second before the door slammed.

Andrea made good on her threat by avoiding Clay for a day and a half. Those thirty-six hours dragged by like weeks, distracting him from his enjoyment of his temporary job.

As an independent naval architect he drew the plans for yachts and then the owners took them to the builder of their choice to have the craft built. More often than not Clay never saw the finished product. This week he'd worked on blueprints for two customers—not his original designs, but adaptations of Dean designs. If he stayed, he'd get to see the finished vessels launched and christened.

Don't go there. You're not staying. Which means you need to focus on Andrea.

Andrea's avoidance of him made his decision to seduce her into returning to Miami with him all but impossible. She'd quit coming in early to have her coffee on the deck, and every time he went looking for her he found her surrounded by Dean employees.

Today, he intended to put an end to her evasive tactics. He rapped on her open office door and the look of consternation on her face when she spotted him confirmed his theory that the minute she saw him head up the dock she made herself scarce. He'd been in the fiberglass building when she arrived this morning and therefore, she hadn't seen him coming.

He leaned against the jamb. "I'm taking Tim fishing this afternoon."

"Why?"

Because he wanted to get to know his little brother. "We have nothing scheduled, and from what Tim said the other day that kid loves to fish as much as I did at his age."

"But Tim's in school."

"Your mother's bringing him over after he gets out."

Andrea blinked in surprise. "My mother has approved this?"

Elaine didn't dare refuse given that Clay knew her secret. "Yes. You're welcome to join us."

She bit her lip. "But I—"

"Have an empty calendar this afternoon. I had Fran check." He ran his gaze over her sedate black pantsuit. If she thought dressing like a nun would make him forget what a few pieces of fabric concealed and how good they were together, then she was mistaken. Men loved mystery—at least this man did. Besides, the suit and the lacy top she wore beneath it were sexy in a subtle way.

"Eve also told me you keep sunscreen and a swimsuit here. Bring them."

Andrea shuffled the papers on her desk and then laid them aside. "Clay, this isn't a good idea. Perhaps another time—"

"Be on the dock by three or we'll leave without you." Clay turned on his heel and left before she could argue.

He would win her back. Failure wasn't an option. And he was counting on her protectiveness of her little brother to bring her to the dock.

Trapped.

Andrea sighed and tucked a stray lock of hair beneath her hat. How had she let herself be coerced into this? Because she hadn't wanted Tim to get any more attached to Clay than he'd already become. Clay would leave and Tim would be hurt. She ought to know.

Clay dropped anchor in a small inlet off Masonboro Island. There wasn't another soul in sight other than an occasional boat passing by in the waterway. Even though they were surrounded by wide open spaces, sharing the small skiff with the man who enticed her to throw caution into the winds was like being locked in a cell with temptation. She couldn't escape unless she trudged through the marshy water to the uninhabited barrier island and took her chances with the foxes and the alligator some claimed to have seen basking on the beach.

Clay's brief red trunks showed his tanned muscular legs, broad shoulders and six pack abs to advantage. Each time he passed by her seat in front of the center console he managed to brush his warm, hair-roughed skin against her and whip her hormones into frenzy. The man was hell on her nerves.

And Tim was in heaven. He hadn't stopped chattering since they'd left the dock. And Clay… Andrea shook her head. She never would have expected Clay to have the patience of a saint, but he answered each of Tim's questions—no matter how foolish or repetitive.

He'd be a good father.

Andrea winced at the stab of regret and focused on the shoreline. Eight years ago she'd thought he'd be the father of her children. But she'd been wrong. Painfully wrong.

Tim tilted his head and laughed at something Clay said, yanking Andrea's gaze back to the fishermen. Her heart skipped a beat at the similarities in their stance and then she shook her head. Damn Clay and his insane allegation that Tim was his son. Because of it she kept seeing similarities—gestures, the slant of Tim's smile, a teasing twinkle in her brother's eyes—between the males that she knew were a figment of her overactive imagination. Tim had probably picked those up from Joseph or copied them from Clay the other day. Her little brother had a budding case of hero worship.

What would hers and Clay's children have looked like? The question caught her by surprise and an old, familiar ache squeezed her chest. *Let it go. The past is the over and you're not going to let it repeat itself.*

"You're turning pink," Clay said, yanking her out of dangerous territory.

"I forgot to put on sunscreen." She reached into her bag and withdrew a tube. Clay plucked it from her hand.

"I can do it," she protested.

"You can't do your back. Turn around."

Not a good idea. Not good at all. But with Tim watching she could hardly refuse without sounding ungracious and rude and Clay knew it. What game was he playing? Reluctantly, Andrea turned. Clay sat behind her on the narrow bench. His thigh pressed against her bottom like sun-baked sand, only firmer. His big, slightly roughened hands descended on her shoulders, and the heat of his touch combined with the sun-warmed lotion stole her breath.

He massaged the upper portion of her back and then dragged languid fingertips down her spine. She shivered. Silently cursing her telling response, she crossed her arms over her tightening nipples. There was no way to hide her goose bumps. His palms glided over her ribs, her waist, the small of her back and then back up again. His fingertips brushed the sides of her breasts. Arousal swirled beneath her bikini bottom and made her breasts ache.

She kept her gaze fastened on Tim, trying to recall why she'd come today, but desire weighted her eyelids. Clay's hands dipped over her collarbone and she ached for him to go lower, to stroke her breasts, to tease her nipples with his lotion-slickened fingers.

She caught herself leaning against him, yanked her eyes open and bolted to her feet. Damn. It. She had absolutely no willpower where Clayton Dean was concerned. It wasn't fair that the one man she couldn't trust would have so much power over her. Why had no other man been able to reduce her to a puddle of need?

Come back to Miami with me, his voice echoed in her head. He didn't mean it. If he truly wanted her back, he'd tell her the truth. And until she knew the truth she couldn't risk the past coming back to bite her. Whatever had driven him away eight years ago still lurked like a shadow ready to enclose her in darkness again—darkness she very nearly hadn't escaped. If not for her friends, her job and later, her baby brother, she probably wouldn't have.

She snatched the sunscreen from his hand. "I can manage the front."

Clay's hot gaze glided from her face to her breasts, her waist and lower, and her double-crossing body responded as if he'd touched her. She wished she'd had a less revealing swimsuit in her drawer, but she'd bought the miniscule black bikini with Toby and the hot tub on his yacht in mind. Not that she'd ever had the chance to wear it. She'd had a feeling that being half-naked with Toby would lead to being totally naked, and that was a step she hadn't been ready to take.

"Sure you don't want help rubbing it in?"

The husky timber of Clay's voice brought a flood of moisture to her mouth and other areas she refused to acknowledge. "No."

"Let me know if you change your mind."

"I won't." But she wanted to. She wanted his hands to retrace the path his hot gaze had taken. Where was her common sense?

"I got a fish!" Tim squealed and Clay immediately left her side to help Tim reel in his catch.

Weak-kneed with relief, Andrea sank back onto the bench. She was in trouble. Big, big trouble. And she had absolutely no idea how she'd survive another six weeks without jumping Clayton Dean.

"I need a favor."

Andrea looked up from the most recent customer satisfaction survey to see Juliana Alden, one of her best friends and partners in the auction scheme standing in her doorway. Juliana stopped by Dean often enough that Eve knew to let her back without buzzing Andrea.

"Sure. Name it."

Juliana entered and closed the door. "Rex is refusing to see me. I know this sounds adolescent, but it's really, *really* important. I need you to go to his bar and see if he's there. I'll wait outside. If you see him you can call me on my cell and I'll come in before he can hide again."

Her uptight bank auditor friend had bought the former Nashville bad boy hoping he could teach her how to have fun, but from the pallor and stress on Juliana's face it didn't look like fun had been on the program. "Sounds easy enough. Are you all right? You're pale."

"Yes. No. I don't know." Andrea's brows rose. The indecisiveness did not sound like Juliana. "I can't talk about it yet. But soon. I promise. Okay?"

Andrea nodded. She, Juliana and Holly had always met once a week either for girls' night out or for lunch, but their auction packages had wreaked havoc on their usual get-togethers. They couldn't even celebrate Holly's thirtieth birthday. But now more than ever Andrea needed the girl talk.

"What about you and Clay?" Juliana asked as if reading Andrea's mind.

If anyone could make her see reason, then Juliana—the queen of logic and level-headedness—could, but Andrea didn't know where to start.

"I slept with him. It was…incredible. I can't get him out of my head. I just *want* him. But I can't risk loving him again because all he talks about is going back to Miami. He even asked me to go with him." The words gushed from her mouth without pause for breath.

Juliana's dark eyebrows lifted. "Would you be willing to go with him?"

"Of course not. Everything that's important to me—my friends, my family, my job—are here in Wilmington. And there's no way I'd leave Joseph at a time like this. Besides, Clay doesn't mean it. He just wants to get me back into bed."

"And you want that too."

"Well…yes, but he's *leaving*," she repeated. "Again."

Juliana sank into the chair in front of Andrea's desk. "Aren't you the one who talked me into buying a bachelor we all knew was totally wrong for me just for the chance to have great sex?"

Andrea winced. "Yes, but that's because you're about to get engaged to a cold fish. You've never had great sex, so you need to see what you're missing before you give up on it."

"And aren't you the one who said women should be more like men and learn to keep love and sex separate?" She held up a hand halting Andrea's protest. "Aren't you the one who said, 'Why should we limit ourselves to self-induced orgasms when there are capable men out there'? Aren't you the one who sings the Tina Turner song, 'What's Love Got to Do With It?' in the shower?"

Andrea cringed and considered crawling under her desk. "That might have been me, but—"

Juliana snorted. "No might about it. Practice what you preach, Andrea, and sleep with Clay while you have the chance. You know he's leaving, so you won't fall in love with him again. It'll just be sex—great sex. But short-term, like a sex vacation."

Andrea frowned. "Who are you and what did you do with my conservative friend? And is sex with Rex really that incredible?"

Color rushed to Juliana's pale cheeks. "Your conservative friend is starting to loosen up a little, and yes, making love with Rex is better than any fantasy I could have imagined. I'll never be happy with vanilla sex again." She rose, looking embarrassed by her confession. "So…can you get away now? I really have to talk to Rex."

"I'll get my keys."

"Andrea, will you think about what I said?"

A sex vacation with Clay. How could she think about anything else?

"What's going on?" Andrea called from her open doorway.

Clay stopped in the hall, parking the hand truck loaded with boxes outside his father's office. "I'm moving my office inside."

Andrea's lips parted and her breasts, covered in a lavender lingerie-style top, rose. Her legs shifted beneath a deeper purple slim-fitting, knee-length skirt and once again she wore seriously sexy high heels. "Oh."

As much as he hated working in the room where his world had crashed, Clay thought he stood a better chance of winning Andrea over to his way of thinking from twenty feet away than from a hundred and twenty yards.

She tucked a long golden lock of hair behind her ear. "Can I speak with you when you have a minute?"

He studied her serious expression and watched her nibble her lush bottom lip—something he'd like to do. "I have time now."

He followed her into her office. She closed the door behind him, walked toward her desk and reached for the matching suit jacket hanging from her chair and then she stopped and turned without donning the concealing jacket.

He silently thanked her for giving him the opportunity

to savor her curves in the satiny fabric. Was she wearing a bra under that top? He'd love to find out firsthand, *hand* being the operative word.

"I changed my mind about dinner."

Surprise yanked his gaze back to hers. "Why?"

Her fingers curled by her side. "Do I have to have a reason?"

"Andrea, you always have a reason, usually an entire list of reasons."

Her cheeks flushed. "Yes. Well. I also start what I finish. I bought your auction package and I'll see it through."

She didn't sound overjoyed, but he'd take what he could get and make it work to his advantage. "I'll set up the date."

"But I have a request. I'd like to keep what happens between us from the staff and Octavia Jenkins. My personal business is just that. Personal."

A needle of regret jabbed him. If he'd learned anything in the three weeks he'd been back it was that his dumping Andrea had been common knowledge at Dean. And in the past few weeks he'd interrupted enough conversations to know that the staff was taking bets on whether or not he and Andrea would end up together or he'd leave her again. This time she wouldn't have to endure the embarrassing gossip because he'd take her with him when he left Wilmington. Although after seeing his father he wasn't sure when that would be.

"Agreed. We'll keep it as private as possible. When would you like to go out?"

"The sooner the better."

Her response jacked his libido up a notch. Now that's more like it. "Tonight?"

"Okay." She nibbled her lip again and then slid into her desk chair. She fussed with the pens on her desk, aligning them in a perfect row, and then she met his gaze. "And Clay? Pack an overnight bag."

Shock dropped his jaw and sent his blood rushing south. He didn't know what game Andrea was playing, but he wasn't about to argue since she'd just made his seduction plan a hell of a lot easier. "Yes, ma'am."

He'd give her a night she would never forget, and he would earn her trust.

A sex vacation. Ohmygosh.

This had to be the craziest thing Andrea had ever done. Sex for sex's sake. Sure, she believed a woman had the right to go to bed with a man without expecting wedding bells, but she'd never tried meaningless sex or even wanted to. Until now.

She pressed a hand over her frantically beating heart, took a bracing breath and opened her front door. Clay stood on the doormat with a duffel bag hanging from his shoulder and a large shopping bag in each hand. He looked edible with his white dress shirt unbuttoned at the neck and black pants hugging his hips. And he smelled edible too, crisp and clean with a hint of lime.

"What's all that?" She nodded at the shopping bags.

"Our date."

"Aren't we were going to Devil's Shoals?"

"I thought we'd stay in tonight." He smiled, a smile filled with seductive promise.

Her pulse stuttered. "Then I hope you have dinner in one of those bags because my cupboards are nearly bare."

"I have dinner…and a whole lot more." His gaze meandered over her loosely upswept hair, her black silk tank dress, her legs and her heels and then back again. "Beautiful and very desirable, Ms. Montgomery."

Her knees weakened at the appreciation in his eyes and the sexy growl of his voice. She suddenly felt hot and damp all over, but that was probably caused by the warm rush of humid air from outside. "C-come in."

She closed the door behind him and tried to catch her breath. "The kitchen's this way. Let me help you unpack."

"No."

She stopped. "Excuse me?"

Clay dropped his duffel bag at the foot of the stairs and then carried the bags to the kitchen and set them on the counter. He returned to her side, cupped her shoulders and steered her toward the sofa. "You relax. I'll handle everything."

A warm puff of breath was her only warning before his lips brushed her bare nape. She tried to face him, but he held fast. "Sit. I'll bring you a glass of wine."

Andrea sat. The sofa faced her fireplace, leaving her back to the kitchen and Clay. Fabric rustled behind her and then something dropped over her eyes. A blindfold? "Wait a minute."

She reached for the black material and then Clay's breath teased her ear. "Trust me."

Swallowing her nervousness, she lowered her hands. Tonight was all about pleasure—physical pleasure. And if Clay wanted to play sex games, then she could be woman enough to play along. The fabric tightened as he knotted it at the back of her head. "This is crazy."

"Trust me," he repeated just before his tongue traced the shell of her ear. She shivered.

That was the problem. She didn't trust him. Not completely. Sure, she knew he wouldn't hurt her physically, but she didn't trust him with her heart. But her heart wasn't at stake tonight, was it? She'd locked it securely away.

No love. Just sex.

And if she repeated it often enough it would be true.

His lips grazed the side of her neck, choking off her ability to reason. She sucked in a sharp breath. His fingertips skated over her shoulders, her collarbone and then dipped to outline the deep V-neck of her dress. Her nipples tightened in anticipation, but he withdrew his hands leaving her with an unsatisfied ache in her belly.

His footsteps retreated to the kitchen. Cabinets opened and closed and then a bag rustled, followed by the pop of a wine cork and a splash of liquid. Footsteps approached and her pulse accelerated. The cool rim of a glass touched her lips. She sipped cautiously. Cool chardonnay—a good one—filled her mouth. Clay lifted her hand and wrapped it around the wineglass stem and then returned to the kitchen.

Andrea drank her wine and listened to the unfamiliar sounds of a man in her kitchen. She heard him extract a plate from the cabinet, but not the clank of pots or pans. He must have brought takeout.

She felt as much as heard Clay join her. And then the sofa dipped as he settled beside her. She inhaled, but before she could identify the tantalizing aromas something warm, moist and slick nudged her bottom lip. She slipped her tongue out to taste. Butter?

"Open."

She obeyed and Clay fed her a morsel. It took only seconds to identify her favorite food, lobster with drawn butter. The next bite revealed Chinese green beans, tangy with soy sauce and ginger, and then a spoonful of wild rice with raisins and almonds. He'd remembered her favorites. She tried to harden her heart, but there was no denying the warmth spreading through her.

With bite after bite Clay satisfied one appetite but

roused another with the brush of his fingers on her lips, his thigh against hers and the occasional press of his arm against her breasts when he reached across her for the wineglass he'd set on the end table.

When he left her again her tensed muscles eased. She sagged into the cushion and squeezed her thighs together. How could she get turned on by this blatant seduction routine? It was ridiculous how easily he'd manipulated her. If she had any sense at all, she'd rip off this blindfold and—

The cushion sank again and adrenaline raced through her. Something cold touched her lips. She opened her mouth. French vanilla ice cream, rich, creamy and delicious, melted on her tongue. But after a few spoonfuls she held up her hand. "I can't eat any more."

Glass clinked as he set the dish down on her coffee table, and then his lips covered hers, a breathtakingly hot contrast to the cold dessert. Her nails dug into her palms as she fought the urge to wind her arms around him. Arousal blurred the edge of reason.

Just sex. Don't get emotional.

All too soon he lifted his head. "I'll be right back."

She heard him moving around the kitchen. A bag rustled and then he climbed the stairs. What was he doing? And why didn't it bother her to have him roaming through her house? She'd never given any other man free rein of her home.

Trust him. And she realized she did in a way she'd never trusted any of the other men she'd thought she might eventually marry.

What felt like ages later but was probably no more than five minutes, she heard him jog down the stairs. Clay approached, captured her hands and pulled her to her feet. He led her across the room and then slipped an arm around her waist. "Careful on the steps."

He guided her upstairs. The sound of water running greeted her when they reached the landing and grew louder as she entered her bedroom. In her bathroom, she inhaled a mixture of flowers and spices. Not her perfume or her bubble bath. Clay released her and turned off the water and then his palms glided over her shoulders, down her arms and back again. He pulled her back flush against his front and his erection pushed against her spine. She gasped and need twisted deep inside her.

"Andrea, if you didn't intend for us to end up in bed together tonight, now's the time to tell me," he whispered against the sensitive skin beneath her ear.

Ohmygosh. She struggled to find her voice. "I did. I do."

His fingers tightened on her arms. "You won't regret it."

That's where he was wrong. She was certain she would and probably already did. This whole blindfold/feeding thing was slipping past the defenses she'd worked so hard to erect.

He found the zip at the back of her dress and pulled downward. Cool air swept her spine. She trembled. Clay eased the straps over her shoulders and then held her hand as she stepped out of the dress.

She squared her shoulders. What did he think of her black push-up bra and sheer, miniscule panties? His groan answered her unspoken question. "You're even more beautiful now than you were eight years ago."

The reminder gave her a twinge of discomfort, but she tamped it down. She wanted to see his face, to look into his eyes and see if he meant the compliment, but she kept her fingers clenched by her side. The blindfold frustrated her.

You're a thirty-year-old woman. Play the game.

His shirt brushed against her thigh as he knelt, and then his fingers curled around her ankle. He removed one shoe and then the other. His fingers skimmed up her legs and briefly cradled her bottom before he flattened his palms over her belly and urged her against his hardness. She rocked her hips to torment him and was rewarded by a low groan. His cheek pressed hers and she imagined him watching the two of them in the wide mirror behind her vanity.

When she'd renovated the house she'd taken a smaller bedroom and converted it into a hedonistic master bath complete with a glass shower stall which they'd used last time he was here and a tub big enough for two on a raised platform. Would Clay join her in the tub?

Desire swirled through her with dizzying force. She'd never been so turned on in her life. She wanted to grab his hand and tuck it between her legs. Instead, she gulped, squeezed her knees together and squirmed.

The cadence of Clay's breathing deepened, quickened. His short nails scraped lightly above the elastic of her panties and then beneath the band of her bra. Her stomach muscles contracted involuntarily and she sucked a sharp breath. With a flick of his fingers the front clasp of her bra gave way. Hot palms cupped her, kneaded her. Her lips parted in an effort to pull air into her lungs. She sagged against Clay, savoring the light abrasion of his hands against her flesh and the rapid rise and fall of his chest against her back. She lifted a hand to stroke his jaw and relished in his smooth, freshly shaven skin against her cheek and palm.

His thumbs buffeted her nipples until she wanted to moan, but then he drew back and whisked her bra from her shoulders. The air stirred around her. His lips sipped from her nape and then inched down her vertebrae, one soft, wet kiss at a time until he reached her panties. He hooked his fingers in the elastic and drew them down her legs. Andrea stepped out of the fabric and waited, quivering with anticipation for Clay's next move.

He cupped her elbow and led her toward her raised bathtub. "Into the tub."

He didn't release her until she'd sunk chest deep into the warm water. The jets turned on and the bubbling, swirling water teased her aroused skin like a lover's caresses. But she didn't want the jets, she wanted Clay.

"I'll be back in ten minutes. Relax." And then his mouth covered hers. His tongue sliced through her lips and stroked deeply, hungrily. Andrea lifted her wet hands to hold him close, but Clay pulled back. He pressed a wineglass into her hand. "Keep the blindfold on and don't move. I don't want you to get hurt."

And then he left her. She couldn't hear his footsteps over the rush of the whirlpool, but it was as if the energy drained from the room.

He didn't want her to get hurt. What did that mean?

Andrea sat up and lifted one corner of the blindfold. Her bathroom glowed in the flickering light of a dozen candles each in its own silver dish. Clay must have brought them, because they weren't hers. The romantic gesture squeezed her heart. Their lovemaking in the past had been mostly hurried encounters. The few times they'd been able to linger had been in the close confines of his sailboat's tiny cabin. There had never been candles or blindfolds, just raw, rushed passion.

Don't fall for him. He's probably perfected this technique on a dozen other women since dumping you.

Leaning back, she tried to recall the pain, embarrassment and confusion of his abandonment, but it wasn't as easy as before.

She released the blindfold and set her wine aside. Her head was already spinning without more wine. If Clay intended to seduce her then he was doing a fine job, but why make the effort when he had to know from her "pack an overnight bag" instructions that they'd end up in bed without all the extra work?

The air swirled around her shoulders and then the whirl-pool jets died. He'd returned. Her pulse raced and her mouth dried. What did he have planned next?

Ten

Clay wanted to be in control, but dammit, he was losing it like some damned high school kid.

All afternoon he'd thought about bathing Andrea, sliding into the big tub with her, pulling her into his lap and lathering every inch of her delectable body with his bare hands, but as soon as he'd undressed her he'd known that wouldn't be possible without coming prematurely, so he'd retreated. Whatever ground he'd gained on his rampant libido by cleaning the kitchen had vanished the minute he reentered the steamy bathroom.

This night was all about Andrea, about showing her how good it could be between them and regaining her trust, but he was about to burst a vein. His gaze narrowed on the eye covering. "You peeked."

She bit her lip. "I—"

"Don't deny it. There's a wet fingerprint on the blindfold." He stroked her cheek beneath the fabric. "Lucky for you I'm a forgiving guy."

Are you? You haven't forgiven your father.

Clay shoved the intrusive thought aside. "Stand."

Andrea rose. Water cascaded over her flushed skin. Droplets quivered on her erect nipples. The ounce of blood circulating in his brain raced south, and his breath whistled through his clenched teeth. Desire pulsed insistently between his legs. He considered throwing the thick bath towel on the floor and taking her right here, but then he recalled the rose petals and the peppermint foot lotion waiting in the bedroom.

Damn. He might not make it through a foot massage.

"How many other women have you spoiled like this?"

Taken aback by her question, Clay paused. He'd had other lovers, but those relationships had always been about sex, the you-do-me-I'll-do-you type. There'd been nothing intimate beyond the physical component. He'd never tried to get to know any of the women on more than a superficial level, but he wanted to get inside of Andrea—inside *her head,* not just her body. Although getting inside her body topped his priority list at the moment—preferably before he shot off like a fire extinguisher.

"None. They weren't worth the effort."

Clay wrapped his hand around her bicep and helped her from the tub and then snatched up the towel and looped it over her back. He couldn't wait. With a swift tug she stumbled against him. Her wet breasts soaked his shirt and her legs spliced with his, dampening his pants. He didn't care.

Her hands slid upward, tangled in his hair and then she yanked him down for a kiss. Clay surrendered. He had no fight left. He opened his mouth, giving her access to devour him. She rose on tiptoe, sliding her pelvis against his. Stars exploded behind his eyelids and a groan rumbled from his chest. He vaguely recalled he was supposed to be drying her, but he made only a halfhearted attempt before he dropped the towel and filled his palms with her warm, damp behind. He loved the feel of her, the shape of her, the taste of her.

He loved her. Period.

Her nails raked down his back. She squeezed his butt and he knew he was a goner. He released her and reached for the buttons of his shirt, but his clumsy fingers weren't up to the task. He swore.

Andrea took over, blindly feeling her way down his chest, opening his shirt and then hooking her fingers behind his belt. Leather slipped free, quickly followed by the hook and zip of his pants. Her palm opened over his stretched boxers and his knees buckled. He sank down on the edge of the tub which put him exactly at breast level.

"Damned fine view," he muttered before opening his mouth over one dusky-tipped breast.

Andrea's fingers tangled in his hair, holding him while he licked, suckled and nipped.

He caressed her waist, her hips, and then his fingers found damp, slick curls. Andrea's nails dug into his scalp and she whimpered. Knowing she was already this hot, this wet for him made waiting almost unbearable, but Clay fought off his need and stroked her.

She shifted her stance, opening for him, and her hips thrust to meet his fingers. Her legs shook visibly. He knew she was close by the flush on her cheeks and her choppy breathing. And then she shuddered in his hand, against his lips and collapsed on him. He caught her, rose and carried her to the bed where he lowered her to the center of the mattress.

She jerked upright, spreading her hands over the sheets. "What is this?"

He pushed her back down with one hand and reached for the condom with the other. The foot massage would have to wait. "Rose petals."

Scooping up a handful, he rained the cool petals down on her skin. Hell, they'd probably leave peach-colored stains on her sheets, but he'd read somewhere that women liked rose petals.

He rolled on the latex, leaned over her to taste the smile on her swollen lips and then hooked her legs over his arms. He found her slick center and thrust home. Her gasp sucked the air from his lungs. When he inhaled, the scent of crushed roses filled his nostrils. He pounded into the tight, slick sleeve of her body. Deeper. Harder. Faster. He ground his hips against hers and when she bowed off the bed, crying out as another climax rocked her, he lost it.

His orgasm knocked the breath from his lungs and made his head spin as if a rogue wave had lifted him and slammed him against the beach. He gasped and groaned and then landed like a washed-up surfer in Andrea's arms. His lungs burned and his muscles disintegrated. He hoped to hell he wasn't crushing her because he couldn't move if his life depended on it.

Her hand smoothed his hair, his face. He lifted a weighted eyelid in time to see her tug off the blindfold. Her satisfied smile melted his heart. "Next time you wear this."

Damn, he loved her. He hadn't thought it possible to love her more than before, but he did. Andrea was a stronger and more confident woman and a kinder and more generous one than the girl he'd left behind. That made loving her even easier than before. And more dangerous.

Leaving her last time had been hard, and he knew with

absolute certainty he wasn't strong enough to leave her again. He'd do whatever it took to keep Andrea in his life—even call a truce with his father.

She wanted him more than before, Andrea admitted with a sinking heart as she lay in bed staring at her ceiling in the early morning light and listening to the sounds of Clay in the adjoining bathroom. And that was scary ground to tread.

It was more than the fabulous sex. Clay listened intently, as if each word carried the weight of a thousand words, not just to her but to each member of the Dean staff—from the high school kid who swept the floors to Peter, the production manager.

The hotheaded high school boy she'd fallen in love with so long ago had become an even-tempered man. Some of the more stubborn employees' unwelcoming attitudes had given Clay plenty of reason to lose his temper, but not once had he lost his cool.

His appeal also lay in the kindness he'd shown to her brother. Surely between Clay's work for Dean and managing his own business long distance he didn't have time to take Tim under his wing. But that hadn't stopped him.

And then there was the way he'd seduced her senses. Yes, she knew what he was up to. By using the blindfold last night he'd put her in the position of having to trust him to feed her, bathe her and pleasure her without going too far or making her uncomfortable. His plan had worked with devastating effectiveness. Why didn't she feel manipulated?

Trust him, he'd said. She wanted to, but how could she when she still didn't know why he'd left her or what she'd done to cause the rift between him and Joseph? What could have been so important that each man would stubbornly stand his ground to the point of forfeiting family? And what would it take to make Clay come clean?

She turned her head and checked the clock. Only a few more minutes before she had to get up and get ready for work. She didn't have time to tie him to the bed and entice the answers out of him. She smiled and wiggled her fingers and toes beneath the sheets. When had she become kinky?

The bathroom door opened and Clay paused on the threshold. "You're awake."

He'd showered, shaved and dressed in charcoal pants and a pale blue shirt. The smell of his cologne drifted to her on a cloud of steam. He looked and smelled edible and she wanted to drag him back to bed, but they had new clients to meet this morning. And she had to get a handle on the soft, mushy feelings inside.

Pull back while you still can.

With a flash of clarity Andrea realized that's exactly what she'd done with every relationship in the past eight years. She'd pulled back. As soon as she started feeling comfortable enough to take the next step she erected barriers or looked for excuses to end it before she got hurt.

She shook off the disturbing discovery and looked up to find Clay studying her. "I'm sorry I didn't get up in time to shower with you."

Passion flared in his eyes. "And then we would have been late for work. We'll make up for it tonight."

She shook her head. "It's Friday. Girls' night out."

His eyes narrowed and his jaw shifted. "Think you could convince my mother to join you if I stay with Dad?"

"Yes. Absolutely." She didn't even stop to think about how she'd accomplish that impossible mission. If it would get Clay and his father together, then maybe they could settle their differences.

"And then I can come here afterward and spend the weekend there—" he nodded at the bed "—with you."

Her mouth dried and her heart jolted into a rapid clip-clop. *You're in too deep. Retreat.* But she couldn't. Not yet. Not until she had her answers. "Sounds promising."

He crossed the room in a few long strides, planted his arms on either side of her, trapping her beneath the sheet, and then he lowered his head and kissed her breathless.

He withdrew and swiped a thumb over her damp lips. "I'll see you at work."

And then he grabbed his duffel bag and left.

Andrea fisted her hands and waited for her pulse to settle. Could she have him in her home all weekend without losing her heart? Other women had affairs that went nowhere all the time. So why couldn't she?

She threw back the covers and rose. This time when Clay left Wilmington there would be no broken hearts, no broken promises and no regrets. Thanks for the memories, she'd tell him, and that's all it would be. Fond memories.

She shook her head and headed for the shower. That was a marketing pitch even she had trouble swallowing. She hoped it didn't come back to bite her.

"Thank you for coming over, dear. I promise I won't be late," Clay's mother said.

"Take your time, Mom." He kissed her cheek and urged her toward the door. "Enjoy girls' night out."

She balked as if suddenly having second thoughts. "But Dora's already gone for the day and—"

"And I have your cell number if I need you. Go. Have fun." Andrea had worked magic on more than just him. She'd called his mother and coerced her into going out.

Heat shot through Clay's veins as he recalled the past

twenty-four hours. Sometime in the middle of the night Andrea had made good on her promise to blindfold him and then she'd driven him absolutely out of his mind. Suffice to say they hadn't had much sleep last night, and he didn't plan to let her catch up tonight or tomorrow night. He shoved his hands in his jeans pockets, adjusting the suddenly snug fit. He had to quit thinking about Andrea unless he wanted to greet his father with a boner.

Clay closed the door behind his mother and waited until her car pulled out of the driveway before joining his father in the living room. He had questions, but surprisingly, the rage he'd felt on his last visit no longer rode his back.

He grabbed the deck of cards off the end table. "Poker?"

Joseph shook his head. "No games. We need to talk about what happened eight years ago."

His father enunciated each word carefully, reminding Clay what Andrea had said about his speech being affected by the stroke. And that's when it hit Clay. He could have lost his father.

Emptiness yawned inside him. He sat down in the wing chair to the right of his father's. As much as he hated hearing about the past, he would have hated losing his father without understanding the dangerous path he'd taken. "Just tell me why."

"No good excuse." His father swallowed hard and looked away. From this side the effects of the stroke weren't visible, and it occurred to Clay that they should have had this conversation eight years ago, but back then Clay had been too hotheaded and too afraid to listen. Afraid of what he'd hear. Afraid he'd find the same selfish bastard lurking inside himself.

"We were having problems, your mother and me.

Business was down, and I was working too many hours and neglecting her. She started sneaking around. Going out three mornings a week, but never mentioned it when I asked her about her day."

Clay's heart pounded like a pile driver. For eight years he'd cursed his father. He'd never considered there might be two sides to the story or that his parents' "perfect" marriage might have been in trouble before his father cheated. Living out of state for five years had kept him out of touch in more ways than just the physical.

"I thought she was having an affair. That she didn't want me anymore. Couldn't blame her. I'd been a testy jackass. Elaine's attention bolstered my dented ego. It went too far. I thought I was getting even, but—" His father's voice broke and his face crumpled. On edge, Clay waited with a knot twisting in his gut for his father to regain his composure. He'd wanted to know the truth and now conversely, he didn't. What would it change? He passed his father a tissue.

Joseph mopped his eyes. "Patricia was taking a stained glass class from that Prescott girl. Andrea's friend. What's her name?"

"Holly." Holly Prescott had been one of Andrea's best friends.

"Yes. Holly. Patricia was making a present. For me. Didn't want to ruin the surprise by telling me where she was going."

Whatever Clay had expected that wasn't it. He'd never condone what his father and Elaine had done, but having heard both sides of the story, he was beginning to understand how two people could make such terrible choices.

He blew out the tension knotting his muscles. "Mom made the seascape hanging in your office window?"

His father nodded. "She wanted to cheer me up."

"It's nice. I'll bring it home. You can hang it here." Clay hesitated, but knew he had to ask. "What about Tim?"

His father's chest rose on a long slow inhalation, and then his jaw shifted and his eyes filled with regret. "He's a fine boy."

"He's your son. You have to see that."

Fresh tears filled his father's eyes. "Wasn't sure. Suspected he might be. Looks a bit like me around the eyes."

"I met him at Andrea's. I thought he was mine."

"No, son, Andrea wouldn't keep that kind of secret."

"He looks like me and he's close to the right age."

His father shook his head. "He only looks a little like you. The eyes. The nose, maybe. The rest is all Elaine. You saw what you wanted to see."

Clay grimaced. Had he been that desperate for a tie to Andrea? Yeah, probably, since he'd just figured out that he still loved her the night before he'd met Tim. "What will you do about him?"

"Nothing. Claiming him would hurt too many people. Harrison is good to him. He loves that boy and Tim worships his daddy. I wouldn't jeopardize that for the world."

"Does Mom know?"

"Don't think so. Hope not. She knows I had an affair, but not when. The affair hurt her enough. Knowing Tim was mine when she couldn't have more babies would hurt even more. She had a rupture when you were born. I almost lost her. A hysterectomy saved her. But it meant no more babies."

"I didn't know."

"Makes her feel less of a woman to be missing parts, so we don't discuss it." Joseph reached across the space between them and covered Clay's fist on the arm of the chair. "I was wrong, Clay. Wrong to cheat. Wrong to ask you to lie. Wrong to drive you away from your heritage." His grip tightened. "But you were wrong to hurt Andrea."

"I'm working on making that right. I still love her, Dad. I want her to come back to Miami with me."

Joseph's hand slid away and his shoulders stooped. "She deserves to be happy and so do you. Here or in Miami."

"What will happen to Dean when I leave?"

His father stared out the window. "I can't return full-time. Doctors tap dance around the truth, but I know. And I want to spend my remaining days with your mother not tied to a desk. If you're not interested in taking over, we'll sell. We're strong and financially stable. We won't lack interested buyers. One of the con-glomerates has already called. They know I'm down and want to take advantage."

Clay's stomach sank like an anchor. "A conglomerate would swallow Dean and close the Wilmington location."

"Probably. But the designs would go on. And the Dean name would still be on the hull."

Acid churned in Clay's stomach. Could he be respon-sible for selling out his grandfather's legacy? For putting a thousand employees out of work?

When he'd returned from Miami he'd wanted the truth to come out, and he'd wanted the guilty parties punished for what they'd done. Now he couldn't see that any good could come from it. His father and Andrea's mother had made a terrible mistake, but they'd done their best to remedy a bad situation and to protect the ones they loved. Exposing the secret would only make the innocents suffer. Andrea. Clay's mother. Andrea's father. Tim.

Clay rose and walked to the window. If he stayed in Wilmington, he'd not only have to live with the secret that had driven him away, he'd never be able to acknowledge his little brother, and he'd have to continue lying to Andrea. She already had trust issues, and who could blame her? Would he ever regain her trust if he couldn't come clean? But he couldn't. The truth had to stay hidden.

"Clay, I almost lost the best thing in my life because I had my priorities wrong."

Clay turned back to his father. "Mom?"

"My family, son. Your mother *and you*. Don't make the same mistake. You have a second chance. And if Andrea makes you happy, then go after her."

His father pulled the walker around to the front of the chair and struggled to stand. It was painful for Clay to watch. He stepped forward to help, but his father waved him away and then he hobbled one arduous step after the other until he reached Clay's side by the bay window.

"I don't expect you to condone what I did. But I hope one day you can find it in your heart to forgive me."

Clay's eyes stung. He wrapped his arms around his father and held tight. "I do, Dad. I already do."

Midnight. The witching hour.

Sand trickled through Andrea's hourglass of time with Clay. She'd decided before he arrived tonight that this was it. She'd grant herself this weekend, and then she'd do the smart thing and end their relationship before it was too late. Before she fell in love with him again. Before he left her again.

The crescent moon cast a dim light into the shadows enveloping the love seat on her back deck. Wrapped only in Clay's arms and the blanket they'd pulled from the bed, she rested her head against his bare chest, nuzzled her nose in the wiry curls on his pecs and listened to the slowing beat of his heart and the crash of the waves on the beach below.

Thirty minutes ago she'd opened her front door to Clay. He hadn't even said hello before kissing her senseless and making love to her quickly and thoroughly on the rug in her foyer. There had been a desperate edge to his silent loving tonight, one she didn't understand, but wanted to. What's more, she wanted to soothe him, to ease whatever had upset him, and that was dangerous because it went beyond just sex and into the realm of caring.

Pull back.

"What happened with your father tonight, Clay?" She regretted the words the minute they left her mouth. That wasn't pulling back. That was wading into deeper waters. Not wise.

His chest rose and fell beneath her cheek in a deliberate breath. "Nothing. It was a good evening."

Nothing? Nothing had made him go off like a sailor who'd just learned he was about to be deployed on an all-male ship for a year? She pushed upright, clutching the edge of the blanket around her nakedness.

"Nothing?" she asked in disbelief.

"Dad and I talked. After dinner we played cards."

Even in the pale moonlight she could tell he was lying. His poker face and his refusal to meet her gaze gave him away.

Pain pierced her and her lungs locked. Deceit wouldn't hurt so much if she was using him for nothing more than the sex vacation she'd planned. Her fingers tightened around the blanket until her knuckles ached.

She'd gone and done it. Gone too far. Fallen in love with Clayton Dean again.

What kind of fool fell in love with a man who wouldn't be honest with her? Her kind, apparently. Squeezing her eyes shut against the sting of humiliation, she bowed her head.

Clay cupped her jaw and lifted her chin. Andrea gritted her teeth and met his gaze. She struggled against the instantaneous response roused by his fingers caressing the sensitive skin beneath her ear.

"Marry me, Andrea."

Stunned, she opened her mouth, but no sound emerged.

"I love you. I never stopped. I want to spend the rest of my life with you." He meant it. She could see love in his eyes and in his hopeful smile.

Her heart contracted and joy erupted over her skin in a shower of warming sparks. She doused it. She'd heard those words from his lips before, and they'd meant nothing. He'd left her. "How can you say that when you can't even be honest with me?"

His nostrils flared and he sat back, lowering his hand to his lap and fisting his fingers. "Some things are better left unsaid."

"This is not one of those things, Clay. You left me. I don't know why. And if I don't know why then I can never be sure you won't leave again."

"I won't. I swear it."

She stared into his steady eyes and shook her head. "I don't need an oath. I need the truth."

His jaw muscles bunched and he looked away. When he faced her again determination firmed his lips and set his face.

He wasn't going to tell her. She knew it before he opened his mouth. "I need you to trust me on this."

"And if I can't?"

"I'll earn it. I'll earn your trust. No matter how long it takes. Give me a chance to prove I'll never hurt you again."

Her rational side screamed, "No, don't give him the opportunity to hurt you again," but her emotional side, the side that still loved him—yes, *still*—asked, "What can it hurt?"

He pulled her back against his chest and brushed his lips across the top of her head. "Give me a chance, Andrea," he repeated. "I promise I won't let you down."

What did she have to lose? She'd already lost her heart.

Eleven

Everything in Andrea screamed a warning about trusting without truth, but another corner her of mind reminded her that her faultfinding and emotional withdrawal from past relationships had prevented her from finding happiness. Hadn't she vowed to break the cycle?

She leaned against the railing of the porch off her bedroom. Seagulls screeched overhead, begging for breakfast. The beach below was deserted at this early hour except for a few shell combers in the distance. The morning breeze, already heavy with humidity, plastered her robe against her front and promised another scorching hot day.

Clay had gone downstairs to make coffee. Waking up beside him felt good and right, as did making lazy love as the sun rose, slanting its warmth across her bed. She loved him. Everything about him. Except for that damned secret.

What was it her mother said? Trust isn't always blind, but it does offer the benefit of doubt?

Andrea caught her wind-tossed hair and held it off her face. Had she offered the benefit of doubt to Clay? No. Maybe he had a good reason for keeping his secret.

Could she love him wholeheartedly—a marriage should never be based on less—knowing he was withholding something that could hurt her? She didn't have the answer. And even if she did, they still hadn't discussed where they'd live if—and that was a big if—they decided to stay together. She refused to desert Joseph and the company at this critical time.

The glass door slid open behind her and the weight of her decision pressed upon her. Clay, carrying a breakfast tray, padded barefoot onto the porch and set his load on the bistro table tucked into the corner. He'd pulled on his jeans, but nothing else. The broad expanse of his back bore a few scratch marks that she'd made during a particularly uninhibited encounter last night. Her face and belly warmed at the memory.

His gaze caught hers. "Paper's here. You're not going to like it."

Andrea cringed. She'd forgotten all about Octavia's column. She reached for the folded paper on the tray. Clay intercepted, catching her hand and pulling her into his arms. Her heart stuttered and her palms flattened against the heat of his chest. How could she want him again so soon, so badly? And how could she let him walk out of her life?

Big hands cradled her hips, pressing her against a growing denim-covered bulge. And then he kissed her. When Clay kissed and held her she had no reservations. They were perfect together. Totally in sync. She tasted coffee, Clay, passion and the promise of a future in his kiss. Did she have the guts to reach for the brass ring knowing she might be knocked from the horse in the process?

He lifted his head and threaded his fingers through her hair. The tenderness in his eyes brought a lump to her throat. "You love me. Admit it."

Andrea's breath hitched. Confessing her feelings was like reaching the point of no return. Once she uttered those words she'd never be able to take them back.

"Andrea, nobody could worship me like you did last night without loving me."

Guilty. Even without the words she'd given away *her* secret. She briefly closed her eyes before meeting his gaze. "Yes. I love you."

His nostrils flared and a smile curved his very talented mouth. He rewarded her with a quick kiss. "You won't regret it. We'll get married as soon—"

She pressed her fingers over his lips. "Clay, we still have so many things to work out. I don't even want to think about a wedding until Joseph's back on the job."

Clay exhaled, released her and strode to the railing. He braced both hands on the wood. The stiffness of his stance sent trepidation racing through her.

"He's not coming back," he said without turning.

Alarm prickled the hair on her arms. "What?"

"Last night he said he wanted to retire and spend the rest of his time with my mother."

"B-but what about Dean?" Her job and a thousand others?

"He plans to sell. He said a conglomerate has already expressed interest. Although how the call got past my mother I don't know."

The point of no return, indeed, she realized with a heavy heart. Even if she played it safe and let Clay walk out of her life again nothing would be the same. No wonder Clay had been so upset last night.

"You could take over," she offered.

He turned. Reservation clouded his eyes. "I don't know if I'm ready to take that step. But if Dean is sold you'll have nothing to keep you from coming to Miami with me."

"Only my home, my family and my friends." Was she wrong to resist change or was her subconscious holding back, trying to wreck another relationship?

He crossed the boards, took her into his arms and nuzzled her hair. "We don't have to make a decision today. Eat breakfast. Read the paper, and then I have plans for that big tub of yours."

The paper. She'd forgotten the article. Again. How did he make her want to forget everything but him? She squirmed free, reached for the paper and flipped straight to the entertainment section and Octavia's article. She skimmed down until she saw her name.

Rumor has it that the dates have been cancelled, but this reporter has learned that Andrea Montgomery and Clayton Dean can't stay away from each other day or night. Will the former (and perhaps current) lovers sail off into the sunset together? We'll soon know.

Andrea flung down the Saturday newspaper and growled in frustration. "The woman has spies. They must be watching the house because you've been parking your car in the garage."

"Your garage has windows."

Was someone watching even now? Andrea pulled her robe tighter around her and scanned the surrounding beach and homes. "I feel dirty."

"Then let me indulge my fantasy. I have wanted to take a bath with you ever since I saw that tub. You have a decadent streak, Andrea Montgomery, and I want to explore every inch of it and you."

The wicked twinkle in Clay's eyes made her body steam. Because her mind was spinning out of control, she grasped on to the one thing that she knew wouldn't let her down. Making love with Clay was never a disappointment.

Clay brushed off the guilt he felt over using sex to distract Andrea. But he had a tough decision to make and he wasn't ready to make it. Stay at Dean or go? Live with the secret or run again?

Andrea loved him. That was all that mattered. They'd work out the rest. He lifted his hands, captured her face and kissed her hard and deep. She melted against him, soft curves to his hard, aching body. His pulse rate shot off the charts in record time.

"Inside," he groaned against her lips and backed her toward the door. Screw breakfast. He'd rather feast on her. He urged her over the threshold and then shut the door behind them. His gaze burned over her robe. Knowing she wore nothing beneath had him hard as a steel beam. Her nipples tightened, pushing at the fabric, and his mouth watered. He kissed her again, skimming his hands over the silky material, cupping the curve of her bottom and her breasts. When she whimpered into his mouth he nearly lost it.

The tie of her belt resisted his attempts to loosen it. He was on the verge of ripping it from her when the knot came free. He shoved her robe over her shoulders and grunted his approval at finally having her naked. And then he bent to capture her breast in his mouth, rolling the tight tip with his tongue.

She clung to him, but all too soon squirmed impatiently and tugged at his armpits. He rose. Her palms skated over his belly, making his muscles jump and contract involuntarily. She made quick work of the button and zipper of his jeans and then she plowed her hand beneath his boxers and wrapped her fingers around his erection.

His knees almost buckled. Fire ignited in his blood and he sucked a breath through clenched teeth. He shucked his pants and then knelt and found her with his mouth, playing her sweet spot until her fingers knotted in his hair. She yanked until he looked up into her passion-hazed eyes.

"I can't stand when you do that. My legs are shaking and on the verge of collapse."

Clay scooped her into his arms and strode toward the bathroom. He set her on the raised ledge of the tub, turned on the water and then knelt at her feet on the plush bath mat. He pleasured her with lips, tongue and hands until she shattered. And then he realized he was about to explode and he didn't have a condom. Damnation. "Don't move."

He sprinted into the bedroom, retrieved what he needed and then returned to the bathroom to find Andrea already in the tub, a satisfied smile curving her luscious lips. That smile was pure fantasy material since he knew firsthand what kind of havoc those lips could wreak on a man. He donned protection and joined her in the hot water. The slippery glide of her legs tangling with his made him grit his teeth and groan. He dragged her onto his lap and speared himself into her tight, hot sheath. Heaven. A lifetime of this wouldn't be enough. He couldn't wait to get here and never wanted to leave.

Her legs straddled his hips. She lifted until he'd almost slipped free before lowering and taking him deeper. Again and again, she shoved him to the edge of sanity and then backed off, stilling until he wanted to come out of his skin, and then she carried him back to the brink.

"Tease." All he could do was kiss the sassy grin right off her lips and hold on for the ride.

His orgasm hit like a tidal wave, slamming him, drowning him, destroying him. He could barely breathe, barely think. Andrea shuddered in his arms as she came again and then relaxed against him. He held her tight, cradling her head against his shoulder, and tried to catch his breath.

Lucidity seeped slowly back into his conscious. He loved this woman. Not just because of the mind-blowing sex, but because she gave unstintingly. Her time. Her talent. Her love. Her heart. How could he give anything less than one hundred percent? He didn't want to see doubts clouding her eyes. But he'd be damned if he knew how he could tell her the truth without hurting her.

He would find a way. He owed her that much. But not now when his brain was totally fried. Limp as soggy seaweed, Clay closed his eyes and rested his head against the edge of the tub. Andrea slid from his lap and into the crook of his shoulder.

He tightened his arm around her and kissed her damp temple. "The article's right, you know."

She jerked out of his hold, grabbed the plastic pitcher from beside the tub, scooped it full of water and dumped it over Clay's head.

Sputtering, Clay jerked upright. "Hey. What's that for?"

"The article may be right, but I don't want my private business to become company gossip again. If I lose the employees' respect, then how can I—" She paused and then her shoulders bowed. "I guess what the staff thinks doesn't matter anymore. Not if your father's going to sell."

Chewing her bottom lip, she climbed from the tub. His eyes tracked her glistening, wet behind—now there was a view he'd never tire of—to the shower stall. She retrieved her shampoo and then slid back into the water. She filled her palm with the liquid and wedged herself behind him. The coconut scent filled his nostrils as she lathered his hair.

"I want it all, Clay. You and me and Dean. Together the way we once planned."

"That sounds tempting, babe, but—" His words choked off as she poured another pitcher of water over his head. "Warn me before you do that, would you?"

Her hands stilled and then combed through the hair at the back of his head. "You have a birthmark."

"Yeah."

"A red crescent shape," she whispered.

Before he could fathom why a birthmark would put strain in her voice she said, "Tim has this same birthmark."

Oh hell. Clay's stomach sank to rock bottom. So much for finding the right words or the right moment.

Andrea scrambled to make sense of what she saw. Why would Tim and Clay have the same birthmark? Coincidence? No, the nickel-sized mark was too distinctive. The same shape. The same reddish color. And hidden in exactly the same place beneath their hair.

"Andrea—"

She lifted her gaze to Clay's and her heart stopped. Dread, apprehension and she didn't know what else filled his eyes. Her heart thumped with deafening force.

That was the secret. The secret too horrible for her to bear.

"You and my mother? No, that's not possible," she choked out, praying she was wrong. "Is it?"

"Hell, no. I would never—"

"Then how?" The other similarities she'd noted between Clay and Tim paraded through her mind. The eyes. The nose. The mischievous grin. The cocky stance. She'd thought Tim had picked up the gestures from Clay or from Joseph.

Joseph. No.

No.

Her mother and Joseph. Everything in her rebelled at the idea of her mother and her mentor together that way.

Andrea crawled from the tub as fast as her shaking limbs could carry her. Her chest tightened and her throat burned. No. Please no. Cold. So cold. She yanked a towel from the rod and wrapped herself in it.

No.

"Andrea, listen." Clay joined her, but she flinched out of his grasp.

A chasm opened in her chest. "My mother and Joseph."

He exhaled and swiped a hand over his face. "Yes."

Confirmation only made her feel worse. "You knew."

"Ye—"

"When? When did you know?"

He snagged a towel and wound it around his hips. "Eight years ago."

"And you didn't tell me?" She paced into the bedroom, stopped and turned to find Clay had followed. Facts fell into place like a complicated jigsaw puzzle. "That's why you left without saying goodbye."

His jaw shifted. "Yes."

Her heart thumped with deafening force. "What exactly happened that day? You came to Dean and then what?"

He looked like he'd rather be anywhere else. "I walked in on them."

"In the office?" she shrieked.

He nodded. "I freaked out. And I ran."

"In the office," she whispered and collapsed on the edge of the bed. Her mother's comment about Andrea's father being her *first* lover suddenly made sense. "How could I not have known?"

They'd had an affair right under her nose. Betrayal and anger swirled like a noxious cocktail inside her. The ones she'd loved and trusted—her mother, Joseph *and Clay*— had lied to her.

"It was a one-time deal."

She jerked her head up. "How do you know that?"

"I've talked to each of them since I came home."

"And you believe them? Why when they've betrayed so many people? Me. My father. Your mother. How could you believe them or cover for them?"

"I do believe them, but I didn't cover for them, dammit." He knelt in front of her and grabbed her cold hands. She tried to pull away, but Clay held tight, boxing her knees in with his elbows. "That's why I left. Because of the affair. I couldn't stomach—" He sucked in a long, slow breath.

"I came home that day to surprise you. I wanted my father to go with me to buy your engagement ring. It was supposed to be an olive branch because we'd soon be working together. I walked in on them. In a clinch." He spat the last three words as if they were distasteful.

"And then everything I believed in collapsed. Two perfect marriages between high school sweethearts. Both lies. And then I got scared. What if I was a chip off the old block like everybody said?"

Clay released her and rose. He strode toward the sliding glass door. "I got in my car and drove around for hours, trying to figure out where in the hell we went from there. And then the doubts swamped me."

He faced Andrea and the agony on his face made her gulp. "You and I had been together for six years and I loved you. Damn, I loved you. But for five of those years we'd only seen each other during summer vacations and holidays. I was afraid we were making a mistake. Afraid I'd follow in my father's footsteps. Afraid I was setting myself up to hurt you that way."

Honesty at last. If she'd known how devastating it would be she would have stuck with the lies.

"So you left."

"If I'd come back, I would have had to lie. To pretend nothing happened. And I couldn't. Andrea, I couldn't look at them and work with them and forget. And I couldn't stand in a church and promise fidelity knowing that behind me sat two people who'd made a mockery of those vows."

She closed her eyes against the sting and swallowed to ease the burn in her throat. "You should have trusted me enough to tell me, Clay."

When she lifted her eyelids he shook his head. "No. You and your mother were tight. As close as sisters. I envied that bond, and I couldn't destroy your trust in her. My father and I already didn't get along. I considered that relationship no great loss."

"You should have told me," she repeated. "Better that than let me agonize for eight years over why you didn't love me enough."

Clay swore viciously and she flinched. "It wasn't you. Babe, it was never you."

"I know that now. But it's too late."

"It's not too late. We'll start over. Here. Today. We'll—"

"And ignore the bomb under the table?" She held up a hand when he opened his mouth. "Go. Now. Please leave. I need time to think." And then, too torn up to watch him walk out of her life a second time, she turned her back on him.

"Tim."

Andrea gasped at the softly spoken name and nausea rolled in her stomach. She'd thought the situation couldn't get any worse and of course, it did. Murphy's Law.

Clay's hands descended on her shoulders. His touch felt warm against her chilled-to-the-bone skin. But she couldn't lean on him. Her thoughts were too tangled. She had to be strong.

"Think of Tim, Andrea. If this secret breaks his world will be destroyed. Your father loves him. Would he if he knew Tim wasn't his?"

Ohmygod. She hadn't even considered that yet.

"I know you're angry and hurt and you feel betrayed. I've been there, but back then we didn't have Tim to worry about. He's your brother. And mine."

She pressed a hand to her churning stomach. She hadn't even put that part of the puzzle together yet. "That's why you wanted to spend time with him."

He nodded. "I wanted to get to know him. Before you lash out think of the innocents who'll be hurt if this secret gets out."

She twisted out of his grasp and covered her ears. "Stop. Stop it. I can't take anymore. Just go. Please."

Clay captured her wrists and pulled her hands away. He kissed her fisted fingers. "We're not done."

Numbness settled over her. She tugged her hands free and hugged herself. "I don't know how we can go on."

"We'll find a way."

She just shook her head and pressed her forehead against the glass door. She heard the rustle of Clay's clothes as he dressed and then his lips touched her nape.

"I love you, Andrea. I never stopped. And I never will." And then he left her.

Just like eight years ago. Only this time she knew why.

And wished she didn't.

If there had been something wrong with her, she could have fixed it. But this… She couldn't fix this.

The only thing she knew for certain was that she understood and forgave Clay for running because she wanted to do the same thing.

Clay hadn't slept worth a damn since leaving Andrea, which was the only reason he was awake when the boat rocked at 5:00 a.m. Sunday morning signaling somebody had come aboard.

It had to be Andrea. Nobody else would knock on his door at daybreak. He tossed off the tangled sheets, jerked on his discarded jeans and raced up the companionway. He took the stairs two at a time, flipped on an outside light and saw her standing in his cockpit outside the doors.

Relief coursed through him. She'd come. Thank God she'd come. He yanked open the door before she knocked.

She silently stepped inside and dropped the suitcase she carried at her feet. The dark circles beneath her eyes looked like bruises on her pale face, and the way she'd ruthlessly pulled her hair back in an elastic band only accentuated the shell-shocked cast of her features. She looked as rough as he felt. He knew exactly what she was going through. He'd lived this tangle of emotions eight years ago.

"You asked me to go to Miami with you. Well, let's go. Now. Today. Juliana and Holly will pack up my stuff and send it to me. I'll sell the house and—"

"Whoa. Slow down." He caught her shoulders in his hands. He had come to one conclusion last night—one he was absolutely certain about. "We can't go."

She twisted free, paced across the salon and then turned and stared at him as if he'd lost his mind. "What do you mean we can't go? Leaving is all you've talked about since you arrived."

"If we leave Dean, my grandfather's dream dies."

"So? What do you care? It's not your dream anymore."

"It used to be. It could be again."

"Our parents lied, Clay. They cheated. And their deceit cost us eight years. How can you stay here and accept that? How can you ever trust them again?"

"I've been running for eight years and I've finally learned my lesson. Running doesn't change anything. I'm through running. This—" He gestured toward the Dean compound. "This is my life. My future. Our future, Andrea. We have a lot of people counting on us."

She shook her head. "How can you forgive them? How can you forget what they did or live with the possibility of the secret blowing up in your face?"

"They made a mistake. An awful mistake. But they've done their best with a rotten situation."

"You're condoning it." She hurled the words as an accusation.

"Never. But I've talked to your mother and my father and I understand how it happened."

"Well I can't."

"Your mother used to be in love with my father."

She gaped at him. "What?"

"They never told us that part, did they? They went on and on about how we were high school sweethearts just like them, destined to be together forever, but they never mentioned your mother and my father dating. Elaine was in love with him before she lost him to my mother. He was her first love. And you know what she told me? You never forget first love. And she's right, Andrea. I could never forget you, and God knows I tried."

A tear streaked down her cheek. "That doesn't make what they did okay."

"No. Nothing can make it 'okay.' Your mother said that when she hit forty she started wondering if she'd made a mistake in letting Dad go and then things went too far."

Andrea wrapped her arms around her chest. Her entire body trembled. Whether it was from cold or shock he didn't know. Clay led her to the sofa, sat down and pulled her into his lap. He tucked her head beneath his chin.

"I don't understand. Joseph adores your mother. Why would he do such a hurtful thing?"

He caressed her stiff spine. "Remember when you started at Dean? Business was down. That was one of the reasons my father and I always argued. I had a slew of big college boy ideas on how to increase sales, and my dad kept insisting the market would turn back around.

"He was working too much and neglecting my mother. And then she started going out and wouldn't tell him where she'd been. He thought she was cheating on him. In some twisted way he was trying to get even by hooking up with your mother. But Mom wasn't cheating. She was taking a class from Holly. She wanted to cheer Dad up with a present."

Andrea's breath shuddered in and then back out. "The piece in his office window?"

"Yes."

"I remember when she gave him that, but still—"

He lifted her chin until her gaze met his. "Andrea, the affair was wrong. There's no getting around that. But they made a mistake which they haven't repeated and each of them deeply regrets it. And as much as I condemn them for lying, they did so to protect the ones they love. You and me. Your father. My mother. Tim."

Sad acceptance settled on her features. "And that's why

you didn't tell me. You were trying to protect me. From this…this gaping dark hole in my heart."

"Yeah. But my running away wasn't entirely their fault. You have to remember I was afraid I'd end up doing what Dad did."

"Do you still feel that way? Do you think you would?"

"No. I'm not worried about following in my father's footsteps anymore. You've been in my heart for fourteen years, Andrea. You're my soul mate. That's never going to change. I love you, and I always will."

Her breath hitched. "Aren't you worried that I'll be unfaithful like my mother?"

He kissed her temple. "No, babe, I'm not. You may yell at me or dump water on my head, but you'd never deliberately hurt me."

She stroked a hand over his jaw and touched her lips to his. "I always thought you left because you didn't love me enough. But you left because you loved me so much."

Clay's throat closed up. She understood. He closed his eyes and said a silent thank you prayer. "Yeah. Too much to put you through what I was going through. I'm only sorry you're going through it now."

"I love you." Tears rolled down her cheeks. She kissed him again, so tenderly his eyes burned, and then she lifted her head. "Where do we go from here?"

"We have to keep the secret. To protect Tim, your father and my mother. And we stay here to pick up the pieces for them in case the story ever breaks."

Her eyes widened. "That's why you were worried about Octavia digging up dirt."

He nodded. "But I don't think it's likely. They've covered their tracks well." He smoothed her hair. "Do you want to talk to our parents? Hear their side of this? I'll go with you."

She chewed her lip and then shook her head. "No. Not yet. Maybe one day. I need time to come to terms with this, so for now, I'd rather they not know what I've learned."

"You got it. Your secret's safe with me." He smoothed a hand down her spine. "On one condition."

"What's that?"

"Marry me. Build a life with me. And let me spend the rest of my days loving you and earning your trust."

A smile wobbled on her lips. "You already have it, Clay. My trust and my heart. But I have my own condition."

"Name it."

"No secrets between us. Ever."

He'd learned the hard way that deceit could destroy the best things in life. He lifted her knuckles to his lips. "You got it."

"Then, yes, I'll marry you."

"You won't regret it, babe, and that's a promise I intend to keep as long as I'm breathing."

* * * * *

BENDING TO THE BACHELOR'S WILL

BY
EMILIE ROSE

Juliet Burns, you have a heart as big as Texas.
I'm truly blessed to count you as a friend.
Thanks for your help.

One

"Another one bites the dust," Holly Prescott grumbled as she watched the second of her two best friends sashay out of the Caliber Club with a newly purchased bachelor by her side.

If you had any sense at all you'd sneak out right behind them. Instead she was stuck here in hooker-high heels and a dress that ought to be illegal—on her, anyway—fulfilling her part of the ridiculous pact she, Andrea and Juliana had made.

How had she let herself be bamboozled into this disastrous plan? Buying men, for crying out loud! She could think of at least a dozen more useful things she'd rather have for her upcoming thirtieth birthday.

So what if she hadn't had sex in so long she'd forgotten how it went exactly? She'd hold on to her born-again virgin status until she'd nixed her tendency to choose men who needed fixing because she couldn't afford any more strays of the two-legged variety. The last one had cost her a bundle and put her hard-won independence in jeopardy. Not that she intended admitting her gullibility to anyone. Too humiliating.

A blast of chilly air from the overhead vent made her curse her clothing for the umpteenth time this evening. Where had her brain been vacationing when she'd allowed her friends to pour her into a dress that looked more like underwear than outerwear? If she had so much as a mosquito bite—or panties—beneath the form-fitting bronze silk, every one would know it.

Crossing her arms over her breasts, Holly scanned the ballroom filled with well-heeled guests. She didn't belong here. Never mind that her father owned the place. She didn't fit in. Story of her life.

"See if I ever trust Andrea or Juliana again," she groused without worrying about being overheard by the women swarming the marble floor. The auction attendees had two hours' worth of free champagne in them, and the normally dignified ladies were too busy screaming their lungs out like rock band groupies to pay any attention to a misfit like her.

On a positive note, their lack of inhibitions could work to her advantage once the bidding on her bachelor began. "Twenty more minutes and I can go home."

"Talking to yourself?" The rich baritone behind her made her cringe. Eric Alden, her best friend's brother, had already read them the riot act once tonight about this foolhardy plan. As far as Holly was concerned, he was preaching to the choir. She didn't need to hear another sermon. But she'd promised to give bachelor bidding the old college try.

Now that her friends had abandoned her, Eric would focus all his cutting wit on her. Might as well cork him before he got started. She turned, but her retort stuck in her throat. *Wow*. How could she have forgotten how good he looked in a tux? His banker-short dark hair looked freshly trimmed and his strong jaw gleamed from a recent shave.

Holly scrambled to rally her brain cells. "I'm cursing your

sister. The dress she and my other so-called friend chose for me is indecent."

Eric's navy blue gaze raked over her, and Holly mentally kicked herself for drawing his attention to her attire—or lack thereof. Before tonight, she didn't think Eric had ever seen her in a dress—certainly not one like this. The nostrils of his straight nose flared, and then he slowly, deliberately circled her, appraising her as if *she* were the one going on the auction block instead of him.

Holly straightened, tucked her tush, sucked in her stomach and prayed he wouldn't guess she was *completely* naked beneath the dress except for the blush coating her skin.

He halted in front of her with only inches separating them, crowding into her personal space. "Definitely indecent. Indecently beautiful."

The husky timbre of his voice combined with his proximity made her heart beat a quick rat-a-tat-tat and sent a weird frisson down her spine. *Hold it. This is Juliana's brother.* Juliana's rule-following, workaholic, socially prominent brother. That triple no-no-*absolutely-no* whammy made tingles of any kind taboo. Holly tried to back up, but the tipsy socialites behind her blocked her path.

"You look lovely, Holly. I almost didn't recognize you without your baseball cap and work boots."

So much for his ego-boosting flattery. Could she help it if her job required protective clothing? "You don't look too skanky yourself, Alden, but then Armani probably helped design your birthday suit, so it's no surprise you look decent in a tux."

Eric's smile seemed a little forced. "If that was a compliment, thank you. May I speak with you a moment?"

She glanced left and then right and found women ogling him on either side. They might ignore her, but they didn't ignore the heir to a banking empire. In fact, they looked as though they'd enjoy nibbling hors d'oeuvres off Eric's naked body. "Me? Sure."

His long fingers curled around her elbow, each one soldering a tendril of heat on her skin. He guided her to the far corner of the ballroom where the noise level registered a few decibels lower and released her. His broad-shouldered frame fenced her against the walls.

"Why are you buttering me up with compliments?" she asked before he said whatever it was he'd dragged her over here to say. At five-ten and wearing four-inch heels, Holly only had to lift her gaze a little to meet him eye to eye—one of the many reasons she never wore heels.

Chagrin briefly flickered across Eric's handsome face. He shoved his hands in pants pockets and leaned closer—close enough that she could taste the mint on his breath—to be heard above the crowd winding up as another bachelor took the stage.

Her mouth dried. *Uh-uh. Cut it out.*

"I need a favor."

Of course he did. Why couldn't a guy say something nice to her just once without having an ulterior motive? She wrestled her wacko hormones into submission and tried to clear her head.

"What kind of favor?" She glanced past him toward the stage. Her bachelor would be up next, and if all went well he'd soon be someone else's bachelor and she could go home. Alone.

"Buy me."

Her gaze snapped back to Eric's. Surely she'd misheard him in the din of screeching women? "Excuse me?"

His body radiated heat, which, perversely, made her shiver. She stepped back—right into the wall. The thump of the cool wainscoting against her spine reminded her that her dress bared her to the waist in back except for the pair of crisscrossed strings that held up the two inadequate triangles of her top.

"Save me from this." He indicated the proceedings behind him with a jerk of his square chin.

Why in the world would he need saving? She didn't know what his date package included, but his company alone would bring a high bid. Eric was a handsome, rich hunk, if you didn't mind buttoned-down, uptight types whom she avoided like she would a communicable disease.

"Why me?"

"Because you're not looking for a wealthy husband."

"Amen." Being his date wouldn't be a hardship, but Holly didn't want a date. Even if she could afford to buy a bachelor she could *not* go out with her best friend's brother without risking one of the most important friendships of her life.

"No can do, Eric. I've chosen my guy. So suck it up and hit the stage. I'm sure you'll make some lucky lady very happy."

His palm curved over her shoulder—her bare save-for-that-string-strap shoulder. Her nipples, damn them, tightened—a fact thin silk couldn't disguise. Embarrassed, she crossed her arms. It definitely had been too long since she'd made love if a simple asexual touch could turn her on.

"Holly, please. I'll give you anything you ask. Just save me from this ridiculous spectacle my mother is forcing upon me."

Ah. Spectacle. Now *that* she understood. Eric had been dumped by his socialite fiancée a few months back. The highly publicized society event of the year had turned into the disaster of the year when the bubbleheaded bride-to-be had literally left him at the altar after screeching a few crushing insults in front of their wedding guests. Eric's pride had to have taken a staggering blow—even if he'd never shown it.

"What would your mother say if you ended up with me, the only girl to ever be kicked out of cotillion?"

His rigid shoulders stiffened even more. "My mother volunteered me without my consent. Her opinion is irrelevant."

Sympathy for him battled with Holly's need to escape. Wasn't she always a sucker for a guy in dire straits? And hadn't she sworn off saving men in need?

She liked Eric, but the VP of Alden Bank and Trust, the largest privately owned bank in the region, represented everything she'd escaped. Pretentiousness. Snobbery. Expectations she couldn't meet.

C'mon, Holly, how can you leave him to the mercy—or lack thereof—of the bidding piranhas? "Your sister would never speak to me again. I promised her I'd bid on 'Light Up The Nights With Franco The Firefighter.'"

Eric's lips flattened. "I met Franco backstage. He's shorter than you and he has the IQ of a rock. He'll bore you senseless."

Why had she never noticed the sensual fullness of Eric's bottom lip? Or that he had lush lashes that looked frivolous on such a no-nonsense male? And why was she noticing now? She cast off the unwanted discoveries. "I don't intend to *date* Franco."

Eric's eyebrows shot up, and he reassessed her outfit with one *l-o-n-g* perusal from those intensely blue eyes. Surprise, speculation and then something she didn't recognize invaded his expression. "Then you're buying him for what? Stud service?"

Holly's mouth fell open and her cheeks caught fire—the curse of a redhead's complexion. Her pride stabbed her with the mother of all stings.

"Do you think I have to buy a man to get laid? I might not be the elegant model-slim sort you usually date, but I do okay in the dating department." If you overlooked her tendency to choose losers. And she'd had her share of sex—none of which rated inclusion in the *Memoirs of a Debutante Dropout* she intended writing one of these days.

He drew back and compressed his lips. "I didn't say that."

Holly gathered what was left of her dignity. "For your information Juliana, Andrea and I wanted to support the charity. No, that's not exactly true. *Your mother—*" she poked his chest "—the event organizer, ordered us to support the charity. So the three of us agreed to bid the trust fund money we'll receive on our thirtieth birthdays on bachelors tonight."

She held up a hand when he would have interrupted and wished she hadn't touched him when her finger wouldn't quit tingling. "But here's the good part. We set a price limit. The fire-fighter will go for more money than we agreed upon. When that happens I'm home free. No bachelor. No broken promises. No unwanted dates."

"And if he doesn't?"

Then she'd be stuck with a guy with more brawn than brains. Worse, she'd be in a financially sticky situation. "He will. He posed for a firefighters' calendar last year. I'll bet most of these women have a copy and want to see if the real Franco lives up to the promise in that G-string."

The crowd roared as the firefighter took the stage. "See. They love him. And they can have him."

Frustration rolled off Eric in waves. He faced the stage and folded his arms across his chest, looking as stoic as a captain going down with his ship. A muscle ticked in his jaw.

Holly waved her numbered fan high over her head, launching what she hoped would be a bidding frenzy. Time inched past as if in slow motion and then the bidding stalled thousands below her maximum allowance.

"Just my luck," she muttered under her breath and then glanced quickly at Eric. She worked alone ninety percent of the time and had picked up the habit of talking to herself—a habit she needed to break before the men in white coats arrived to cart her to an asylum somewhere. But if Eric had heard her, his face didn't show it.

The audience remained unresponsive despite the MC's attempt to draw more bids. Resignation settled over Holly like a cold, wet blanket. She was going to be stuck with a male blond bombshell—one she couldn't afford—all because of a tequila-induced promise and a case of pride that wouldn't let her admit to her friends that thanks to not her first bit of misplaced faith she needed her trust fund money to live off.

"You don't want to be here any more than I do," Eric said without turning his head.

"You got that right. My life is almost perfect. Why would I want a man to screw it up?" More than one already had.

She tightened her grip on the wooden handle, but before she could lift the fan to bid again Eric's fingers curled around her wrist, trapping her hand by her side with a firm grip. Her knuckles brushed his hard thigh and her stomach did that taboo fizzy thing again. No doubt he'd feel her sprinting pulse beneath his fingertips.

"Buy me, Holly, and we can skip the dates. I'll reimburse you whatever you pay and you can use the money for veterinary bills or buy yourself a truckload of pet supplies for that menagerie of yours."

Holly's dogs always needed something. How wise of him to hit her where it counted. But then she'd never doubted Eric's intelligence—except for the day she'd heard about his engagement to Prissy, the pretentious witch. Tempted more than a little, she considered his offer while the MC launched into another recitation of Franco's physical assets.

Holly had promised Juliana and Andrea that she'd bid on *a bachelor* tonight. Eric was one. What's more, she didn't think there was another man on the docket who would exceed her price limit. So she had a choice. Eric and reimbursement, or Franco and financial difficulties in the months ahead. Either way, she'd be stuck with a bachelor she didn't want. But doing a good deed, getting out of the dates and holding on to her money seemed like a win-win-win proposition.

She lifted her gaze to his. "No dates. You swear it?"

"Yes. Buy me, and if my price exceeds your limit—"

She snorted inelegantly and punched him lightly in the biceps. "Jeez, Eric, you have a big ego if you think you'll go for more than ten grand."

"—I'll cover the cost no matter how high," he continued as if she hadn't interrupted.

Juliana and Andrea would be miffed, but surely she could

make her friends understand. Guilt rode Holly like a hair shirt for twisting the bet to fit her needs, but buying men hadn't been *her* idea. She'd argued against it from the moment of inception and been outvoted. "All right, Eric. I'll buy you."

As soon as she said the words, the MC whipped out a copy of the sexy calendar and Franco stripped down to the thong he'd worn in the picture with a bump and grind worthy of a Chippendales dancer. The bidding frenzy Holly had expected erupted.

When the gavel hit, her stomach sank. Her bachelor's price had exceeded her limit. She could have been scot-free, but instead she'd been burned by the second promise in one night.

"How about a kiss to seal the deal?"

The reporter's remark drew Eric's attention to forbidden territory—Holly's wide mouth. The siren-red shade of her lipstick could give a man all kinds of ideas about what she could do with those lips and where she could use them to optimal advantage—if he was inclined to think that way. Eric wasn't. Not with Holly.

So why did his brain engage the idea of tasting her like a heat-seeking missile locking on to its target?

Judging by Holly's open-mouthed stare she wasn't any more enamored of the request than he was. And then Holly's eyes narrowed and her lush lips compressed. She shook her finger at the reporter. "Octavia Jenkins, don't play games with me."

"I'm just doing my job, girlfriend." Octavia motioned for them to move closer while her photographer pointed his lens.

"You know her?" Eric asked against Holly's temple as he wrapped his arm around her waist to pose for the picture they apparently couldn't leave without. His palm found warm, *bare* skin at the base of her spine. He quickly shifted his grip to her fabric-covered hip, but her thin dress did nothing to mask her body heat. His hand burned, and that burn spread up his arm and down his torso.

"She's one of my students," Holly replied *sotto voce*.

His sister had mentioned that Holly, a commercial stained glass artist, taught classes in the craft to subsidize the care and feeding her overpopulated pet collection. That's how he'd come up with the idea to offer her money for her animals. "Is that going to be a problem?"

"Not if I can help it." Holly forced the words through the patently false smile she aimed at the photographer.

"C'mon, folks, this isn't a firing squad. Kiss for the camera," the reporter cajoled.

Kissing Holly appealed far more than it should. Eric blamed the unwanted attraction on her seductive dress and dangerously high heels. Holly had always been the girl next door who wore jeans or shapeless sweats. She'd never been a girlie girl. But tonight there was no doubt that she was all woman. A generously endowed woman. His gaze lifted from the smooth ivory curve of her breasts to her mouth.

"Don't even think about it," Holly all but snarled through her clenched teeth. Pink dotted her cheeks, and her toffee-brown eyes sparked a warning.

Was the possibility of kissing him so repulsive that she couldn't tolerate even one platonic peck to pacify the pushy reporter? The idea slipped under his skin like a splinter.

She shoved an errant curl behind her ear, and Eric noticed the polish on her short nails for the first time—the same dark red as her lips and toenails. He'd never known Holly to wear nail polish or makeup, and he'd certainly never noticed her doing anything with her shaggy, boyishly-cut copper-colored hair. Tonight it curled in sexy disarray, looking as if she'd just crawled out from under an enthusiastic lover.

In fact, he'd never seen Holly look so desirable and she smelled… He filled his lungs. She smelled like a woman who didn't wear cologne to mask her subtle, natural scent. He slammed the vault on his unacceptable thoughts.

The reporter motioned them even closer. Holly shook her

head, lowered her arched eyebrows and glared at the photographer beside the reporter. "You have three seconds to take your picture and then we're out of here."

The shutter clicked.

"Excuse us," Eric said to the newshounds and then cupped Holly's elbow and steered her toward the exit.

Octavia kept pace with them. "Covering and reporting on your dates is going to be the highlight of this assignment for me, Holly. Just think of all the additional business the newspaper exposure will bring your way. Consider it free publicity. And of course, because you are my friend, I have a vested interest in the outcome of your dates."

The last phrase sounded like a warning to Eric, but before he could demand the reporter clarify her meaning Holly muttered a curse. A chorus of screams erupted behind them, drowning out whatever she said next. Holly stopped and pointed to the stage. "Look, Octavia. Another bachelor sacrifice. Go do your job. Good night."

The newspaper duo turned back. Holly slammed out the front door, veered off the sidewalk and trekked unsteadily across the thick grass toward the golf course. At nearly midnight the area was deserted and lit only by a slice of June moon. Eric followed because he needed to make arrangements to repay Holly.

She stopped and bent so abruptly he almost fell over her. He caught her hips to steady them both. The nudge of her bottom against his groin as she removed her shoes and the suggestive position with her bare back sunny-side up played hell with his hormones. He released her and put a few inches between them.

He hadn't slept with a woman since Priscilla had dumped him four months ago. Not because he mourned his ex-fiancée or their aborted relationship, but because with the pending merger between Alden's and Wilson's, another privately owned bank, he hadn't had time. The result of his abstinence reared its head.

And then Holly straightened, with sexy heels dangling

from her fingertips, and resumed her course. She plunked down on the bleachers at the edge of the eighteenth green and then instantly sprang back up and flattened a hand to her bottom. "I'm wet."

His heart slammed against his chest. So maybe the idea of kissing him hadn't turned her off. And why did that excite him? He shifted his stance to hide his body's reaction.

She lightly punched him in the stomach and glared. "From the dew on the bench, Casanova."

He *wasn't* disappointed. If anything, he was embarrassed. At thirty-six he shouldn't be so transparent or so easily titillated. Besides, this was Holly, a plain spoken tomboy and Sam and Tony's baby sister. Even if she had been revealing sexual arousal, he'd have done nothing to alleviate it. There was an unspoken rule between friends. He didn't date their sisters, and they didn't date his. Anything beyond dating qualified as grounds for an ass-kicking. He might be six-five and a solid two hundred and twenty pounds, but he didn't want to go two against one with Holly's brothers for something he could easily avoid.

Besides, the Caliber Club was one of Alden Bank's largest commercial accounts. Antagonizing the Prescotts could cost Alden's business.

Holly turned, giving him a clear view of damp fabric clinging to her perfectly shaped butt. There were no panty lines. He bit back a groan, drew off his tux jacket and spread it over the bench. After a moment's hesitation, she sat on his coat, tipped her head back and met his gaze. "We have a problem."

"Besides the reporter?" And his unwilling and unwanted surprise attraction to Holly.

"The reporter is the problem. Eric, you and I each work with the public. Our businesses rely heavily on our reputations. If we renege on these dates, Octavia will report it in her Saturday column, and we're going to come out looking like welshers. Trust me, I know Octavia's twisted mind. She'll make each of us a laughingstock. I know that's something I'd like to avoid. I'm guessing you would, too."

On the heels of the humiliating end to his engagement. She didn't say it. Didn't have to.

His dented pride didn't relish another lashing in the press, and with the bank merger closing in on the final stages Eric couldn't afford bad publicity without adversely affecting Alden's bargaining power. Why hadn't his mother considered that before involving him in this fiasco?

"Why didn't you mention your relationship with the reporter before?"

Holly took a deep breath and blew it out slowly. The play of moonlight and shadow over her cleavage drew his gaze. He'd always known Holly had a broad-shouldered, athletic build because he'd spent countless afternoons playing ball in the driveway with her two older brothers a decade and a half ago. Holly had often joined them to even the numbers. She was fast on her feet and had a decent hook shot, if he remembered correctly. But what he hadn't realized years ago was that her breasts matched her generous height and firm muscle tone. His pulse accelerated. Damn.

"Because I didn't know Octavia would make this personal. Besides, me buying you was *your* idea, remember? My plan was to leave the auction alone tonight."

He lowered himself beside her on his coat. Their shoulders and thighs brushed. Sparks ignited, but he ignored them. Tried to, anyway. He saw where this was headed and couldn't see any way to avoid it. "Your recommendation?"

"We go through the motions. If Octavia is around then I want you to treat me exactly like any other date. If we're lucky she'll soon lose interest in torturing me. If luck's against us then it's only eleven dates. We'll survive. Somehow," she said with a total lack of enthusiasm.

She'd *survive* dating him? The comment ripped the scab off

his wounded pride, and Priscilla's comment echoed in his head. *The only place you don't bore me is in bed.* If he'd bored his tra-ditional-minded ex-fiancée, then he'd turn a free spirit like Holly comatose, and her friend would report it in the paper. Another public humiliation.

Damned if he dated Holly. Damned if he didn't. "I can't treat you like my other dates."

"Why in the heck not? Am I such a toad?"

She was far from a toad, but commenting on her unique beauty would be unwise. "I sleep with most of the women I date by the third evening, if not sooner."

Her lips parted and then closed. Her throat worked as she gulped. "Not this time, pal. You got the raw end of the deal. I'm not your type."

"Nor I yours, I imagine."

A smile played over her lips. "Not even close. But it's just dinner and stuff, right? What can go wrong?"

What indeed?

As if in answer to the question, the automatic sprinklers erupted. After a shocked gasp Holly looked skyward. "That was a rhetorical question."

She snatched up her shoes and then zigzagged through the spurting nozzles like a running back headed for the goal line. Eric grabbed his coat and jogged after her. She stopped on the sidewalk edging the parking lot. Her hair and gown were drenched and plastered to her body. Grass clippings clung to her bare feet and mascara streaked down her cheeks, but instead of complaining Holly laughed and once again looked skyward.

"This is what I get for trying to pull a fast one on my friends? Okay, okay, I get it. I'm sorry."

Eric couldn't think of a single woman he'd ever known who would have had anything less than a complete meltdown over having her evening and probably her dress ruined. He extracted a handkerchief from his pocket and offered it to Holly.

"Thanks." She blotted her face. Droplets glistened on her eyelashes as she grinned up at him. "I don't suppose you have a beach towel tucked in there do you?"

That unabashed grin twisted something in his gut. He caught himself grinning back. "Not tonight."

Gravity carried a rivulet over her collarbone and between her breasts. His gaze followed and his smile faded. Wet fabric molded Holly's body, tenting over her beaded nipples and dipping into her navel. He'd found her satiny dress sexy before, but seeing the fabric adhered to her curvaceous damp body like a second skin ratcheted his response up a level—right into the danger zone. He swallowed hard.

And that's when it hit him. He'd miscalculated.

His safe way out of the auction had become a minefield of trouble.

Two

Dumped and deserted. A situation with which Holly was becoming all too familiar for her liking.

She shoved her wet hair off her face, plucked at her stuck-on dress and faced Eric. Water had turned his white silk shirt almost transparent. She could see the dark whorls of his chest hair and even the small brown circles of his nipples. Warmth she couldn't blame on the humid June evening settled low in her belly.

Good grief. You've seen him without a shirt before. That might have been years ago, but still, what's the big deal? Shaking off the unwanted fascination, she met his gaze. "Could you give me a ride home? It appears my cohorts have abandoned me."

Looking tall, dark and better than any male model she'd sketched in her university Live Art class, Eric motioned toward a black Corvette. "Certainly. We still haven't finalized the repayment of your *substantial* bid."

A smug smile twitched the corners of his mouth. Holly rolled her eyes. "Go ahead and gloat. I know you're dying to."

He smiled and looked so much like the guy she'd had a crush on in her teens that it sucked the breath from her lungs. "I've never been happier to waste fifteen thousand dollars."

She snorted. "You guys and your egos. I should have let Prissy have you."

His smile vanished, and she wondered if having his ex-fiancée join in the bidding had surprised him as much as it had her. Or maybe he'd wanted her to let Prissy win him?

"Thank you for outbidding her."

Holly tried to gauge his sincerity, but couldn't. Had he loved Priscilla Wilson? Had his heart been broken when she'd dumped him so cruelly? Or was his sister right? Juliana swore her brother couldn't squeeze a drop of emotion out of his calculator heart with a juicer. "I promised and, good or bad, I always keep my promises."

He opened the passenger door and cupped Holly's elbow as she lowered herself into the leather seat. She wished he'd quit touching her. Each time he did, something tightened and twisted inside her.

She directed him toward her house and twenty minutes later he parked beside the white picket fence surrounding her home. She climbed from the car before Eric could open her door, and a chorus of barks reached them.

"It's okay guys. It's just me," she yelled through cupped hands, and the barks turned from warning to welcoming.

Eric stood with his hands on his hips, appraising the farmhouse. Because she lived alone, Holly had installed several area lights to keep the yard well-lit. The scent of gardenias, honeysuckle and moon flowers saturated the humid night air.

"Not the ramshackle hovel you expected?"

His gaze landed on hers. "It's nice."

Pride filled her chest. Her maternal grandfather had built the house for his bride back in the 1930s. Since moving to the farm seven years ago, Holly had steadily made upgrades both inside and out as money permitted. She'd turned the barn where cows and horses used to take shelter into kennels with dog runs and converted the carport behind the house into her work studio. A local farmer leased all but ten of the five hundred acres and kept her supplied with all the corn, cucumbers and tomatoes she could eat.

She paused beside Eric at the base of the stairs leading to the wraparound porch. "I know what they say behind my back, you know. That I live out here in disgrace, exiled to my grandparents' farm because I don't know how to behave in polite society."

Moonlight played off the sharp planes of Eric's face, casting shadows beneath his cheekbones. "This doesn't look like exile."

"It isn't. It's home. C'mon in." She climbed the steps and unlocked the front door.

She'd had men in her house before, but usually they were misfits like her. Eric, according to his sister, lived in a professionally decorated place in an upscale Wilmington waterfront community. Holly had learned from the wealthy housewives who'd taken her stained glass classes that even her extensive renovations couldn't bring this old house up to yacht club neighborhood standards. But she loved her home, her refuge.

The front door opened into a miniscule foyer with stairs leading to the unfinished attic space directly ahead. When her grandparents had built the house, they'd intended to finish off the upstairs as the children and the need for additional bedrooms arrived, but they'd only had one child, Holly's mother, so the expansion had never happened. Holly's living room lay to the left and her bedroom immediately to the right. "Would you like coffee or something while I change?"

"No thanks."

The sound of canine nails clicking on hardwood floors approached from the kitchen and then the mutts surrounded them. "Down, Seurat and Monet."

"You named your dogs after painters?" Eric bent to scratch each dog's scruff.

"Yes. Seurat is dotted and Monet's colors blend with no

defined lines. They're staying inside while recovering from surgery. They need homes if you know anyone who'd love a mutt." Fat chance of that. Eric's contemporaries preferred pure-breds.

"And you have them because…?"

"I live in the country. People dump their unwanted pets out here all the time, and then, of course, others have heard that I'll foster unwanted animals, so…" She shrugged. "I have the vet check them over and neuter them and then I try to find someone to adopt them." She gestured to the sofa and chairs. "Have a seat in the den. Give me a minute to get into some dry clothes and then we can work out the date details."

Holly stepped into her bedroom, leaving Eric to find the den on his own, and pushed the door almost closed. She peeled off her damp, clingy dress and then draped it over the corner of her grandmother's cheval mirror. The ceiling fan overhead stirred the air, causing chill bumps to rise on every inch of her body. She scrubbed her upper arms while she debated whether or not she had anything clean to wear. When had she done laundry last?

"I have to confess, Eric, that until the MC described your auction package I didn't even know what your dates would be." She raised her voice to be heard through the quarter-inch door gap as she bent over her T-shirt drawer. With her booming, un-ladylike voice—a curse, according to her parents—Eric would be able to hear her from the den.

And then she heard a familiar creaking hinge and straightened abruptly. Her gaze darted to the mirror. Seurat had pushed open her bedroom door, and Eric was not in her living room. Instead, he stood exactly where she'd left him, and right now he was getting an eyeful of her naked backside and a clear view of her front side reflected in the mirror.

Holly snatched the wet dress from the mirror, clutched it to her chest and spun around. But the wet fabric bunched and stuck and refused to cover what needed covering. Eric, damn him, didn't look away. In fact, his dark gaze raked over every exposed inch of her skin.

Her heart stuttered like a jackhammer. "Excuse me."

Holly lunged forward, shut the door, forcing it past the sticking upper corner and leaned against it. That hadn't been revulsion in Eric's eyes. Worse, the heat swirling in her stomach like a water spout didn't remotely resemble shame or disgust.

The only thing worse than getting involved with another needy man would be getting involved with a man who came from a world where she'd been a complete failure, a world to which she'd have to crawl back amidst a chorus of "I told you so's" if she couldn't locate the ex-lover who'd suckered her into borrowing against her trust fund and loaning him money.

Oh, man, why hadn't she broken her promise to buy Eric and bolted when she'd had the chance?

Promises were the pits.

Eric's sister stormed through the office door early Monday morning without bothering to knock. "What are you doing?"

"Good morning, Juliana. I'm working on an account analysis to determine which of the branches we'll have to consolidate when the merger goes through." His sister had a vested interest in the Alden Bank and Trust-Wilson Savings and Loan merger—an interest she'd jeopardized Saturday night by buying the wrong bachelor. "One of us needs to think about the merger."

Anger darkened Juliana's complexion and glinted in her eyes. "I meant with Holly. Besides the fact that she's my friend and therefore off-limits to you, how dare you take advantage of her generous nature by conning her into buying you? She deserves a man who'll sweep her off her feet and treat her like the special person she is. *You* don't know anything about romance."

Her verbal stiletto nicked his ego. His ex-fiancée had shouted similar words and a few other choice phrases at him instead of the traditional "I dos" in front of their wedding guests right before she'd stormed back down the aisle. Alone and unwed.

"And what about you? You should have bought Wallace Wilson, your fiancé, instead of that bartending biker. You know what a tight-ass Baxter Wilson is and how concerned with appearances he can be. He'll be offended that you didn't buy his son. Did you even consider the ramifications of your actions before you chose unwisely, Juliana?"

"Wally isn't my fiancé yet, and this is not about me. This is about you. You go through women faster than you go through neckties. I do not want Holly to be one of your discards."

"I have no intention of becoming involved with Holly more than superficially. Neither of us wants to go on the dates, but her reporter friend is pressing the issue. We'll go through the motions until Octavia Jenkins loses interest. My goal was to avoid vicious gossip which could be detrimental to the merger, and I thought Holly would be a safe alternative to a marriage-minded female."

And he'd never been more wrong in his life. Even though Holly had pulled on jeans and a baggy T-shirt Saturday night, once more camouflaging her generous curves, he'd kept seeing her naked and his usual razor-sharp concentration had taken a hiatus. As much as he disliked loose ends, he'd been relieved when the phone rang and Holly had had to rush out to pick up his sister before they finalized the date details.

He'd called Holly this morning and scheduled a date for tomorrow night. It had taken him promising to bring her a reimbursement check for the auction cost to get her to agree.

"Holly? Safe?" His sister had the nerve to laugh. "You don't know what you're in for."

"What is that supposed to mean?"

"It means, big brother, that Holly isn't one of your usual dim-witted debutantes. She's not going to be impressed with your stock portfolio or the fact that you play tennis with the mayor and golf with a judge. She's more interested in what's on the inside than net worth or connections, Eric, and you, like our mother, have a calculator for a heart."

Surprised by his sister's unusual vehemence, he rocked back in his executive chair. "You don't think I'm capable of showing Holly a good time."

"Frankly?" She folded her arms and cocked her head. "No."

His competitive instincts, never far from the surface, reared. "Then prepare to eat your words, little sister."

Eric had enjoyed his dinner at one of Wilmington's finest restaurants as much as he always did, and yet the only enthusiasm he'd seen from Holly had been for her crème brûlée. Throughout the rest of the meal, she'd appeared tense and uncomfortable.

He signed the credit card slip and rose. Apparently eager to leave, Holly sprang to her feet without waiting for him to pull back her chair, thereby proving his sister's prediction true. Holly wasn't enjoying the evening. Eric was determined to change that.

Keep the client happy. He'd decided the safest approach to this series of dates would be to consider Holly a client. They had a verbal contract, and she'd paid for his services even if he had a check for a one-hundred-percent refund in his pocket. He didn't mix business with pleasure. The one time he had—his engagement to Priscilla—he'd been burned.

You've never seen any of your clients naked.

He locked the safe on that thought. Outside the building, he cupped her elbow. She stiffened. "Would you care to walk along the waterfront?"

Her hesitation shoved another splinter into his ego. "Sure. Why not?"

The moon ducked behind a cloud, but the streetlights illuminated the area well enough for a stroll. Holly wore flat shoes tonight, along with a simple black dress that in no way resembled Saturday night's seductive number but that did nothing to erode the memory of how she'd looked wearing sinfully high heels and nothing else. Holly had an amazing figure. Not Rubenesque by any means, but not fashionably slim, either. She had curves, womanly, generous curves that begged a man to map her topography with his hands. With his mouth.

He ran a finger beneath his suddenly restricting collar and loosened his tie a fraction of an inch.

Holly's long stride down the cobblestoned sidewalk would leave a shorter man in the dust. Eric kept pace beside her until she halted abruptly in front of a gift shop window. A Haunted Historic Wilmington Tours poster held her attention. He shoved his hands into his pockets and waited for her to move on, but then she looked over her shoulder at him. The excited sparkle in her eyes knocked the wind out of him.

"Want to? It starts in ten minutes."

He'd rather shred money. But his pride demanded he show Holly a good time and thus far he'd failed to deliver anything more than a fine meal and stilted dinner conversation. If this tourist fodder entertained her, then he would—what had she said Saturday night?—*survive* it. "I'll buy the tickets."

Thirty minutes later, Holly inched closer to him in the shadowy interior of the theater allegedly haunted since the 1800s. Since the tour began, she'd startled at every squeak and gasped along with the other gullible fools on the tour as they followed their guide through the drafty and dimly lit area beneath the stage. Goose bumps covered her skin. She shivered and rubbed her upper arms.

Who'd have expected practical Holly to believe in ghosts? Eric took pity on her and put his arm around her shoulders. A mistake, he realized an instant later.

Holly burrowed against him, her breast pressing against his ribs, and she stayed as close as she could and still walk the creaking floor boards. Her scent filled his lungs and her hair tickled his jaw. The warmth of her in his arms roused the specter of his libido and sent it drifting through his blood like a hot phantom breath. It took every ounce of concentration to focus on the guide's macabre spiel instead of the woman plastered against him.

At the conclusion of the tour, he had to admit that if he'd been a more susceptible sort he'd have enjoyed their talented host's shtick, but Eric was a cynic. Smoke and mirrors didn't interest him. He preferred cold, hard, provable facts. But the excited flush on Holly's cheeks and the twinkle in her eyes made the price of admission worth every penny.

On the sidewalk in front of the building, she took one last look over her shoulder as if she expected an evil spirit to chase after them from the theater, and then she grinned at him. "Thanks. That was awesome."

Her wide, unrestrained smile reminded him of the girl she'd been back when they'd shot hoops in her driveway and of the idealistic fresh-out-of-university fool he'd been at the time. Was it only fourteen years ago that he'd first joined Alden's? It seemed like a lifetime since he'd realized his father was a source of amusement to many of the bank employees—a figurehead who did whatever Eric's mother told him to do like a well-trained dog. A man more excited by a good cigar or a round of golf than a P&L statement.

The day he'd heard the laughter in the break room, Eric had decided that he would never be the butt of jokes. He'd be man enough for both his father and himself, and he'd succeeded until Priscilla made a fool out of him. Now the reporter's coverage of this damned auction package could sink him faster than rising interest rates could the stock market and with equally devastating results. What in the hell had his mother been thinking when she'd inflicted this on him?

"I'm glad you enjoyed the tour."

Holly's eyes widened at the unintended sharpness of his voice and then she averted her gaze. "I guess we should head back. I have an early start tomorrow."

He led her back to his 'Vette and then pointed the car in the direction of her farm. Damn. Any points he'd gained with the ghost tour had been lost with one bitter comment. "Tell me about your business."

Holly flashed him an I-know-what-you're-up-to glance. "You mean you haven't read my file?"

"You have accounts with Alden's?"

Another hesitation. "Several. I work primarily with commercial concerns, but I also do windows for private homes. I teach stained glass classes once a week, not just because I enjoy sharing my craft but because those same women who take my classes often commission me to do windows for their homes, tell their friends about me or recommend me to the boards of the organizations to which they belong, which in turn leads to more commercial accounts." Her entire body became animated as she discussed her work.

"Smart advertising," he acknowledged.

"I think so."

"You like making windows better than working at the Caliber Club?"

"Oh, yeah. No comparison."

The nuances in her voice raised questions such as why would she leave a secure, well-paying job, one with limitless advantageous connections, for the financially risky venture of crafting stained glass windows? He turned into Holly's driveway and spotted a dark sedan parked in the shadows beneath a large tree. His curiosity would have to wait. "You have company."

"Great." Her sarcastic tone implied otherwise. "It's Octavia."

The reporter and the photographer beside her in the front seat waved as they drove past, but made no move to get out of the car.

"What do they want?"

Holly stared at her knotted fingers in the dimly lit car. "To see the end of our date."

Eric's spine prickled a warning. "Pardon?"

Holly took a deep breath and then lifted her wary, toffee-brown gaze to his. "Women talk when they're working on their projects in my class. Octavia believes the first kiss foretells the future of any relationship."

He'd have to kiss Holly good-night. The news sent a rush of adrenaline through him.

Holly bit her lip and lifted her chin. "Eric, I realize you probably had no intention of kissing me good-night, and as much as I hate the idea of a mercy kiss, could you kiss me and make it look good? It'll keep her off our backs. This week, anyway."

Moisture flooded his mouth and his pulse pounded like a marching band headed toward the end zone located below his belt. He jerked a nod because the words on the tip of his tongue, *my pleasure*, were forbidden and just plain wrong. He exited the car, and for once Holly waited for him to open her door and assist her out.

With a hand at the small of her back, he guided her up the walk, the stairs and then stopped on her doormat. She turned toward him, and in the soft glow of her porch light she took a deep breath, clearly bracing herself to endure his kiss.

Bracing herself. As if she expected kissing him to be an ordeal. Eric's pride roared in protest. He inhaled once, twice, willing his irritation away and his knotted muscles to relax. What he needed was technique. Smooth, controlled, seductive technique. He'd be damned if any woman would *endure* his kiss. He'd settle for nothing less than total capitulation.

He lowered his head until only a fraction of an inch separated their mouths and waited. Waited for Holly's breath to sweep over his chin when she exhaled. Waited for his pulse to steady. And when his heart accelerated instead of slowing, he relented and brushed his lips over hers with a featherlight touch. The spark of electricity jolted him. Curious, he took another cautious sip, and current shot down to his toes. Judging by Holly's gasp, the feeling wasn't one-sided. He settled his mouth over hers, sinking into the lush softness of her lips. Her fingers clutched his waist and her tongue flicked against his and then quickly withdrew.

Any thoughts of controlled technique vanished. Eric banded his arms around her, molding the long length of her body against his as he delved deeper, stroking the satiny warmth of her mouth, tasting rich crème brûlée and even richer Holly. His fingers tightened on the curve of her waist, and his palms prickled.

Holly felt good—too good—in his arms. Her pelvis nudged his as she shuffled closer. His response was instantaneous and enthusiastic.

Unacceptable.

Unforgivable.

Embarrassing.

He was too damned old to get aroused from a dead-end kiss. His only hope was that Holly hadn't noticed. He gripped her upper arms, lifted his head and put a few inches between them.

"Good night." His voice sounded strained and no wonder. His lungs weren't working.

"'Night." She licked her lips and raised her lids to reveal slightly dazed eyes.

Instead of releasing Holly and stepping away the way his brain ordered him to do, Eric found his arms encircling her, pulling her closer. He kissed her again and again. He couldn't help himself. Even as he consumed her mouth, his conscience shouted, "What are you doing?"

Her arms twined around his neck, pressing her soft breasts against his chest. His fingers glided upward from her waist. He had to feel her weight in his hand, to cup her fullness. *Had to*.

The sound of a car starting and crunching down the gravel driveway barely registered, but the barking dogs hurling themselves at the other side of the front door managed to infiltrate the haze clouding his mind. His hand stopped inches short of its target. He lifted his head and swore.

Holly stiffened, jerked her hands from around his neck and pushed against his chest. She looked past his shoulder. "Octavia's gone. I, um, think that probably convinced her."

She licked her lips again and need clawed at him, but Eric released her and stepped away.

What in the hell had just happened?

Whatever it was couldn't happen again.

He, more than anyone, knew that strong emotional attachments made a man weak. If he ever needed a reminder, all he had to do was look at his henpecked father.

He backed away from temptation and left as quickly as he could and still maintain his dignity. Two miles down the road, he realized he still had Holly's check in his pocket, but he couldn't risk turning the 'Vette around. Until tonight, no woman had ever rattled him enough to make him forget that money and the power attached to it made the world go round.

Who'd have thunk it?

Holly leaned against the inside of the door and sank to the floor. Monet and Seurat crawled all over her, jostling for attention. She absently scratched them while willing her pulse to slow.

If anybody had told her uptight Eric Alden's kisses held more sexual promise than the pages of the *Kama Sutra*, she'd have laughed. And darn it, she could not turn the page to see what the next chapter revealed.

How unfair that when she finally met a guy who could singe the toes out of her panty hose, he was the one man she couldn't have. Not only had she tried and failed to fit into Eric's world, she'd promised Juliana after the auction that there was nothing sexual about buying her brother's date package.

Those melt-her-mascara kisses had made a liar out of her. Her body still hummed and her lips wouldn't stop tingling, no matter how hard she bit them. If he'd been anybody but Eric, she would have invited him in for more than a nightcap, thereby breaking her born-again virgin vow. But she'd promised herself she wouldn't settle for anything less than happily ever after next time. If such a thing existed. And she had her doubts. Waiting for a prince—a prince who didn't need fixing or financial assistance—to love her and all her foibles hadn't worked thus far. Better to do without a man altogether than be disappointed yet again.

Holly shoved to her feet and dodged the dogs all the way to her kitchen. She'd have to do a better job of keeping her distance from Eric Alden. She sifted through the pile of magazines and junk mail that had piled up on the counter while she was finishing her current project until she found the bachelor auction brochure. She read over the eleven enchanted evenings promised in Eric's date package to refresh her memory and groaned. "Talk about monotonousness. Jeez."

As long as he didn't kiss her again, then his offering of meals at stuffy see-and-be-seen restaurants where even the wait staff had condescending attitudes would make ignoring the chemistry between them easy. Each date would be a reminder of the world she'd left behind—the world that had turned on her when she'd dared to sully her hands at manual labor.

Juliana and Andrea were the only friends who'd stuck by Holly when she'd said to hell with being miserable doing what was expected of her, quit her job at the Caliber Club and moved to her grandparents' farm. Being happy was more important than being accepted.

Eric thrived in society with all its restrictions, expectations and conventions, but Holly was a debutante dropout who'd suffocated until she'd escaped. He was a banker who lived by the bottom line, and she was a bleeding heart who'd given away more than she could afford, a situation illustrated by her current predicament. One she needed to address ASAP.

Despite the smoldering kisses, she and Eric couldn't be a more mismatched pair—a fact she'd better not forget if he ever hit her with another one of those break-her-celibacy-vow kisses.

Three

Holly tried to ignore the coffee klatch going on behind her as she double-checked the measurements of the living room window she'd been hired to replace.

If she hadn't left the Caliber Club behind, she could have been one of this group. But instead of designer duds and jewelry that cost more than her Jeep, she wore chain store jeans, simple gold stud earrings and a Timex. As usual, she didn't fit in.

But you're not here to fit in. You're here to work at a job you adore.

"What made you bid on Eric, Holly?"

The metal tape measure retracted so fast it almost cut Holly's finger. She faced her client, a woman a few years older than herself, and searched for an acceptable answer. The truth wasn't an option. Finally, she shrugged. "Why not? He's good-looking."

"And good in bed," one of the other women said.

Holly's gaze zipped to the ultrathin, high cheekboned brunette. The woman scanned her friends' faces. "Oh, please. I am not the only one of us who shared Eric Alden's bed before marrying my husband. And Eric was absolutely fabulous between the sheets, wasn't he?"

Three of the six heads nodded. Holly struggled to keep her jaw from dropping. These women had slept with Eric? Holly blew a floppy hank of hair off her forehead and turned back to the window to hide her consternation. Why was she surprised about the affairs? The upper class was its own school of predatory fish, inbreeding and feeding off one another. That was one of the many reasons she'd chosen to get out.

And Eric was…well, sexy in a take-charge kind of way.

"But why did *you* buy him, Holly? Handsome or not, he's hardly your type," her hostess pressed. Charlise Harcourt had been one of Holly's students for the past eighteen months, so she'd met Lyle, the mistake who'd run off with Holly's money.

Think fast. Why did women want wealthy alpha males? "Um…to be treated like Cinderella?"

The women nodded like bobble head dolls, and Holly struggled to conceal her disgust. As far as she was concerned, Cinderella and all her fairy-tale-princess cousins needed to get off their duffs and learn to solve their own problems rather than wait around for a guy to swoop in and do the job.

"Eric can certainly be Prince Charming as long as you remember the party ends at midnight. He isn't the type to commit to any woman who can't further his career."

An unspoken, "And that's not you," hung in the air.

"That bank is his wife and his mistress, too," the brunette said. "A mere woman can't compete."

"Look at his engagement," a third woman chimed in. "That was no love match. Eric was willing to marry to cement the bank merger. Too bad Priscilla wasn't smart enough to hold on to what she had. I'd take a lifetime of great sex and bottomless pockets over love any day. That's what friends, personal trainers and tennis pros are for." A suggestive laugh followed the words.

TMI. Way too much information. Holly quickly stashed her tools. "Ms. Harcourt, I'll have a rough sketch of the design you described ready for your approval early next week." Her cell phone rang. "Excuse me."

Holly turned her back on the women. "Rainbow Glass. This is Holly."

"We need to set up our next date."

Eric. Her heart clogged her throat and her back itched with the knowledge that a half-dozen pairs of eyes stared at her. "Twice in one week?" she whispered.

"The auction package stipulates two dates per week until this is done."

Why hadn't she bothered to read the fine print before jumping into this? Because she'd been certain she could get out of the dates, that's why.

Conscious of the eavesdroppers behind her she carefully weighed her words. "I can live with that. But I can't talk now."

"I have your check." He didn't take the hint.

"That's what you said last time." As long as she deposited the money and transferred the funds before her credit card bill came due, she'd be okay. She nearly laughed aloud. A banker bought on credit. No doubt Eric would be appalled.

"Do you need it now? I can run it by your house during my lunch hour."

"I'm not there. I'm *working* and I need to get off the phone."

"Tonight, then. I'll pick you up at six." That sounded more like an order than a request, but she couldn't call him on it with a roomful of gossipers behind her.

"Fine. Tonight. Whatever." She hung up without waiting to see if he had more to say, and then turned to say her goodbyes. The knowing smirks on the women's faces turned her cheeks into fireballs. "I'll get back to you with the preliminary drawing. Have a good afternoon."

Charlise walked her to the door. "Holly, have a great night, but don't forget what we said."

As if she could.

Eric Alden. Good in bed.

Not something she needed to know.

Eric had never had to work so hard to hold a woman's attention. Frustrated by his failure, he glanced at Holly and then turned his Corvette down Carolina Beach Road, heading toward her house. He hoped the reporter wasn't waiting for them because another kiss wasn't on his agenda. Too risky, and he wasn't into risky ventures.

During dinner, he'd exhausted every topic of conversation from weather to work to Holly's brothers. They'd found very little common ground other than the physical awareness between them that each seemed determined to ignore.

His mother had planned the auction package and the dates behind his back, but she'd done so knowing his preference for quiet restaurants, spectacular food, a good wine list and exemplary service. Clearly those qualities didn't rate as high on Holly's list.

Would he have to pull another tourist attraction out of his hat to salvage the evening? And what did he know about tourist spots except whether they were a good financial risk when the owners submitted loan applications?

Holly straightened abruptly, her gaze fastening on the brightly lit miniature golf place. She hadn't shown that much animation all night. Before he could think twice Eric steered his car off the highway, found a spot in the gravel lot and killed the engine.

Holly eyed him as if he'd lost his mind. "I don't remember this being part of your date package."

"Neither was the haunted theater tour." He thrust open his door. By the time he rounded the hood, Holly waited for him on the sidewalk. She'd worn another figure-concealing outfit tonight, but it didn't matter how loosely the paisley skirt and blue-green top fit. He'd seen the generous curves Holly concealed. Unfortunately. It didn't help that the irregular skirt hem fluttered around her legs in the balmy evening breeze, reminding him exactly how long and sleekly muscled her limbs were.

"I'm going to kick your butt, you know. I'm good."

The excitement shining in her eyes hit him hard and fast. He blamed the swift adrenaline rush on his competitive nature. "Don't issue challenges you can't back up, Ms. Prescott."

He paid the fee, chose a ball and selected a club. Holly took the putter away from him and wiggled her fingers at the clerk behind the counter. The guy dragged two clubs with longer shafts from under the counter. That Holly knew the guy had a secret stash made Eric wonder how often she'd frequented the place.

Holly handed Eric a putter. "Have you ever played?"

No, but he played golf and he putted well. How hard could miniature golf be? Too bad he didn't have his custom-fitted clubs with him. "Don't worry about me."

"Would you care to make a wager?"

He rarely gambled. "Like what?"

"If I win, we substitute one of my favorite restaurants for one of the stuffy places on your list."

"You didn't enjoy tonight's meal?"

She wrinkled her nose. "The food was good, but every time I took a sip of wine the waiter rushed forward to refill my glass. It got to the point where I didn't want to drink anything because it made extra work for him, and I had no idea how much I'd had to drink."

"He gave exceptionally good service and was rewarded for it. That's his job."

"Good or not, it's disconcerting to know someone is watching your every move. Jeez, what if I'd picked up the wrong fork?" She lined up her putt and talked right through it. "And what if you and I had been on a hot date and we wanted to be alone? Having Don hover, however nice and attentive he was, was like having a chaperone."

Eric had never had the kind of date she described. Even if he'd known the woman in question would end the evening in his bed, he had never noticed or minded the interruptions. He never allowed himself to become that needy for a woman's attentions. And he never would.

"How can you relax and enjoy your meal when the whole point of eating in a place like that is being seen by the right people?" Holly's ball rattled in the cup.

Eric frowned at the L-shaped green. Her statements had surprised him so much he'd forgotten to study her technique. "There isn't a straight shot. How did you make a hole in one?"

She shrugged. "Physics. You have to bank the ball off the right spot in the wall. Like billiards."

Billiards he understood. He lined up, tapped the ball and missed the cup by inches. Holly's lipstick-free lips curved. Had he ever dated a woman who didn't excuse herself immediately after the meal to freshen her makeup? Holly hadn't bothered. She'd been too eager to leave the restaurant. And him?

Eric gritted his teeth, studied the artificial turf, lined up and then stroked again. And missed.

"Don't give up now. It's a par three," she said too cheerfully, clearly anticipating a victory. The constant awareness of her made concentrating difficult, but he focused and made the shot. "Eric, relax. It's just a game."

Just a game. Clearly, Holly didn't remember from their basketball games how badly he hated to lose.

Seventeen holes later, she'd trounced him, truly and embarrassingly trounced him, and her grin as she bounced back to the car was wide enough to drive a truck through.

"You made that look easy," he said before turning the key in the ignition.

"And I'm sure you've heard the cliché, 'Appearances can be deceiving.' This is the course closest to my house, so it's familiar terrain. How else would I know Ira kept the good clubs behind the counter?"

Card shark. Pool shark. Was there such thing as a miniature golf shark? Because without a doubt he'd been hustled, and he had only himself to blame. He'd underestimated Holly. He wouldn't again.

Traffic was light. In twenty minutes he could drop Holly off, head home and study the latest merger data in preparation for tomorrow's meeting. Why didn't that plan appeal?

"What other sports should I avoid if I want to escape total humiliation at your hands?" Her chuckle washed over him like a warm summer breeze, and her scent tantalized him in the close confines of the car.

He needed to buy her a bottle of perfume. Smelling an expensive concoction worn by thousands of women would be easier than knowing the alluring scent filling his lungs was uniquely Holly's. He cranked up the air-conditioning.

"Just be glad Octavia wasn't there to witness your loss or she'd have eviscerated you in her Saturday column. She has a thing about dominating men. But your secret's safe with me."

Holly had evaded his question by bringing up a larger issue. He let her get away with redirecting the conversation to focus on the gauntlet ahead. How could he escape kissing her again? Not just tonight, but each of the next nine dates? "Do you think she'll be waiting at your house tonight?"

Holly flashed him a guilty glance. "I didn't tell her about the date."

Satisfied that he could end the date without a casualty, he nodded. "Neither did I."

"According to the auction's fine print—which I finally read this afternoon—we're supposed to tell her about each date ahead of time so she can observe if she wants."

"She saw the end of our last date." The memory of Holly's kisses brought a flash fire of heat. "We'll tell her next time."

By then he'd have devised a few evasive techniques. He turned down Holly's driveway. A canine chorus shattered the silence. "Something wrong?"

"Probably just a raccoon or a possum sniffing around the barn for food, or maybe just the sound of a strange car, but I always check the kennels before going to bed, so soon I'll know."

"You check them alone?"

"What? You think I need a bodyguard to protect me from the boogeyman?"

She lived in a rural, sparsely populated area, and while her yard might be well-lit, there was no telling what or who could hide in the shadows of her outbuildings. And why did he care? Holly wasn't his concern. "I'll walk with you."

"That's really not necessary, but c'mon if you insist. You might decide to take someone home with you tonight."

His gaze jerked toward hers. "Pardon?"

"A four-legged someone," she clarified. "I have a Shepherd mix that would be perfect for you. He's picky about his food and full of himself, too."

The comment shouldn't have surprised him. Holly had needled him subtly, but consistently throughout the evening, like an adversary trying to pull an opponent's head out of the game. Why did he tolerate it? He didn't have an answer, but he suspected it had something to do with enjoying a woman who didn't agree with everything he said. Dating a woman who dared to challenge his opinions was a novel experience. Money, he'd discovered, not only brought power, it bought people. But not Holly.

He followed her to the barn. She flicked on the lights and he stopped in surprise. He'd expected to see wooden stalls as weathered as the exterior, but instead the structure had been gutted. A concrete floor stretched from end to end, and a half-dozen spacious chain-link kennels lined either side of the wide aisle.

Each cage held at least one dog and a plush bed for each mutt. The closest held a lab-type bitch and her pups. "These are all strays?"

"Yes. It's disheartening how some people can discard a loved one when she no longer suits them."

She? Eric's gaze sought Holly's face, but she'd turned away. She was talking about the animals, wasn't she?

She walked along the aisle dispensing dog treats and chatting with each occupant for a moment before pulling a lever that opened exterior doors to the dog runs surrounding the barn. Apparently, each kennel had a private run.

"Your renovations must have been expensive, and upkeep must be costly."

Her gaze hit his and her cinnamon eyebrows arched, disappearing beneath shaggy bangs. "Why do you think I agreed to buy you? You promised money for my family. Thanks for the check, by the way."

He'd given her the check the moment he'd arrived this evening, leaving no chance for another oversight.

But what did she mean by referring to these mutts as her family? *Her family* owned the most prestigious country club on the east coast, complete with a marina and an award-winning golf course. "You're welcome."

"See anyone you want to take home? They've had all their shots and been neutered except for Cleo. She can't be spayed until the pups are weaned in a few weeks."

"I don't have time for a dog."

Holly stepped into the bitch's cage and lifted a fat black puppy. "How can you resist an adorable face like this one?"

The dog's face didn't interest him half as much as Holly's as she nuzzled the squirmy ball of fur. There was an overwhelming sense of satisfaction in her eyes and a softness in her features he hadn't seen before, as if she'd finally let her prickly guard down. "You enjoy caring for these mutts."

She looked up at him through copper-tipped lashes. "Everybody needs love."

She shoved the pup into his arms. He stiffened. "I don't think—"

"A dog would help you unwind, Eric."

He held the mutt and made a mental note to take the suit to the cleaners tomorrow. A long pink tongue swiped his chin. Yuck. "I don't need to unwind."

She snorted. "This from the guy who had a white-knuckled grip on his putter. Give me a break, Alden. You're as tightly strung as a clothesline."

He'd never owned a dog or even a fish. His mother hadn't allowed pets of any kind in her professionally decorated home. But he had to admit holding the warm, wiggly creature wasn't entirely unpleasant—if the mutt would quit trying to French-kiss him.

Holly grinned, took the pup back and returned him to his pen. She lavished attention on each of the remaining littermates before letting herself out of the kennel.

"Okay, if I can't convince you to take a friend home, then I guess we're done here."

"We could post bulletin boards in the bank branches showing the dogs you have for adoption." What in the hell was he saying? Banking was business. There was no room in his bank or his life for sloppy sentiment and that's what these castoff mutts evoked.

Holly's eyes widened in surprise. "That would be great, but I have a feeling your mother will veto that idea."

That lifted his hackles. Margaret Alden ran the banking chain with an iron fist, but on this he would not bend. He'd never let his mother dominate him the way she did his father. Holly wanted to find homes for her menagerie and he had the power to help her.

"It's a public service and good community relations. She'll agree." He'd make damned sure of it.

And before he did something else stupid like kiss that wide

smile off Holly's unpainted lips, Eric turned on his heel and headed for his car. Holly had him using sentiment instead of sense, and that was a dangerous practice he had no intention of continuing.

Entering Alden Bank and Trust as a customer was one thing. Showing up at the main branch on Friday morning and demanding to see the VP without an appointment was another.

Holly felt the curious gazes of countless bank employees like glass slivers in her back as she climbed the wide marble staircase leading from the main floor to the offices on the second-floor balcony. The weight of those stares added ten pounds to the load she carried.

Her heart thumped harder. Why did being here make her nervous? She'd grown up in affluent circles surrounded by the community's movers and shakers, and she'd visited Alden's corporate offices before. In fact, Juliana's office lay on the opposite side of the balcony overlooking the lobby. Holly glanced that way and saw her friend's dark head bent over her desk. The glass-walled offices on this floor reminded Holly of cages at a zoo. How could Juliana stand it? Holly knew she'd go nuts locked away and on display.

Holly followed the directions the teller had given her to Eric's office and caught a glimpse of him through the open blinds as she approached the desk of the woman guarding his domain. Before she could tell his dragon of an administrative assistant that, yes, she was the pushy broad who'd dared to ask the teller to call up and announce her arrival, Eric looked up from his desk. Holly's pulse stuttered and her steps slowed as their gazes met through the glass.

Great kisser.

Good in bed.

Girl, don't even go there.

She wished the women had never told her of Eric's prowess

between the sheets. That was the last thing her I-haven't-had-any-in-a-long-while body needed to hear. Her dates with Eric had nothing to do with either kissing or sex, but her deprived hormones seemed to have trouble getting the message. She'd even dreamed about him last night. Ridiculous, considering all she wanted to do was get through these dates so she could focus on locating Lyle and her money.

But seeing Eric's face relax as he'd cuddled the puppy had gotten to her. She had a feeling he had no idea how uptight he was, but for a split second Wednesday night his rigid control had slipped, and she'd caught a glimpse of the guy he used to be back in the days when they played basketball in her driveway. Back before he'd become the kind of man who'd marry to profit the bank.

Through the glass, she saw Eric rise, circle his big desk and open his door. "Good afternoon, Holly. Come in."

She wasted a smile on his prune-lipped assistant before ducking into his office.

Another one of those hand-tailored suits accentuated his broad shoulders, flat belly and height. This one, in storm-cloud grey, brought out the blue of his eyes. His white shirt accentuated his tan and his burgundy tie screamed conservative. Definitely a hunk—if you liked the type. Which, of course, she didn't. She liked a guy who knew how to have fun, one who didn't live in a world where keeping up appearances was more important than happiness or where connections were more important than kindness. One who followed his heart instead of his head.

Her gaze skimmed over his office. Oyster-grey carpet. Black desk. Black leather chairs. Why did the lack of color surprise her? Other than Eric's tie, there wasn't a speck of color in the room. Even the original charcoal sketches on the walls were black-and-white.

Holly suppressed a shudder. She loved color and couldn't live without it. That's why stained glass excited her. The permutations of color and pattern were limited only by her imagination, which had been grand enough to get her into all kinds of trouble ever since she'd invented her first imaginary friend at four years old. A few years later, Andrea and Juliana had replaced Amethyst, her imaginary pal, and the three of them had been tight ever since.

"Holly?"

She blinked away the memory. Eric stared at her with one dark eyebrow raised in question.

"I have the dogs' pictures. A friend at a framing gallery helped me mat and mount them. I'll stop by every Friday to swap out the photos." She'd chosen the classiest frames from the discounted and discontinued styles so the pictures wouldn't wreck her already iffy budget or stick out in the marble bank interiors. She didn't want to give Eric's mother any reason to refuse to hang them. "I have one for each Wilmington branch. Five in all."

He took the frames from her and his fingers brushed hers. That taboo tingly feeling fizzed like champagne in her belly. He rested them across the arms of a black leather wing chair. Holly bit her lip as Eric flipped through them. There were six dog portraits per frame. The teenager who worked part-time helping Holly tend the kennels had helped her wash and groom each dog, and then Holly had taken the pictures with her digital camera. The project had turned out better than Holly had expected. Even the homeliest dog looked handsome and appealing.

"I'll see that these are hung in each branch's vestibule."

"Thanks." She should go. But her feet stayed fixed to the carpet. She'd realized as she stared at the ceiling last night waiting for her body to cool after that absurdly sensual dream, that Eric might be able to help her find Lyle. Indirectly, of course, because she couldn't tell him the whole truth.

Ask him.

How could she without giving away too much?

But you need help.

No disputing that truth.

"Have you ever used a private detective?" There. She'd asked.

Eric's eyes narrowed. "Yes. The bank has employed a few. Why?"

"I'm, um…trying to track down someone I used to know."

"I can recommend a couple of good ones who won't pad their expenses. Have a seat." He moved behind his desk, sat and clicked his mouse. He pulled a pad of paper forward and wrote down a couple of names and addresses.

Holly perched on the edge of the second leather chair and tried not to fixate on his long-fingered hands or the dusting of dark hair at his cuffs. She didn't want to think about those hands and what they'd almost done Tuesday night. The skin along her ribs prickled with the memory of his touch.

She accepted the page, folded it and tucked it in her shirt pocket, hoping the crisp stationery would hide her taut nipple. "Thanks."

Concern darkened his eyes. "Holly, are you in trouble?"

Financial trouble, yes. She could scrape by a while longer, but the dogs' upkeep plus routine living expenses were pushing her to the limits of her budget each month.

"Everything's peachy." Except for the missing money. "Business has never been better." Also true.

How could she have misjudged her ex-lover so badly? She'd been convinced Lyle's business plan was a sound one and that his intentions were genuine. Otherwise, she never would have loaned him that much money.

But pride wouldn't let her admit even to her closest friends that she'd been taken for a fool and lost the nest egg she needed to carry her over during the winter months when business took its usual cold-weather downturn. Unlike her friends Juliana and Andrea, Holly didn't have a bulging bank account. She'd spent a small fortune over the years renovating the farm. And yes, she did have a teensy problem—okay, not so teensy—with giving assistance to those down on their luck.

"Like I said, I'm just looking for an old friend."

Eric didn't look as if her forced smile fooled him, but thankfully his phone buzzed before he could interrogate her further. He pressed the intercom button to answer. "Yes?"

"You're expected in the boardroom in five minutes," an emotionless voice said.

Holly twisted in her seat and saw his sour-faced admin watching them through the glass.

"Thank you," Eric replied.

"I'll get out of your way." Holly vaulted to her feet and headed for the door. "Thanks for working me in."

"Not a problem." Eric reached it first and held the door closed with one splayed hand. The subtle tang of his cologne teased her nose and tickled something a whole lot lower. "When are you free again?"

She cursed the stupid, telling catch of her breath. "We already had two dates this week."

His slow smile made her cheeks heat. "Next week."

"I'm free most evenings." Didn't that sound pitiful? She bit her lip. But heck, born-again virgins didn't date. Too risky.

Holding her gaze, he inclined his head. "I'll set something up and give you a call."

"I'll look forward to it." Not. But the flutter of her pulse said differently. And wasn't that the worst news she'd had all day? Why oh why did she have to have the hots for Juliana's brother? Had to be the celibacy thing.

He opened the door and motioned for her to precede him. "I'll walk you out."

"Not necessary. I know the way." And she needed to get out of his magnetic field before she found herself stuck to him.

"The boardroom is in the same direction."

"Oh. In that case…"

They hadn't taken ten steps before his mother came out of her office. Her cool gaze raked over Holly and then her mouth stretched in a diamond-hard smile. "Good afternoon, Holly. Working today?"

Holly's face burned at the barb. Okay, so maybe she had come straight from her studio, but her jeans and T-shirt were clean. "Yes. I've been working on the window for the new women and children's wing at the hospital."

Mrs. Alden managed to look down on Holly without being openly rude—it was a skill the filthy rich perfected and one Holly detested. Once upon a time, Holly had been a welcome guest at the Alden home, but that door had been firmly closed when Holly turned her back on society and all it entailed. And while she'd love to tell the bank president where she could shove her condescension, Holly couldn't. Mrs. Alden had too much power in the community from which Holly drew commissions.

"Mother, Holly brought the pet adoption signs I told you about."

Mrs. Alden's lips flattened. "About those—"

"I'll take care of them," Eric interrupted firmly. Clearly, his mother wasn't thrilled at the prospect of hanging them on the premises.

By all reports, the woman was a ball-breaker, and the number she'd done on Juliana's confidence with her controlling ways made Holly want to pop the banking barracuda upside her perfectly coiffed head. Why Eric hadn't bowed to her by now, Holly had no idea. His father had certainly caved.

But jeez, wouldn't Margaret Alden make a witch of a mother-in-law? Good thing Holly had no intention of going there.

Four

Would Octavia live or would Octavia die?

Holly swung her Jeep into a parking space beside a newspaper rack and leaped from the vehicle, digging for quarters in her cut-off jeans pocket as she loped across the pavement. She shoved the coins into the machine and yanked out a Saturday paper. Her newspaper subscription had been an early casualty of a tightened budget, but today's paper held the first segment of Octavia's coverage of the auction, and therefore Octavia's fate.

Holly's hands shook as she flipped to the appropriate page and then *bam!* The Love At Any Price? headline winded her, but the picture of her and Eric in a lip-lock on her front porch sapped the strength from her knees. She sank down on the Jeep's front bumper.

Death. Long. Slow. Torturous. Octavia deserved nothing less for putting that picture in the paper.

Holly scanned down the article, skipping over the bits about Juliana and Andrea—she'd come back to her friends' parts later—until she found her name.

Can a gifted stained glass artist bring color to a man who sees only green? If the soldering fusion between laid-back Holly Prescott, owner of Rainbow Glass, and ascetic Eric Alden, heir to the banking empire, is any indication then my guess is Mr. Alden will soon be humming "Color My World," and the former debutante will be dusting off her company manners. Do opposites attract? This reporter is willing to bet the bank on it.

Through the angry roar in her ears, Holly heard a cell phone bleating. Hers. She dragged herself around to the side of the Jeep to answer it, but when she saw the name on caller ID she almost didn't. In the end, duty and resignation won. "Hi, Mom."

"Holly, please tell me what the article says is true. Have you finally come to your senses and chosen an appropriate man? I was so pleased when you bought Eric instead of that crude firefighter. I hope this is a sign you've seen the error of your ways."

Holly gritted her teeth. "The article is pure fiction. You know it and you know why."

Her mother's disappointed sigh carried over the phone connection. "You could try to fit in instead of flagrantly ignoring your father's and my wishes."

Holly's skull tightened at the familiar refrain. Her mother had married money, and she was convinced Holly should do the same. "I think I'll pass. There's more to life than bagging a wealthy husband. Besides, if that's my sole ambition, then what am I supposed to do for the rest of my life once I've accomplished that illustrious goal? Wait until the first husband kicks so I can practice my skills again?"

"Hollis Cameron Prescott—"

Whoa. When her mother dragged out the full name Holly knew she had to cut her off or suffer a long, boring lecture and the resulting union full of miners with dull pickaxes in her head. "Mom, I'm double parked. Gotta run. Talk to you later."

Holly disconnected and flopped in the driver's seat feeling only slightly guilty for having cut her mother off. The early-morning sun shown down on her skin and she cringed. She kept the Jeep's top down and the doors removed unless inclement weather threatened. This morning, she'd been in such a rush to buy a paper that she hadn't bothered to apply sunscreen. She reached into the backseat for a baseball cap and pulled the brim over her eyes, hoping to avoid a red nose. Her pale skin didn't tan. It freckled.

She skimmed the rest of the article, whistled in surprise over Octavia's audacity and then dialed Andrea's number. Busy. She tried Juliana. Also busy. She hoped her friends weren't suffering a parental tongue-lashing because there was no way anybody would be happy with this article except maybe the newspaper's circulation department. And Octavia had better watch her back. Holly wouldn't be the only one wanting to drench the reporter in maple syrup and stake her to a red ant hill.

Holly dug through the miscellaneous mess in her glove compartment until she located the business card Eric had given her, flipped it over to the private numbers he'd written on the back and dialed.

He answered on the second ring. "Alden."

"We're sunk," she said without preamble.

"Good morning, Holly." His voice sounded deep and rough and winded. Holy moly, what had she interrupted? An image of broad naked shoulders flashed on her mental movie screen. *No, no, no, don't go there.* If Eric's Friday night date had stayed over for breakfast then she didn't want to know.

"Back atcha. Did you see Octavia's article and the picture?" What time was it, anyway? She looked at her wrist and realized she'd left her watch at home. No surprise, since she'd barely taken the time to brush her teeth before racing out the door.

"Not yet."

"Suffice to say, you'll be hearing from your mother. Mine's already called me. Did I, um…wake you?"

"No. I always work out in the morning before breakfasting and reading the paper."

Structure. She suspected he had too much of it while she, according to her father, could use a little more.

"Just so you know, I'm on my way to kill Octavia. When the cops come knockin', do me a favor and say it was justifiable homicide."

"Holly—" His voice held a note of caution.

"Relax, Eric. I'm kidding. I may have flunked Debutante 101, but I haven't enrolled in Intro To Ax Murder yet…although I'm suddenly developing a keen interest in the subject."

She thought she heard Eric chuckle, but she was probably mistaken. Eric didn't chuckle. Not anymore, anyway. He used to. His gravelly, from-the-gut laugh used to be one of the most attractive things about him.

"Give me a minute. I'm getting the paper." Seconds ticked past before she heard pages rustle. "Where are you?"

"At a convenience store. Why?"

"Are you close enough to swing by for coffee and a strategy session?"

She glanced at her less-than-lovely attire. But hey, she wasn't trying to impress Eric. Right? Besides, if he saw the real her, then maybe he'd turn down the voltage on his magnetism. "Sure. Think the guard at your gate will let me into the neighborhood?"

"I'll call and tell him to expect you."

"See you in a few." She disconnected, blew out a slow breath and put the car in gear. "Well, Holly, your day started in the toilet. Will it go up from here or get flushed?"

Twenty minutes later, the guard at the entrance to Eric's prestigious neighborhood cast a doubtful eye over Betsy, Holly's bumblebee-yellow Jeep. He took Holly's name and then opened the mechanical gate.

"Jeez, you'd think he'd never seen a car from the last decade before. Betsy, I think he's afraid you'll drip oil on his pristine pavement," she muttered as she drove away from the guard-house. "He doesn't realize you're too polite to drool."

She followed the flat, winding road until she found Eric's place, a stunning Mediterranean-style home complete with arched windows, creamy stucco walls and a terra-cotta tile roof. She turned Betsy into the driveway. "Nice, but what does he do with that much house?"

Three tall arches framed the portico, but despite the perfectly manicured lawn and color-coordinated flower beds, the house wasn't at all fussy or feminine. No, this was definitely a man's house—right down to the tall palm trees flanking the entrance like giant phallic symbols. Oh, yes, the house suited Eric to a *T*. Stylish. Expensive. Immaculate. Big.

Don't go there. Shaking her head, Holly climbed from the Jeep, pitched her hat into the backseat and ruffled her hair. "Unlike your place, which is a homey hodgepodge that doesn't quite fit any style."

"Talking to yourself again?" Eric asked from the porch.

Dang. Her cheeks warmed. Squinting into the sunlight, she located him in a shady corner of the porch. "Always do."

He held a coffee mug in his hand—a fact she nearly missed because of his attire...or lack there of. His gym shorts were... well, *short*, baring way too much muscled, hair-dusted thigh. His tank top revealed bulging biceps and broad, corded shoulders. The results were devastating.

Holly hadn't seen Eric decked out in anything less than custom-tailored perfection in a very long time. Her mouth dried and her pulse thumped erratically. If she avoided his face, which showed the lines of stress he'd acquired over the past decade plus, then from the neck down Eric looked even better than the guy she used to have a secret crush on. *Used to* being the operative words.

His navy blue gaze traveled from her T-shirt to her cut off jean shorts, down her legs—which, thank God, she'd waxed—to her flower-bedecked flip-flops and then back up again. Heat rippled over her skin.

Wasn't days shy of thirty too young for hot flashes?

"Coffee?" He held open his front door.

"That'd be great." Holly stepped inside and caught her jaw before it dropped. She'd been in her share of minimansions, but Eric's place took top honors. Marble floors swept from the front door all the way to the French doors a basketball court's length away. From the foyer, she could see a swimming pool and the inlet behind his house. The entire center of the house soared two stories high, and the only thing interrupting the open space was a bridge, supported by marble columns, which divided the huge foyer from the gargantuan living room and connected the left half of the upstairs with the right. On her left, stairs curved upward in a graceful sweep of marble flooring and wrought-iron railings.

Not bad, although a stained glass window over the entrance could warm the space up a bit by adding color to the white morning light streaming through the clear panes already in place. Ditto the trio of high windows at the rear of the house. Working on two-story scaffolding would be a bit tricky, but she'd done it before. Not that Eric had asked her opinion.

"Nice place. Kind of big for just you, though, isn't it?"

"I entertain clients frequently."

Right. A showplace. She knew all about those. A house you lived in, but you didn't really *live in*. No kicking off your shoes beside the sofa or tossing your jacket over the newel post. Everything had to stay as perfect as a model home. She'd grown up in that kind of house and knew it wasn't her thing. If she couldn't relax at home, then where could she?

He led the way past a home office on the left and the dining room on the right—both very formal affairs, with gleaming dark wooden furniture—to the huge kitchen-den combination. "Have a seat."

Holly slid onto a suede-cushioned, wrought-iron bar stool at a work island larger than her kitchen table. The polished granite countertops were cool under her elbows. "My mom thinks landing you is a huge improvement over my usual dates. I'm predicting your mother is going to have the opposite reaction. You might want to suggest she up her aspirin intake so she doesn't have a stroke."

"Don't worry about my mother." He slid a full mug and a sugar bowl in her direction. "I have milk, but no cream."

"Black with a pound of sugar's my poison." She accepted a teaspoon and doctored her brew.

"Describe your usual dates."

She nearly spewed coffee. "My usual? Hmm. Guys who need help finding their place, I guess."

"Bums?"

She fought a wince. *Bum* was her father's word. "Not exactly. Just guys down on their luck or in transition. It's not like I pick up hitchhikers or derelicts or anyone dangerous."

"Strays like the dogs you collect."

She suspected the warmth of her cheeks wasn't solely caused by the steam rising from the coffee. "Some might say that."

Some did. Juliana and Andrea, in fact.

He tapped the lip-lock picture in his open copy of the paper. "We need a strategy to get through the next nine dates without this happening again."

She pointed with her spoon. "Hey, you kissed me."

"You asked me to."

Why had she come here? She didn't need this. "Only the first time. And you could have faked it. No tongue action necessary."

"Are you saying you didn't enjoy my kisses?" he asked in a low don't-mess-with-me voice.

She had to be red to the roots of her hair. "I'm not dumb

enough to deny something that was obvious even to a woman sitting in a car a hundred yards away. I mean, jeez, how much practice do you get? You're pretty good with those lips, Alden. But like you said, it can't happen again."

His stillness reminded her of a predator about to pounce. *"Pretty good?"*

She shrugged, wishing her words hadn't come out like a challenge. For crying out loud, she had older brothers. She knew better. And she didn't want Eric to kiss her again.

Really, she didn't.

Nope. Not at all. Nosiree.

And the only reason her pulse was racing now was because she'd just guzzled half a mug of coffee. Caffeine rush. Yep. That's the reason.

For several seconds, Eric's darkened gaze held hers. Her mouth dried. Electricity popped and crackled between them, and when his gaze shifted to her mouth her lungs constricted. If he kissed her she was sunk—not just because of the volatile chemistry between them, but because she missed being held, missed being the recipient of someone's undivided attention and missed being wanted, needed and accepted.

He turned away abruptly and Holly exhaled a pent-up breath. Eric opened the fridge, extracted a mountain of ingredients that he piled on the counter and then he pulled a pair of frying pans from beneath the work island. "Have you eaten?"

She had to clear her throat to jump-start her voice. "No."

"Eggs and Canadian bacon?"

"You're going to cook for me?" Had a guy—other than in a restaurant—ever cooked for her? Usually, she was the one who made sure others had three squares a day.

"I promise you won't need medical assistance as a result."

He delivered the words without so much as a twitch of his lips, but laughter sparkled in his eyes. Well, well, whatdayaknow, Eric hadn't lost his sense of humor after all.

"I'll risk it. I'm sure you're insured." She yanked the paper forward and scanned the other couples' pictures. Octavia clearly had a thing for first-date kisses. No surprise there. And Holly truly hoped Andrea's and Juliana's good-nights were half as good as they looked on paper and that the dates and the men attached to them didn't backfire on them.

She lifted her gaze from the steamy pictures. "About our dates... I guess you're going to have to come in every night when you bring me home. Octavia can't see good-night kisses—or the lack thereof—through a closed door."

He set the bacon on to heat in one pan and then single-handedly cracked eggs into a bowl. "Good idea."

"You just have to stay long enough to make her think she's missing something."

He dropped an egg on the floor, but made no move to clean it up. Instead, his dark blue eyes lasered onto hers. "Is there a reason why she needs to think she's missing something?"

How much could she tell him without totally humiliating herself? "Octavia's a little worried about my personal life."

He grabbed paper towels, mopped up the spill and pitched the mess into a stainless steel trash can tucked beneath the overhanging counter. "Why?"

Oh, heck. Why had she lifted the lid on her dirty laundry hamper? "Because I've sort of sworn off men for a while."

"At the risk of being redundant, why?" He turned back to the stove to scramble the eggs. Each swirl of the spatula flexed and shifted his tight buns.

He expected her to string sentences together with a riveting view like that? Puh-leeze! Sitting here and watching him had the effect of a clanging alarm clock on her hibernating estrogen cells. She needed to hit the Snooze button. Pronto.

So...what had he asked? Oh yeah. "I need to get my life straightened out before I worry about someone else's. Um, can I make toast or something?"

Any distraction would be welcome.

He opened a built-in bread box and extracted a bag of bread—the bakery variety, not the grocery store kind—and then rolled up another door to reveal a stainless toaster. "Help yourself."

She climbed from the stool and circled the island. Working beside him shouldn't make her edgy. She'd shared a kitchen with a man before. But none of the men from her past had made her stomach feel all warm and swishy, as if she'd guzzled hot coffee too fast, and none had been so totally and completely wrong for her—even though they hadn't ended up together.

She started the toast and lifted her gaze skyward. *Okay, joke over. This isn't funny anymore.*

"Is your need for a P.I. related to your decision to straighten up your life?"

Holly stiffened. "Yum. Smells delicious. I haven't had Canadian bacon in ages. My mouth is already watering. I can't wait—"

"Holly." His direct gaze pinned her in place.

Darn. So much for changing the subject. "Sort of."

"Is it or isn't it?"

"It is," she reluctantly admitted.

"And?"

She winced and debated blowing him off, but she'd been carrying this burden a while and she needed advice. Who knew money better than Eric? Maybe there were options she hadn't considered yet. "If I tell you, then you have to swear to keep the info to yourself. I don't want my friends or my family to know."

Ten full seconds ticked past before he inclined his head.

"I, um…loaned my ex-boyfriend something and I want it back."

"He stole from you?"

"No. I *loaned* Lyle some money. He left town and I haven't heard from him."

"How much money?"

She grimaced. He wasn't going to like this. "Fifty grand."

Eric's shoulders squared. "With what collateral?"

She shifted in her flip-flops, regretting her confession. "None."

"Holly—"

"He had a sound business plan. I believed he could make it happen. So I borrowed against my trust fund to back the venture."

Eric's expressionless banker's mask dropped into place. She could practically see the wheels turning in his mind as he divided the eggs and bacon onto two plates. Holly added the toast.

The hard-eyed, flattened-lip moneyman faced her. She wanted the guy with the humor in his eyes back. "Is he typical of the men you date?"

Nothing like zeroing in on her foibles. Why lie? "Typical as in I loaned them money? Yes. But never that much before."

"How long has he been gone?"

The ham melted in her mouth. Would it be rude to ask him to shut up and let her eat before he spoiled her appetite? Yeah. Probably. "Thirteen months."

"Do you have the loan terms in writing?"

She hid her grimace behind her coffee cup. "Sort of."

"Holly—"

She held up a hand to stop him. Clearly there was no *maybe, sort of* or *kind of* with Eric. Something either was or it wasn't.

"Okay, yes, but it's a handwritten agreement. We didn't have it notarized and there is no specific repayment schedule. Eric, I know I messed up, but I really…trusted him." And she'd been burned. It wasn't the first time someone she cared for had turned on her. Her own family, for example. Would she never learn? The only one she could truly count on was herself.

"Why didn't you come to me before making this loan?"

She shrugged and swallowed a mouthful of eggs. "Because you represent the bank."

"And banks lend money."

"But you probably wouldn't have in this case. Besides, it was my money I wanted to lend. Well…it will be soon. For a little while, anyway."

"Then you should have consulted a lawyer. Have you called the police?"

"No! I told you. I don't want my friends and family to get involved."

"The man stole from you, Holly."

"We don't know that for sure. All I know is he wanted to develop some prototype thingy and then apply for a patent. Just because I haven't heard from him in over a year doesn't mean my money is gone. Patents take a while."

Eric exhaled. "You are entirely too trusting. You can't save the world one man or dog at a time."

That did it. He'd killed her appetite. She shoved her almost empty plate aside. "Oh m'gosh, you've turned into my father."

"You could have tried talking to your father before loaning the money. Colton is a savvy businessman."

"Are you kidding? The only discussion my father wants to have with me is the one where I tell him I was wrong to leave the Caliber Club and beg him to let me come back."

"Would that be so bad?"

"Yes! I tried working there. Every part of the job that interested me was declared beneath me. I'm too creative to limit myself to choosing which ink pen to use each day. I need to design, to get my hands dirty, to be part of the process. That's what feeds my soul and keeps me going. I'd rather die than sit behind a desk for the rest of my life."

His nostrils flared and his spine straightened. "Every business needs good managers."

Eric sat behind a desk. She'd insulted him and that hadn't been her intention. "And there's nothing wrong with that if it fulfills you, but being the Caliber Club event manager didn't fill me up because it was only a glorified title. The only real planning I was allowed to do was on paper. I was expected to delegate the fun stuff to a staff so capable they didn't need a figurehead supervisor butting in. Maybe if I'd been allowed to become more involved, I wouldn't have been left feeling so…empty and useless. Face it, Eric, I'm the blue collar duck that hatched in the white collar swan's nest."

He finished his meal in silence and then he laid down his fork. "How tight has this financial mistake left you?"

His quick shift caught her off balance and she cringed. Should she try to bluster her way out of this? She had a feeling Eric wouldn't fall for it, so she owned up, "I could use the money. Like you said, the dogs are expensive."

"Stop by the bank Monday. I'll help you establish a line of credit."

"Thanks, but no thanks. I've already borrowed enough, and I don't want to jeopardize the farm by using it as collateral. It's my home." And the only place she truly felt as if she belonged. If she absolutely had to, then she could sell some acreage, but then she'd end up stuck in the middle of a subdivision. Ick. "When my trust fund money comes through later this month, I'll pay off the loan."

"Will you have enough left over to see you through?"

Did he have to be so perceptive? "No."

"Then I'll make you a personal loan for whatever you need."

How long had it been since someone had tried to take care of her? Touched and choked up, she covered his hand on the bar. Awareness traveled through her fingers and up her arm to pool deep in her belly. Okay, so touching him wasn't a good idea. She withdrew her hand. "I truly appreciate that, Eric, but I'll find a way to make a little extra money."

She didn't know how yet, but she would. Right now she needed to get out of here before her stupid prickling eyes leaked. She vaulted to her feet. "Wow. Look at the time. I have to run. Set up our next date and call me."

Eric caught her hand, trapping her by his side with a warm, firm grip. "I'll call the P.I. You'll be hearing from him."

"I called yesterday. I can't afford him."

"I can." And then his big hand squeezed hers. Sensation bubbled through her veins. "Holly, I'm going to help you whether you like it or not."

"You don't have to do that."

"That's the price for my silence. Otherwise, I go to your father."

Anger flushed the pleasure right out of her system. Holly yanked her hand free. "You sneaky buzzard. You promised to keep this between us."

She shoved her plate in the sink and glared at him. "I'll find a way to repay you whatever the P.I. charges whether *you* like it or not. Count on it."

Manners be damned, Eric let Holly go without walking her to the door. He remained on his bar stool, hands fisted on the counter to keep from grabbing the woman.

Otherwise the gratitude glistening in Holly's tear-filled eyes combined with her skimpy attire would have led him to making a bigger mistake than he'd made when he kissed her goodnight. That's why he'd deliberately antagonized her by mentioning her father. He wouldn't betray her confidence. Once he gave his word he kept it, but she obviously didn't know that.

His gaze dropped to the picture in the newspaper and heat rushed through him at the memory of Holly wrapped around him like a sweet-smelling honeysuckle vine. "*Pretty good*, my ass."

He'd come close—too close—a few minutes ago to making her admit his kisses were better than *pretty good*.

He'd been intimate with more women than he could name since being seduced at fifteen by a college girl intent on sinking her artificial nails into the Alden fortune. She'd been the first of many intent on getting his ring on their finger via his bed.

He enjoyed sex. What man didn't? But he could take it or leave it. Why did *this* contrary female get to him and make him want what he couldn't have?

Holly didn't dress to impress him. Her ragged shorts—damn, he'd had no idea her legs were that long—and her loose T-shirt proved that. He suspected she looked the same when she rolled out of bed in the morning as she had when she'd rolled into his driveway. Rumpled. Makeup free. Dressed for comfort rather than success. Had she even brushed her windswept hair? God knows she didn't watch her tongue. In fact, he wondered if her outspokenness ever cost her commissions.

Holly Prescott was the real deal. Honest. Outspoken. And a sucker for strays. His money didn't turn her on. But his kisses had—a fact she'd been more than happy to share and one he wished she'd kept to herself. He was experienced enough to know she'd been with him through every kiss Tuesday night, but he was also smart enough to ignore the forbidden desire between them rather than let it cause problems.

Because of his friendship with her brothers and hers with his sister, a temporary alliance between him and Holly would be out of the question, but anything long-term would be a disaster. Without a doubt he and Holly would burn up the sheets, but outside of bed…

He shook his head and carried his dishes to the sink. Holly Prescott would be a career liability and his career always came first. If he ever contemplated marriage again, then he'd choose a quiet, graceful woman who knew how to conduct herself appropriately. Someone like he'd believed Priscilla to be. He hadn't loved his ex-fiancée, but he would have married her because she was exactly the kind of wife a bank VP needed by his side. Poised. Polite. Connected. Circumspect… At least she'd been circumspect until the aborted wedding day. He hadn't seen her vitriolic and ill-timed rejection coming.

His relationship with Holly was inappropriate, inconvenient and definitely temporary, and it must remain absolutely nonsexual. With the merger in the works, he could not afford such an outspoken partner.

Eric reached for his phone. He had dates to plan. Dates that did not include kisses, gratitude, skimpy attire or a reporter determined to make a fool out of him.

Five

Dress casually. By whose standards? Hers or Eric's?

Holly rifled through the clothing in her closet Monday evening. Somehow she didn't think dinner with Eric in which-ever stuffy place he'd made reservations tonight would ever be a jeans and a T-shirt affair—her idea of casual.

Luckily, Andrea and Juliana insisted on a girls' night out most Fridays, so Holly had clothes, but other than one little black dress, everything she owned screamed with color and pattern. Eric, the king of black, white and gray, would have to deal with that. She settled on a silk wraparound dress in shades of flame—oranges, reds, golds with a touch of cobalt. It should have clashed horribly with her hair, but it didn't because one of the swirls was the same copper as her hair.

She'd barely tied the knot at her waist when the doggy chorus coming from the barn alerted her to Eric's arrival. He was on time and she was running late because, after teaching her class this morning, Holly had had to drive a hundred and fifty miles to pick up a particular shade of iridescent glass for her current project. The right glass for a project could either make or break the piece. She didn't skimp on glass, regardless of the cost.

The memory of the ribbing and grilling she'd endured from her students—particularly Octavia—made her wince. Holly had finally threatened to shut off the power to their soldering irons if they mentioned Eric or his sexual prowess again. Their constant chatter had been like talking to a dieter about chocolate cheesecake. Just plain cruel.

After raking a comb through her floppy I-can't-do-anything-with-it-so-why-try? hair and slicking on a fresh coat of cherry lip balm, she stabbed her toes into a pair of low-heeled beaded sandals and raced for the door. She opened it in time to see Eric in a white Polo shirt, khaki slacks pressed to a knife-edge crease and leather boating shoes, climbing her porch stairs.

Casual looked good on him. Her heart thumped like a rubber mallet against her rib cage.

"Good evening, Holly."

Goose bumps chased over her skin at the rich timbre of his voice. *Dang it. Stop that.* "Hi. You said casual, but I didn't know how casual, so this is what you get."

"You look lovely." And when he treated her to one of those slow, sweeping glances she felt attractive and feminine right down to her unpolished toenails.

Why had other men never looked at her that way? Why did it have to be Eric off-limits Alden, whose gaze aroused her like a lover's caress? Her house must be haunted because a ghost wrapped both hands around her neck and squeezed off her oxygen supply.

"Thanks," she croaked through her constricted larynx and grabbed her purse from the hall table. The sooner they started this date, the sooner it would be over. Without a good-night kiss. And that was *not* disappointment weighting her stomach. It was simply hunger. She'd missed lunch.

"No Seurat or Monet tonight?"

She pulled the door closed behind her. "No. They've healed enough to go to the kennels."

He didn't say anything else until after he'd turned the car onto the road. "You talked to the P.I."

It wasn't a question, but she responded anyway just to drown out the sound of her pulse drumming in her ears. "Yes. He stopped by this morning. I gave him some photos and copies of all the documents."

"Good. Wes is quick and thorough. You should have answers soon." Except for the growl of the powerful engine, the rest of the short drive passed in silence, and then he turned down a street that made the fine hairs on her skin rise in alarm. The gated entrance of the Caliber Club loomed ahead.

She refused to dine in her family's establishment under the watchful and judgmental gaze of her father and brothers. "Uh-uh, forget it. I'm not eating here."

He nodded to the security guard as he passed and drove by the sprawling club toward the marina. "We're having dinner on the yacht. Catered and served by an unobtrusive waiter."

While she appreciated that he'd heard her earlier comments about hovering waitstaff and substituted a private dinner for one on the stuffy date list she wasn't so sure that being alone with Eric was a good idea. "Is that really wise?"

"Octavia and her reporter won't be able to take pictures if we're miles out to sea."

"Good point. I'm surprised she didn't insist on riding along."

The grin he shot her punched the breath right out of her lungs. Wicked humor glinted in his eyes. "She suggested it. We might leave the dock a little earlier than I led her to believe. If she can get past the guard, then she'll arrive just in time to see us fading into the distance."

Holly sputtered a laugh. Octavia wouldn't like that, but Holly did. She especially liked seeing Eric smile, but she didn't like the glow that flash of white teeth set off inside her. "You're a smart man, Eric Alden."

"So I'm told." He climbed from the car. Holly tried to get out, but he'd locked her in. She squirmed impatiently while he rounded the hood, stopped by her door and pushed the remote control button to unlock her door, and then he extended his hand. She just didn't get this whole man-woman thing. For Pete's sake, she could open her own doors.

"Tricky, Alden. Very tricky. I can see I'm going to have to watch you." His long fingers curled around hers, initiating a tickle of awareness she'd just as soon not have traveling along her nerves. She pulled her hand free.

He cupped her elbow—darn him—and guided her down the dock past sleek, expensive vessels. She'd been on the Aldens' yacht before, but not with Eric. In fact, she, Juliana and Andrea had taken advantage of the hot tub on the upper deck a few weeks ago.

The moment she stepped on board, the slight vibration of the engines beneath her feet told her the captain was already at the helm. At a signal from Eric, several club staffers hustled to release the ropes and before she knew it, Eric had whisked her into the salon and away from shore like a captive on a pirate ship.

Huh? Where had that metaphor come from? Eric was far too polished to be a pirate, and she wasn't a helpless captive. The stylish eighty-foot yacht wasn't even close to a creaky pirate's galleon. But her pulse quickened nonetheless as the marina faded from sight. Her gaze took in leather seating, glass tabletops, and gleaming wood furnishings, as elegant as any luxury home or hotel suite.

"Riesling?" Eric offered her a goblet of pale golden liquid.

"Sure. Thanks." She curled her fingers around the stem. "So here we are. Now what?"

"Dinner will be served as soon as we clear the inlet. Help yourself to hors d'oeuvres, if you like."

Holly sipped her wine and studied the artfully displayed fruits and canapés on the coffee table. Despite her hunger, for some crazy reason her stomach protested the idea of eating. How dumb was that? She couldn't possibly be nervous. Could she?

This wasn't romantic. It was only a boat ride, and she'd taken dozens of boat rides before. Heck, her father owned a yacht almost as long as this one and each of her brothers regularly participated in the marlin tournaments with their big fishing boats.

But telling herself an evening cruise with Eric was nothing special and making herself believe it were totally different. The set up was too cozy. Too intimate. Tension hummed through her and her mind emptied of polite conversation. Where was an intrusive waiter when you needed one? She'd almost prefer being stared at in a pretentious restaurant to being alone with Eric knowing there were bedrooms below deck.

What was with her rebellious hormones, anyway?

She shook her head, trying to banish her students' comments, but buzzwords flashed in her head like neon lights. *Eric. Bed. Sheets. Hot.*

Stop.

"Holly, sit down and quit worrying."

She glanced at him and made a face. "Obvious, huh?"

"It's just the two of us."

She snorted. "No kidding, Einstein. That's the problem."

He inhaled sharply. "Do you always say what you think?"

"Usually. It beats tiptoeing around a situation and getting nowhere." She sipped her wine. It didn't wash away the tension knotting her throat. "Eric, this…*thing* between you and me can't go anywhere."

If he tried to deny there was something between them she just might smack him. After she dumped her drink on him.

"I assure you the only item on the agenda tonight is a shared meal away from prying eyes. Relax, Holly."

The sad part was that his smooth, deep voice made her want

to relax, but as soon as she did she'd be in trouble. She'd left the life of wealth and privilege behind not because she didn't like the beautiful things money could buy, but because that material-focused life smothered her and skewed her priorities, making it too easy to judge people by what they owned instead of who they were beneath the gilt. She couldn't afford to let it lure her back for even one minute.

Being one of *the* Prescotts of Wilmington, North Carolina came with a boatload of restrictions and expectations that trussed her up more effectively than a straitjacket. She'd actually learned to like being the family reject because nobody expected anything from her.

She perched on the edge of the leather sofa and Eric sat beside her—not close enough to touch, but close enough that the tang of his cologne invaded her senses.

She searched her brain for a safe topic. "Is your mother peeved that you ended up with me?"

"I can handle my mother."

"Juliana can't."

"That's because my sister goes about it the wrong way."

"There's a right way to handle Margaret Alden?" Oops.

But Eric didn't seem to take offense. "Yes, my mother respects those who have the backbone to stand up to her. Juliana tries too hard to please her. But my mother is not our problem. Octavia is. She won't be as easy to elude next time."

Holly sighed. "No. In fact, this morning in class she said she thought we'd be her juiciest story, and that she planned to stick to us like fuzz on a peach. That's why I enjoyed ditching her tonight so much."

"I have a strategy."

"I'm glad to hear it." But Holly didn't want to talk about them, their next eight dates or the kisses they needed to avoid. She wanted a safer topic like politics or religion, but she'd settle for something closer to home. "Back to your sister… You might be willing to sacrifice yourself by marrying for the sake of the family business, but Juliana shouldn't. She's never been in love before, so she doesn't know what she's missing by settling for safe and boring Wally—the wimp—Wilson. The banks can merge without a marriage to seal the deal, you know. Businesses do it all the time without human sacrifice."

"Have you?"

Holly blinked. "Have I what? Been a human sacrifice?"

"Been in love," he replied, ignoring her sarcasm.

She told herself to look away, to break his dark ensnaring gaze, but she couldn't. Why would he care about her pathetic love life? "Too many times to count." An exaggeration. "But this isn't about me."

"Why didn't those relationships work?"

She sighed. If she answered his questions, then maybe she could get him to listen, and if he listened, then maybe she could convince him to talk some sense into his sister before her best friend made the worst mistake of her life. Holly kicked off her shoes and tucked her feet beneath her, settling in to tell an old, boring tale.

"Once my boyfriends realize that my family really has written me off as a lost cause, they start a campaign to convince me to heal the breach. When my swallowing my pride and taking a job I don't like becomes more important to the man in my life than me being happy, I wise up and get the message. It's the Prescott cash and prestige he's after, not me. So…end of relationship."

"How many?"

"Excuse me?"

"How many men have tried to change you?" The tension—and was that anger? —in his voice made the fine hairs on the back of her neck stand on end.

"None of your business. But just so you know, not all of them were my lovers. I'm kind of picky about who shares my bed." She twisted on the sofa. Her knee nudged Eric's thigh and those annoying and distracting taboo tingles hop scotched up her leg.

Cut it out, already. She shifted away again because touching him was *so* not a good idea.

"I admit I wasted my twenties looking for love, but next week I'll be thirty and I intend to be a lot smarter from now on. If I can't be happy with myself, then I'll never be happy with a man—no matter how great he is. That's why this—" she gestured to the two of them "—is totally messing with my head. I could never be happy with you, so being sexually attracted to you is an aggravation I just don't need."

A muscle ticked in Eric's jaw. His knuckles whitened on the stem of his glass until she thought he might break the crystal. His gaze drifted from her eyes to her mouth and then slowly over her breasts, waist, hips and legs. Holly's nipples tightened and lava-like heat bubbled beneath her navel.

How did he push her buttons without even touching her? However he did it, he had to stop.

"Eric, I have been celibate for over a year, and I am hanging on by a thread. If you don't quit looking at me like you want to strip off my clothes and lick me like a lollipop, then I'm going to launch myself at you, and we're both going to be sorry. Naked and sated and probably covered in rug burn from this fine Persian carpet, but sorry."

His navy eyes snapped back to hers. He swore, shot to his feet and crossed the salon, putting as much distance between them as he possibly could and still stay within shouting distance. Sexual energy rolled off him in waves, rocking her from clear across the room.

"Are you trying to provoke me?"

Holly exhaled slowly, straightened her legs and shoved her feet back into her shoes. "No. I'm sorry. But I've never had to deal with this in-your-face magnetism before and frankly, it sucks. Especially since it's *you*."

His stance turned rigid and she realized that she'd insulted him again, but then he wiped a hand over the lower half of his face and laughed—a strained bark of laughter, but laughter nonetheless. "I never know what is going to come out of your mouth."

Wow. He's really something when he laughs. Too sexy for words. "But you do know what I'm going to put in it."

He reared back and his chest expanded. His pupils dilated to almost obliterate his irises.

Oh, spit. Would she never learn to think before she spoke? "I meant dinner, Eric. Is it time to eat yet?"

Eric set down his drink and shoved his hands into his pants pockets. A muscle in his jaw twitched wildly. "By all means let's feed the one appetite that won't get us in trouble."

Irreverent.

Irrepressible.

Enticing as hell.

Holly Prescott energized and aroused Eric in an inconceivable and unacceptable manner.

What was he going to do with her?

He mechanically ate his lobster bisque, shrimp scampi and lemon meringue pie while debating his dilemma and discreetly observing the confusing woman across from him. How in his detailed calculations could he have been so mistaken as to believe Holly would be a safe way out of the auction?

She looked up. "What? Do I have meringue on my nose or something?"

"No. I'm glad to see you're enjoying the meal instead of picking at it the way you do in the restaurants."

"The food is delicious."

Was it? He'd barely tasted his.

She grimaced. "And the only one staring at me here is you."

Perhaps he hadn't been as discreet as he'd thought. "Forgive me. I'm not used to seeing you look so lovely."

"Save your flattery, Eric. It won't get you anything but trouble."

Where had he gone wrong? He pushed his unfinished dessert away and reviewed the misleading evidence. Holly came from the same social class as he. Hell, he'd practically watched her grow up, although she'd been off his radar screen for more than a decade. She'd attended the same schools and deportment classes as his sister, and had been Juliana's best friend for more years than Eric could recall. But Holly's candor bore absolutely no resemblance to his reserved sister's rule-abiding, conservative behavior. How could two women with the same background be polar opposites?

The parameters of his and Holly's relationship had been firmly established. Because of the newspaper coverage, his options were limited. They would date because they had to or risk negative media exposure, and they would ignore this inappropriate attraction, which he likened to Hitchcock's bomb under the table. But Holly seemed determined to drag the bomb out into the open and to not only shake the package but to dance around it like a damned Maypole. Sooner or later, it would explode if she didn't quit rattling it—*and him*—with her verbal artillery.

If she were an employee, he could have her transferred out of the realm of temptation. If she were a regular date, he'd simply quit calling. Correction. If she were one of his regulars, he'd have bedded her by now, thereby quenching his thirst for her peculiar appeal and allowing him to move on and focus on the merger.

When had he lost control of the situation? How could he regain the upper hand? Treating her like a client wasn't working. Reminding himself she was his friends' baby sister wasn't, either. He needed a new strategy. But how could he make Holly respect the conventions of a platonic and businesslike relationship when flaunting societal rules seemed to be her forte?

By keeping her off balance? But how did one go about keeping Miss Unpredictable herself off balance?

Dealing with his overly aggressive mother had taught him that when an adversary pushes, you not only repulse the attack but you drive for the advantage. Victory was the only option.

He suspected Holly used her bold verbiage to keep people at a distance. So tonight when he walked her to the door he'd call her bluff, and like a playground bully, she'd back down soon enough when he volleyed her reckless advances right back at her. Bluffing wasn't only a poker skill. It was a business strategy he'd employed often and successfully. If Holly Prescott wanted to play hardball, she'd chosen the wrong man to challenge.

As soon as she laid down her fork, he rose. "If you're finished, I'll tell the captain to return to port."

Forty minutes later, Eric turned the Corvette into Holly's driveway and drove past the reporter's sedan. He parked his car and escorted Holly up the front steps with his plan firmly in place. His heart quickened in anticipation of a successful outcome and his first good night's sleep since the auction.

"Invite me in."

Holly looked over his shoulder in the direction of Octavia's car, sighed and unlocked her front door. "C'mon."

He followed her inside, but before she could flick on the entryway light, Eric elbowed the door closed, caught Holly by the shoulders and backed her against the wooden panel. Against the proverbial wall. Her muscles knotted beneath his fingers.

"Hey!" Moonlight filtered through the stained glass side-lights flanking the door to illuminate the surprise in her widened eyes.

"Holly, if you insist on throwing the attraction between us in my face, then I'm going to believe you want me to act on it."

He heard her gasp, caught a quick flash of white teeth as her mouth dropped open. "Say what?"

Eric erased the distance between them until only the width of a dollar bill kept him from full body contact and dipped his head until her swift breaths puffed over his lips. He attributed the hammering of his pulse to the adrenaline rush of his attack.

"You've mentioned your prolonged celibacy and threatened me with rug burn tonight. Are you hinting, perhaps, that you want me to take the initiative and snap that thread by which you claim you're hanging?"

Holly tipped her head back so quickly it thumped against the door. A wince crinkled the corners of her eyes before she narrowed her wary gaze on his. "Do I seem like the subtle type to you?"

No. And that was the problem. If she'd been subtle and followed the rules of appropriate behavior, he wouldn't be applying these unorthodox means to get her to back down.

"You seem like a smart lady who knows how to get what she wants, and you've plainly stated you want me." Her scent and body heat ensnared him. Eric knotted his muscles, fighting the flash of desire and struggling to maintain his strategy, but even his legendary control couldn't dam a southerly blood flow.

Holly wet her lips and the urge to kiss her consumed him. Not part of the plan. He rallied against it and wished he could see well enough in the shadowy entry to gauge whether or not his scare tactics were working.

"This pirate thing has clearly gone to your head."

Damn the woman. Couldn't she be predicable just once? Why wasn't she cowering or, at the very least, squirming and begging for freedom? Her palms splayed on his chest, but she didn't push him away.

He'd probably regret asking, but he couldn't understand her convoluted thinking. "What pirate thing?"

"Just because you whisked me onto your ship and out to sea tonight doesn't give you the right to ravish me."

Ravish me. The words blasted through him like a cannonball and his teeth met with an audible click. The idea appealed. Too much. He swallowed hard. "I don't hear you saying no."

Say no, dammit. Scream at me. Slap me.

"No," she whispered and then her tense shoulders relaxed and her features softened. Several heartbeats later, she added, "You don't."

Shock imploded his plan and his strategy disintegrated.

Before he could gather his defenses and plan a new offensive Holly rose on tiptoe and pressed her lips to his. *Damnation*. The tantalizing drag of her mouth over his weakened his resistance. Her tongue eased between his lips. Retreated. Advanced. He locked his jaw against her sensual assault. Her fingers curled and unfurled against his pecs, and then she wrapped her arms around his waist and tormented him with the sweet pressure of her soft breasts against his chest.

Another miscalculation. He'd made too many of them with this woman. *Retreat*. But his muscles weren't following his commands. His body had locked and loaded.

With a groan Eric surrendered and opened his mouth to meet each parry of her silky tongue. He splayed one hand over her bottom and pulled her hips flush against his. If she wanted to play with fire, then she ought to know his fuse was already lit. But instead of shying away from his rigid arousal, Holly moved against him, shifting her hips in a way guaranteed to annihilate any willpower he might have had left.

He couldn't think, couldn't reason his way out of this through the haze of passion hanging over him. He could only feel the warm lushness of Holly's curves against him, the sweep of her hair against his palm, the hunger she'd unleashed on him. *In him*. He devoured her mouth, trying to satisfy a craving that had been growing since that first kiss. But he couldn't get enough of her. Her taste. Her scent. Her softness. He raked his hands up her sides and down again, mapping and memorizing her womanly terrain.

His fingers bumped over the knot at her waist. His conscience flashed warning signs, but he ignored them and swiftly released the knot. He drew back scant inches to take a ragged breath, and the front of her wraparound dress gaped, revealing the lacy edge of a scarlet bra. A blaze ignited in his groin. He should have known Holly wouldn't be the white cotton type. Her fingers kneaded his biceps as he hooked the fabric of her dress with his fingers and separated the panels to reveal more of her creamy skin and a pair of skimpy panties in the same seductive red lace.

"Beautiful," he muttered under his breath. And then his hands found bare skin. Satiny. Hot. He caressed her belly, her rib cage, and finally, he cupped the full globes of her breasts and scraped his thumbnails over the beaded tips. The noise she made—half moan, half growl—detonated an explosion of need deep in his gut.

What happened to scaring her off?

And then Holly lifted a leg and hooked it around the back of his. His mind blanked and his knees nearly buckled. His fingers found the bra's front clip and released her breasts. She filled his palms, but he needed more. He needed to taste her. Eric bent his head, and took her dusky areola into his mouth. Her flavor went straight to his head and her scent filled his lungs.

He raked his palm up the back of her smooth thigh and shoved his hand beneath her panties to cradle her bottom. Soft. Warm. And he was so damned hard and hot. He traced the damp heat between her legs and stroked her slick folds. Holly's fingers clenched in his hair as he suckled and caressed her.

"Oh yes, right there," she rasped. "So good. Feels so good. Please, please. Now, Eric. Now. *Now.*"

Her hoarse voice ratcheted up his response. He was seconds away from ripping open his fly and taking her against the door when her palm framed his jaw and lifted his mouth to hers.

"I can't wait." She kissed him hotter and wetter than he'd ever been kissed before, and then she shattered and shuddered against him. He swallowed her cries.

Panting, she let her head fall back against the door. Her hands clutched his shoulders. He dragged his gaze from the mesmerizing rise and fall of her breasts to her heavy-lidded eyes and reached for his belt buckle with his free hand.

Holly's fingers covered his. "Do you have a condom? We don't want a souvenir of tonight."

An ice-water shower couldn't have sobered him more than

her words. His hand stilled. A condom. No, damn it, he didn't have a condom. Why would he when this wasn't supposed to happen?

What in the hell are you doing, Alden?

Eric jerked his hand from Holly's panties and yanked the sides of her dress closed, but it was too late. The image of her generous curves and satiated expression had been seared onto his retinas. His pulse roared in his ears and throbbed in his groin. His body screamed for completion, but he'd be damned if he'd let a woman make him lose control. Losing control meant becoming weak like his father. A puppet to his passions. A slave to emotion. A fool for a woman's whims.

Holly had called his bluff and he'd folded. He had to find a way to push her away, to end this sensual cat-and-mouse game before it was too late. "Your itch has been scratched. Perhaps now we can return to the dates as planned."

The dazed passion in Holly's toffee-colored eyes turned to confusion and then hurt and then anger. She straightened and clutched the sides of her dress together. "You bastard."

"*Your* bastard, Ms. Prescott, for eight more evenings. But I'll be damned if I'll be your gigolo." He cupped her shoulders and shifted her away from the door and then yanked it open. "Good night."

Six

Lying, even lies of omission, never paid off, Holly grudgingly admitted. Telling her friends she couldn't afford to buy a bachelor would have been so much less embarrassing than facing Eric again.

She blew a hank of hair off her forehead and trudged from her Jeep to the bank. Eric must think her completely pathetic. First, because she'd thrown herself at a man who clearly didn't want her, and second, because she'd gone off like a cherry bomb with a very short fuse. The memory of how she'd clung to him, begged him to take her and how she'd dissolved in his very talented hands made her skin broil, and it had nothing to do with the cloying summer heat and humidity.

So much for her no-sex vow. But was that any surprise? She liked sex and climaxed more often than not.

Never like that.

Had she ever been turned on that quickly? No. Why now and with Eric, of all people?

Just her luck to finally find a guy who could locate her buttons and press them very effectively, but who was forbidden. The button-pushing *couldn't* happen again. Even if Eric were interested—and he'd made it clear he wasn't with his nasty gigolo comment—she couldn't risk falling for him and giving up the independence she'd fought long and hard to achieve. She didn't fit in his world. Never had. Never would. And no longer wanted to try.

Not that he'd asked her to.

As unobtrusively as possible, Holly slipped into the vestibule at Alden's main branch to swap out the dog photos. She'd deliberately delayed coming to the main branch until Friday's lunch hour when the bank would be its busiest because she didn't want to run into Eric. With this much traffic into and out of the building, surely she'd be lost in the crowd.

She nodded at the security guard posted by the door and quickly got on with the job, but her usually nimble fingers complicated the simple task. Remove a picture. Tape a new one to the matting. How hard was that? Very hard when her fingers fumbled as if she were wearing heavy-duty welding gloves. *Faster. Faster.* One picture down. Five to go.

She glanced quickly over her shoulder and faked another smile for the watchful guard, but he was too busy talking into his radio to notice.

She took a quick peek through the glass doors at the two-story interior of the bank and marble stairs descending from the office level. No Eric. Whew. Her brazen behavior Monday night shamed her so badly she'd screened her calls all week. Eric had called twice to set up a dinner for tonight. She'd ignored his messages. Sooner or later, they'd have to resume the dates, but not yet. Please, *please* not yet. She wasn't ready.

Did that make her a coward? Probably. Too bad.

The vestibule doors opened and closed, ruffling the pictures as customers came and went. Holly kept her chin tucked and ignored them. *Faster. Faster.* One picture left. There! Done.

The door opened again and she sensed someone stopping behind her. She hoped it was a potential pet owner interested in the dog photos she'd removed from the frame and piled on the counter, but the hair prickling on the back of her neck said otherwise. With a sense of dread, she looked over her shoulder and froze. Eric. Her pulse skipped erratically and her mouth dried. Darn it. Why did her bells have to chime for him?

Tall. Dark. And taboo.

He stood stiffly in the marble vestibule, wearing another designer suit that fit his broad shoulders and lean hips to perfection. His emotionless banker face gave nothing away, but the hands fisted by his side shouted seeing her wasn't a pleasure.

Don't think about where those hands have been.

Too late. One particularly pushy part of her body was practically shouting, "Yoo-hoo, remember me?"

Eric's dark gaze drifted over her tank top, her too-tight-because-everything-else-is-dirty jeans and flip-flops before retracing his path. She cursed her beading nipples and hoped he wouldn't notice or that he'd attribute them to the air-conditioning vent overhead if he did.

Mortification burned her face. "Um, hi, Eric."

"You haven't returned my calls." The rumble of his voice slid over her skin like velvet. She suppressed a shiver.

"I've been busy." Eager to make a quick escape, she fastened the back on the frame. "How did you know I was here?"

He inclined his head toward the guard. "Denny had instructions to notify me when you arrived. We have eight dates left, Holly, including one tonight."

Darn and blast. Done in by a spying guard. "No can do. This is Friday. Girls' night out. I always have dinner with Juliana and Andrea." Not that she'd been able to get a hold of either of them to find out if dinner was on. "Maybe we can get together in…a week or two?"

Maybe by then she wouldn't relive the heat of his kiss or the magic in his fingers every time she closed her eyes. Her blood simmered anew at the thought, and the seam of her tight jeans abraded sensitive territory. She turned her back on Eric and stretched to rehang the picture.

Long, suit-clad arms reached around her, bracketing her shoulders as he grasped the frame and hooked it over the nail. The length of his torso briefly blanketed her with heat and his thighs and hips nudged the crevice of her buttocks like a spooning lover. She sucked in a quick breath and a hint of his cologne made her dizzy.

Don't lean back. No matter how badly you want to. And boy did she want to.

And then he moved away, taking warmth and temptation with him. Hallelujah. Reluctantly she turned, hugging herself. "Thanks."

His impassive expression didn't change. Did she get to him at all? No fair if she didn't. He should be at least half as addled by this forbidden attraction as she was.

"Cancel your plans. I'll pick you up at six."

"Eric, I don't think—"

"My college roommate is coming into town. He wants me to meet his fiancé. They're only in town for tonight. Tomorrow they leave on a cruise for the Bahamas."

Tension eked from her shoulders. They wouldn't be alone, but Eric would still have to drive her home, and she'd have to revisit the scene of her shame all over again. Good grief, she'd had a hot flash every time she'd walked through her foyer this week. Today was the first day the sight of her front door and the memories attached to it hadn't turned her on. Much. "Can I meet you at the restaurant?"

"No. Karl's fiancé is an artist. You'll enjoy meeting him."

Her temper sparked. "So you Duke alums can talk serious stuff without us artsy flakes interrupting?"

Eric's jaw muscles bunched, released and bunched again as if he were chewing on his temper. He waited until several customers exited before replying. "I need an open-minded date."

That was a compliment, wasn't it? So maybe he didn't think she was a total idiot. Loose, but not stupid? She grimaced.

"Holly, fifteen thousand dollars and the secret you want me to keep say you'll make yourself available." His implacable tone warned her not to argue and made her hackles rise, and then she replayed what he'd said and blinked.

"Wait a minute. Did you say *him*?"

Eric moved closer—right into her personal space. Holly couldn't retreat with the bank table right behind her. "Karl is gay. I don't know of anyone else who wouldn't be patronizing or rude to him and Nels, his partner. Or are you homophobic?"

"Of course, I'm not." Darn. Darn. Darn. She couldn't think of a good reason to refuse. "I'll be ready at six."

"Don't do anything I wouldn't do," Karl called out.

"Well, that leaves the field wide-open," Nels added in a voice thick with sarcasm.

Eric threw back his head and laughed, exposing the strong column of his neck. His white teeth flashed in the parking lot lights.

Holly chewed the inside of her lip and studied him. His deep, from-the-gut laughter combined with the lack of tension on his face reminded her of the guy she'd had a crush on fifteen years ago. The guy she might be developing another crush on.

Girl, you are in real trouble if you let that happen.

It was only a crush, wasn't it? These weird, twisted feelings could hardly be anything more, since he and she would be disastrous as a couple. Any moron could see that. The banker and the bohemian. Not a pretty picture.

But wasn't days away from thirty too old for crushes?

So what was this, then? An old-fashioned case of lust? She'd never experienced one of those, but she'd heard and read about them, and gosh knows Eric kept her body humming.

Looks like a duck. Quacks like a duck. Is a duck.

Okay, so this is lust. Deal with it.

But how?

By ignoring it, dummy. What other choice do you have?

"Have a great trip," she called out. Karl and Nels waved goodbye and drove off, leaving Holly alone with her date. Oh, joy. Not.

Dinner in a local microbrewery restaurant had been fun, not only because Karl and Nels had been entertaining, but because they'd brought out a side of Eric Holly hadn't seen in a very, very long time. An extremely attractive side.

Eric's I-know-how-to-have-fun expression transformed into the more stoic banker face right in front of her. She shook her head, mourning the loss. "You should do that more often."

A line formed between his dark eyebrows. "Do what?"

"Relax and have fun with your friends."

"They live four hours away in Charlotte." He motioned her toward his Corvette without touching her. He hadn't touched her all evening, and while just last week she'd wished he'd quit cupping her elbow, tonight she'd missed the courtly gesture. Dumb. Dumb. Dumb.

"What do you do for fun, Eric?"

He unlocked the door, seated her and then rounded the hood and folded his length behind the steering wheel before answering. "I play golf and tennis."

"*Pfffft*. I know all about those kinds of matches. My father and brothers play, and those games have nothing to do with fun. Business deals are negotiated on the greens. I meant the kind of outing where there's nothing on the agenda except a good time. Like tonight."

"Holly, I work sixty to seventy hours a week. I don't have time for goofing off—especially with the merger pending."

"You should make time or else—"

"Spare me the 'all work and no play' clichés. I've heard them." He turned the car onto the road. A streetlight revealed his flattened lips.

He'd heard them from his ex-fiancée, Holly recalled. In fact, all the wedding guests had heard them just before Priscilla had hurled her bouquet and boulder-sized diamond at Eric and stormed out of the church in her megabucks designer gown.

Holly cringed at the memory and searched for a new topic. "How did it feel to know your roommate was gay? Were you uncomfortable?"

"I didn't know for two years. By then, I knew Karl and trusted him. His preferences weren't an issue. And no, I was never uncomfortable. He respected my choices as I did his."

So Eric wasn't as uptight and narrow-minded as she'd believed, and he must be very sure of his masculinity not to feel threatened by sharing a room with a gay man.

Her opinion of him hiked up a few notches and that wasn't a good thing. She didn't need to add liking him to the hormone rush poisoning her thinking, but he made disliking him a little more difficult with each date. Sure, he'd threatened to share her secret with her father, and the gigolo comment had really knocked her sideways, but Eric was also helping her solve her Lyle problem, and he'd suggested the doggy posters. So he wasn't a totally ruthless jerk.

Too bad. She wouldn't have the hots for a hard-nosed jerk.

She twisted in her bucket seat to observe him. "Were you ever…you know…tempted to…try his way?"

Eric's head snapped toward her so quickly it was a wonder he didn't plow the car off the road and into a tree. "My God, is there nothing you won't ask?"

She shrugged. "Not really. But for what it's worth, I've never wanted to swing that way. I'm strictly into guys."

"Thank you for sharing that with me." His words, forced through clenched teeth, implied anything but gratitude.

"You didn't answer my question."

He turned the car into her driveway, parked behind her Jeep and then met her gaze. "No, I have never been interested in having sex with a man."

"Just curious." Holly scanned her yard. "I don't see Octavia's car."

"I informed her of the date."

"Maybe she's haunting another couple tonight. She can't be everywhere at once." Holly tried the car door and once again found it locked. Eric really had a hang-up about this gentleman thing. She fidgeted in her seat until he unlocked and opened her door, but she avoided his hand and climbed out without assistance. "We're off the hook. You don't have to walk me to the door." She stuck out her hand. "I had a great time tonight."

Eric ignored her hand. "I always see my dates to the door."

Feeling a little foolish, she lowered her arm. "Right. And you always sleep with them by the third date, but we've broken that rule. Want to break another?"

He remained silent and unblinking.

Holly sighed and led the way. Well, darn, she'd tried, but she would not invite him inside—back to the scene of the crime, so to speak. "I'm going to sit on the porch swing and enjoy the evening for a while. So…thanks again for dinner and for introducing me to your friends. I had a good time. Good-night, Eric."

She traversed the length of the porch and plunked herself down on the swing. Instead of taking the hint and leaving, Eric followed and sat beside her.

She'd shared the porch swing with countless others, male and female, canine and feline, but the seat had never felt so narrow. She toed it into motion, but the gentle sway failed to soothe her the way it usually did. Tonight she was too aware of the man connected to the thigh and shoulder brushing hers and hypersensitive to the warmth of his body and the subtle fragrance of his cologne.

"You're very talented," Eric said.

She blinked, hoping to clear the sensual stupor enclosing her. "Hmm?"

"Your work at the restaurant."

"Oh. Yeah. Thanks." She'd done the entry doors for the brewery as well as several inside decor pieces. During the meal the owner had come over to the table to greet her and then informed everyone seated in their section that Holly was the artist responsible. Bless him. She'd handed out a few business cards as a result, and if she was lucky she might get a much-needed commission or two from the exposure.

Eric stretched his arm along the arched back of the swing and angled his big body to face her. Holly's chest tightened and she inched forward. "You know, you and me and moonlight is not a good idea. You should go."

"We need to revisit the ground rules before our next seven dates."

"You have too many rules. Rules for the auction. Rules for behavior. Rules for our dates. Whatever happened to just living each day as it comes?" The straitjacket conventions were one of the reasons she'd ditched her old life.

"Rule number one. You will return my calls promptly. Preferably within twenty-four hours. Number two. No more of your outrageous come-ons."

Rule number two brought a flood of embarrassment to Holly's cheeks. "Come-ons? Are you kidding me? I have not been flirting with you. If I had you'd know it."

"Number three. If you choose to ignore the rules, you will accept the consequences. Is that clear?"

Anger rushed up her spine in a hot wave. "FYI, Eric, I run off at the mouth when I'm nervous. And yes, I tend to speak my mind. I happen to find you attractive, and I'm not hypocritical enough to lie about that, but that doesn't mean we should jump each other every time we get the itch."

"There you go again." He hooked an arm around her shoulder.

"Hey! Wait a min—"

His lips sealed her protest and her pulse rate rocketed into the stratosphere. Eric took possession of her mouth with the mastery of the pirate she'd accused him of being on their last date. Firm.

Commanding. And oh, so skilled. Holly fisted her hands against his chest, but somewhere in the adrenaline rush she forgot to slug him.

Her lips parted and his tongue sliced through the opening. Hot. Slick. Sinful. Good heavens, the man knew how to kiss the reasoning right out of her. A moan bubbled in her throat. Somehow, her disobedient fingers ended up tangled in the crisp, short hair at his nape, and *somehow* her leg ended up draped over his. Eric's warm palm traversed her thigh to splay over her hip and then her world shifted.

Holy moly, the banker rocked her boat.

She reveled in his firm, sure caresses over her bottom, waist and ribs. When his thumbs teased the undersides of her aching breasts, she shivered and arched against an impressive erection.

Erection?

Huh?

She lifted her head to gasp for breath, pried open her heavy-lidded eyes and found herself straddling him with the hem of her hyacinth dress hiked up to expose the crotch of her purple panties.

Oh m'gosh. How had she ended up in his lap? Had she climbed on board or had he put her there? She couldn't remember. How did he do that to her? Her face burned. Wanton again. Jeez.

"Okay, okay, wait." She pressed her hands against his collarbone. His chest rose and fell rapidly beneath her palms. At least she wasn't the only one turned on tonight. She wriggled off him and backed away from the swing yanking her skirt down as she retreated.

"Eric, we're not going to keep doing this. Me getting all hot and bothered and you going home with an impressive piece of lumber in your pants."

A pained expression crossed his face. "Holly, do you ever edit your thoughts?"

"There's nothing wrong with being honest," she snapped

back. "If you ask me, that's one of the things that's wrong with society. We tell too many polite lies because we don't have the guts to be honest, and then people end up snickering and talking behind someone's back. Betrayal by the ones we thought we could trust hurts far more than the truth would have."

Understanding softened his eyes.

She grimaced when she realized how much she'd revealed. From sex to sob story in sixty seconds. Talk about a mood killer. Which was probably a good thing. No. Definitely a good thing. "The point is, this can't keep happening."

"You have the power to stop it. If you'd follow the rules—"

Shaking her finger at him, she advanced. "Oh, no you don't. You are not pinning this on me, Eric Alden. I do not make a habit of wrapping myself around a man. In fact, I have never had trouble keeping my hands or my lips off anyone before. So this is *your* fault."

His gaze sharpened. "I never go where I'm not wanted."

She growled in frustration. "I never said I didn't want you. But I shouldn't. I have too much to lose in getting tangled up with you."

"Like what?"

"My best friend. Me." She cursed her loose tongue and quickly retreated to the far end of the porch. She hated that he rattled her so easily. "Forget I said that."

Boards creaked as Eric crossed them, and then Holly felt his heat and presence behind her. Darn her internal radar for picking up his signal so strongly.

"Explain."

She sighed. Since she'd already humiliated herself what did she have to lose? She turned and, as usual, Eric had invaded her personal space. She backed into the railing. Trapped.

"For the first time in my life, I like where I am and who I am. My home. My job. My friends—most of them, anyway. Octavia is making it *really* hard to like her right now." She swiped a lock of hair from her forehead. "Anyway, I want to still like myself when our dates are over."

"And you won't if we become…intimate." His eyes, as dark as a moonless night, nailed her in place.

"Probably not. Heck, I don't know. Between you and the money I loaned Lyle, I have stupidly put everything I've worked for these past seven years on shaky ground. Unless I find Lyle and work out some kind of repayment, then I could very well end up crawling back to the Caliber Club and begging for a job—just like my daddy wants me to. I learned the hard way that I don't fit into that world. *Your* world, Eric. And this thing between you and me…well, it only complicates an already complicated situation."

He shoved his hands into his pants pockets, but the rigidity of his face and body belied the casual pose. "What can I do to help?"

"You're already helping by paying the private investigator. As for us…" She shook her head. "I don't know. Half the time, my common sense tells me to get as far away from you as possible, to cancel the remaining dates and deal with the fallout from Octavia's negative publicity, even though it will result in lost revenues that I can't afford right now. The other half of the time, I think we should just do it and get over it already."

"Pardon?" Eric rasped.

Oops. "Forget it. I'm just a little panicked and I'm not thinking straight."

"Holly—" He reached for her.

Holly dodged around him, fled across the porch and stabbed her key in the front door. She stepped inside and turned on the threshold. "Eric, go home before we make a really big mistake."

And then she closed the door in temptation's face.

Eric stood on his front porch and glared at the Saturday paper. How in the hell had Octavia Jenkins pulled this off? She had to have high-placed connections to get last night's photos in today's paper.

Usually the Lifestyles section was planned well in advance, and last-minute photo and story insertions were saved for breaking news. Holly straddling Eric's lap and kissing him senseless was *not* news.

Hunger dug its talons deep into his flesh and his blood pumped harder as he studied the grainy black-and-white photo. Holly's long fingers were tangled in his hair and her lips slanted over his. His hands weren't visible because they were under her skirt clutching her derriere. He ought to be thankful that wasn't clear, or the picture would have bordered on pornographic.

The paper crumpled as he clenched his fists against the memory of her soft skin. He stomped into the house and punched the button on his coffeemaker with enough force to send the machine skidding several inches across the counter.

He wanted Holly Prescott.

Why? She was absolutely nothing like the women he usually chose. She wasn't sophisticated or acquiescent. She didn't even like the same type of restaurants he did. He couldn't blame his hunger on abstinence because he'd been four months without sex before, and it hadn't kept him semi-aroused 24/7 nor had him ready to claw out of his skin and into hers at the slightest provocation.

Holly and the very traits that made her entirely wrong for him turned him on. Her limitless energy and her outspokenness had slipped under his skin, and during dinner last night she'd utterly charmed Karl and Nels.

And him.

Damn.

Until Holly, he'd never met a woman he couldn't understand. Just when he thought he had Holly pegged, she turned the tables on him. Not only had his aggression not sent her scurrying for cover as he'd hoped, but last night he'd discovered, compliments of the P.I.'s report, that Holly Cameron Prescott was full of hidden surprises.

When Eric had returned home after their date last night, he'd found copies of the documents pertaining to Holly's loan to her ex waiting in his fax machine. Wes had also included a copy of Holly's college transcripts—not that Eric had requested that information, and he didn't want to know how Wes had obtained the transcripts without Holly's permission.

With Holly's scent still clinging to his skin and clothing, Eric had examined the documents and discovered Holly had majored in business and minored in studio art. She'd graduated with a 4.0 average—a far cry from the ditzy flake her brothers painted her as being. And she was as careful in her business as he was in his. The business proposal, written in Lewis's handwriting and signed and dated by him, looked completely legit.

Eric had been surprised to realize Holly wasn't a sappy bleeding heart. Damned if he wouldn't have loaned Lyle Lewis money, too. The man appeared to be a good risk. But whereas Eric would have insisted on collateral, Holly had settled for a stake in the profits of Lewis's invention. Risky, but potentially more profitable in the long run.

The coffeemaker gave a last gasp. Eric blinked back to the present and poured himself a cup. Last night's discoveries only increased his admiration of Holly, and that wasn't a benefit.

Seven more dates. How would he survive them without becoming more deeply involved?

He snatched up the phone and jabbed in Holly's number.

"Rainbow Glass. This is Holly."

Her voice made his pulse trip like an adolescent's. "Have you seen the paper?"

A frustrated groan traveled through the connection. "Yes. And this time I'm truly going to kill Octavia. She was there last night, lurking in the shadows like a sniper."

"A sniper?" Holly's word choice surprised him.

"Yes, waiting to take us out with one shot. What else would you call today's article? Do you expect anyone to look at that and see us as serious business people? Jeez, I'm riding you like a porn star. My mother will have a conniption."

Eric clamped his jaw shut at her typical over-the-top description. He couldn't prevent the flares shooting off in his bloodstream. Holly was right. This was serious. He reread the relevant section of the article.

The Queen of Denial takes on King Midas. Who will be the victor? From where this reporter stands sharing the throne looks like a lot of fun.

He didn't like being compared to the greedy king. "Why does she call you the Queen of Denial?"

Silent seconds ticked past. "Because she says I'm trying to forget my roots. Which is complete hooey. It's not like I've changed my name or moved to a commune or something." Her sigh carried across the connection. "Look, Eric, I don't know how to avoid Octavia short of leaving town."

An idea struck him. "I have a house on Bald Head Island. Let's spend the weekend there. We'll fulfill a few more dates out of Octavia's sight and the photographer's camera range. I'll pick you up in an hour."

He set the phone down on Holly's sputtering protest.

Thirty uninterrupted hours together would put an end to this unorthodox attraction one way or another. Either he and Holly would end up in bed together and satisfy their curiosity, or they'd totally alienate each other before leaving the island. He hoped for the latter, because the former would cause no end of complications.

A dangerous plan, but definitely worth the risks.

Seven

"We have a noon lunch reservation," Eric said as he strode away from the Bald Head Island ferry terminal with the purposeful stride of a magnate on the way to close a billion-dollar deal. "That will give us time to drop our bags at the house before returning to the club. Our tee time is at three and our dinner reservation is at seven."

Holly rolled her eyes and strolled beside him on the dock, towing the two-wheeled cooler she'd insisted on bringing despite Eric's insistence that they wouldn't need food in the cottage. He planned to eat out for every meal. Ugh. She refused to shower and dress for every meal. Besides, beach air always made her hungrier than usual. "You have a schedule?"

"Of course."

She should have expected a guy who could plan an island getaway in less than an hour, convince the ferry boat captain to ignore their lack of reservations on a Saturday morning and who'd arrived at her house dressed for a beach trip in chinos pressed to knife-edge crease and a crisp short-sleeved oxford shirt to have a freaking agenda.

Some vacation. She hadn't put her work on hold and scrambled to find care for the dogs to come over here and hobnob with the rich and famous. No way. She suppressed a shudder.

"We're on an island paradise, Eric. We don't need an agenda."

"I've reserved a tennis court for tomorrow at nine. We'll leave on the one-thirty ferry," he continued without breaking stride literally or verbally.

She snatched the strap of her weekend bag which he'd hung over his shoulder and yanked him to a halt. Other ferry patrons parted and flowed past them like a school of fish. "No."

His surprised look made her wonder if anyone ever dared to defy him. He guided her out of the pedestrian traffic. "No?"

"That's what I said. Stop and smell the salt air, for crying out loud. You left your suit at home. Now act like it." She rejoined the queue headed toward shuttle service and the golf cart parking lot. The only vehicles allowed on the island besides service vehicles were golf carts and bicycles. No cars. Her idea of heaven, since not having Beemers or Benzes as status symbols was something of an equalizer.

Her flip-flops slapped on the wooden dock. "Cancel the reservations—at least my half."

Eric kept pace beside her. "What do you suggest we do for the next thirty hours?"

"Nothing. Or as close to nothing as possible."

She couldn't see his eyes through his Oakley shades, but his scowl said he thought she'd lost her mind. "Nothing?"

"Yes. Isn't there a nature trail somewhere around here? I wouldn't mind walking that. I'd love to bicycle around the island, and maybe we could rent a canoe and paddle through the marshes or go fishing."

In her privileged youth she'd known others who had vacation homes here, but somehow she'd never accepted their invitations to visit the exclusive island off the North Carolina coast. Right after Eric hung up this morning, Holly had gone online and visited the island's Web page before packing her bags. Though she'd never admit it to Eric, she'd printed out island maps just in case he wouldn't show her what she wanted to see.

"Hiking, biking and canoeing are your idea of nothing?"

"Well, honestly, I'd love to doze on the beach under an umbrella for a couple of hours and then tackle the rest."

Energy and frustration rolled off him in waves, but he kept his gaze steadfastly directed ahead.

"Eric, do you ever just kick back and relax, dig your toes in the sand and let the tide roll in?"

His jaw muscles flexed. "Of course."

She stifled a laugh. He was such a bad liar. "Good. Because that's what I plan on doing for the rest of the weekend, and if you want this trip to substitute for some of our dates like you told Octavia it would, then it would help if we were together just in case she tracks us down."

She stopped in front of the golf cart lot and gawked. There were carts of every size, shape, color and level of luxury. One even had a Rolls-Royce grille. So much for the generic equalizer. She shook her head and faced Eric. "Do you own a fishing rod or do we need to rent that, too?"

He shoved his glasses into his thick hair and stood toe-to-toe with her for several seconds, his nostrils flaring, his lips flattening, and arguments chasing through his eyes, then he said, "We'll get the cart first. The rental shop is on the way to the house."

She beamed. "Great. Why don't you cancel the reservations while I shop?"

Thirty minutes later, Holly had rented two rods, one for her and one for Eric, even though he insisted he wasn't going to fish, and she'd made arrangements for a pair of bicycles to be delivered to his address. Eric helped her load the rods and other paraphernalia into the golf cart and then he steered away from Bald

Head Village and into the island. They drove past a lighthouse and a chapel. Holly snapped pictures with her digital camera and made a mental note to explore both buildings before leaving tomorrow if time permitted.

Eric tracked her gaze. "Old Baldy was built in 1817 and is the oldest standing lighthouse in North Carolina. Federal Road was the original supply road from the landing to Old Baldy."

"Where is your cottage from here?" Eric swerved to avoid another golf cart hogging the middle of the road as it passed. The driver was too busy talking to someone in the backseat to watch where he was going. The sudden move jostled Holly against Eric. His bare forearm singed her skin. She scooted away as far as the bench seat allowed and struggled against the urge to see if she could massage the residual warmth away.

"On the opposite side of the island."

Even with Eric as a hormone-rousing distraction beside her, Holly felt the tension drain from her muscles as they drove deeper inland. Everything about the island moved at a slower pace, especially once they left the village and the tiny harbor behind. Towering oaks met to form a canopy above the road, and without traffic noise the sounds of wildlife nearly drowned out the quiet whir of their vehicle. She heard crickets, frogs and birds, but not the same varieties she could hear from her own porch.

Flashes of color in the dark foliage made her camera finger twitchy. She could get dozens of window design ideas here. This weekend could be great for her creativity, and consequently her career. She only hoped it wasn't disastrous for her personal life.

"The nature trail's on your left."

She turned her head in the direction Eric indicated.

They passed a variety of cottages from new to older and palatial to small and quaint. Where would Eric's be on the spectrum? When he finally turned into a crushed oyster driveway, Holly gasped and grabbed his arm. "Stop."

Eric braked hard, jerking the cart to a halt. "What?"

"*This* is your place?" She sprang from her seat, tipped her head back and gaped at the surprising structure in front of her. How utterly charming and un-Eric-like. She snapped a series of pictures.

"Yes."

"It's the antithesis of your house in Wilmington." The beach house was cozy, inviting and totally informal. A wide covered porch practically shouted, "Welcome home."

The two-story house stood on pilings like most coastal homes in an area where hurricane flooding was a possibility. The clapboard siding had been painted in the palest gray possible—like the inside of an oyster shell—with snowy white trim and a smoky blue front door. Two gables faced forward, and a wide dormer window occupied the space between them in the steeply pitched roof. Fish-scale shingles decorated the area above the windows in each gable—a whimsical touch for such a practical owner.

She could hear the ocean although she couldn't see it as she walked up the driveway, twisting her head left and right to take in the rolling dunes and the dense trees flanking and shading the house. "How close are we to the beach?"

Eric rolled the cart slowly beside her. "The house is ocean-front. I bought it in foreclosure. It's a good investment and should have an exceptional return when I sell—"

She held up her hand in a stop gesture. "Don't spoil it for me by telling me money motivated your purchase. Let me believe you saw this adorable house, fell instantly in love with it and bought it because you couldn't live without it."

He removed his sunglasses, tucked them into his shirt pocket and leveled his navy eyes on her. "Of course."

The touch of sarcasm in his voice made her wrinkle her nose and stick out her tongue. She should have known sentiment hadn't influenced his purchase. "I absolutely adore it. Show me the inside. We can unload later."

He parked the cart in the carport beneath the house and led the way up the stairs. The covered entry led into a hardwood-floored foyer and then a spacious den. "There are four bedrooms and three bathrooms on this floor. The main living area and the master bedroom are upstairs."

The house smelled a little stuffy, but Holly barely noticed as she stared past Eric. The amazing view of the beach and the Atlantic Ocean beyond the dunes and sea grass pulled her across the den to the wall of windows. She fumbled with the door latch and stepped out onto a wide porch spanning the rear of the house. She could barely see the neighbors' houses through the trees. A deck upstairs provided shelter to part of the porch from the blazing sun, and stairs leading down to the sand called to her. *Later,* she promised.

"This is gorgeous. How often do you come here?"

"A couple of times a year."

Which explained the stuffy smell and the lack of personal items scattered across the flat surfaces. She turned on him. "You own a slice of paradise and you only visit twice a year?"

He shrugged. "Work comes first."

"You need a hobby, Eric. One that makes use of this fabulous place." She went back inside and, without waiting for her host, climbed the stairs to the top floor and crossed an expansive great room to look out at the ocean. The exterior walls were practically all glass, making her feel almost as if she were standing outside, and the view from this higher vantage point was even more spectacular than the one from downstairs. "Wow."

She turned a full circle, taking in the sand-colored leather sofas, glass tables and pickled oak flooring. The dining room and a kitchen with enough counter space and cabinetry to make a serious cook drool occupied the street side of the house, but once again, there were no personal touches to stamp Eric's personality on the house.

Eric stood in the center of the room and nodded toward an archway. "My bedroom's through there."

His neutral tone drew her gaze. She looked into his eyes and saw what, exactly? A dare? An invitation? Whatever it was gave her goose bumps and made her stomach muscles tighten.

Come into my parlor, said the spider to the fly.

Yes, and we all know how that turned out.

"Good to know. I'll choose a room downstairs."

A totally wasted day, Eric decided. He could be analyzing the merger data he'd shoved in his suitcase or making connections at the Bald Head Island Club. Instead, he sat in a chair on the sand in front of his cottage with a cold beer—compliments of Holly's cooler—in his hand, watching Holly's ass.

And a fine one it was, too.

He bit back a snort of self-disgust and reined in his inappropriate thoughts. In the three hours since they'd arrived, Holly had reduced him to a frat-boy's mindset. Beer. Women. Sex.

He was a leader, not a follower, but since landing on the island he'd followed wherever Hurricane Holly led. If he left her to her own devices, he feared she'd spin off her own little tornado and wreak havoc on his unsuspecting neighbors.

At present, Holly stood knee-deep in the surf, fishing rod in one hand and a baseball cap covering her coppery hair. Her swimsuit— a two piece in eye-popping neon green—covered more than his dates' bikinis usually did, but the bottoms—boy shorts, Holly had called them—hugged the lower half of an hourglass figure with mouthwatering devotion. And every time Eric recalled the way the underwire top cradled her full breasts, he had to take a swim.

He checked his watch. How long before he had to test his self-control again by applying more sunscreen to her back? The first time he'd massaged the lotion into her supple ivory skin had nearly overpowered him.

Oh, yes, he wanted Holly Prescott, and remembering why a quick affair with her was a bad idea was becoming harder with each passing minute. He needed to write down the bullet points for future reference before he forgot them.

"Hey, cut it out," Holly called and kicked a shower of cool water in his direction. "No clock-watching. You should have left the Rolex in the cottage."

"Have you changed your mind about the golf game yet? The fish aren't biting."

She reeled in her line and trudged toward him through the shallow waves. Her thigh muscles flexed and her ample breasts jiggled just enough to make him wish he had the strength to look away. Sweat speckled her chest and trickled down her cleavage. One droplet dangled above her navel like a diamond belly button ring. He ached to follow the droplet's trail with his tongue. His fingers contracted and the beer can crumpled in his hand, spilling cool liquid over his fingers.

"C'mon, Alden, the world won't end if you kick back for a few hours. There's nobody on this island you need to impress today. No clients to schmooze. No deals to broker. Give it a rest already. Let's hike the nature trail. It should be cooler in the shade of the forest."

Since they'd arrived she had yet to practice what she preached and kick back in a chair on the sand. She'd been a constant blur of motion. How did she stand still long enough to create her stained glass pieces? He had to admit the detail in the panels at the restaurant had surprised him. Holly was an extremely talented artist. Somehow that piece of information was never included when anyone condemned Holly's "shameful bohemian lifestyle."

And her family wanted her to give it up.

A tide of something that felt an awful lot like pride surged in Eric's chest. He crushed it. He deserved none of the credit for Holly refusing to buckle to parental and societal pressure. But after seeing her art, he was glad she hadn't.

Admiring her courage will bring nothing but trouble.

He pushed out of the low chair and rose. How could he salvage the day and postpone being alone in the cottage with her when she'd insisted he cancel their reservations? His plan—to schedule every second of their day—had been sabotaged. He'd nearly swallowed his tongue when she unpacked enough food from her cooler to feed them for the entire weekend.

"Perhaps we could swing by the club for a cocktail after our hike." He offered her a towel, hoping she'd cover up. She hitched it around her hips, blocking only half of her remarkable attributes. He was too old to have to fight so hard to keep his eyes off a woman's breasts, but fight he did.

She snorted and shook her head. "I don't think so. Tequila is what got me into the auction in the first place. I swear I'll never drink another margarita as long as I live."

"Holly, the other option is to spend time in the beach house. Just the two of us. Alone."

She blinked, swallowed and pursed her lips. "How about if we drive to that ice cream parlor after dinner instead?"

Something cold in what should be a crowded family atmosphere would be even less intimate than the club. "Excellent suggestion."

When had eating ice cream become foreplay?

Holly licked the last bit of double chocolate raspberry truffle ice cream from her fingers and tried to pretend she hadn't noticed Eric's dark eyes following each lap of her tongue as she consumed her dessert. Despite the families surrounding them at the tables outside the quaint little shop, the ice cream wasn't the only thing melting on this balmy Saturday night.

She shifted in her seat and squeezed her knees together, but the hum of arousal stubbornly stayed put. She'd been overheated ever since Eric had stripped down to swim trunks this afternoon. A desk jockey shouldn't have six-pack abs, mile-wide shoulders and deep pectorals. And his legs and butt…whew. Lean. Muscled. Tight. *Wow*.

The banker had a bodacious body. Who'd have thunk it? She hoped steam wasn't spewing from her ears and panties.

She cleared her throat in an effort to shake off the barnacles clinging to her larynx. "Do you think Octavia will find us?"

Eric paused with his spoon cradled in his long fingers. "The auction rules required me to tell her we were coming to the island and to give her our itinerary, but we have several things working in our favor. One, you changed our itinerary."

"Demolished, you mean," she said with an unrepentant grin.

"Yes. Two, she has nineteen other couples to follow who are not on this island. Three, unless she rents a boat and a slip in the marina, the ferry is the only way to get here. Because she's not a property owner, the captain is less likely to overlook her lack of a reservation on a peak season weekend and allow her on board. Lastly, there are no hotels. She'd have to make it a day trip."

He chased down the last chocolate chip from his single scoop of mint chocolate chip in a bowl and slid it between his lips. Just one more difference between them. She was a double-scoop-cone person, and he preferred the neater single serving in a bowl. But he was a closet sensualist, she'd discovered. He'd savored each bite as if it were nectar, holding it in his mouth for several seconds before swallowing, as if he were letting it melt on his tongue.

Her decadence versus his self-control. Did he ever lose that control? And if so, where? Bed?

Don't go there, Holly.

The memory of the women's comments about Eric's sexual prowess sent another ripple of heat over her. Holly sipped her water, hoping for a cooling effect. It failed. "Did you ever consider breaking the rules and not telling Octavia we'd left Wilmington?"

He set his spoon in the bowl and pushed both to the side. Slowly. Deliberately. Was he as deliberate at everything? Say... pleasing a woman, for example.

Jeez. Quit acting like a dog in heat.

"We are already bending the rules by not going on the dates described in the program."

Holly wagged a finger. "Ah, but the fine print says substitutions are allowed when necessary. I consider dodging my back-stabbing former friend necessary."

"She's doing her job."

"By printing articles full of sexual innuendo and hiding in the dark to take private photos?"

"Put your personal opinions aside and consider the situation from a business perspective. Which will sell more newspapers? Standard dates or erotic encounters?"

"Yeah, yeah, I get that, but it's not the truth."

"Isn't it?" Those two quietly spoken words hit her like a stun gun. Instantly, electricity arced between them. "The pictures were real, Holly. Your friend is calling it like she sees it. No matter how much we might prefer otherwise, there is no libel involved."

"I never expected you to take her side."

"I'm not choosing sides. I'm suggesting you examine the situation objectively and look at the articles from a marketing standpoint. Octavia Jenkins is an ambitious journalist who wants her byline in as many homes as possible."

"I know that, but I still feel betrayed. I guess I should be thankful she didn't hear your gigolo crack or my name would be mud, because as sure as the sun's going to rise tomorrow, she'd print it."

He grimaced. "I'm sorry."

Her eyebrows shot into her hairline. Eric apologizing? Unbelievable. "Don't apologize unless you mean it."

"I mean it."

"Then why'd you say it?"

The sounds of other couples gathering their broods and busing their tables as the ice cream parlor closed for the night filled the silence between them. Holly's pulse accelerated with each passing second. "Eric, quit searching for the politically correct answer and just spit it out. You should know by now that I respect honesty more than anything."

His jaw shifted and then he exhaled. "Because you're not the only one hanging on by a thread."

Shocked, she gasped and gaped, but Eric continued. "I'm attracted to you and I'm fighting myself. I don't need to fight you, too. I was trying to push you away."

"But…but…" The sudden hormone infusion into her bloodstream deep-fried her brain. She couldn't think, couldn't find words to express the maelstrom inside her. "But I—"

She what? Why couldn't they be together again? *Ba-bump. Ba-bump. Ba-bump.* Her heart thudded hard and fast. Oh yes, because she couldn't be a part of his world and didn't want to lose Juliana's friendship.

But Eric hasn't asked for a permanent relationship, has he? And his sister doesn't have to know, does she?

Holly shrugged off the naughty imp trying to get her into trouble. "You thought giving me the big O against my front door would push me away?"

"My intention was to call your bluff. I went further than I intended because I—" His fists clenched on the tabletop. "Because in the heat of the moment I lost sight of my objective."

His grudging admission stunned her. So Eric hadn't been as cool or controlled that night as he would have liked her to believe. "You want me? *Me?* A graceless, redheaded amazon?"

His dark gaze locked with hers, and the passion simmering in his eyes stole her breath. "So badly even my hair is rigid."

Heat *poofed* inside her like a gas grill igniting. "Wow. When you're honest you're *really* honest. I, um…like that…I think."

Let it go, Holly. Walk away. Let Eric be the voice of reason since your thinking is clearly incapacitated at the moment.

But she couldn't drop it. She'd never been as physically attracted to anyone as she was to Eric Alden, and she'd been on enough diets to know denial only made the hunger worse. If she indulged in her craving, she'd get over it.

She crumpled her paper napkin in her fingers. "So why are

we sitting here when we could be at the cottage…getting to know each other better?"

His nostrils flared on a sharp inhalation. "You're the one who said you had too much to lose for us to get together."

"Right. I do, but only if we try to frame this relationship with hearts and flowers and make it last long-term. Short-term, on the other hand, could be good. Very, very good, I suspect, given what I've already sampled."

His eyes narrowed, but she didn't wait for a reply.

"Have you ever heard that Toby Keith song about what happens in Mexico staying in Mexico? What if what happened on this island stayed on this island?"

Something sparked in Eric's eyes and then his banker face shut out all emotion. "Too risky."

"And you never gamble?"

"Only when the odds are in my favor."

She propped her elbows on the table, rested her chin on her linked fingers and looked up at him through her lashes. "And what part of a no-strings-affair weekend isn't in your favor, Mr. Alden?"

Eric swore under his breath and scanned the surrounding area. The families had cleared out. Only the two of them remained at the tables. "Holly—"

"We'll need condoms. I didn't bring any. Did you?"

"No," he barked harshly. Before crushing disappointment and embarrassment totally overwhelmed her, he added, "But the island store should carry them. And it's open," he glanced at his Rolex, "for another ten minutes."

Her pulse tripped. Air whooshed from her lungs. She dragged it back in. "Then let's go."

They hastily dealt with their trash and headed for the golf cart at a speed walker's pace. Within moments Eric parked the golf cart outside the store.

"Last chance to change your mind." His voice sounded deeper, thicker. That was her only clue that he wasn't as calm as he appeared.

"Not going to happen." Wise or not, she'd chosen her path.

"Would you like to come in with me?"

She shook her head. Her knees were shaking too badly to leave the cart. How idiotic was that? "Surprise me."

Eric disappeared into the shop. To keep second thoughts from making her punch the Go pedal and race—as fast as a battery-operated vehicle would go, anyway—away from her decision, Holly turned on the golf cart's radio and tuned into a country station. She sang along with Chris Cagle, Kenny Chesney and then Gary Allan before Eric exited the store with a bag in his hand.

Her heart stalled. Was she making a mistake? Possibly. Probably. But it wouldn't be her first or her last. Apparently mistakes were her forte.

Eric climbed into the cart, held her gaze for one long, breath-stealing moment and then the vehicle shot forward into the darkness. The moonlight didn't penetrate the tree canopy in places. Rabbits, possums and a deer darted through their head-light beams. Normally, Holly would want to stop and watch the wildlife. But not tonight. Tonight, she trembled with desire for the man beside her, and judging by the quick, singeing glances Eric shot her way, he felt the same.

It took forever to cross the island and another eon before Eric rolled to a stop in the carport. Silence, except for the insect and frog chorus, closed around them.

"Last chance," he repeated roughly.

She gulped and rubbed her damp palms against the legs of her shorts, but made no attempt to get out of the cart. "You already said that."

He remained facing forward. His hands tightened on the steering wheel until his knuckles turned white in the dim light. "If I kiss you out here, we won't make it inside."

The rough whisper nearly incapacitated her. Holly couldn't

move. Couldn't breathe. Her muscles tautened and heat hissed from her pores. "Would we get in trouble for that?"

As if in answer to her question, another golf cart passed on the narrow road, its headlight beaming through the night. The passengers tooted the horn and waved. Holly and Eric woodenly returned the greeting.

Eric laughed low and sexy and shook his head. He turned his head, and his tight smile made her blood sing. "Definitely."

Oh m'gosh. She was actually nervous. She couldn't recall the last time she'd been nervous about becoming intimate with a man besides the initial he's-going-to-see-me-naked moment. This was so much more than that. "Y-your bed or m-mine?"

"Yours is closer." His voice sounded as thick and dark as molasses.

"Alrighty, then." And still neither of them moved. Holly's heart hammered against her ribs and her pulse drummed deafeningly in her ears. Would he get out of the cart already? If not, she was going to look way too eager when she raced up the sidewalk ahead of him.

Not even a hint of breeze stirred the air beneath the house. Her skin dampened and her clothing clung. She wished she'd showered away the sweat, sand and sunscreen from the beach and the nature walk before going to the ice cream shop. Oh, ick. Eric was probably used to sweet-smelling *clean* women. "I, um…should probably shower first."

Eric's chest rose as he inhaled deeply. "My shower is large enough for two."

Hooo, boy. Were her legs steady enough to climb three flights of stairs? Maybe. Maybe not. "Okay."

His head turned and his gaze locked with hers. "Or there's one on the beach side of the laundry room. Smaller. But closer."

Her breath hitched. "Down here?"

"Yes."

"Outside?"

"Semienclosed."

"Private?"

His Adam's apple bobbed as he swallowed. "Private enough."

"How far?"

"Twenty feet."

Holly dampened her suddenly dry lips. "I think I can make it that far."

Another one of those bone-melting chuckles rumbled from Eric's throat. "Same here."

He wanted her. He really, *really* wanted her. Every tense line of his body, the granite edge of his jaw and the steadiness of his dark eyes broadcast his need. Something blossomed inside Holly with the knowledge, and her nervousness transformed into pure hunger.

"So…what are we waiting for?"

Eight

Eric gave sanity one last chance to take a stand. When it failed to make an appearance, he grabbed the bag of condoms with one hand and caught Holly's fingers with his other. He tugged her across the golf cart's bench seat.

She stumbled from the cart and fell against him. The electricity from the navel-to-breast contact crackled over him, short-circuiting reason and finesse. Holly's head tipped back and her gaze locked with his. Desire darkened her toffee-colored eyes and parted her lips. She dampened them with the tip of her tongue, sending need slicing through him like a bolt of lightning. His blood pressure spiked with dizzying speed. He gritted his teeth as his control wavered.

"This way." His voice came out hoarse, as if he'd swallowed a bucket of the pulverized oyster shells crunching beneath his quick footsteps. By the time he reached the outdoor shower behind the house and flicked on the dim overhead light, his lungs bellowed as if he'd run twenty miles uphill instead of taken twenty-odd steps across level ground.

He dragged Holly into the cramped dressing area, pitched the condoms onto the bench seat, caught her shoulders and pushed her against the adjacent fiberglass shower wall. He couldn't wait another second to cover her mouth with his. She opened immediately, met the thrust of his tongue instantly and wound herself around him with gratifying swiftness. Their teeth and noses bumped, but Eric couldn't slow down, couldn't rein in his hunger or find his usual finesse.

He devoured her mouth, suckled her bottom lip, stroked her waist, hips and back, and then he tangled his fingers in her silky, short hair, angled her head and kissed her harder, deeper, breaking the kisses only when he had to suck air into his burning lungs.

He tunneled his hands beneath her tank top over her rib cage and encountered a bra he couldn't get around. Backtracking, he found the hem of her shirt and yanked upward. The stretchy fabric snagged below her breasts. Frustrated, he released her mouth and drew back a fraction. "How do I get this off?"

"Bra...attached." Holly punctuated her words with incendiary sips and nips along his throat and jaw. "Hooks...in...back...underneath."

His fingers found and fumbled with the unfamiliar fastening. If his hands didn't quit shaking, he'd never get her naked. *Naked.* The thought of having Holly naked in his arms didn't help the situation. He forced himself to inhale a slow, steadying breath and then hissed it out through clenched teeth when she bit his earlobe. Other than his first time, he couldn't recall a single occasion in his thirty-six years when he'd been this agitated, this eager. And like his first time, this was going to be over before he dropped his pants if he didn't find a measure of control.

Her top loosened. *Finally.* Eric ripped it over her head and pitched it behind him. Without patience. Without finesse. And then her full, round breasts were right there in front of him, inviting his touch, waiting for his mouth, and he didn't give a damn about anything except stroking her warm, satiny skin, thumbing the puckered tips and tasting her.

He dipped his head and traced the dusky circle with his tongue before pulling her deep into his mouth. Her fragrance, a potent cocktail of salt, coconut suntan lotion and pure Holly filled his nostrils and went straight to his head like a snifter of Courvoisier cognac.

She made a mewing sound, and her head lolled from side to side as he tested her weight and suckled. Her fingers clenched spasmodically in his hair and a shudder rippled over her. But the lull only lasted seconds before Holly pulled his shirttail free and pushed his Polo shirt over his belly, shoulders and head. Her short nails scraped through his chest hair and his muscles contracted involuntarily. She twined her arms around his waist, and then her soft breasts fused to his chest.

He'd never been a breast man, but in that moment she converted him. Eric groaned and struggled for control, but Holly cupped his cheeks and rose on her tiptoes, her hard nipples searing a path across his chest. She fed him one drugging kiss after another.

The grind of her belly against his erection nearly snapped his fortitude. He couldn't wait. He forced his hands between them. The button on her shorts gave way, and then he shoved his hands beneath her shorts and panties, urging the barricading garments over her rounded bottom and down her long, long legs. Holly kicked her clothing and her flip-flops toward the dressing area and stood before him naked. She reached for him again, but he caught her hands and held her away from him to savor her lush ivory curves and her neatly trimmed auburn curls in the dim light. "Incredible."

She bit her lip. "You don't have to lie."

He saw doubt in her eyes before she ducked her head. "I'm not lying. Holly, you are…like an exquisite piece of art."

A tentative smile quivered on her swollen lips. Eric released her, kicked out of his boat shoes and reached for his belt. Holly's hands covered his.

"Let me."

Her fingers delved behind his buckle, pulling the leather free. The zipper slid down with tantalizing—torturing—slowness and then she eased his khaki shorts and briefs over his hips.

"Hoo boy." She cupped his hard flesh and stroked him from base to tip.

Eric sucked a sharp breath and squeezed his eyes shut as desire throbbed insistently beneath her wandering hands. "Holly," he groaned. "Watch it."

The sexiest laugh he'd ever heard washed over him. "I plan to do more than just watch."

He thought he'd explode. Survival instinct had him knocking the shower nozzle with his elbow. The cold blast of water on his back gave him a modicum of control.

Holly jumped and squealed, "Jeez."

"You wanted a shower."

"Not a cold one." She wiggled beside him, rubbing the chill bumps on her upper arms. He would have believed it impossible for her pebbled nipples to tighten more, but he enjoyed being wrong.

The water warmed. He caught her waist and dragged her beneath the spray with him, saying a silent thank-you to the cottage caretakers who kept the liquid soap dispenser hanging on the shower wall filled. The unit yielded a palm full of citrus-scented shower gel. Eric slicked it over Holly's shoulders and then turned her face to the wall and massaged more down her spine. His arms encircled her, pulling her lathered back to his front and smoothing his hands over her breasts, belly and the curls between her legs. He refilled his hands with shower gel and stroked her until her slippery bottom gyrating against his erection nearly made him come. Shoving her beneath the spray was his only defense.

She sputtered and turned on him, planting her hands on his chest and backing him toward the shower seat. "Two can play that game, buster."

And then she drove him out of his mind with her soapy, talented hands and deft, persistent touch. She washed his neck, shoulders, back and chest. The slight scrape of her mild calluses as she slicked palms over his body reminded him Holly was no pampered socialite. She worked with her hands, and those hands were quickly arousing him to the breaking point. When she reached for more soap, Eric knew he had to intervene before she washed away what was left of his reasoning power. He snagged the condom bag, broke open the box and withdrew a wrapped package.

Holly reached for it. "Let me."

"No." He ground the words out. "Not this time." He rolled on protection, sat on the bench and tipped his head against the shower wall. He wanted to kiss her again, but he didn't think he could withstand another encounter with those lips. "Come here."

Holly didn't hesitate. Bracing her knees on the seat on either side of him, she straddled his lap and lowered. He gripped her hips and then snagged her gaze. "Slowly."

The slick heat of her teased his tip and then she eased over him a fraction of an inch at a time without breaking eye contact. Her pupils expanded. Her lips parted. Her face flushed. And her breasts rose as he filled her halfway. Her expression of pure hedonistic delight made him clench his muscles and pray for the ability to hold out long enough to pleasure her.

"I can't wait," she whispered before dropping swiftly and taking him completely. She rose and repeated the process. Once. Twice. A third time.

"Stop." He banded his arms around her wet body, mashing soft curves against his hard torso.

"Stop *now?* Are you *crazy?*"

"Trust me on this," he forced out through gritted teeth and

then punched the soap dispenser with his right hand. He lathered her again. The bubbles drifted downward. He traced the path with his fingers, between and then over her breasts, and then he delved into her curls and found the soft button that made her gasp and arch her spine. Water drummed on their heads and shoulders, rinsing away the foam as quickly as he created it until only the puddle of suds where their bodies joined remained.

He captured a nipple in his mouth and Holly squirmed and whimpered, "Eric, please!"

He stroked and suckled, eased her up his shaft and back down again. Deeper. But slowly. Ever. So. Slowly. Each rise and descent shoved him further away from sanity. He trembled with the effort to hold on as Holly writhed impatiently against him. And then she cried out and shuddered. Her internal muscles squeezed him, and Eric's tenuous control snapped. He thrust as deep and fast and hard as he could. The explosions started in his groin and imploded throughout his body like a volley of charges in a building demolition until he slumped like a frameless crumpled heap beneath Holly.

And then all went still in the shower stall except for the echo of labored breathing and patter of cooling water raining down on their sated bodies. Holly sagged against him, her head resting on his shoulder, her quick pants scorching his neck.

He slapped off the water and the humid summer night closed in around him. Damn. The night was warm, but the chill of humiliation doused the heat of passion. "I apologize."

Holly stiffened and lifted her head. "For what?"

She had to ask? "Going too fast."

She leaned back without disconnecting their bodies. "Was it good?"

A bark of self-deprecating laugher shot up his throat. "You couldn't tell? It was so good I lost it like a virgin. You?"

A grin widened her mouth and danced in her eyes. "My

scream didn't give me away? Let me give you a pointer for future reference, Alden. You don't apologize when you've made a woman scream your name."

Eric smiled, truly smiled, in a way Holly had never seen him smile before. He looked relaxed and happy. Something went squishy inside her. It certainly wasn't him. His big hands caressed her bare bottom, stirring ashes that had barely begun to cool, and what should have been soft wasn't. He shifted his hips and she gasped at his renewed vigor.

Oh, boy, could I ever get used to that.

And then it hit her. No, she couldn't. Tomorrow they'd leave the island and forget this ever happened.

No big deal. She could handle it. There was nothing wrong with a sex-only relationship. Guys did it all the time.

Most women don't.

Yeah, but you're not most women. If you were, you'd have been happy in your old pampered life, delegating the dirty work and living the carefree, empty existence of a trust fund baby.

She closed her eyes to hide her turbulent thoughts and opened them again when Eric's teeth grazed the side of her neck with an eroticism that made her heart pump faster.

Okay, so she might have a teensy problem in the future seeing Eric across a crowded room at some stuffy society function and pretending he hadn't given her mind-melting orgasms. But she'd get over it. She had to, or risk everything she'd worked for. And while she wanted more of the magic Eric's very talented hands and generously endowed body promised, she needed a few seconds to get her thoughts straightened out.

She pushed against his shoulders. "You want to carry this upstairs? Your legs must be numb from me straddling them."

"Nothing about me is numb." He punctuated the comment with another breath-stealing upward thrust.

Wow. "I'm a big girl."

"And a perfectly proportioned one." His palms outlined her shape, stopping at her ribs so his thumbs could drag over her nipples. Her stomach tightened.

If he kept saying stuff like that, she was going to forget this was just sex. She punched his shoulder. "Let me up."

Eric released her and Holly found the floor one foot at a time. She didn't feel empty without him inside her, damn it.

Her legs were the numb ones. She wobbled. Eric rose and held her waist until she found her balance. She hugged her arms over her breasts, tried to ignore his gorgeous naked body and focused instead on the pile of sweaty, sandy, crumpled clothing on the floor. Putting them back on held zero appeal.

"There should be some towels in the laundry room." He treated her to a spectacular piece of scenery as he bent over, picked up his pants and fished the house keys out of his pocket. She dug her short nails into her palms and fought the urge to stroke his bottom. Eric straightened and unlocked a second door in the dressing area, one she hadn't noticed before. But then she had been somewhat distracted earlier. He disappeared inside and returned seconds later with one pale gray beach towel hitched around his hips and another extended in his hand.

"Thanks." She quickly looked away from the thick ridge beneath his towel and wrapped herself in the bath sheet. "So…um…"

Boy, was this was awkward. And she had no one but herself to blame. She'd laid the ground rules. It wasn't Eric's fault she was…a little confused. She wanted him. And she didn't. He'd made her feel so amazingly good. And yet he was wrong for her on so many levels.

He lifted her chin until she reluctantly met his gaze. "Holly."

"What?"

"I worry when you don't speak your mind."

For once she didn't want to share her thoughts. Her Miss Smarty-pants defense came to the rescue. "I'm just wondering if you're as good on top as you are on the bottom."

Surprise widened his eyes, and then his pupils expanded and his nostrils flared. A predatory grin stretched across his mouth. "You're about to find out."

Holly didn't want to move, didn't want to wriggle out from under the heavy male arm and calf pinning her to the mattress or leave the warm cocoon of Eric's bed. But the peal of the doorbell meant one of them had to get up and apparently, that someone was her.

Eric lay comatose beside her. No surprise there. A tired smile curved her lips. They'd stayed up half the night making love— having sex—and had already had round four—or was it five?— this morning. Her banker was definitely good in bed. And it didn't bother her one bit that those other women knew it.

Liar.
And he's not your banker.
He is for six more hours.

She eased sideways and stood beside the bed, granting herself five seconds to savor every luscious, rumpled, beard-stubbled inch of him, and then she scanned the floor of his bedroom looking for her clothing. Nada. The bell rang again. She filched the short-sleeved dress shirt he'd worn yesterday from his closet and buttoned it as she jogged down the stairs. The shirttail flopped against her thighs and a draft cooled her bare bottom. Eric's lingering masculine scent surrounded her.

She opened the front door to…no one. A kaleidoscope of brilliant colors drew her gaze to the Welcome mat. She blinked. Flowers in a crystal bowl that sparkled like a prism in the early morning light. Hmm.

"Must be a misdelivery," she muttered. Hoping to catch the delivery person before he departed, she snatched up the arrangement and stepped toward the railing. The Happy Birthday message on the envelope stopped her in her tracks.

Today was *her* birthday. And while many were aware of her

birth date, of those people only Octavia knew Holly was on the island. Tension invaded her muscles. "Damn. Damn. Damn."

And here she stood on the porch in Eric's shirt and nothing else in plain view of any viper with a camera. Wouldn't that make a lovely photo in the Saturday paper? Not.

Clutching the flowers and scanning the landscape for her traitorous friend, Holly backed hastily into the cottage and barged straight into a solid wall of muscle. Strong arms enfolded her and pulled her against the heat of a bare chest. A bristly kiss prickled her neck and spiked her pulse rate.

"Happy Birthday," Eric murmured in her ear in his middle-of-the-night-one-more-time voice.

She spun around. "You know?"

"Why else would I send flowers?"

The flowers weren't from Octavia? Holly thrust the bowl into Eric's arms and plucked the tiny envelope from the foliage and opened it. "Happy 30th. Eric."

She closed her eyes and pressed the card to her chest as emotion rose in her throat. Relief that Octavia might not be here with her intrusive camera mingled with warm fuzzies. Eric had bought her flowers.

Don't make more out of this than there is. He probably sends women flowers all the time. Keep it casual.

"Holly?"

She met his gaze, wrinkled her nose and bumped the door closed with her hip. "I thought they were from Octavia and I freaked a little. How'd you know? About my birthday, I mean."

He'd pulled on navy shorts and nothing else. His dark hair looked exactly as she'd left him. Rumpled and sexy. And the sight of his sinful mouth surrounded by a heavy morning beard left her hot and bothered. She knew how good that stubble felt in certain sensitive places—places that prickled like crazy at the prospect of a return visit.

"You mentioned it last week. I asked Juliana the date."

Juliana. His sister. Her best friend. That was a guilt trip Holly didn't want to take this morning. She stomped on the memory.

Juliana's, Andrea's and Holly's birthdays were only weeks apart. Normally, they celebrated each other's birthdays together, but this year the auction packages had interfered. They'd promised to make up for it once the dates were over. "When did you have time to order flowers?"

"Yesterday while you haggled with the shopkeeper over the best bait to use."

Before they'd decided to sleep together. Her throat tightened. He couldn't do nice things like that or she would have trouble forgetting this interlude.

Who are you kidding? You're already going to have trouble.

"Thank you."

"You're welcome. While you were getting the door, I called the ferry terminal and changed our reservation for the last crossing tonight. Since it's your birthday I thought we'd hang around long enough to do the other things on your list. Bike around the island. Rent that canoe and paddle Bald Head Creek. But first," he lifted a hand and traced a finger along the buttons she'd left open at the top of her borrowed shirt, "I think we need to try my shower."

Heat and desire pinged and popped inside her like kernels in a bag of microwave popcorn. It didn't look as if her craving for Eric was going to be nearly as easy to satisfy as she'd thought.

Playtime over. Eric closed a mental door on the weekend and carried his and Holly's bags down to the golf cart Sunday night.

It was hardly surprising that the muscles between his shoulder blades knotted tighter with each step he descended into the humid night air. He'd been more relaxed this weekend than he'd been since he'd joined the family business and found out about his father's weakness, but now he'd have to pay the price for wasting forty hours during which he should have been preparing for the meeting with the merger negotiation team tomorrow. Baxter Wilson was an SOB to deal with, and he'd be looking for any sign of weakness on Alden Bank's part. It was Eric's job to minimize those weaknesses and play up Alden's assets at the bargaining table.

Behind him the dead-bolt clicked as Holly turned his key in the lock. That's exactly what Eric needed to do. Lock the vault on the attraction between them. Holly had made him forget his priorities.

He glanced over his shoulder in time to see her lift the cooler. All he had to do was look at her and he wanted her again. Work be damned.

He'd let her get too close, but he was not his father. He would never allow a woman to lead him around by the balls. It was time to reestablish the boundaries that he'd ignored. "Leave that, Holly. I'll get it."

She snorted. "Oh, please. Do I look fragile to you?"

No. She looked strong and capable and as sexy as hell in her cut-off shorts and another one of those built-in-bra tank tops. She had a fresh dusting of freckles across the bridge of her nose and over her shoulders because they hadn't been as diligent with sunscreen as they should have been during their afternoon outdoors.

He dumped the bags in the cart, met her at the bottom of the steps and took the cooler from her. She smiled up at him, and her scent drifted to him on the night air. He set his jaw against the temptation to steal one more cherry lip balm-flavored kiss, because if he did he might end up dragging her back upstairs, or God forbid, back into the shower behind the house. Electricity crackled through him at the memory of their shared shower. Eric fortified his resolve to ignore the attraction between them from this moment forward and headed for the cart.

"Are you sure we don't need to clean the cottage?" Holly strolled down the driveway and then turned to take another look at the house. If it weren't dark, no doubt she'd pull out her camera. She'd taken pictures all over the island claiming she needed the photographs for work, but work didn't put a blinding smile on your face like the one she'd worn today. "We should at least strip the bed and take out the trash."

"The housekeeping crew will take care of it." This idyllic interlude had to end. Now. He had to get back to the real world before it was too late.

If they went back inside, he might not have the strength to leave without making love to her again, and if they made love again, he might not want to let her go. He'd had the best sex of his life this weekend, but there wasn't a woman in Wilmington less suited to being a banker's wife than Holly Prescott.

He needed a woman who knew the importance of powerful connections, one who knew how to keep a lid on her emotions. Holly wasn't just outspoken. Her expressive eyes revealed too much. No wonder she'd hated the Caliber Club crowd. The members had probably read her thoughts and eaten her alive.

He settled on the bench seat of the cart and glanced at his watch. They were cutting it close. "Holly, we need to leave now to make the ferry."

"Right." She took a few steps in his direction and stopped. "Um, Eric, we might have a problem."

"What?" Impatience and frustration made his tone sharp.

The hurt look on her face hit him square in the chest. She folded her arms. "Tire's flat, Einstein."

He launched from the vehicle and circled to her side. The front passenger side tire bulged on the ground beneath the rim. "Damn."

"Do you have a pump or an air compressor or a spare?" Practical Holly. She saw a problem and tried to fix it. He admired a woman who didn't wait for a man to do her dirty work.

"No." At home he would never be as lax with his car, but here on the island he left the trivial details to the maintenance crews. He wasn't here often enough to need tools.

He raked a hand through his hair. If they didn't leave now,

they'd miss the ferry—the last ferry off the island tonight. He pulled out his cell phone. "I'll call for the shuttle service."

The operator picked up. Eric explained the problem.

"I'm sorry, Mr. Alden. The shuttle is booked for tonight. By the time we have one available you'll have missed the ferry."

Beside him Holly stretched, lifting her arms above her head. She leaned left, then right. The moonlight caught a sliver of pale skin between her tank and shorts, teasing him until his mouth dried. He turned his back on the tempting sight. "I have to get off the island tonight."

"I'm sorry sir. Unless you can call a neighbor to give you a ride, then I can't help you."

He ground his teeth in frustration. He didn't come to the island often enough to know his neighbors. The bikes had already been picked up and the terminal was too far to walk. He and Holly were stranded. He cursed his accelerating pulse. "Then change our reservation to the first ferry in the morning and have the shuttle service pick us up."

"Yes, sir. I'll take care of that for you. The shuttle will pick you up at 5:45."

"Thank you." He snapped the phone shut and tried to deny the anticipation percolating through him like a straight shot of caffeine.

Holly rocked back on her heels. "We're stuck until tomorrow?"

"Yes," he snapped and silently cursed. If he had any sense at all, he'd send Holly to a guest room.

"Well, don't hurt yourself jumping for joy over another night with me."

Holly's sarcasm scraped his raw nerves. That was the problem. Part of him was elated by the prospect of another night in Holly's arms, in the slick glove of her body. And that was bad. The strength of his need for her made him weak.

"You may set your own hours, but I have an important meeting tomorrow." He couldn't afford to lose his edge in the merger negotiations, and he needed to be at the office early in the morning to bone up on details.

She planted her fists on her hips. "Eric, I may not have a staff that relies on me, but I have to work tomorrow, too. I have contracts to fulfill, and I have my Monday class to teach. I know staying another night is inconvenient, but barking and growling at me and giving yourself an ulcer over a few lost hours when you would have been asleep anyway isn't a good idea. We'll still be home in time to make it to work before nine."

"I need to call Tina and tell her I'll be delayed again and see if she can handle the dogs until I get home."

You're an egocentric jerk, Alden. You considered no one but yourself. His jaw shifted. "I'd forgotten your dogs."

"They haven't forgotten you. Thanks to the pictures in the banks, four of them have new homes with loving families and all the puppies are promised as soon as they're weaned."

Holly dropped to her knees beside the tire. "Hey, look at this. The valve cap is off and lying beside the tire. My guess is someone deliberately let the air out. Three guesses who."

Eric expelled an angry breath. "Jenkins."

"You're good." Holly straightened. "So have we reached the point where I can plead justifiable homicide yet? Because I really want to wring her neck."

His lips twitched. How did Holly do it? She made him smile when he was seriously irritated. It wasn't the first time. But it needed to be the last. He had his future mapped out and it didn't include a woman who knew how to knock him off his career track.

He shouldered their overnight bags and headed back up the stairs, mentally ticking off fingers as he climbed. If he counted yesterday morning on the beach, the midday hike on the nature trail, last night's trip to the ice cream parlor, today's bike ride and canoe trip as dates five through nine, then he only had to get through two more outings with Holly before he could walk away.

And that last date couldn't come too soon.

Nine

The studio door opened behind Holly fifteen minutes before her students were due to arrive. "Is it safe to come in?"

Octavia. Holly stiffened and carefully laid the sheet of water glass on the work surface before she faced the door. "Traitor."

"I'm trying to help you, Holly."

Holly choked a sound of disbelief. "By making a fool of me?"

"No, by showing the world and *you*, my blind friend, that you're a beautiful, desirable woman who deserves better than the schmucks you usually end up with." When Octavia got riled, her dark eyes sparked flames and her coffee-colored skin flushed as they were now.

"Oh, puh-leeze."

"Did you or did you not spend the weekend in hunky Eric Alden's bed?" Octavia held up a hand before Holly could answer. "Before you feed me a bunch of baloney, you need to know that the hickey on your neck is telling its own story."

Holly fought the urge to rip off her heavy leather gloves and cover the offending spot that, judging by the burn, had to be flashing like a red streetlight.

"How does spying on me and printing shocking photos and sexual innuendo in your article make me look good? It makes me look like a tramp to everyone except my mother. *She* thinks that seeing my body fused to Eric's means I'm over my 'little rebellion' and ready to meekly return to the family fold because I'm finally dating what she considers an 'acceptable man.' She left three messages on my phone this weekend telling me how proud she was of me for settling down. Little did she know I was boinking her banker when she left those messages. And if that's not annoying enough, she's planning a couples' dinner party for Eric and me and his parents."

"Holly, you've practically cut off all ties with your family."

"With good reason. They consider me an embarrassment and a failure."

"Then prove them wrong by showing them how good you are at what you do instead of hiding your head in the sand. It's time to stop being the Queen of Denial. This is your heritage, and you'll only ever have one family."

"Good. Because one's more than I can handle." She flipped on the overhead ventilation and the fan roared to life. "Do you intend to work today or just yammer nonsense?"

"When I was fourteen, my parents were murdered on our own front porch in a gang drive-by shooting."

The bald statement stopped Holly mid-step. Shock and sympathy rippled through her. "I didn't know. I'm sorry."

"Yeah, well, here's the deal. I was an angry and resentful kid who hated my parents and considered them the dumbest creatures on Earth…until they were taken from me. I was pouting in my room after another screaming match when I heard the gunfire. By the time I reached Mom and Dad, it was too late. They were gone. After that, I was shuffled from one resentful relative to another. It didn't take me long to figure out how lucky I'd been to have had parents who cared about me and wanted the best for me. Like yours do for you, Holly."

Holly's anger toward Octavia deflated like a balloon. She hid the sympathy in her eyes by aligning glass-cutting tools on one of the six tables set up for her students. "Octavia, it's not the same."

"It is. There's animosity between you and your folks. Make your peace while you still can." Octavia crossed the workspace to the rack where Holly kept lightweight coveralls for her students and pulled a jumpsuit like the one Holly wore over her shorts and T-shirt. Protective clothing was a must when working with glass, leaded solder and corrosive flux. "And for your information, my articles are not fiction. The chemistry between you and Eric is so strong it registers on the Richter scale."

"Yeah, well it did before he went all pinstripe on me," Holly blurted and then immediately regretted it.

"What do you mean?"

Holly hesitated. "When exactly were you on the island and how much did you see?"

"Raymond and I came over Sunday afternoon in time to see you two return on the bikes and disappear into the cottage, fused together like copper foil and solder. We left on the last ferry Sunday night—thanks to two people who missed their reservation and freed up seats." She winked.

Holly tried to tamp down the sparks ignited by the memories of her time on the island, but she didn't have much luck. They smoldered low in her belly like the embers of a forest fire waiting for a whiff of breeze to reignite them into flames that could wreak more devastation.

From the first time she and Eric had made love—*had sex*—Saturday night until pack-up time Sunday evening, Eric had dedicated himself to relaxing as diligently as he worked at his job. She fought a smile because it had clearly been hard work for him to unwind. It shouldn't be. Everyone needed balance in their lives. Work and play.

Who would balance Eric when she was no longer part of his life? She shook off the question. *Not your problem.*

"Raymond? Is that your tall, skinny photographer sidekick?"

Octavia ducked her head, but not before Holly saw her blush. Interesting. Holly would have to dig into the Octavia-Raymond relationship once she wasn't in knots over Eric. "Yes."

"And you and Raymond are responsible for the flat tire?"

Octavia shrugged. "Guilty. I thought you two need more time together."

"Why? This relationship is temporary."

"Maybe it doesn't have to be. Maybe Eric is the bridge between you and your family. And it's clear as glass that you guys are into each other."

Holly snorted. "I thought you were an investigative reporter hiding behind that lifestyles byline. How could you possibly get your facts so wrong?"

"I don't think they are. Now explain what you meant by him going pinstripe."

Holly hesitated. She'd known Octavia for years, and until this auction ordeal she'd trusted her. She needed to talk to someone. Juliana was out because she was Eric's sister, and Holly hated to put Andrea in the middle. "Off the record?"

"Off the record," Octavia agreed.

"Eric was with me Sunday night, but he wasn't *with me*. If you know what I mean. We shared a bed and our bodies and the sex was top-notch." She paused. "Well, it would have been top-notch if I didn't have Saturday night for comparison. But it was as if…as if he'd already turned back into Eric Alden, VP of Alden Bank. He held something back. He wasn't the same guy I was with before the flat tire."

Octavia pursed her lips. "Was he angry at me for stranding you and taking it out on you?"

Holly shook her head. "I think he was having delayed morning-after regrets, an 'Oh, hell, what have I done?' moment."

"Holly, you don't know that for a fact."

"I don't need him to spell it out. I received his give-me-some-space message when he barely grunted hello this morning." The ferry and car rides home had been silent and tense. Eric hadn't been rude. Far from it. He'd been solicitous. Too solicitous. The kind of solicitous that you'd be with your great-grandmother. By the time he dropped her off this morning she'd been so on edge she wanted to scream.

"Isn't Alden's bank in the middle of a big merger? Maybe his mind was on work."

"Yeah, Juliana's wrapped up in the merger, too, but I can't believe that's all there was to Eric's abrupt change."

"Well, my friend, if you really care, and I think you do, then you'll have to pry his reasons out of him, and you have several more dates to get your answers. Don't walk away as easily as you did from your family."

Holly bristled. Admitting she could never be the daughter her parents wanted had been hard. Incredibly hard. "It wasn't easy."

"But mending fences can be. Make peace with your family, Holly, and while you're at it, give Eric a chance."

Luck finally gave Holly a break. Her other students arrived, cutting her tête-à-tête with Octavia short.

Unfortunately, luck couldn't do anything toward blocking Holly's tormenting thoughts—one in particular. She had a sinking feeling she was in too deep with a man she could never have.

The meeting was going to hell, and if Eric didn't get out of here soon, he was going to tell Baxter Wilson to go screw himself.

Holly wouldn't hesitate to take the pompous windbag down a notch.

Neither would he. Eric laid his pen on the table. "Your demands are ridiculous and there is no way in hell that Alden's will settle for a forty-percent share in the merged company."

His mother's head whipped toward him, shock and displeasure over his aberrant outburst clear in her eyes. She stood. "Gentlemen, it's time to break for lunch. We'll resume our discussion this afternoon."

Eric shot to his feet, crossed the room and opened the boardroom door. The moment he did, his administrative assistant sprang from her desk and hustled over to hand him a pink message slip. Eric scanned the note and crushed it in his hand. The P.I. had found Lyle Lewis.

He had to call Holly and then they needed to confront the SOB who'd taken advantage of her. The sooner the better. By next week Eric's obligations to Holly would be fulfilled and he wouldn't have to see her again. He ignored the sudden tightness in his chest, pivoted and faced his mother. "I'll be out of the office this afternoon."

"Excuse us a moment, Baxter." She indicated Eric follow her across the balcony and into her office and then closed the door. "What is the meaning of this? You've been surly and rude to Baxter all morning. And now you're bowing out of the negotiations? It looks bad enough for Juliana to miss today's meeting. You cannot do the same."

"Wilson isn't negotiating, Mother. He's scalping. And if you agree to his demands, then you're a fool." What in the hell was wrong with him? As a rule he enjoyed tough negotiations, but today he was happy to have an excuse to walk away from the table.

His mother stiffened. "I have no intention of coming in second place. Baxter is posturing. He knows Alden's is the stronger of the two banks, and you will get back in there after lunch and prove it with your data."

"I have a personal matter to attend to."

His mother's mouth pinched. "The negotiations come first."

Correction. His mother's ambition to head up the merged banks came first. And until recently Eric had felt just as strongly on the issue. "Pull our offer off the table, Mother."

"Are you out of your mind? We need this merger if we're to become the largest privately owned bank in the southeast."

"Let Baxter know we're willing to walk away."

"But we're not. What if he calls our bluff?"

"He won't. He needs the merger more than we do." Eric checked his watch. Would Holly be at home?

"I'm not willing to risk it."

"Then you're on your own this afternoon. The data is on my laptop. You're welcome to it." He reached for the doorknob.

"This has something to do with that Prescott girl, doesn't it?"

"That's none of your business."

"It is if she costs us this merger. I wouldn't be surprised if that bohemian wasn't also behind your sister's refusal to buy Wallace Wilson at the auction. She is a bad influence on Juliana."

"Mother, I suggest you keep your erroneous opinions to yourself."

"Do not let her pull you down to her level."

Anger burned up his spine. His mother wasn't saying anything he hadn't heard others say before—Holly's own family, in fact—but he couldn't stomach it today. "If you think Holly is beneath you, then you are mistaken. Don't. Cross. Me. On. This."

Eric yanked open the door and stalked out.

Thirty minutes later, he pulled up in Holly's driveway and parked behind her Jeep. He'd tried phoning, but she wasn't answering any of the numbers he had for her. He rapped on the front door, but no one answered.

Her car was here and as far as he knew, she didn't own a second vehicle. That meant Holly had to be here. He considered checking the kennel, but the sound of country music led him along the wraparound porch. He found an attached building behind the house. An intricate stained glass sign hanging from a post proclaimed it Rainbow Glass. Flower beds flanked the slate walkway and surrounded a separate gravel parking area. He hadn't expected such a professional setup. That's what he got for letting her brothers' derogatory comments about Holly's hobby influence his opinions instead of getting the facts.

Eric opened the door and stepped inside. A tune about the wrong truck parked in a woman's driveway filled the air. At the back table, someone in baggy overalls and a welding helmet soldered two metal rods together. Eric couldn't tell if the body beneath the shapeless clothing and concealing helmet was male or female. He scanned the room searching for Holly. His gaze roved over completed stained glass pieces hanging along the walls. They came in all shapes and sizes and ranged from elaborate to simple. Holly definitely had talent, and while he wanted to examine the work more carefully, right now he needed to find Holly and then Lewis. Perhaps the welder knew how he could reach Holly.

He shielded his eyes from the glare of the welding torch, stepped deeper into the studio and called out, "Excuse me."

The welder's head lifted abruptly. The torch went out. A heavy work-gloved hand raised the metal and glass mask. Holly. Surprise, followed by desire, flashed through Eric. How long would it take before his engines didn't rev at the sight of her?

"Uh…hi." She set the torch aside and pulled the helmet off her head. Sweat slicked her hair to her skull. She yanked off her gloves and raked her fingers through the damp strands. "Why are you here? We've finished our dates for this week."

He'd spent the better part of the last two nights making love with her when he should have been sleeping, and yet he'd never felt more alert. "The P.I. located Lyle Lewis."

Her toffee-colored eyes widened and her lips parted. "And Wes called you?"

"Yes."

She frowned. "Why?"

"I told him to keep me informed. Lewis is in Raleigh. If we leave now, we can be there in two hours."

"We?"

"I'm driving."

She folded her arms and set her chin at what he'd come to recognize as her argumentative angle. "I thought you had an important meeting today."

"I did. But this needs to be settled, and I don't want you confronting him alone."

She crossed the room, stopped in front of him and extended her palm. "Hand over the address. I can do this and you can go back to work."

"No."

"No?"

"He took advantage of you, Holly. I intend to make sure that doesn't happen again." His accompanying her had nothing to do with wanting to punch the dumb ass who'd been stupid enough to walk away from Holly's love and thoughtless enough to leave her in a financially vulnerable situation. Eric considered resolving the matter penance for betraying his friendship with her brothers and for using Holly. No, he hadn't taken her money the way Lewis had, but he had selfishly used her body. And wanted to do so again. He crushed the unwanted thought beneath his wingtips.

"Not necessary. Eric, I'm a big girl. I can fight my own battles. Just give me the address."

"I owe it to Sam and Tony. I would expect them to do the same for Juliana."

She scoffed. "Your sister is too sensible to ever need bailing out."

True. Juliana was cautious and reliable. At least she had been until she'd bought a washed-up country music singer bar owner at the auction. His mother was right to be concerned that Juliana's purchase might jeopardize the merger. The incident had certainly soured Baxter Wilson's mood and made the pompous banker more cantankerous than usual. But his sister wasn't the issue at present. "How quickly can you be ready to leave?"

"When would we get back?"

"That depends on how soon we locate Lewis, but my intention is to return tonight."

She chewed on her bottom lip. Eric's mouth watered. Would she taste like cherry lip balm today?

You're not going to find out. Kisses are over. Dates will be strictly hands off from this moment forward.

But the resolution didn't stop his blood from pooling behind his fly when Holly reached for the zipper of her overalls and lowered it to her crotch.

Knowing he would never have her again didn't stop his groin from throbbing when she stepped out of her boots and shimmied the baggy worksuit over her shoulders and hips to reveal a skimpy tank top and another pair of disreputable cut-off shorts. Her moves were as erotic as a striptease, and he didn't think she had a clue about her power over him. He hoped not.

Swearing their affair was over didn't stop him from devouring her hourglass shape with his eyes. She turned her back to hang up her discarded clothing and bent over to shelve her boots, presenting him with the delicious curve of her backside. He clenched his teeth hard enough to risk a dental emergency and fisted his hands against the urge to cup those sweet cheeks. One weekend hadn't been enough to do more than whet his appetite. He still wanted her. But he couldn't have her.

"I need to call Tina to be on standby just in case we don't make it back in time to feed the dogs," Holly said from her bent over position and then she straightened and turned before he could tamp his desire. Her gaze met his and her breath caught. She swallowed and wet her lips. The thin fabric of her top peaked over beading nipples.

"Eric?" she whispered.

He took a mental and physical step back, jerking his gaze away from temptation and landing on a complicated floral design window.

"Do you keep a portfolio of your work?" His voice came out as raspy as an obscene phone caller's.

"You betcha. I have to have something to show to prospective clients." She dragged a large folder from between two file cabinets and then motioned for him to follow her into the house through the back door. They passed through a mud room, the kitchen and into her den. She laid the folder on the coffee table and pointed at the sofa. "Park it right there. You can look at my work while I change clothes and pack a bag—just in case."

His mind flashed back to the night when she'd changed clothes after the auction and he'd seen her lush curves naked for the first time. His mouth watered and his pulse quickened.

"We'll make it back." Come hell or high water. The alternative meant spending another night with Holly. His heart thumped in frustration.

Not anticipation.

Or so he assured himself.

"Do you still love him?" Eric asked from the driver's seat.

Holly ripped her gaze from the brick apartment building near the university campus where supposedly Lyle Lewis had secreted himself and focused on Eric. A nerve twitched in the sharp angle of his jaw. His eyes looked dark, fathomless, giving away nothing of his thoughts.

Did she still have feelings for Lyle? Or had she worried more about the missing money than the missing man since he'd disappeared? Coming on the heels of her weekend with Eric, Holly couldn't make heads or tails of her jumbled emotions. She'd certainly never been as physically aware of Lyle, or any man for that matter, as she was of Eric. "I don't know."

Eric held her gaze for several seconds and then jerked an abrupt nod. "Let's go."

Holly accompanied him to the ground floor apartment. She was an emotionally and physically strong woman. So why was she glad to have Eric by her side? She stopped him with a hand on his arm a yard shy of the door. "Eric, I knew when I invested in Lyle's project that there was a risk of failure. So if the money is gone…it's gone. And I just have to accept I screwed up. Again."

His hard expression softened. He lifted a hand toward her face, hesitated and then dropped it before making contact. She wanted him to touch her. Yearned for it. Ached for it.

That couldn't be good.

"Holly, if Lewis had walked into the bank and presented the detailed business plan he gave to you, then I would have approved the loan, too."

She didn't know which surprised her more: Eric's reassurance that she hadn't been a fool or his revelation that he'd seen her paperwork. "Let me guess. Wes gave you copies of my files."

"Yes. I wanted to know if you had any legal recourse."

Should she be peeved or pleased that Eric cared enough to investigate the details of the transaction? Her father and brothers would have condemned her without delving deeper. Before she could make up her mind, Eric rapped hard on the door.

Seconds later, the panel opened and there stood Lyle, her former lover. Holly stared, waiting for some rush of emotion, but there was none. Her heart didn't slam against her ribs the way it had when she'd looked up from the lead cames she'd been welding and spotted Eric in her studio. Instead, she looked at the man she'd once cared about and noticed that he wasn't as tall as she remembered. His jaw wasn't as strong, nor his shoulders as broad. He was still cute in a geeky kind of way, but being near him didn't raise her temperature. And he looked young—much younger than the twenty-five she knew him to be.

Had she robbed the cradle or what? "Hi, Lyle."

Surprise and genuine pleasure lit his eyes before he grabbed her and hugged her. "Holly. It's great to see you."

She stood in embrace and felt…nothing. Wasn't that weird? Hadn't she considered a future with him? Maybe even marriage? He held her at arm's length, glancing at Eric and then back at her. "But why are you here? How could you have heard the good news already? Did the attorney call you? I asked him to wait."

"What good news?" Holly asked in confusion.

Eric's hand lifted to the small of Holly's back. Static electricity sparked from his fingertips, skipped through her middle and out to her extremities.

Lyle observed the gesture and studied Eric. "Who are you?"

"Eric Alden. Ms. Prescott's financial advisor."

Holly opened her mouth to dispute his claim, but bit back the words. Eric hadn't touched her since leaving the island. And now he was. Was he staking a claim? No way. So why did the thought flush her with excitement? She and Eric were not and never could be an item.

He was just showing a united front. Right?

"Holly? Did you think I wasn't going to…that I'd cheat you?" The hurt on Lyle's face and in his voice reminded her why she'd become involved with him in the first place. Lyle needed someone to believe in him—a sentiment with which she was all too familiar. Come to think of it, that was probably why she'd chosen each of her boyfriends.

Hmm. Her date selection criteria needed a serious overhaul.

"I didn't know what to think, Lyle. You left with fifty thousand dollars, no goodbye and no forwarding address. And you haven't called in thirteen months. I had to hire a P.I. to find you."

"Has it been that long? I guess that does look bad, but I've been caught up in the project, and I didn't want to call until I could prove your trust in me wasn't misplaced. Come in." He waved them into a small, dimly lit apartment and down a narrow hall. He stopped in a cramped kitchen and lifted a stack of papers from the table. "I've spent most of my nights perfecting the project and my days trying to find a buyer. I worked a deal with the chair of the university's mechanical engineering department to let me to use tools in their workshop.

"Getting the patent took longer than I expected, but it finally came through last month. I've been negotiating the sale of my invention, but I wanted to wait until I'd signed the contract before telling you. My lawyer has looked over it and says it's a good deal."

"May I?" Eric extended a hand.

Lyle hesitated and when Holly nodded handed over the document. She should read the contract herself, but at the moment her train of thought seemed to be a little…derailed.

She couldn't help comparing the men while Eric read the contract. Lyle was a soft-spoken dreamer who'd talked endlessly about his inventions, his plans and his future. Holly had been excited for him, and she'd wanted to support him and help make his dreams come true. Two things her family had been unwilling to do for her back when she'd wanted to leave the Caliber Club and open Rainbow Glass. If not for inheriting the farm and the first of several trust fund payments on her twenty-first birthday, she never would have been able to quit her job to pursue her craft and open her business after l-o-n-g miserable months working at the club.

Eric, on the other hand was a confident overachiever she just *wanted*. Period. He rarely talked about his work. She suspected he internalized way too much, and somebody needed to teach him how to relax. But on several occasions he'd quizzed her about stained glass, and each time he'd listened to her responses—something her family seemed disinclined to do. They were too busy dismissing her livelihood as a quaint hobby.

Being with Eric made her feel good about herself and her work, and when she was with him she didn't feel like a misfit. She felt talented, capable and desirable.

Uh-oh. You're treading dangerous ground, girl. Keep it up and before you know it, you'll be falling in love with him.

Her stomach burned like a blowtorch. Was she falling for

Eric? No. No. *Please* no. Even if he asked her to—and he hadn't—she couldn't go back to that world. She'd be better off dating her string of losers than reverting to being the loser. And she'd rather lose fifty grand to Lyle than lose her heart to a man who would only shatter it like a pane of glass.

She stared at Eric, her stomach churning and burning. Their gazes locked, but his banker's face gave nothing away. "You've earned an exceptional return on your investment."

She blinked, dragging her thoughts back from the edge of disaster to the present. "Huh?"

"Your initial share will be a million before taxes."

Holly gulped, glanced at a beaming Lyle and then back at Eric. "A million *dollars*? No more money woes?"

"No." Approval briefly warmed Eric's eyes and then his banker's mask fell back into place and he turned to Lyle. He reached inside his coat pocket, extracted a business card from his wallet and offered it to Lyle. "My attorney has copies of the agreements you and Ms. Prescott have already signed. He is willing to take whatever steps necessary to enforce them and to make certain Ms. Prescott gets the agreed-upon compensation. Please have copies of all the current contracts forwarded to him at this address. And I suggest, Mr. Lewis, that you keep Ms. Prescott, your principal investor, abreast of any future developments or relocations, or you'll be in violation of your agreement and we'll file a lien against you."

"Y-yes, sir." Lyle looked totally intimidated by Eric, and who could blame him? Eric had gone pinstripe again and when he did that he was more daunting that a Marine drill sergeant. Lyle's widened and worried eyes sought Holly's. "Uh, Holly, can I talk to you a minute? Alone?"

"Sure. Eric, could you wait for me in the car?"

Eric's chin lifted a notch and his shoulders squared. She thought he'd refuse. Several seconds ticked past, and then he abruptly pivoted and left them.

Lyle waited until the door clicked shut. "Thanks for believing in me, Holly. I'm sorry I didn't keep in touch. I just forget everything when I'm lost in a project."

"I understand and you're welcome." She stared at Lyle, and he stared back. An incredibly awkward silence yawned between them. What did you say to a man you no longer loved? "Thanks for the memories" just didn't cut it. Wanting to escape, Holly eyed the door.

Lyle's gaze followed hers. "I guess I've been replaced. Your 'financial advisor' seems pretty territorial."

Denial sprung to the tip of her tongue. Eric territorial? No way. And she didn't want him to be. Did she? Nah.

Lyle laid a hand on her shoulder. "It's okay, Holly. What we had was good, but I always knew you deserved better than an inventor whose income and attention span are hit-and-miss at best. You're a caretaker. I'm glad you finally found a guy who can take care of you."

"Take care of me!" Her anti-Cinderella psyche rejected the notion. She'd never believed in fairy tales, never believed in waiting for a guy to ride to her rescue—mainly because they never showed up. And if they did, there'd be strings attached. She'd learned the hard way to count on herself and no one else. "I can take care of myself."

"I know you can, but sometimes it's nice to have someone to lean on."

"No thanks." She knew what happened when the pillar of support was yanked away. "And you're wrong—dead wrong—about Eric and me."

Ten

Walking out the door and leaving Holly with her lover was the hardest thing Eric had ever done.

Harder than standing in front of four hundred wedding guests while Priscilla screeched her emasculating insults loud enough for everyone within a five-mile radius of the church to hear.

Harder than learning his father was a mindless puppet.

The late afternoon sun beat down on his head while he paced beside the Corvette. Sweat dotted his upper lip and trickled down his spine. He peeled off his suit coat and tossed it in the car.

Why was leaving Holly with Lewis so hard?

Surely Eric hadn't been foolish enough to become attached to her. But why else would he have acted like an ass, thrown his weight around and issued threats—threats he fully intended to back up should the need arise? Loyalty to her brothers? No, dammit. Because he wanted to put his fist through something.

How could Lyle Lewis forget Holly for thirteen *months?* Eric couldn't keep her out of his head for thirteen minutes—all the more reason to get the dates over with and walk away.

Two dates. They could knock another one out tonight with dinner on the way home. And then there'd only be one. The thought brought no relief from his inner turmoil.

Holly exited the apartment with Lewis on her heels. She paused on the doorstep and turned to hug the man who'd so easily forgotten her. Lewis kissed her and Eric's gut burned. The two of them separated, shared a few words and a lingering look.

Eric clenched his fists. Holly Prescott was not and never would be his. He had no right to feel possessive. But he did.

He circled the car and yanked open the passenger door before the urge to damage Lewis's face overcame him. Eric worked out with a punching bag every morning, but despite that he'd never been a violent man, never been in a fistfight. His reputation depended on him maintaining control, but if Holly didn't get in the damned car soon, he'd lose his tenuous hold on civility.

Finally, Holly approached. The need to drag her close and wipe the other man's taste from her lips with his own mouth swelled inside Eric. With colossal effort he clamped down on the urge.

Jealous.

The word pierced his grey matter as he circled the Corvette. He repelled it but it plunged right back in.

My God. Was he jealous?

He sucked air into his lungs and considered the possibility. He couldn't be jealous, because jealousy implied an attachment he refused to allow himself. He lived his life by reason not emotion. He wouldn't have it any other way. Otherwise he'd end up like his father, a weak yes-man.

He could not afford to get emotionally involved with Holly. His ridiculous fascination with her had to end. Immediately. The question was, how did he evict her from his head? He pointed the car toward the highway and focused on keeping it between the lines while his thoughts spun out of control.

"Could we stop for food somewhere? I missed lunch and I'm starving."

Holly's question penetrated his ruminations. "Yes."

He took the next exit and pulled into a restaurant parking lot at random.

Holly observed him from under copper-tipped lashes. "Not your usual style, Alden."

"No, but it's yours."

"If by that you mean good food and a casual atmosphere, then yes."

He followed her inside and sat across the booth from her at a table beside the window. He ordered the daily special the waitress suggested. Whatever he ate would likely taste like paper anyway. He looked out the window straight into the front entrance of a hotel no more than thirty yards away.

Holly. Hotel. Two words that had no business occupying the same brain simultaneously. And yet he couldn't shake the idea. No matter how hard he tried to focus on the brightly lit, family-oriented restaurant, the hotel pulled his gaze like a high-powered magnet draws metal filings.

"Eric," Holly reached across the table, caught his jaw in her fingers and turned him to face her. "If you keep looking at me like that and then at the hotel I'm going to have to jog over there and ask them if they rent rooms by the hour."

Her impudent candor didn't shock him nearly as easily as it once had. His gaze melded with hers and arousal pulsed through his body. Her touch burned his skin. In seconds he was as hard as the steel pedestal supporting the table between them.

"Holly—"

She released his jaw, held up her hands and leaned back. "I know. Edit my thoughts."

No, don't. He was beginning to like her wayward mouth. It kept him on his toes. But admiring her candor, her vitality and her generosity was a path strewn with land mines. Before he could pry a reply out of his clearly demented mind, the waitress arrived, deposited their salads and drinks, and then left.

Holly lifted her fork, toyed with it a few seconds before meeting his gaze. "Since we can't discuss what each of us is really thinking about, tell me why the merger between Alden's and Wilson's is a good thing. From everything Juliana has said, working with Baxter Wilson on a regular basis sounds like a surefire way to increase your headaches."

He had to admire Holly for laying her cards on the table and then giving him something else to focus on besides certain disaster—a quickie in the hotel next door. "The merger will bring both power and prestige."

"And power and prestige are that important?"

"They're the axis on which the world rotates."

She lowered her fork. "That's why you were going to marry Priscilla. Not because you loved her or wanted to be with her, but because of the power the merger would bring."

He hated admitting it now. It made him sound callous and mercenary. "Yes."

"That's sad, Eric. Because once the trappings of money are stripped away and it's just the two of you naked in bed, you should like and respect the person you're with."

He conceded the point with a nod. Marrying Priscilla would have been a mistake not because she'd turned into a vindictive witch when she found out he hadn't scheduled the months-long world tour for their honeymoon that she'd demanded, but because he deserved better and so did she. The only thing they'd had going for them was good sex, and in comparison to making love with Holly even that hadn't been all that great.

Holly toyed with a cherry tomato. "Do you really believe he who dies with the most wins? Because what happens if the money goes before you do? You have to like the person you've become if you're going to have any chance of starting over."

A voyage Holly had made successfully already. His admiration of her climbed another notch, and even though he knew he shouldn't touch her again he couldn't stop himself. He reached across the table and covered her hand with his. "You're right. But please, no more references to getting naked."

She grinned, alleviating the negative atmosphere. The rest of dinner passed without incident, but even though she drilled him on the potential pitfalls of the merger, proving her business degree hadn't been wasted, Eric remained conscious of every pass of Holly's pink tongue over her lips, the rise and fall of her breasts beneath her thin shirt and the building next door and the two hundred or so beds it contained. How he carried on coherent conversation he didn't know.

He'd never wanted a woman with this all-consuming desire. And that made it all the more treacherous, all the more imperative that he end this relationship as soon as possible.

They lingered over the surprisingly delicious meal, dessert and then coffee. Considering he needed to get home, call his mother and find out how—*if*—the afternoon's negotiations had progressed, Eric found himself disinclined to get back on the interstate and even more reluctant to say good-night to Holly.

One date left, and then his obligations to her would be satisfied. He didn't even have to worry about her financial situation because her investment had paid off handsomely, and his lawyer would make sure she was remunerated. Where was the joy his imminent freedom should bring?

Holly pushed aside her empty coffee cup, propped her elbows on the table and rested her chin on her linked fingers. "Do you ever wonder if the sex between us is so good because we're totally wrong for each other?"

Blindsided by the question, he swallowed. Hard. Would he never be able to anticipate the way her mind worked? The woman kept him perpetually off balance. "*Good?*"

Her eyes sparkled with laughter at his insulted tone. "Phenomenal then, if you insist on an ego-stroking. Do you think we can get through another date without ending up in bed together? Because I gotta tell you, Eric, if you were telekinetic, a room key would have flown across the parking lot and landed in your hand already." She folded her napkin and placed it on the table. "Or am I reading you wrong?"

Why deny the obvious? There was enough fire in his gut to launch him to the hotel like a rocket without his feet ever touching the asphalt. Eventually, that fire would go out, but apparently, not tonight. "You're not."

Honest. Intelligent. Beautiful. Educated. What else could a man ask for in a lover? Remembering the reasons why Holly was not banker's wife material became more difficult with each passing second.

She tilted her head and waggled her eyebrows. The naughty gleam in her eyes had him bracing himself. "So whatdaya say? What happens in Raleigh stays in Raleigh?"

"Holly—" He bit off his protest and fisted his hands. Who was he trying to fool? He wanted her. Hell, he ached for her. And soon he'd have to say goodbye. Why not enjoy the time they had left? And in the process, maybe he could quench his thirst for this full-bodied redhead. "Absolutely."

Why did this feel like goodbye?

And why did that trouble her?

Holly wanted Eric to hurry, to vanquish the ache in her belly and breasts. And keep it gone. But he lingered over every kiss, every touch, as he removed her clothing in the shadowy hotel room lit only by a trickle of sunlight leaking through a gap in the closed curtains.

Eric's fingers traced her spine and she shivered. His tongue laved the hollow beneath her ear and then his big hands cradled her breasts and thumbed the tight tips, making her bite her lip on the whimper plowing its way up her throat.

She didn't want to want him like this, didn't want to be hypersensitive to the hot touch of his hands, his mouth, his tongue. They'd made love—*had sex*—often enough over the weekend that she could no longer blame her over-the-top response on her extended celibacy stint. The novelty should have worn off by now. But it hadn't. Not even close.

She blinked in an effort to clear the sensual fog enfolding her in a total whiteout and realized, as his fingers parted her curls with unerring accuracy, that she was completely naked and covered in goose bumps and he was completely not.

"Um, Eric, one of us is overdressed."

He eased away—oops, had her nails dug those crescents into his forearms?—and ripped back the covers on the bed. His passion darkened gaze caught and held hers as he reached for his tie and loosened the knot. Transfixed, Holly watched his slow, deliberate movements, and when her lungs burned she remembered to inhale. He draped his tie across the back of the desk chair and then deposited his shoes and socks beneath it.

The man had sexy feet. How was that possible? Feet weren't sexy. They were just…*feet*. And in Eric's case, *big* feet. To go with the rest of him.

Eric opened the top button of his short-sleeved white shirt, revealing a whorl of dark chest hair. The second and third buttons parted, playing a sexy game of peekaboo with a wedge of taut, tanned skin stretched over perfect pectorals. As the wedge widened, Holly's mouth dried. And then the shirt joined the tie. Not a moment too soon.

Eric reached for his belt. A heavy jungle beat drummed through Holly's veins and she realized she was trembling. Weak-kneed, she sank onto the edge of the cool-sheeted bed. Her breasts ached. She clenched her fists against the need to touch them or any other part of her body clamoring for attention. She squeezed her thighs together. Had she ever been this turned on?

Eric lowered his zipper, apparently one tooth at a time.

Could he possibly go any slower? C'mon, c'mon, c'mon, I'm

dying here. She swallowed again, but her mouth remained desert-dry. Why? Why did *he* have the ability to do this to her when no one else could?

His charcoal dress pants slid to the floor, leaving behind extremely tight black briefs. Oh, man.

"I never took you for a tease, Eric," she croaked.

He hooked his thumbs in the elastic waistband and peeled off his briefs and then circled his fingers around his thick shaft and stroked. "This is no tease. It's a promise."

Hooo boy. The Chippendales had nothing on the banker. She was so hot it's a wonder her pores didn't whistle like steaming tea kettles. And if he didn't move faster she'd melt into a puddle on the sheets.

So what are you waiting for? Hurry him along.

Holly reached out and wrapped her fingers around his and towed him forward by his hot, silky flesh. She dampened her lips and then leaned forward to take his engorged tip in her mouth.

His breath hissed and his fingers tangled in her hair. She ran her tongue over him, savoring his taste, his smooth texture, his heat and his deep-bellied groan. She stroked and suckled another groan out of him and then—*hallelujah*—he tumbled her back onto the bed and slammed his mouth over hers. *'Bout time.*

His thigh jammed between hers and his splayed hand rasped a path from her knee to her curls. Bingo. He found the magic button and plied it with her wetness until she bowed off the mattress. She tore her mouth away to pant for air and gasped again when his teeth grazed her nipple.

He was good at this—too good at this. And the thought of turning him over to some dim-witted, money-grubbing socialite once this affair ended chafed.

She didn't want to let him go.

Don't go there.

She clamped down on her intrusive and unsettling thoughts as Eric delighted her with his mouth and hands, suckling, nipping and caressing her right into madness by pulling back each time she teetered on the brink. She raked her nails up his back, trying to get him inside her, but instead of up he went down. His mouth burned a hot, damp trail from her breasts to her navel and then lower. One blunt finger traced her auburn curls.

"Did I mention how much I like this?" he rumbled against her hip bone.

Gulp. "No. Bikini wax experiment."

The heat in his gaze made the pain of creating a tiny triangle worth it.

"Sexy. Like an arrowhead pointing to the promised land."

She squirmed, hinting at the hunger she waited for him to satisfy, but Eric didn't take the hint. He traced each corner of her curls, each fold of her moist skin, and then finally, finally, bumped over the bull's-eye. Her body tensed in anticipation. *Thank you.*

But her gratitude was short-lived as his hands wandered elsewhere, leaving her hovering on the edge of ecstasy. She whimpered in frustration and then cried out as his mouth consumed her. *Yes, yes, yes.* In seconds, release racked her, bowing her body and fisting her hands in the sheets. Hard on the heels of her first orgasm, he sent her soaring again. When the ripples died down she collapsed on the sheets and pried one heavy eyelid open.

Eric smiled back at her from between her legs, a sexy, glistening smile. "You're not shy about your pleasure."

As if she could help herself. Was that one more thing she did wrong? "Am I supposed to be?"

"No." He rose and reached for his wallet, withdrew a condom and applied it. Bracing himself over her body, he eased between her legs. "Don't change. Not one thing."

His words suffused her with a warm glow. And then he filled her with a long, slow glide, relighting the fire she thought he'd extinguished seconds ago. His deep kisses and deeper thrusts fueled the heat until she exploded like a Molotov cocktail with the sound of Eric's orgasmic groan in her ears.

She drifted back to the mattress like a pile of ashes, savoring the weight of his sweat-dampened body melded to hers.

Don't change. How long had she waited to hear someone say those words?

But why did it have to be Eric who said them?

Eric, the one man she couldn't be with unless she did change. For them to stay together, she'd have to give up everything she'd fought so hard for in the past seven years. Her independence. Her career. Her I-don't-give-a-damn-what-they-say-about-me shell. To be with him, she'd have to conform to society's rigid constraints. Eric's wife—not that he'd asked—would have to be a pillar of the community, an example other women could admire and respect, a fund-raising maven and a society icon. A rebel and an outcast like her would never do.

Shock pulsed through her in sobering, chilling waves. Was she actually considering trying to change for him?

Had she lost her mind?

No, you've lost your heart.

Oh, no. Holly bit her lip until tears stung her eyes. She'd fallen in love with Eric Alden, and she didn't want to let him go. But could she bear the price of holding on?

"I've done a bad thing," Holly blurted as soon as Andrea opened her front door on Wednesday evening.

Andrea grimaced. "That makes two of us."

Holly blinked at her friend's worried tone. Concern for Andrea nudged her own troubles aside. "What happened?"

Andrea shoved back her blond hair with an unsteady hand. "Nothing I can talk about yet. Come in."

"But—"

"No, this is about you. You're ready to discuss your mistake and I'm…not. Want a martini? I found a new recipe using Godiva liqueur and raspberry vodka."

"Sounds good, but not tonight. I have to drive." Besides, if she drank she'd probably cry like a baby and then pass out. Worry had kept her from sleeping more than a handful of hours since her discovery Monday evening. Holly sank onto the sofa and took a bracing breath. "These dates haven't turned out like I expected."

"I think it's safe to say none of us got what we planned for out of this bachelor auction. I'm sorry I ever suggested it. Go ahead. Say, 'I told you so.' You were against this from the beginning."

"Gloating never occurred to me, but maybe I could help if you'd tell me wha—"

Andrea held up her hand. "No. You talk. I'll listen."

"I don't want to drag you into the middle of this, but I don't know where else to turn." Holly stared at her knotted fingers. "I think I've fallen in love with Eric Alden."

Andrea gasped, but Holly forged on. "How stupid is that? I can't fit into his world. I just can't."

"Holly, you already do."

"Oh *puh-leeze.*"

"I don't know why you insist on drawing a line between your current life and your old one. Yes they are tremendously different lifestyles, but you go into these women's homes all the time and they come to yours. How many of them have been taking your stained glass class for years? I've been in some of your classes, Holly. There's more bonding in there than metal and glass."

Holly stiffened. "You're wrong."

"No, you are if you don't recognize the friendships for what they are. Yes, there are a few old biddies who look down on you because you work with your hands, but the majority of these women you claim you could never be one of *like you.* They take your classes, let you decorate their homes, introduce you to their friends, and they share intimate secrets they'd never share with the 'hired help' you believe yourself to be."

Jealousy twisted her stomach as she recalled the information shared about Eric. She shook her head to clear the thought. "Okay, maybe that's true, sort of, in a twisted kind of way, but…what about Juliana? She'll never forgive me for sleeping with her brother."

"If you make Eric happy, she will."

Holly snorted. "As if I'm ever going to get the chance to make that happen. And what about my family? You know how they frown on my 'little hobby.'"

"Your family is trying to force you into the cookie-cutter mold they understand, but I think it's because they worry about you."

"Oh, c'mon. You don't seriously believe that?"

"Yes, I do. Your mother worries about your safety out there in the boonies, and your father is old-fashioned. He has an overwhelming need to manage your finances until he hands you off to some other guy for safekeeping."

Holly bowed her head and crushed her bangs between her fingers. It was time to come clean with the whole truth. "Maybe my father had good reason to worry about my finances."

"What do you mean?"

"I should never have agreed to buy a bachelor. I couldn't afford one." She winced at Andrea's shocked expression and continued. "I make a decent living with Rainbow Glass, but I spent all my trust fund money past and present on the dogs, my renovations and my lost-cause dates. I chose the firefighter because I thought he'd go for more money than we agreed on and then I'd be off the hook."

"No. Juliana and I chose the firefighter for you."

Abashed, Holly confessed, "With a lot of prompting from me. I really didn't think he was sexy. I thought he was built like a fire hydrant. I prefer my men long and lean—"

"Like Eric."

"Uh, yes. Anyway, the bidding stalled, and I panicked. I

thought I'd be stuck with Franco. And then Eric offered to re-imburse me if I bought him. Since I'd borrowed against my trust fund to finance Lyle's invention, I jumped at the chance to get out of debt. I never intended to date Eric, but Octavia backed us into a corner and then…I, um…fell for him."

Andrea's eyes filled with sympathy, not condemnation. "Oh, Holly, why didn't you say something about the money?"

"I was ashamed. I was trying to make it on my own, to prove to my family that I wasn't the empty-headed twit they thought I was, and that was about to blow up in my face. I wanted to hang on to my independence and my pride as long as I could."

"Do you need money? I can give you—"

Embarrassment scorched her cheeks. "No, but thanks. Eric hired a P.I. to help me locate Lyle, and it turns out my invest-ment in Lyle's invention is about to pay off big-time."

"So we've circled back to the problem. Eric. You'll accept as-sistance from him but not your family?"

Holly smothered a groan. "It's not the same. There are strings attached to my father's help. I'd have to go back to the club."

"Your father loved having you work there. He used to brag about having all his children under his roof again."

"But that's it. I wasn't *working*. I was being paid an exorbi-tant salary to twiddle my thumbs while everyone else was busting their tails for a fraction of my salary. It wasn't fair."

"No. It wasn't. So what makes you think you love Eric?"

Holly blinked at the quick subject change. She knew all the reasons why Eric was wrong for her. What made her think they had even a slim chance of a long-term relationship?

"Besides sex so hot it curls my hair?" She slapped cold hands to her hot cheeks. "Please, don't tell Juliana I said that."

Andrea smiled. "I promise. Besides sensational sex…"

"He treats me like an equal instead of a nitwit, and he listens. I mean he *really* listens, and he understands that Rainbow Glass isn't a quaint hobby to fill my single years. It's a business. He even looked at my portfolio, something my family has never bothered to do." With her heart in her throat she looked up at her friend. "Andrea, he makes me feel good about being me—even when I'm nervous and running off at the mouth."

"In other words, your wall-building comments don't stop him."

"Wall-building? What's that supposed to mean?"

"Holly, I love you like a sister, but I've watched you use outrageous comments to push people away for years. It's as if you're trying to run them off before they can dump you."

Speechless, she gaped. "I do that?"

"'Fraid so. Your relationship with Eric sounds like something worth fighting for. Will you?"

Anxiety gnawed Holly's stomach. "What if I fight and fail?"

"Not trying is the same thing as failing, isn't it?"

"And we both know how much I hate being a failure. So…I guess I have my answer and my work cut out for me."

Eleven

Eric couldn't concentrate worth a damn today. Or yesterday. Or the day before. As a matter of fact, he'd been distracted everyday since Monday. His feelings for Holly—whatever they were—had come between him and his work. No woman had ever done that before. And he didn't like it.

His final date with Holly was Friday night, a dinner with her parents, and while he should be pleased to be relieved of his obligations, he wasn't ready to let her go. Would he ever be?

He leaned back in his desk chair, twisting his favorite Mont-blanc pen in his fingers and looked through the glass wall of his office. He spotted his father making one of his rare appearances at the bank. Just the person Eric needed to see. He needed answers. Answers only Richard Alden could provide.

Eric bolted to his feet and crossed the reception area to his father's barely used office. "Dad, do you have a minute?"

"Certainly, son. Thursday's always slow. Come in."

What day wasn't on his father's business calendar? Eric kept his comment to himself and struggled to find a way to phrase the question he'd come in here to ask so that it wouldn't come out as an insult, but his usual diplomacy deserted him.

His father gestured to the leather visitor chair.

Eric closed the door and sat. "Why do you let Mom walk all over you?"

If his rudeness caught his father off guard, Richard didn't show it. "It's taken a lot of years for you to ask. I know you lost respect for me once you started working here. And yes, I know what they say in the break room. I kept waiting for you to come to me and ask if the rumors were true. But you never did."

He waved away any denial Eric might have made—not that Eric could deny the truth. He hadn't asked because he hadn't wanted to hear his father admit he was weak.

"Son, I let your mother run the show because I love her. Pleasing her makes me happy."

"But this is *your* bank. Your name's on the door."

"It's *our* bank. Your mother's family's bank merged with my family's bank thirty-eight years ago. My side happened to have controlling interest at the time and therefore claimed naming rights. But your mother loves Alden's more than I ever did. She's a better custodian of it than I ever could be. So I do what I have to do to keep my finger on the pulse, but I leave what happens inside these walls to your mother. That way, we're both happy."

"It doesn't make you feel—" *Emasculated*. But Eric couldn't say it, couldn't hurt his father that way.

"Inferior? No. I'm a salesman, not a number cruncher. Your mother handles the nitty-gritty and she excels at it. You and Juliana take after her more than me in the respect that you prefer the business side to the personal side of operations. It wasn't always that way. You used to be quite a charmer back in your days as class president and captain of the basketball team. I envisioned you successfully combining my role and hers. But lately…" He shook his head. "All you think about is the bottom line."

Eric's shoulders stiffened.

"Eric, I'm happy to do my part outside the offices, and if people underestimate me in the process, that's their problem and yours. I'm good at working the people side of the business. I schmooze and lure new and lucrative clients—" his father pulled a cigar from his humidor, snipped off the tip and studied the rolled tobacco "—and I work behind the scenes to convince Wilson Savings and Loan's board of directors to support your mother as president and you as VP should the merger go through."

Stunned, Eric watched a wily smile widen across his father's face. "You've talked to Wilson's board?"

"Just a friendly round of golf or two and a few dinners at the club, but I've managed to lure each of them into our corner. Baxter's an SOB and everyone wants to see the back of him. He'll be given a nominal position or forced into retirement."

Eric stared at his father and a new respect for him welled in Eric's chest. Richard Alden wasn't the powerless puppet he appeared to be. He knew how to play hardball, but he wielded his influence behind the scenes instead of going for the glory. "You sly devil. I had no idea. I thought—"

"You thought I was a henpecked husband because you listened to gossip," his father said around the unlit cigar clamped between his teeth. "I do what's good for the bank."

Eric's smile faded. He'd misjudged Holly because of what others said. He'd also misjudged his father. He should have been more direct—the way Holly would have been—and gone straight to the source.

"Mother tried to marry me off for the good of the bank, and now she's doing the same to Juliana. You've never said a word either for or against that plan."

His father shrugged. "A business-merger marriage worked for your mother and me. You had a lucky escape, and only Juliana can determine how her relationship will turn out."

A lucky escape. Yes, with hindsight Eric could see that he had, indeed, been lucky not to be tied to Priscilla. He hadn't realized how lucky until Holly had disrupted his carefully structured life.

"You didn't mind being bartered like a stock option?" he asked his father.

"No. I was crazy about your mother from the moment I met her. She was dynamic and courageous—not to mention gorgeous. She didn't follow in anybody's shadow. I admired that and still do. She's a tigress, my Margaret. Chances are she wouldn't have looked twice at me if I hadn't been forced on her. We're an unlikely pair, but we make a good team." Richard rose. "One of these days I hope you'll find as good a match as I did, someone who admires your strengths and complements your weaknesses."

Could that special someone be Holly? Or would he bore her out of her mind and drive her away twice as fast as he had Priscilla?

At times like this, Holly wished she were a heavy drinker. A stiff shot of something would make dinner with her parents easier to endure and might even give her the courage she needed to talk to Eric afterward. She planned to lay her heart on the line tonight. And then he'd either crush it by saying goodbye or accept her love and give them a chance.

"Please come in, Eric," her mother said in the foyer. "I'm sorry your parents couldn't join us tonight."

"They send their regrets," Eric's deep voice replied.

Holly's stomach knotted with tension. She clutched her wine-glass tighter and stared at the highly polished brass andirons in the empty fireplace—empty because exposing her mother's all white decor to soot and wood was too risky.

Four days had passed since the hotel quickie. Four days of Holly agonizing over what she was going to do with the knowl-edge that she'd fallen in love with her best friend's brother, a man who represented the life she'd fled. But she'd always believed in taking risks for something she believed in, and she believed she could make Eric happy. He needed someone to remind him to unwind as much as she needed someone who believed in her. With everything he'd said and done, Eric had proved his faith in her.

Maybe Andrea and Octavia were right and Holly could have it all: Eric and her career.

Pretty bold of you to assume Eric's interested in something permanent with you.

She turned her head as he entered the living room with her mother. Holly's love for him squeezed the breath from her chest. Dressed in a navy suit that flattered his wide shoulders and lean hips and a white shirt that accentuated his tan, Eric looked edible—much more palatable than the stuffy, stilted meal her mother was likely to serve.

He greeted her father and then Eric's gaze met and held Holly's. Her heart thumped its way into her throat as he crossed the room. His long fingers encircled her hand. The warmth of his touch sent goose bumps chasing over her skin and a rush of moisture to places that had no business moistening with her parents in the room. She loved him and it terrified her. She had so much to lose.

"Good evening, Holly."

"Eric." She leaned closer and lowered her voice. "I'm sorry I couldn't talk Mom out of this. I'd rather our last auction date be private. Afterward, can we…talk?"

Heat filled in his eyes and his fingers tightened. "Yes."

Desire swirled in Holly's belly. It was as if the room shrank down to the two of them, as if her mother and father had vanished. The memories of Monday night's lovemaking flushed Holly's skin and dried her mouth. Eric couldn't look at her as if he wanted to eat her up and feel nothing for her, could he? She searched his face looking for a hint that he felt more than desire.

"Drink, Eric?" her father asked, shattering the intimacy before

Holly found her answer. "I have a new bourbon from a private distillery you should try."

Eric released her hand and turned. "Thank you, Colton, I will."

Her father poured and crossed the room with the highball glass. "We were proud of Holly for having the good judgment to buy you at the auction. I hope this month has been…pleasant."

Tolerable, his tone indicated. Holly gritted her teeth.

"Yes, sir. You have a charming daughter."

"No need to sugarcoat it, son. Holly's a handful, but let's face it, she's not like my boys who know their duty and understand their roles in the legacy of the Caliber Club. But Holly can learn. I'm counting on you to convince her to come back to work for me."

Eric paused with the glass inches from his mouth. "I wouldn't even attempt it. Have you seen Holly's work?"

"A few pieces," her father said dismissively.

"She creates magic with metal and glass."

Eric's praise filled Holly with a warm glow.

"I'm sure her window-making is a fine hobby."

"No sir, Holly's art is her career, and her work happens to be part of the architecture of several buildings around town. I hadn't realized how much of a presence she had until I saw her portfolio. I'm surprised you haven't commissioned a piece for the Caliber Club before now."

Eric's pronouncement shocked Holly speechless. Gratitude welled up in her…and then the doubts crowded in. Guys didn't flatter her unless they wanted something, and each of the boyfriends she'd dumped had tried to mend the breach between her and her family because they'd wanted a piece of the Prescott wealth and prestige. Was that Eric's aim?

Power and prestige are the axis on which the world rotates, he'd said Monday night. Did that mean Eric couldn't love her without her family's clout? Was that why he'd helped her with Lyle? To gain points with her family? To secure the Caliber

Club's business? Eric had been willing to marry Priscilla, the pretentious witch, for the good of Alden's Bank. Was dating Holly more of the same?

Pain squeezed her heart. She looked away from the face she'd come to love and right into her father's. Holly recognized the speculative gleam in eyes the same brown as her own. Her father thought he had a fish on the hook—a point he proved by trolling a sales pitch any used car salesman would envy. Only her father wasn't selling cars. He was trying to sell his daughter.

Embarrassment mingled with uncertainty.

It was going to be a *l-o-n-g* night.

"Holly's children will certainly be…imaginative," Nadine Prescott said with a fond smile for her only daughter as the maid cleared the brandy glasses away.

Holly's children. The minute Nadine said it, Eric knew that's what he wanted. A life with Holly. Children with her. The discovery sent his thoughts reeling.

He'd fallen in love with irreverent, irrepressible and enticing-as-hell Holly Prescott. He'd once thought her the worst possible candidate for a banker's wife. Now he realized she was the best and the only one he'd consider. He *loved* her. Love. Something he'd sworn he'd never let happen to him.

He loved that she still believed in people, whereas he'd lost faith long ago. She was also honest, intelligent, beautiful and educated. Her smiles energized him, and her touch made him as randy as a frat boy on Friday night. And he'd come to love her wayward mouth…which, now that he thought about it, had been silent for most of the evening. Concerned, he sought Holly's gaze.

She bolted to her feet. "Quit shoving me down Eric's throat! We're only dating and you're practically naming our children. Daddy, do you think I can't land a man by myself? Do you really believe I'm so unlovable that you have to buy one for me?"

"Princess, I'm not—"

"What do you call it when you promise Alden's the financing for that megamillion dollar expansion you plan to build? Or when you guarantee a free yacht slip and first choice of the new condos?" And then her turbulent gaze turned on Eric. "Is that all I was to you? Another business alliance? Another Priscilla?"

The pain in her voice tightened a vise around Eric's chest until he could barely breathe. Nadine and Colton had spent most of the evening entertaining Eric with anecdotes of Holly's childhood antics, from her imaginary friend to her attempts to best her brothers. Colton's mention of the expansion into luxury condos overlooking the club's marina had been news to Eric. He stood. "Holly—"

Every last vestige of color drained from her face. "Not that you asked, but I'll get married if and when I find a man who loves me for me, not for the perks that come with being linked to a Prescott."

I do. But Eric clenched his teeth on the words and watched her storm from the room. An icy sensation crept over him. Priscilla's denunciation and desertion had dented his pride. Holly's crucified him. How could she believe he'd use her for business purposes?

Because you almost married Priscilla for the sake of the bank. Self-disgust riddled him. *You're a real prize, Alden. A prize idiot. And you're a damned fool if you let Holly get away.*

He gathered himself and turned to his shocked hosts. "Thank you for dinner. Good-night."

He followed Holly out and caught up with her in the circular driveway. She was already in the driver's seat of the roofless, doorless Jeep with the engine running. Her fingers clutched the steering wheel with a white-knuckled grip, and her dark, wounded eyes warily watched his approach.

"Holly, I didn't date you for the Alden's sake."

Her bottom lip quivered. "Yes, you did. We both acted out this charade so Octavia wouldn't cause trouble with our businesses. The question is, how far were you willing to go for your precious bank, Eric?"

How could he argue with facts? "I didn't know about the condos until tonight."

"Do I look dumb enough to believe that? Guys never say nice things to me or about me unless they want something from me. And you and my brothers are so tight you probably know what they have for breakfast each morning. I'm sure they let that little detail slip." She faced forward and reached for the gearshift. "You're good in bed, Eric, but not good enough for me to sell myself."

Déjà vu. He knew what was coming next. At least this time there wouldn't be four hundred witnesses. Eric granted himself one last chance to memorize every detail about her and then took a bracing breath. "Thank you for a memorable month, Holly. We both know I can't be the laid-back guy you're looking for, so it's best we end it now."

Her gasp pierced him and her pain-filled eyes made him waver. Was he wrong? Wasn't she getting ready to dump him?

He conquered the urge to rescue her bottom lip from her teeth, but lost the battle to wipe the lone tear from her cheek. "I hope you find the man you're looking for. But do me a favor. Don't lend him any money."

She choked out a laugh and covered his hand, pressing his palm to her cheek. "I think I can safely make that promise."

She curled her other hand around his lapel and tugged him forward until his lips touched hers. Eric had scant seconds to savor her softness, her taste, and then she shoved him away. Desire pulsed through his breaking heart. It took every ounce of his strength to straighten instead of yanking her into his arms.

"Be happy, Eric." And then she drove off and left him shaking so hard he could barely stand.

Loving Holly hadn't made him weak. Losing her had.

With a hollow ache in her chest Holly sat in front of her computer screen studying the digital photos she'd taken on Bald Head Island.

She'd done it again. Fallen into her old habit of rescuing men. And once again, it had burned her. But saying goodbye had never hurt this much because this time she'd opened her heart and not just her wallet.

She traced a finger over an image of Eric's laughing face and her breath hitched. She was too tired to maintain her anger, and besides, any anger should be directed inward. She'd known they were a mismatch from the beginning. The banker and the bohemian.

But who would remind Eric to take time for himself now that they were over?

She would. If not in person, then she'd do so by proxy. Her pulse kicked faster. Sitting up straighter, Holly blinked her gritty 3 a.m. eyes. She had to get some sleep before her Monday class arrived, but first she had to find the right picture. She scrolled through the images until she found the perfect one—a shot of Eric's island house surrounded by dunes and swaying sea oats. She'd turn this photo into a window he could hang in his office, and maybe when he looked at it he'd remember their time together. And her.

She swallowed the sob clawing at her throat and reached for a pencil and paper. The project would be large and detailed, and it would take an incredible number of hours. But what else did she have to do? She couldn't eat or sleep, and she'd finished her last commission two days ago—the morning of the disastrous dinner with her parents. She couldn't move forward on anything else until her clients approved the preliminary sketches.

She was still bent over the full-sized drawing when the studio door opened behind her hours later.

"Is it safe to come in?" Octavia asked.

Surprised, Holly swiveled on the stool, stared at her friend and then looked at the clock on the wall. She'd been at this for seven hours? "It's ten already?"

"Girlfriend, you look awful. Did my article peeve you that much?"

Holly grimaced. She'd forgotten to buy this week's paper. "Actually, I haven't read it."

"What happened?" Charlise pushed past Octavia, opening the studio door wider to reveal the rest of Holly's students on the threshold.

Emotion bubbled inside Holly, but she suppressed it and stood to stretch her stiff muscles. She forced her mouth into her most professional smile. "Good morning, ladies. I guess I got caught up in my new project and forgot the time."

All eight women crowded around her to get a look at the poster-sized image she'd sketched and colored and the inspiration photo beside it.

"It's gorgeous. Whose house is it?" Charlise asked.

When Holly couldn't make her voice work, Octavia replied, "It's Eric's house on Bald Head Island."

Just hearing his name made Holly's bottom lip wobble. She bit down hard to stop the telling motion, but she was too late. The sympathy in the other women's eyes was almost more than she could take.

Charlise put an around her shoulders. "Oh, Holly, we warned you not to fall for him."

Holly lifted her chin and gritted a smile. "I'm fine. Really. Shall we get to work?"

Charlise gave her a hard stare. "You're not fine. You look like you've been at this all night. You need a shower, breakfast and a nap. Octavia will keep an eye on your class."

Holly examined the concerned faces surrounding her and realized Andrea was right. These women were her friends, and any lines between them were lines Holly had drawn.

She'd exiled herself. How dumb was that?

If she'd been wrong about being an outcast, then what else had she been wrong about?

* * *

"Excuse me. I need to see Eric," Holly tried to step around the bank guard at lunchtime on Friday, but he planted himself between her and the marble stairs leading to the executive offices of Alden's bank. She wasn't going to let something as trivial as the lack of an appointment stop her.

He eyed the large parcel in her arms and shook his head. "Mr. Alden is in an important meeting, Miss…?"

"Prescott. You know my name because you've spied on me before, Denny. Call him out."

His cheeks turned ruddy. "Ma'am I don't think—"

"Do it or I'll start shrieking for Eric at the top of my lungs. And my daddy always said I had the bellow of a bull elephant on the rampage when I cut loose."

Denny stared as if gauging her sincerity. She smiled, but it felt hard and brittle. A week of sleep deprivation would do that to you.

Denny turned away and spoke into his radio. Holly couldn't hear what he said. For all she knew, he could be calling the police to haul her to jail. A moment later, he turned back and waved her forward. "He'll meet you upstairs, Miss Prescott."

"Thank you." Holly climbed the stairs. Nervousness twisted her stomach and the window she carried seemed to gain ten pounds with every tread. A door marked Boardroom opened as she reached the landing and Eric, looking to-die-for handsome in a dove-gray suit, stepped out.

Holly's courage took a nosedive. She took a deep breath and willed it back. Her anger had lessened over the past week and her heartache…well, it was manageable once in a while.

"Holly." His banker's face gave nothing away, but his gaze roved from her face to her feet and back again. She hadn't slept more than a handful of hours since they'd said goodbye, and she'd had to trowel on makeup to cover the dark circles under her eyes. She'd attempted to tame her unruly hair and worn her tame black dress and a pair of real shoes instead of her beloved flip-flops. He indicated the frame with a dip of his head. "More dog pictures?"

"No. A peace offering. I didn't give you a chance to explain Friday night before I condemned you, and isn't that exactly what I always accused my parents of doing?" She shifted nervously in her pumps. "Look, can we go to your office? This thing's heavy."

He immediately took it from her and then strode toward his office. Holly followed, forced a smile for his sour-faced assistant and waited until he'd closed his door. He rested the frame on the arms of the wing chair just as he'd done with the dog pictures. Had that only been three weeks ago?

Holly knotted her fingers and swallowed to ease the dryness in her mouth. "I made this for you to remind you to dig your toes in the sand and let the tide roll by once in a while." Eric's lips flattened and she continued in a rush. "That's not because you need to change, Eric. You don't. You're perfect exactly as you are. But until you have someone to remind you to balance your life, I thought you might need a nudge every now and then."

When he made no move to unwrap her gift she moved forward. Her hands shook as she ripped off the protective brown paper. And then she backed away and waited…and waited. "I thought maybe…maybe you'd remember how good it was between us on the island."

Eric silently studied the window. His Adam's apple bobbed. Holly's nerves twisted like spaghetti on a fork. Did he like it? Did he hate it? His expression gave nothing away.

Unable to bear the suspense, she glanced over the black-and-charcoal office searching for the right place to hang the piece and then her heart stalled. She reluctantly dragged her gaze back to her window. It was her best work yet. She'd poured her love into each piece of glass, copper and lead, and it showed. But the vibrant piece, with its peach-washed sand, indigo water and azure sky, didn't fit into Eric's monochromatic office any more than Holly could fit into his life.

She'd only been fooling herself. Had she honestly believed that seeing Eric again today might lead him to forgive her for judging him unfairly and convince him to give their relationship another try?

Well, Holly, you've screwed up and built another wall where you shouldn't have.

Her eyes stung, but no face-saving smart-ass quips came to mind. She yanked open the door and fled. Her heels clattered across the marble floor and down the stairs. Almost there. Almost there. She wanted to get outside before she lost it.

"Holly Prescott," Eric's voice reverberated through the open two-story bank. Holly kept running. "Will you marry me?"

What? Stunned, she skidded to a halt near the exit and spun around to see Eric at the top of the stairs. His gaze locked on hers and didn't waver as he descended. A hush settled over the busy bank as the patrons around them stilled and stared.

Her heart thundered so hard she was certain she must have misheard. *No way* had Eric proposed with the Friday afternoon customers crowding the bank. Not after his public humiliation with Priscilla.

The customers parted, clearing a path for Eric's purposeful stride. Holly struggled to catch her breath.

"Are you crazy?" she whispered as soon as he reached her side.

"Yes. Crazy about you." He took her cold left hand into his warm grasp. "I love you, Holly, and I want you beside me to remind me to relax once in a while."

Her mouth fell open and she searched his face. "Me? Graceless, redheaded amazon me?"

He smiled and stroked her cheek. The love she saw in his eyes squeezed the breath right out of her. "Irreverent, irrepressible and enticing-as-hell you."

"But—"

He laid a finger over her lips. "Honest, intelligent and beautiful you. You love me, Holly. I can see it in your window."

She closed her eyes, gulped, and then met his dark gaze again. "Yes. I love you."

It felt good to say it. Scary as hell, but good to finally have it out in the open.

His nostrils flared as he inhaled. "And you'll marry me."

"Eric—"

"I swear I didn't know about the condos."

Holly winced. Boy, had she ever been wrong about her family's feelings. Andrea had been right. They did love her and wanted the best for her.

"I know. I'm sorry. My father came to my studio yesterday because I haven't been answering my phone. He told me he could see how much I loved you Friday night, and that he was doing whatever he could to give his baby girl what she wanted."

A tear streaked down her cheek. And Eric was all she wanted. But would she be enough for him? "Eric, I can't be a Stepford Wife. I'll always be a sucker for strays, and I'll probably continue saying the wrong things."

"I don't want a Stepford Wife, and I love your candor. I could use a little of it myself." He gently thumbed the tear from her cheek. "Holly, I'm not asking you to change or to give up Rainbow Glass or your home. I'm asking you to make room in your life for me."

Eric was offering her love and acceptance in both worlds— the one she'd left behind and the one she'd created for herself. He couldn't possibly know how much he tempted her. "Your mother hates me."

"His mother will love you," Margaret Alden rasped from behind Eric, startling Holly back into awareness of where they were and their eavesdropping audience. "If you make him happy and if you'll let him return to the boardroom long enough to sign the last paper finalizing the merger."

"Mother, the paperwork will have to wait," Eric said without turning. "She hasn't said yes."

"Of course, she hasn't. You haven't proposed properly. Get on with it."

For a moment, her self-assured banker looked adorably confused, and then a slow, devastatingly sexy smile curved his lips. He dropped to one knee and pressed a kiss to the back of Holly's hand. The touch of his lips made her pulse flutter.

"Holly Prescott, will you do me the honor of becoming my wife and let me spend the rest of my life loving you and your wayward mouth?"

Love swelled inside her. She knew how hard this public display had to be for him, but Eric didn't flinch. He loved her. He really, *really* loved her. The emotion was clear in his eyes and in his willingness to endure this spectacle. She tugged his hand. "Eric, get up. Everyone's watching."

"Not until you say yes. Rescue me, Holly. Bring color into my world, and remind me there's more to life than work. Say yes."

Fighting an ecstatic smile, she pressed her lips in a considering line. "I've sworn off rescuing men, but I guess I can make an exception. For you. Just this once." She stroked his face, savoring the slight rasp of stubble along his jaw and the love in his eyes. "Yes, Eric, I'll marry you if you let me spend the rest of my days loving you…and your incredibly sexy, talented mouth."

His lips curved in a grin. He rose, caught her in his arms and planted one of his trademark melt-her-mascara kisses on her. The bank patrons and employees cheered. Slowly, Eric lowered her feet to the floor.

Holly blinked when she saw Juliana standing beside them wearing a huge smile. "Holly, I've always loved you like a sister. This makes it official."

Holly hugged her best friend and sent a silent thank you skyward. She'd gambled it all—her career, her friendship and her heart—and she'd hit the jackpot.

Epilogue

Love At Any Price
By Octavia Jenkins

Love can be found in the strangest of places. It usually shows up when you're not searching for it and at the most inconvenient time.

It is with both joy and regret that I pen this last install-ment. My only regret is that this assignment had to end. The joy comes from the magic of seeing couples fall in love. Not all of the twenty couples participating in the bachelor auction found happiness, but a good number did, including yours truly.

This reporter is going to take two weeks to get hitched and honeymoon in Vegas with the man this series brought me, my trusty cameraman and sidekick Raymond. I will return mid-July with exclusive photos and the story of a triple wedding taking place in the Bald Head Island Chapel.

Until then…just call me Cupid.

* * * * *

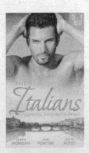

MILLS & BOON®
By Request

RELIVE THE ROMANCE WITH THE BEST OF THE BEST

A sneak peek at next month's titles…

In stores from 21st August 2015:

- **His Virgin Bride** – Melanie Milburne, Maggie Cox & Margaret Mayo

- **In Bed With the Enemy** – Natalie Anderson, Aimee Carson & Tawny Weber

In stores from 4th September 2015:

- **The Jarrods: Inheritance** – Maxine Sullivan, Emilie Rose & Heidi Betts

- **Undressed by the Rebel** – Alison Roberts

Available at WHSmith, Tesco, Asda, Eason, Amazon and Apple

Just can't wait?
Buy our books online a month before they hit the shops!
visit www.millsandboon.co.uk

These books are also available in eBook format!